GOD'S WILL

L. B. STEPHENS

Copyright © 2018 Lee Ball
All rights reserved.
ISBN: 9781980222347
ISBN-13: 978-1985446748

I would like to thank my two wonderful boys, Jason and Aidan, my family for all the love and support they have given me over the years, particularly my mother. Huge thanks must also go to Dawn, Andrew Booth, Ann Aspinall, Stuart Winfield (for the excellent cover) and to David Pickering for his superb editing, good advice and helpful suggestions.

For Dawn...

The gay morn breaks,
Mists roll away,
All Nature awakes
To glorious day.
In my breast alone
Dark shadows remain;
The peace it has known
It can never regain.

Charles Dickens, *Lucy's Song*

God's Will

1

There it is again. It has to be them.

They have chased him, beaten him, dragged him through the black mud. He can recall their shapes above him, ghosts in the mist, but nothing more. The man now lies motionless in the creek, the rising salty water at his lips, not knowing who he is or why he is there. It was the fog that saved him. Of course it was. How else could it be explained? He has no recollection of escaping their clutches, only brief flashes of the horrific assault remain. Now they roam the marsh howling for their loss, their final victory thwarted for a moment by the thick swirling mist.

But why can't he remember anything?

He can only presume his escape was made with his final reserves of strength, because there is nothing left in him now. Other than a cold-induced shuddering he can't move a muscle in this watery grave. He is too beaten, too numb to save his own skin now. The only hope is that the fog will thicken and that they give up their pursuit.

Who are they? Why is he here? Half-remembered images surface and then are pulled back down into the depths before he can fully comprehend what they mean. In their wake, a dark residue, like thick oil on crystal clear water, tells him that he is guilty of some awful crime and this outcome was inevitable. He just doesn't know what that crime was.

A movement, a shape—a robin, boldly hopping around the muddy bank, first on a dead branch, then a stone, then his arm, which he now realises is twisted to an impossible angle. The bird tilts its head quizzically, cautiously wondering what this wheezing creature is, half submerged in the freezing winter tide, coated in mud.

God's Will

The man's face is so swollen from the unremembered attack he can just about see through one eye. He gets a final view of the world through an eyelid-puffed frame. The robin on his broken arm is possibly the final living thing he will ever see.

The man coughs, splutters and releases a groan that sends the little bird fluttering into the air. It is soon back. This time it comes closer, its head slanting left to right, up and down, demanding to know if this barely living thing has anything in its larder for an empty belly on an early winter morning. Another cough, another phlegmy rumble, but the bold robin holds tight. Despite the shaking beneath its feet and the moaning filling the air, it holds on, and the man wonders why.

Trying to work out what I am, little bird? I'm not sure I can tell you, but if I were you I wouldn't hang around to find out.

A gust of wind comes down the narrow creek like an invisible wave, sending the bird into the air again. It hovers, briefly, and then turns before disappearing into the reeds nearby that sway gently in the thinning fog. There is nothing to stay for here, not now the tide is rising across the man's lips.

The water is so close to the man's mouth he cannot stop the gurgling of panic in his own throat. He is a bystander at his own demise. As the fog slowly dissolves, it changes in colour and hypnotises the man on the bank. First white, then grey until finally mustard, like a yellow vapour. The flashing navigation lights of a jet twinkle in the morning sky and dip towards a sloping shoreline dotted with trees, cows, and a house on a hill, the faint glow of light at a window. Someone is warm and snug, he concludes. Below the house he makes out a trio of poplars, now ghostly through a filter of fog, pointing to the sky.

It comes again. That mournful hum so deep it penetrates the land beneath him. He scans the horizon one final time and notices how the

God's Will

poplars below the house have increased in number. Now there are five. He frowns, puzzled. Two of them are smaller, nearer and descending the hill towards him. He laughs inwardly as the salty water seeps past his pursed lips and spills down his throat, chasing the life from his lungs

Hurry, death. They have found me again.

God's Will

Six weeks earlier...

God's Will

2

The portly man looked nervously up and down the stairwell he had just climbed before reaching into his pocket and taking out the letter. Although he had read it a dozen times since its arrival a week before, he read it again, searching for some important detail he may have missed.

But he had missed nothing at all, he concluded. How could he with such a simple message?

Dear Mr Denby,

Although you don't know me I am aware of you and your recent 'bad luck'. Because of your difficulties I also realise how desperately in need of money and security you must be. I can offer you those things in abundance if you are willing to work for me. I have a job that will pay handsomely if you are suited. For more information call at the above address next Wednesday at 8pm.

No signature.

That was the bit Denby was having trouble with. Even though he had repeatedly told himself it was probably an oversight or that it didn't matter, there was a part of him that knew that it mattered a great deal.

He pushed the letter back into his inside pocket and checked his watch. It was exactly eight pm. Eight pm, on Wednesday, 3 January.

The address given was Flat 7, 183 Broadstairs Crescent, Brixton, London. And that was where Denby in his camel-coloured overcoat now stood. He had decided that if this shabby stairwell in the shabbiest part of town was any indication, it was certainly not the home of a wealthy businessman. There was something wrong with this whole

God's Will

business, his old bones sensed. But, as the letter correctly stated, he was desperately in need of money, and he knew from bitter experience how rare opportunities like these were.

From behind other doors along the short hallway he could hear people talking, televisions, music, but nothing came from behind the one before him. Not a thing. Outside the wind howled and a cold breeze ran around the stairwell. Denby shuddered, cleared his throat and knocked on the door. The sudden vibration triggered a small flutter of dried paint off the wood, one jade-coloured sliver drifting down past his face in cold evening air that had found its way inside. Before it could land on the tiled floor Denby heard footsteps and took a step back, to do what he didn't know. Maybe to run. But run from what?

A bolt snapped back, a chain was released from its holding and a key was turned before the door opened a crack. There was someone standing there, but it was just too dark inside for Denby to see who. The old man could feel panic overtaking him and he wanted to run, but there was something in the shadows of the apartment that fixed him to the spot.

'Mr Denby,' said a low steady voice. 'Thank you for coming. Won't you please come in?'

As the door closed behind Denby it felt like he had walked into a cold vacuum, as if he had entered a fridge. There was light spilling into the hallway but he still couldn't make out the man's features, nothing at all in fact but his height, which he estimated at well over six feet. A formidable figure, then.

'I'm just through here,' uttered the man, ducking into a larger room.

Denby followed and took in the stale damp smell of the place as he did so. It reminded him of his previous home and he trembled at the association. He rubbed his hands together and tried to gather his thoughts.

God's Will

'The letter mentioned employment. I am sixty-three, you know, and struggle with go it. It's an interminable hell—'

'All in good time,' the stranger interrupted. 'Can I get you a drink? I don't have much. Sherry, port... or maybe a little brandy?'

Denby suddenly felt much more at ease and smiled broadly. 'I wouldn't say no to a brandy.'

'Of course you wouldn't. Won't you take a seat, Denby?'

Of course I wouldn't? And Denby, is it? Well, I'll be blowed!

The abrupt change of tone put Denby even more on edge. Everyone he knew called him by his surname. He actually preferred it, but coming from a stranger—this particular stranger—didn't sit well with him. But he decided not to comment upon it.

He sat down and his eyes swept the medium-sized apartment. Other than a single leather armchair, a tall walnut dresser and a three-bar electric fire, the room was bare. No ornaments, no paintings, no sense of home, and no way for Denby to get an impression of the man before him. The lack of warmth troubled him. A single lightbulb hung unadorned from the pale, cracked ceiling.

The stranger opened a cabinet in the dresser to reveal a bottle of cheap brandy and a single glass. As the man opened the bottle, Denby noted that he wore slippers, old-fashioned brown slacks, a white shirt and a shepherd's check cardigan. He simply couldn't understand how the man could appear so comfortable in this chilly, unwelcoming place. Denby felt at a complete disadvantage but was unable to do anything but wait and see how the situation unfolded. Outside the wind howled and the rain that had just begin to spit on his arrival had turned to hail and was hitting the windows hard. It was as if he had gone back in time thirty or forty years. The only proof that he hadn't was a small silver-cased mobile phone that he noticed sitting on the windowsill.

God's Will

The stranger filled the glass halfway, then turned. Like his frame his face was long and narrow with wide dark eyes.

'They forecast snow,' Denby said, trying vainly to sound relaxed.

'It's more like a monsoon.'

'And you would know, of course,' the stranger observed sarcastically.

Denby was finally aggrieved enough to respond. 'Now listen here, I don't have to take that tone. I was invited here to–'

'I was referring to your childhood in Bengal.'

Denby was in the process of rising to walk out but this nugget of information from his past shook him and he sank back down.

'How the hell do you know about India?' said the man brushing strands of greying hair across his balding scalp, self-consciously.

'I know a lot about you. I know about your schooling at Buckmaster, your university days at Cambridge, your parents' messy divorce, your first dalliance back in eighty-five with the rent boy in a public toilet in Hammersmith—and of course I know all about your hard drive full of images of abused children that led to your arrest and the resulting two-year custodial sentence.'

For the first time since his arrival Denby felt genuine fear. Was this some type of trap? He had heard about these internet detectives and how they tracked paedophiles down, like it was a sport.

'Who are you?'

'I am Mr Lamb. You don't know me, and after this business is complete you won't see me again,' the man said firmly, finally passing him the glass and walking over to the glowing bars of the fire. 'I am very aware of you, however, and your time in Pentonville Prison—but your crimes are of no interest to me. I have invited you here to present you with a proposition.'

God's Will

Despite the cold air in the room Denby was feeling very hot. He took a large mouthful of the brandy and looked at the window. The dusty grey net curtains, dimly lit by the streetlights on the road outside, gave no solace. As the storm raged outside, Lamb rocked on the balls of his slippered feet and stared down at him.

'Paedophile,' he said softly. 'A strange word that twenty years ago most people had never heard of. But now it fills the populace with fear and loathing.'

'Let me tell you now, I have served my time and I have nothing to hide–'

'Other than what you can offer in any potential arrangement between us, I have no interest in you whatsoever, Denby. What crimes you have committed are of no concern to me.'

Placing his hands in his cardigan pockets, Lamb slowly paced the carpet before his guest. Denby watched him for a moment before finishing the brandy and placing the empty tumbler on the arm of the chair.

'Well, what is this job? I'm a busy man. I've got things to do.'

'No you haven't. You are currently living at a bed-and-breakfast in Muswell Hill and you spend your evenings drinking with a group ex-cons and general wasters in Soho.'

'And what if I do!'

'Tell me about your current home.'

'It's a place the probation services use for low category ex-convicts struggling to find a home. It's a temporary measure, but it's comfortable enough.'

'Paedophiles can be low category?' Lamb inquired, topping up the empty glass.

Denby was about to protest but he knew it was futile. In the eyes of the world he would always be a paedophile.

God's Will

'Not sure why I was sent there,' he mumbled, 'but I'm happy to be away from that damned secure unit, being watched all day. Might as well have been back in prison.'

'You have been there for six weeks now. By my estimation you must have spent your savings already and will soon be running into debt—if the cost of brandy is any indication, that is.' Lamb walked back to the electric fire. 'Very soon you will have a housemate. Very soon a man will join you at your little home for ex-cons. I want you to watch him and report to me wherever he goes and whoever he contacts. For that I will pay off any debt you have and give you three hundred pounds a week, plus expenses.'

Denby wasn't quite expecting such an easy line of employment. 'And all I have to do is tail him and report back?'

'And tell no one.'

'How long will this go on for?'

'As long as it takes.'

'Who is this man?'

Lamb stopped pacing and stared at the fire. 'His name is Greene. Thomas Greene.'

Denby twisted the end of his moustache into a fine point and shook his head. 'Never heard of him.'

'No, you wouldn't. Nobody would. Because his name recently changed. He was once known as Sickert. Thomas Sickert.'

Denby, who was in the process of finishing his second brandy, spluttered. 'Thomas Sickert? You don't mean–'

'Oh, but I do.'

'Now hang on. Sickert is a killer! He was involved in the Steiner business. That little girl... and all the rest of it.'

God's Will

'You mean the murder of little Lottie Steiner. And by "all the rest of it" you are referring to those terrible things he did to her. The conspiracies are endless. Did he really gobble her all up, I wonder?'

'Him and the other chap... Solomon? Anything is possible with minds like that. Butchers, the pair of them!'

'And you differ from them how, Denby?'

'I've never harmed a child in my life! I look... looked at images, nothing more. And before you say it, the young fellow in the toilet assured me he was seventeen!'

Lamb laughed softly to himself. 'I do apologise. That was uncalled for. Forgive me. Now what do you say to my proposition?'

'After that remark I've a good mind to tell you what to do with it.'

Lamb picked up the bottle and topped up Denby's glass a third time. There was no resistance. 'I understand. But I haven't finished yet.'

Denby took up the glass and it hovered at his lips. 'Go on.'

'If this partnership proves fruitful and your work leads to a satisfactory outcome, I will give you fifty-thousand pounds.'

Derby mouthed the words to himself, then drank the brandy in one go. Outside the rain seemed to have eased for the first time since his arrival.

3

The beaten man from the estuary is lying on an ancient four-poster bed adorned with the original curtains, the pattern so faded it is impossible to discern the artist's original design. Other than the bed and a single chair at its side, the room is decorated with dusty ornaments and faded prints. There are sprinklings of ceiling plaster on the bare floorboards

God's Will

and there are white, powdery trails where rats have scurried around the room and out onto the landing.

The man lies huddled on the lumpy mattress beneath layers of old, stained blankets, like a one-sided crucifix, his left arm pointing away from his body, the other splinted at a right angle across his chest. There is a dull ache from his right ankle but he lacks the strength to investigate. His mud-knotted hair is dry but his face is clean, the aftermath of the brutal attack clear to see.

Not for him, though. His eyes are mounds of black-blue flesh, like alien fruit, sealed tight, rendering him blind for the time being. He lives in a world of inexplicable noises and glimpses of flashing inner light.

He can hear the fire that burns in the hearth and the sound comforts him a little. It crackles and pops as if to say *hang on, stay in there, I am at your side,* but the only sound he can make in reply is that of his teeth tapping uncontrollably in his head. The freezing fog from the estuary has found a home inside him. It has warped his thinking and brought on a temporary dementia. It has his tongue, too; he can't utter a word. And, like a monotonous bass line, he hears that repetitive moaning out on the estuary. Maybe it is this sound that whips up the storm of panic in his chest. He coughs and chokes, and draws air in weakly through his partially opened lips. Then he gets his breathing back under control and his pain eases. He wants to speak, to call out, to find out where he is and what has happened, but he doesn't have it in him. Not yet. For the time being he must wait.

Motes of dust drift across his eyeballs. To him they are searing comets, turning his darkness into a universe of blazing activity. When he tries to focus on them they shoot out of view at enormous speeds. Sudden supernova bursts of light blind his inner vision and pain darts through his head. The sound of the rats scurrying beneath the bed

God's Will

increases his fear until, somewhere in the distance, he hears birdsong. He recognises the lilting song of a robin.

Is that you, my little friend? How do you like me now? Shaking like an epileptic, bird, broken and bruised to hell... Can you tell me who brought me to this not so wonderful hospital, with rats for porters? I did a terrible thing, my friend. A terrible, terrible thing.

Why these words? Why?

He can only wonder at this for a moment because right now he has other pressing concerns. New sounds have just joined the opus—creaking floorboards and footsteps.

Someone is coming.

4

Retired Inspector Reid sat at the kitchen table and noted how very clean it was. He didn't have a kitchen. He didn't even have a house. He didn't have much, least of all his health. He felt rough, shaky. It had been going on for some time but recently it had got a lot worse. He was at an all-time low. The return of his host distracted him briefly from this malaise and he forced a tight-lipped smile onto his lips. The other man was wearing a t-shirt with words that up until now he couldn't read. Now he could. *Keep Calm and Drink Ale.* Reid smacked his lips, then picked up the mug and took a sip of the milky, sugary tea. It made his spirits rise, ever so briefly.

The other man was Stockwell. He was short, with thick limbs and a shapeless, rectangular torso and black receding curly hair. Reid watched him for a moment but was unsure how to broach his real reason for being there. So far he'd lied. He needed access to this retired

God's Will

prison officer. Until the previous day he hadn't even been aware of Stockwell's existence. It would in fact have been true to say that he wouldn't have cared if Stockwell existed or not. Were it not for a chance meeting.

Billy Ruffle had been convicted of masterminding a series of bank jobs in the mid-seventies, and it was Reid who had put him behind bars. On the day of his conviction Ruffle had promised to get his revenge. Reid had to thank a twenty-year stretch and God's intervention for a change of heart. They had met by chance near Reid's flat the previous day, but instead of performing an act of retribution, Ruffle had explained how he was saved. He had found deliverance from evil in the shape of our Lord Jesus... and could he buy Reid a pint?

Sceptically, Reid had accepted. It was a decision that would change the rest of his life.

He took another sip of tea and then spoke with half-closed eyes. 'I'm sorry to say, I've told you a half-truth.'

'I don't follow...' said Stockwell, warily.

'I'm not writing a book about Thomas Sickert. My name is Reid. I was the investigating officer at the time of the kidnapping.'

'Christ,' said the other man, 'I see. That was a long time ago. What do you want with me?'

'Information. You were at Brixton.'

'That's right.'

'I met an ex-con yesterday. Billy Ruffle.'

'Reverend Ruffle? That God-botherer?'

Reid conceded he knew all about Ruffle's conversion and they talked about him and shared knowledge of other felons before Reid got to his point.

'Ruffle told me that you escorted Sickert to see Solomon at the hospice the night he died. Is that true?'

God's Will

'Yes, true enough. No secret there. What about it?'

'Solomon was dying of lung cancer and was taken from Broadmoor on the Isle of Wight to a London hospice. Did he ask to see Sickert, or was it the other way round?'

'Solomon asked to see Sickert.'

'I see,' said Reid, looking off, as if this changed what he knew about the case, 'and it was granted?'

'Yes, every prisoner has the right. It's down to the governor. It was granted.'

'Have you been questioned about this before?'

'Yes, a couple of boys from the Met came and wanted to know if the two men had spoken. And I'll tell you what I told them. I wasn't cuffed to him. That was Verecker.'

'I see. Where were you?'

'I sat outside at the door.'

'What time did Solomon die?'

'Eight o'clock.'

'Very precise?'

'I was finishing at eight. I was clock-watching. That was when the door opened and that's when Verecker told me. The doctor went in and he was dead. What more can I say?'

'And Verecker said there was nothing spoken between the two men?'

'That's what he said. You can rely on Verecker. Have you spoken to him?'

'I'm having a few problems locating him.'

'Took early retirement like me. I haven't seen him for years. This isn't about the Steiner gold, is it? You trying to locate it?'

Reid frowned. 'There is no gold. There never was.'

Stockwell grinned. 'Plenty of rumours say otherwise.'

God's Will

'You have no idea where I can trace Verecker?'

'Try the prison service. Explain you're ex-police. I'm sure they'd be able to help you.'

Reid reached into his pocket and took out a small wad of £20 notes. He placed it on the table between them. Stockwell picked it up and drummed out a rhythm on the polished table top.

'If you can find out for me, I'll double that.'

'I call in the Officers' Mess from time to time. I'll spread the word.'

The drumming suddenly stopped and Stockwell pointed the roll of notes at Reid. 'Isn't Sickert to be released soon?'

'Yes,' Reid said forlornly, as if the fact had placed him under the heaviest burden in his life, 'yes, he is. Today.'

One week after the clandestine meeting between Lamb and Denby, the subject of their discussion walked free from Brixton Prison. It was late winter, and Londoners were preparing for a cold snap that had been widely predicted by forecasters. As the last of the released men hurried past him, Thomas Greene (for his own safety he had now to erase any evidence of Sickert) moved from the spot he had stood on for more than a minute and walked beyond the shadow of the prison walls. He was afraid to move and walked slowly, tentatively. Ripples of soft light ran before his eyes and he felt nauseous. Nothing was real to him, and he was certain of nothing. He walked a little further but stopped again as he looked up at the overwhelming, white sky above him. It was so vast it seemed to press down on him, stopping him from joining the handful of other released men as they hurried off. It seemed so easy for them, those who had chosen petty crime as a way of life, but for him, a man whose only conviction had resulted in a life sentence, it was a unique sensation. It was one strong enough to take away his breath and force every thought from his mind.

God's Will

Then something caught his eye.

A solitary snowflake caught in the wind circled him like a bright white moth. If it wasn't for the dark prison walls he might not have seen it against the whiteness of the sky. Thomas Greene, the convicted kidnapper and murderer, the one-time gangster, was transfixed by its movement. At any other time in his life it wouldn't have meant a thing. But that day, that first day of freedom, he felt it was significant, and he focused everything he had inside him on that tiny white flake as it swirled and twisted in the wind. Soon it was joined by another and then another, and before long glittering white specks were filling the air. Somehow the sight calmed his thinking and his vision became clear again. Rubbing the melted snow from his beard and shaking the thin layer of snow from his shoulders, he looked back at the building that had been his home for nearly a decade, then set off through the cold.

Greene spent his first day of freedom in central London. It wasn't planned. He didn't have a plan. On the bus into the city he recognised so much that he thought lost in the horror of the past. But London was all he knew. He wandered aimlessly throughout the day, occasionally finding solace in an old pub or café he knew. Much had changed, and he had changed, too. Uppermost in his mind was Larry, but he had to learn to forget him now. He was gone, and if Greene was to have any kind of life in freedom he needed to find a different way of being.

On three separate occasions Greene found himself drifting towards Soho. That was his past. That was where it all began, and its pull was almost unstoppable. Somehow he fought it off until later that evening when he made the slow but unavoidable journey towards his new home in Croydon. It was a bail hostel, although few of these establishments dealt with bailees. Now they had another purpose. Much of their

God's Will

activity was aimed at rehabilitating offenders and reacquainting them with basic life skills after many years in prison. Greene was all of that.

The snow had stopped now but it had took hold and was at least three or four inches deep—a rarity for London. Greene stamped the slush from his feet at the door and looked up at the sign. Needham House was exactly as described by his probation officer. It was a red-bricked monstrosity resembling a Victorian workhouse. Seeing it up close, he wondered if that was its original purpose. Inside he was greeted with distant applause, a cough and the smell of disinfectant. It was very warm and, despite his apprehension, he was thankful to be out of the cold. As there were voices coming from a room ahead of him he walked towards it tentatively. More applause. A TV quiz show proved the source, and he understood that the pattering of hands was not for his arrival. A man sitting in a group around the television turned to face him. Suddenly Greene felt very alone and out of place.

'You've got to register,' the man said, too loudly. In a moment everyone was staring at him. 'You need to see Brian.'

For a moment Greene could only stare back, unable in any fashion to muster a response. It was a voice somewhere along the corridor that distracted him. Somehow it was a voice he knew well. He just couldn't put his finger on it because it was out of context. It was an odd sensation, a feeling that put him at odds with this new place. It was a voice that recalled the emptiness and despair of a life without hope. It stirred negativity within him. It evoked the suffocating smells of men's sweat, shit and piss. He wanted to leave, but something in that voice held him back and forced him along the corridor to a small office. There he found a man he knew very well indeed. Verecker, the screw who had befriended him at Brixton. The one who had been with him the night Larry died

God's Will

For a moment Greene simply looked at him, aware now that he didn't want to leave. Verecker's face reminded him of his time with Larry. It was the only the link he had.

Verecker was talking to an elderly man and didn't notice Greene at first. When he did, he didn't seem to recognise him.

'Can I help you?'

He didn't remember him? It hadn't been that long. Verecker had retired only a couple of years previously. Greene hadn't heard from him since, but then why would he? Inside, the screws were the enemy. Even if some of them were compassionate types, Greene didn't imagine one of them would feature in his life on the outside.

Telling the old man to leave and asking Greene to close the door when he had, Verecker got up.

'Hello, Tom.'

Greene suddenly understood what was happening and smiled weakly. 'Hello, Mr Verecker.'

'Sorry about that,' Verecker said, shaking his hand. 'Due to your...' He paused awkwardly.

'Infamy?'

'*Past*, I was going to say. Because of your past, we must be careful. Best if it seems I've never met you before. You now have to live your life as Thomas Greene. Sickert is no more.'

Greene nodded and Verecker smiled softly before offering him a seat.

'This is different, Mr Verecker,' Greene observed, sitting down.

'Enough of that. It's Brian here. Yes, I prefer it to walking the landings. Here I help men; I don't lock them up. It suits me.'

It fitted him perfectly. Greene had always sensed some hidden sadness within Verecker. He believed it stemmed from the job, which

God's Will

he seemed to have drifted into by mistake but had been too polite to complain about.

It took Verecker ten minutes to explain the rules of the house and what Greene could and could not do under his probation. Greene's probation officer had repeated it to him so many times he almost knew it off by heart, but he listened anyway. He was happy to feel safe and warm.

'Now then,' said Verecker eventually, stacking the paperwork into a tidy pile, 'that's all the official stuff out of the way. Now let me tell you roughly how things will work. You won't be here long, that's for certain. In fact, if it wasn't for a last-minute hitch you wouldn't have been here at all. I only got a call you were coming yesterday morning. There's a chap at the Home Office by the name of Malory who is dealing with your case. In the next couple of days he'll have found you alternative accommodation, and the sooner the better. There's a chance you could be recognised here. You have aged, and the beard might help, but a notorious face is rarely forgotten. Sorry, but it's a fact. Don't worry, though, I don't think you will have any problems. You're not on a programme, so you are free to come and go as you please. There's a small allowance, so get out and reacquaint yourself with the world.'

'Why no register?'

'As I recall, you were convicted of killing a man, not a child.'

Greene remained stony-faced and stared back at him. 'You know what I mean...'

'Society may have you down as a child molester, Tom, but in the eyes of the law you are a simple everyday killer. Sorry to be blunt, but it's a fact. Now, unless you are about to confess to some heinous crime that has been hitherto undocumented, I suggest you stick with that and begin to rebuild your life. Shall we take a look at your room?'

God's Will

5

Days pass and the bedridden man shakes no more. He has survived his brief hibernation and sensation has finally returned to his muscles. This endotherm is ready to live again. There is much pain in his splinted arm and right ankle, but it is bearable. But his eyes... what in God's name is happening there? It feels as if the rats have climbed aboard the bed and are gnawing at his eyelids, trying to look inside.

Agony, pure agony.

Someone has been attending him during his recuperation. Through dream like memories he recalls being fed and cleaned. His eyes have been bandaged and twice he has been led to a toilet, his aching ankle forcing him to hobble like an invalid. Why is he still alive? Could it be that the shapes he saw before he passed out were not his attackers but his saviours? It's the only explanation he can reach. On each splutter and cough, someone comes to his aid. They sit him up and pat his back, like a mother would a baby. It's an effective response and within a short time the coughing stops and he catches his breath again. He wants to speak, he longs to know where he is and what has happened, who they are and what they plan to do with him. But, most of all, he wants to know *who he is*.

As his strength improves so does his visual memory. Faces and places appear in his head like a slideshow, but there is no sense of what they imply. He knows they are distant shadows of his early life but why they leap through the darkness randomly, triggering different emotions and overshadowing his recent past, he does not know. Although it is from some clouded perspective he is fully aware that a large part of it is due to some terrible act he is solely responsible for. He tries to raise his

God's Will

hand to rub his stinging eyes but someone stops him. He catches his breath and pants for air. He suspects the person has spoken but his mind is lagging behind and by the time he realises they have, he has forgotten what they have said. Fingers touch his face and brush across his brow. There is no tension there. This is a gentle, caring hand. The same fingertips follows the contours of his head and lift it softly from the pillow. A glass is put to his lips. Much of the water dribbles down his chin but enough of it finds its way inside. He splutters but he is grateful. Footsteps on the floorboards fade and his nurse has gone. In time the crackles and pops in the hearth remind him of happier times. There were *some*, he recognises, some light amongst the darkness.

Slowly he is becoming conscious of the world beyond his room, the constant scurrying and squealing of the rats, the tapping at the window of a branch from a tree or bush, the clatter of a cart on cobbles on a yard outside, the shriek of a magpie, the caw of a crow and the cackling of geese. The distant moaning has stopped now. Footsteps and voices in other parts of the house tell him that there are at least two other people in it. Every few hours his carer appears and unceremoniously drops wood for the fire on the bare floorboards, waking him from his slumber. It is the same person who tends to his wounds and sits at his side. How he knows this he is not sure. Possibly it is through the heightened perception this sudden blindness has given him, but most probably it is because of the smell. Whoever these people are, they are not big on personal hygiene.

This house he cannot see or touch has become real in his mind. To break the monotony he imagines leaving his bed and exploring it. He walks along corridors, looks out of windows across a fogless marsh. He watches the robin in the branches of the tree that taps at his window. He imagines a winding lane that leads across the estuary where he was found. Because of the creaking floorboards and cobbled yard and the

God's Will

cart he suspects the house is old and for the first time he wonders if this is the house he saw with the light at its window out on the marsh. He also wonders where his attackers are now.

Was the moaning from them? What are they? Monsters of some kind? Beasts?

For the sake of his own mental stability he tries not to dwell on these thoughts for too long. He longs to unburden himself of this pain. And what of the faces that grow clearer by the hour, those images that parade through his mind? One appears often and brings with it contrasting emotions. A man, a handsome blond-haired man in his mid-twenties. He is smiling—but is he smiling with warmth or mockery? Then there is the little girl in the pinafore dress and hair in pigtails, the one who never smiles but stares at him with accusing eyes. This in turn brings a wave of emotion flooding over him, filling gaping holes in his memory.

He is woken by the robin outside his room, its eloquent song soothing him in his distress. He doesn't know why, but he knows it is the one from the marsh.

I did a terrible thing, my little friend. A terrible, terrible thing.

Why these words?

With this question comes a sudden revelation. A name. A bold, clear Christian name, followed swiftly by another, a surname. It is a name he knows in an instant to be his own.

My name is Sickert. Thomas Sickert.

6

God's Will

Greene had hardly slept. There was so much going on in his head he just couldn't settle. To his own amazement he realised he missed his cell. That security had been pivotal to his existence behind bars. One of the ironies of prison life was that even though he was surrounded by criminals, a foot-thick metal locked door made invasion in the early hours extremely unlikely. To remedy his current fears he had jammed a chair under the door handle.

Having little appetite and not wanting to encounter small talk in the communal dining area he decided to go out and get a coffee. On the way to the main door he encountered the old man who had been with Verecker the previous evening.

'Brian needs to see you. I was just coming to find you.'

'Is he in his office?' Greene replied, aware of the man studying his face.

The man didn't answer and the stare intensified. 'You look familiar. Where were you? Brixton? Pentonville?'

Greene remembered Verecker's comments about his notoriety. He rubbed his thick beard self-consciously before turning away.

Verecker was sitting at his desk, busy with paperwork when Greene walked in. He asked Greene to close the door, but before he could speak again Greene reran the incident with the old man. To his surprise, Verecker chuckled for the first time since his arrival.

'Frank? Memory like a sieve. But as you're leaving us I wouldn't worry about it.'

'So soon?'

'I got a call this morning.' He passed Greene an envelope. 'There's money and a debit card and pin. You will have a fortnightly allowance paid into that account. You'll also find the address of your new accommodation. Malory tells me it's a small bed-and-breakfast catering

God's Will

for low category ex-cons, so nobody there should show any interest in you.'

'Who is this Malory?'

'Your guardian angel. Be thankful someone is looking out for you.'

'Don't monsters like me normally get a new identity *and* a new home?'

'Haven't you heard about the economy? It hasn't improved much since you were sentenced in the seventies.' He said it with an empty smile that caught Greene's attention.

'Is everything okay?'

Verecker gave a sigh. 'I'm afraid my mother's not doing too well. She's had a number of strokes. She's very weak. They've done everything they can.' He got up, walked round the table and placed a hand on Greene's shoulder. 'But that's not your problem, so get on your way. And good luck.'

As Greene left he was thankful they had had that brief time together. Verecker's pain briefly overshadowed thoughts of his own hopeless future. Perhaps they overshadowed them a little too much, for as he flagged down a taxi he was unaware of another car starting up along the road, its occupant studying him closely.

Greene's new home was in Muswell Hill, but if it was anything like the previous place he was in no rush to get there. It had started to snow again and by the time the taxi had dropped him off on Charing Cross Road it was coming down heavily. He found a cafe and ordered a large cappuccino. Somewhat taken aback to receive very little change from a fiver, he found a seat at the window and watched this new world through the glass, wondering if this was how his life would be from now on—an endless sequence of moves from one place to another without any say-so from him. Forever looking over his shoulder. He

God's Will

spent the next hour trying to be positive, but his heart wasn't in it. He left shortly after that, feeling without purpose and out of place. This London seemed very different from the one he remembered. The dark, soot-coated buildings had all been cleaned up. There was a new shine to the city. It seemed the coffee shop he had just visited was one of a chain that had replaced the plethora of individual cafes dotted all over the city back in the seventies. He didn't know this place anymore. Maybe it was time to forget London?

Off Charing Cross Road he found Cecil Court, a walkway of small, elegantly fronted bookshops he had visited with Larry many times. Other than the books forced on him by school he hadn't read anything of substance in his life. Larry had changed all that. His flat in Mayfair had been a mine of literary treasures. Larry was a frustrated teacher and their early relationship had been Pygmalion-like. Despite the lukewarm response of his pupil, Larry, reciting prose at all hours, had slowly converted his young charge and before long, to his own surprise, Greene's love affair with literature had begun. Now, more than at any point in his life, he needed to occupy his mind. He didn't want to think about who might recognise him and what they might think and what they might say. Back in his cell he had been able to hide away from the world, but that protection was no longer available. Perhaps the power of prose would do the trick. If his terrors were to be kept at bay he had to force his mind into a rigid exercise programme. He believed reading could solve a lot of his problems.

With half-a-dozen books under his arm, Greene made his way to the till. There he discovered a young shop assistant cowering under a barrage of complaints from a brawny woman with tattooed eyebrows and a faux fur that had lost a number of skirmishes with moths. As Greene got closer he realised that the problem stemmed from the young girl's inability to trace a copy of a book that had apparently been put to

God's Will

one side. The sound of raised voices troubled him and this, combined with the gloom from the poor lighting in the shop, roused up his former pessimism. He felt an urge to throw down the books and run out into the fresh air, but just at that moment, as he turned his head away from the counter, he noticed a sign towards the back of the shop. The words called to him. Those words were *True Crime*.

Greene knew there would be something involving his own past there. He also knew there would be no good him reading any of it, but in seconds he had travelled the length of the shop and was scanning the long lines of hardbacks. It didn't take him long.

There was more than he expected. The first one was simply called *The Steiner Murders*. Another, which intriguingly had him and Larry related, was called *Twins from Hell*. Try as he might, Greene couldn't pull his eyes from Larry's gaze. Even from the grave Larry had some unworldly hold upon him.

Then there was a noise behind him, a voice. Greene turned to find the young assistant smiling up at him. God knew how long he had been standing there. She had clearly spoken but he had missed it and all he could hear now were footsteps out in the lane and the traffic on Charing Cross Road. Knowing she would speak again, he took the opportunity to study her pale complexion, her cherry-red lipstick and the short bob that reminded him of Lizzie Minelli in *Cabaret*. He half expected her to break into song à la Sally Bowles, but she didn't.

'I've got to nip out and there's no one to cover. Sorry…'

'It's okay,' he said. He realised he still had the book with him and Larry on the cover.

The girl glanced at it before looking back at him. 'Did you want that one as well?'

'As well?' he replied, faintly.

'As well as the ones you put on the counter?'

God's Will

'No,' he muttered, sliding it back into the vacant space.

'I don't blame you.' His bemused gaze forced her to expand on the comment. 'Those crime books. Depressing if you ask me.'

'Very,' Greene conceded as he made for the door. 'Very depressing indeed.'

For a man starved of freedom for decades, Thomas Greene made a valiant attempt at balancing the books in the hours that followed. He was more woozy than drunk. The cold air, like a slap across the cheeks, had quite a sobering effect. Initially the booze had given him a boldness that he had almost forgotten, but it didn't last. He knew what he should do, but no amount of alcohol was going to give him the strength to do it; to escape the city that had defined him.

He was now in Muswell Hill, his new home. It was only ten o'clock but the streets were deserted. The freezing conditions, it seemed, had cleansed them of all activity. Again Greene was reminded of how alone he really was. No doors, no lights out, yet still he was a prisoner. He didn't want to be here. He had had enough structure and daily ritual for one lifetime, but he was old and tired and lacked the strength to keep on against the grain.

The heavy snow that had briefly abated, allowing a golden sunset, had returned. Walking up the path to the address given to him by Verecker, he listened to the dull sound of his feet in the deepening snow. It padded the sound of his breathing around his ears, and the cold exposed the moisture in his breath. As he knocked on the door, a car, the same one that had followed him throughout the day, slowly passed along the road. As if a part of him sensed he was being watched, Greene was about to glance back when a bulb burst into life in the hallway. A diffuse shape moved towards him, the patterned glass of the door transforming it into some oddly shaped creature. When the door

God's Will

opened it revealed quite the opposite, however. In front of him stood an attractive dark-haired woman roughly ten years younger than himself.

'My name is...' For a brief moment he almost gave his real name, but then he quickly recalled his rather plain non de plume. He also remembered Verecker's words. *You are Sickert no more.* 'Greene,' he muttered. 'Thomas Greene. I believe you have a room for me?'

'I was expecting you earlier,' the woman said, barely allowing him to finish. Her smell was a mixture of cigarette smoke and cheap perfume, a combination he knew well.

'Yes, sorry. I... had a couple of appointments.'

'Yes, I can smell them,' she muttered coldly, sniffing at his breath. She was quick, he had to give her that. Standing back against the opened door she flicked her head back nonchalantly. 'You better come in.'

As Greene passed the woman in the hall she looked up and down the street as if his arrival was part of some illicit rendezvous. Maybe it was, he concluded. What would the neighbours think if they knew a notorious killer had just joined the community? For a moment he was uncertain where to go, so he waited for her to close the door and walk to the living room at the end of the hall. From the way she threw out her hips he got the sense that she was out to impress him. If she was, she had been successful. There was something he found appealing about her wholesome shape under the cheap polyester dressing gown as it swished against her well-formed backside. It reminded him of someone he once knew.

'Don't mind me,' Greene said as she turned off a flat screen TV on the wall.

'I don't,' she replied coolly. Then, as if it was some sort of natural reflex, she gave him an empty smile that disappeared as quickly as it had appeared. 'I'm sorry. I'm a little tired. I waited up for you.'

God's Will

'It's appreciated.'

'A man deserves a drink on his release,' she acknowledged.

Greene wondered what they had told her about his past. Her next comment told him she either knew nothing or she was a good actress.

'Have you been away long?' Before he could answer she waved her hand in the air. 'Ignore me. It's none of my business. I'm a bit out of practice. I only started up again recently. Things are a little more organised now. Bed-and-breakfasts are used less and less these days. I spoke to Mr Malory this morning and he's explained the general situation. I believe they're struggling to find places anywhere else at the moment. The usual merry-go-round.'

Greene was taking all of this in but his mind was distracted. He was thinking of another woman from another time. It was the eyes and hips that did it.

'I'm Angie.'

'Hello, Angie,' Greene said, with a weaker smile than he had intended.

'You eaten?'

'I had a bite earlier.'

'I see. You smoke?'

Greene hadn't smoked for years, but nearly took one from her anyway. It took an effort to remember that tobacco had little currency outside prison establishments.

As Angie lit up, Greene studied the room. Straightaway he was unimpressed. Inside he had been led to believe that there had been an interior design revolution in Britain. Well, if there had, nobody had bothered to inform Angie. Her world seemed to consist wholly of cheap ornaments and battered self-assembly furniture. Although the television was one of the latest flat-screen affairs, it was smaller than the one he had back in the seventies. There were other doors leading off the living

God's Will

room, but only one was open, to the bedroom. Angie caught him looking and walked over to pull the door shut. Her eyes met his for a moment and then dropped away.

If this was the usual first encounter most newly released felons had with the outside world Greene couldn't help but feel the probation service had excelled themselves. Angie was in her late forties, but still alive with that beguiling mystery that women of a certain age exude. Like some weathered temptress she studied him, one arm across her surprisingly narrow waist and the elbow of the other resting on it. Greene couldn't help noticing the shape of her large breasts and a milky white thigh teasing him through a split in her dressing gown. He looked away, only for his eyes to settle on a familiar print of a South American beauty in scarlet robes staring smugly back at him, as though sensing the tension in the room. He was outnumbered.

He was about to ask the way to his room when there was a commotion in the hallway. Greene turned as the door opened and a white-haired man with a ridiculously wide moustache stumbled in. His overcoat had a slight dusting of snow on the shoulders.

'By George, it's brass monkeys out there! Hello,' the man exclaimed, noticing Greene. 'A new arrival?'

He took off his overcoat and threw it on the sofa. From the smell of his breath Greene concluded he wasn't the only one who had had *appointments* that day.

'Thomas Greene,' he said, this time without hesitation.

There was a brief pause as the old man stared back at him. Greene put it down to the booze.

'This old reprobate, Mr Greene,' said Angie, picking up the coat and shaking off the snow, 'is Osbert. But everyone calls him–'

'Denby,' said the old man, offering his hand and giving the broadest of smiles. 'Osbert Denby at your service.'

God's Will

7

'Good old girl, Angie,' Denby muttered, winking at Greene who sat opposite him at the breakfast table. 'Salt of the earth, she is.'

The living room had been turned into a dining room. The sofa that had previously taken up a prominent position in the centre of the room had been relegated to a side wall and in its place stood a medium-sized dining table where Greene observed Denby at close quarters for the first time since their drunken introduction. He responded to the old man's observation with a smile that wasn't much more than a brief turning-up of the sides of his mouth. He returned his attention to his plate. He had too much of a hangover to do much else. He had barely touched his breakfast. He transferred his focus to the view through the window.

The snow clouds had gone now and the sky was a deep royal blue, but there was still snow on the ground. In the sunlight that somehow reached the overgrown back garden, the living room seemed a little less drab than before, and the dark-skinned beauty in the print on the wall looked a little less assured. Greene watched Denby's comical moustache dart from side to side and listened as he spoke. But he wasn't *really* listening; he was too caught up in his memories. He remembered the last time he was free, those final days before Lottie's kidnapping, and all the madness that ensued. There was something in Denby's voice that did it. He was very well-spoken, and that triggered something within him—again, something from his past. He just couldn't remember what or who. He wondered what crime Denby had committed.

God's Will

Everything around him had age to it, his host and Denby included. The old man seemed like a character from an old film, and Angie a character from a seventies TV show. The only thing that told him he was in the present was the baying studio audience on the TV ridiculing a man for apparently sleeping with his sister. How the world had changed. The sauciest daytime TV ever got in his day was *Cooking with Fanny*. When Angie reappeared from the kitchen to clear the table, Denby played mother by cheerfully topping up their cups from a large teapot. A moment later he was bawling with laughter, pointing at the TV.

'Seems the young fella has been sleeping with his big sister! My God, he must be desperate. Look at the state of her!'

Greene didn't reply but he got a sense from Denby's sudden change of expression a moment later that he was about to ask a question. He wasn't wrong.

'So, tell me, Thomas, what are your plans now you're out?'

Denby's frankness took Greene by surprise, but he quickly guessed the reason for it. Once you had done time at Her Majesty's pleasure you never quite trusted anyone again. He was probing, tentatively finding out about his new housemate. Verecker had said it was a house for low category ex-cons, so old Denby was probably a failed fraudster or something equally unexceptional.

Greene told him that he intended to take things easy, slowly reacquaint himself with the world, but the truth of it was he didn't have a clue what he was to do. Even though there had been a three-decade opportunity to plan for a life in freedom, he genuinely didn't know. Maybe it was superstition? If he didn't think about it, he wasn't tempting fate to stop it happening. But happen it did, and here he was, free to do whatever he wanted. The thought appalled him.

God's Will

He rallied and sipped his tea, thinking about this man Malory. Had he chosen this place because it was tucked away, with few tenants? Either way he was thankful. It was a definite improvement on Needham House.

'Now why don't you leave Mr Greene alone now, Denby?' Angie suggested. 'I'm sure he doesn't want to put up with your cross-examining all morning. What will you do today, love?'

She was dressed now not in dressing gown and slippers but in high heels, white blouse and pencil skirt. Greene was still somewhat taken aback by Angie's morning attire and her changed attitude towards him. During the night her scowl had transformed itself into a warm, almost girlish smile.

'I hadn't really thought about it. Not quite sure where to start.'

'It's often like that at the beginning. Just take it easy. Take each day as it comes.'

It was a cliché, but bound with so much warmth that he simply had to smile. She was the epitome of homespun philosophy, but that was fine by him. He had always found that particular kind of advice strangely reassuring.

'And the sun's shining. That's always a good sign, I say. The sun shining on the righteous and all that…'

It was an ill-advised observation to make in a home for ex-cons and they all seemed to be aware of the tension it provoked, especially Angie. She seemed frozen to the spot, a tower of dirty crockery balancing in her right hand. It was Denby who came to her rescue. Denby, of all people.

'I think you'll find that on a cloudless day the sun shines on everyone.'

God's Will

After breakfast Greene felt tired and went to his room for a nap. It lasted all of twenty minutes. A nightmare. He knew he was awake but it was still there, playing in his mind. He got up and paced the room but it was only when he splashed cold water on his face that it eventually began to fade. He sat on the end of his bed and sobbed. He knew why it was there.

He had dreamt that it was night and that he was standing before a large house. Leading to the door of this house was a long path, with swathes of brilliant white marguerites on either side. Fooled by the glow of the moon, they shone like stars in the darkness. Slowly he walked forward. He was afraid, yet he continued because he was aware of some strong sense of responsibility. He was there for a reason. As he reached the door he stopped. Something was wrong. Despite the late hour the door was open. Not much, but enough to see that the moon had pierced the darkness from the far end of the hallway. He went in, his heart racing. He stopped. There at his feet was the bloodstained body of a man. The silver light had transformed the corpse into some ghastly apparition and he wanted to run, but he couldn't. Although the man's face was beaten to a blur, he knew this man. He could tell from the fair hair and the high suntanned brow, now red and blue, mottled with clotted blood in the moonlight. The urge to run was intense, but he couldn't because he knew he was there for a reason.

Five minutes later Greene was out of the front door. He hadn't planned to go anywhere, but he was so haunted by this hellish dream he knew he had to keep his mind active. But where to go? There was only one place. Soho, or thereabouts. Why he believed he could ever keep away was anyone's guess. He blamed Denby. Before his fateful morning siesta it had dawned on him who he reminded him of. He had once known a solicitor by the name of Fenton, a slug of a man, fat and greasy and in the pocket of most criminals he knew. Fenton's part in

God's Will

Lottie's kidnapping may have been minimal, but he was a link in the chain. Whatever happened to Fenton, anyway? Whatever happened to the rest of them, these characters in a horror story? Greene tried to push the association to the back of his mind. He was good at that, focusing himself. Keeping his thoughts clear and positive had kept him sane. Prison had deprived him of his freedom, but inside he had got it all worked out. At the beginning there had been all kinds of horrors running amok in his head. Those final days of freedom had been as wild as he had experienced at any point during his time in London. And that was saying something. He knew that if he wasn't going to lose his mind he had to take all the madness, all the horror of those final days, and lock it away behind walls higher than any worldly structure. And until that morning he had been very successful, but he was now aware of something stirring deep inside that inner prison as he walked the streets of London and thought of the likes of Fenton. He could feel it as it stirred to life, as it slithered in the darkness, as it hissed like a waking beast. It was from this that the nightmare had been born.

Off Charing Cross Road Greene found Cecil Court once more, the walkway of small elegantly fronted bookshops he had visited the previous day. The Liza Minnelli lookalike he had spoken with was leafing through a magazine on the counter as he entered. He closed the door and instantly sensed a different atmosphere. The gloom had gone; the bright morning and razor-sharp beams of sunlight had seen to that. Particles of dust stirred by the draft swirled in the light and through the patterns his eyes converged on two words at the far end of the shop. The same ones he had seen the previous day.

True Crime.

The girl closed the magazine and smiled as she recognised him.

'You back again? I saved your books.'

God's Will

'Books?' he whispered, unable to look at her.

'You left them,' she said cheerfully, conjuring a small pile of paperbacks and placing them on the counter. 'Were there any more?'

'Er, yes. Just one,' Greene muttered, walking to the far end of the shop.

He located the book he wanted and made his way back, then hurriedly handed it over, hoping a quick transaction would avoid unwanted small talk, especially any regarding the hardback the girl now had in her hand.

'The Steiner Murders? There was something on the TV about that the other night,' she commented, holding the book in both hands. 'One of them has just got out, they say. Sickert I think his name was. Some say they shouldn't be let out. Killers like that. Child murderers.'

Greene found himself fascinated by the views of a stranger on the subject of his own infamy. 'What do you say?'

'Difficult to know, really,' she replied.

'How so?'

'There have been so many miscarriages of justice recently I often wonder when I hear about convictions.'

Greene's eyes narrowed and he was suddenly aware of the myriad of noises that pass for silence in a city. 'Do you think they may be innocent?'

'I didn't say that.' The girl looked directly at him for the first time. 'What do you think?'

'I... know a little of the case. I'm a... a journalist,' he lied, his eyes fixed on hers. 'But I know this much. The majority of men in prison are guilty of their crimes, and that Thomas Sickert *is* a murderer. It's a sad fact.'

God's Will

The girl frowned, then took the money and gave him the books. Greene felt bad; not for himself, but in the way he had affected her mood. He felt a sudden urge to redress the balance.

'It may also interest you to know that I have spoken to a lot of these criminals and some of them, even the most notorious, feel terrible guilt for their crimes.'

He gave her a long gentle smile he wouldn't have thought possible even the day before, and then he walked out of the shop into the sunshine of a London morning.

Mid-afternoon, Greene found himself in a pub he and Larry had once visited regularly, The Marquis of Granby on Rathbone Place, just off Oxford Street.

Ordering himself a pint of bitter and a beef and horseradish sandwich, he found a table near the window and took out the books he had bought. Larry had converted him from trashy novels into an avid reader of high-end literature. He ran his fingers along the bindings of the paperbacks. Anthony Powell, Olivia Manning, Julian Mclaren-Ross. The feel of a book in his hands normally gave him a warm, reassuring sensation, but it was the other book, the hardback with the sensational title that drew his attention and stirred in him an altogether more negative emotion.

Greene pushed the other books aside and placed the hardback squarely on the table before him. The cover had a picture of himself and Larry superimposed over images of Steiner, Lottie, Olga Hotlz the nanny, Larry's white Jaguar and Radstone House, Larry's family home, the finale for the killings. He opened it to find an image of him and Larry sitting by the riverside at Radstone. They looked a little like Charles and Sebastian from *Brideshead Revisited*, he thought. He remembered the photograph well and was certain that it had been in his

God's Will

possession for some time. He wondered how it had ended up in the author's hands. He leafed through the pages but in the end he came back to the same picture because it was the only one of them together. How handsome they both were. Larry was wearing a white tennis top and white shorts, while he was in pale linen trousers and a black silk shirt unbuttoned to the navel. It surprised him to see how toned he was. He guessed it must have been taken around seventy-four of seventy-five. He attempted to recall who had taken the picture, but his head was spinning and he needed to take a large gulp of his beer to clear it.

Would he ever rid himself of Larry's pull? On this busy junction of Rathbone Place and Charlotte Street, watching the steady flow of lunchtime traffic, he realised he didn't want to be rid of it. It was too intoxicating. In a way, this was why he was here. He hadn't thought about it until that moment, but it was under this perpetual gaze of restaurants, pubs, offices and listed buildings that he had really got to know Larry. It was in the Wheatsheaf, directly across from him, that he had amassed such happy memories of wild nights with Larry's rag-bag of bohemian friends.

By the time Greene emerged from the pub later that day he was muzzy-headed thanks to the five pints of bitter he had consumed. Instead of going straight ahead towards Oxford Street and getting a bus back to Muswell Hill, he turned left along Charlotte Street. It was early evening and the crescent moon was hanging low, competing unsuccessfully for prominence with the BT Tower, which glowed like some gigantic lighthouse against the darkening inky sky. Halfway along the street a flurry of snowflakes forced him to stop and look up. It was a moment or two before he realised it was only the wind shaving layers of settled snow from windowsills and eaves and not another fall. He thought back a couple of days to Brixton, his former home. In the

God's Will

same moment a car stopped on the road beside him and he heard a voice he recognised. He slowly dipped his head to see inside the car.

'Can I offer you a lift, Mr Greene? Or do you still prefer Sickert?'

Greene's caution quickly turned to disdain.

'Inspector Reid...' he muttered with a groan. 'I wondered how long it would be.'

8

Soon there is a pattern to the days. Each morning Sickert is woken by the chorus of birds outside his room. He listens carefully for the lilting song of the robin. His robin. He needs a friend now. In between those times he coughs up gritty phlegm—he suspects he's swallowed a few bucketloads of mud from the estuary—he aches, he sleeps, but mostly he wonders what his story is and who has done this to him.

If it wasn't for his the terrible pain in his eyes and his ankle he would get up and find a way to escape, but he knows he wouldn't get far. So for now he bides his time.

Strength is not only growing in his body; his mind is growing stronger, too. He is finding a way to control his negativity. He plays games, practises mental arithmetic, tries to remember the spelling of awkward words. He knows some poetry and, for some odd reason, he can recite a great deal of Shakespeare. Was he an actor? Was he once a performer of some kind? Despite this positive development, a sense of depression hangs over him. It is stronger when certain images enter his brain, like the man with the blond hair and the little girl. Only now they are animated. Now he can see them both walking, gesturing to him. But *why*?

God's Will

A wheeled carriage of some kind travels through the house towards Thomas Sickert's room. He can't make sense of the noise. A carriage, inside a house? Plaster and dirt crunches beneath its hard wheels and the unoiled axle squeaks as if to say *clear the way! clear the way there!* The sound gets louder and louder and as it does so fear grows inside the man on the bed. He tries to sit up but he doesn't have it in him and flops back onto the pillow. The noise reaches a deafening crescendo before stopping, suddenly, before him.

For a full minute, nothing. No words, no movement. Sickert senses the presence of more than one person, but they don't speak. Not a word. They are studying him, like an insect under a microscope. He has no courage. Not an ounce.

'Move me closer to the fire, Philip, and close the door.'

At last. A woman, then—and she's not in a carriage but a wheelchair, of course! Sickert tries to assess the situation, but he is still too afraid. He is completely at their mercy.

He quickly estimates the woman to be elderly. Seventies, eighties? She speaks slowly and her voice is soft and gentle, yet hoarse. Is she ill, perhaps? He suspects so as she coughs occasionally. Her cough is different from his own. She does it to clear her throat, not her chest. There is something familiar in the way that the other person, Philip, moves around that tells Sickert he has been his carer since his arrival.

'Now stoke the fire. We need more food and water. And see if there is any brandy left The Napoleon.' Philip does not move from the spot. Sickert hears the old woman patting his arm and adopting a softer, reassuring tone. 'There's nothing to worry about. Our patient will not hurt us.'

Sickert's eye dressings are changed and ointment is liberally applied. The combined smells of the strong balm and Philip's unwashed state almost makes him wretch. He recovers quickly and, after a small

God's Will

intake of food—cheese, dry bread and a little brandy—he is propped up onto his pillow. With the door closed, the temperature has risen two or three degrees and for the first time the patient feels warm. The pain in his eyes has reduced. The ointment is working. It is no longer a stabbing sensation. Instead, the pain now throbs across his eye and brow; it is distracting but tolerable. You could almost say he was feeling comfortable, comfortable enough to speak for the first time. He parts his bloated lips.

'Please don't hurt me…'

'No one will hurt you now.'

'Who are you?'

'Who I am is unimportant just now,' the woman replies, grandly.

Sickert's voice is hoarse, like the woman's, but without her energy and tone of authority. 'Where am I?'

She ignores the question. 'What brought you here?'

'I…' His voice trembles. 'I can't remember.'

'What *do* you remember?'

Sickert thinks for a moment and clears his throat. The effort triggers acute pain in the centre of his chest. He finds just enough strength to mutter a response. 'Nothing of the present. A little of the past.'

'Your own past?'

'What do you mean?'

No reply. Just another long silence, punctuated by the occasional pop and fizz from the fire.

'What brought you here?' she repeats.

'I can't remember. I wish I knew.'

'Tell me what you do recall.'

'I remember the… beasts. They have done this. I got away. Somehow I escaped.'

God's Will

The old woman doesn't reply. Again Sickert wonders if this pair are party to his nightmare. More whispers and a cacophony of sounds emanating from the ancient wheelchair convey to Sickert an image of the old woman and Philip in spirited conference.

The old woman coughs again before speaking, slowly. 'Describe these beasts.'

'I can only remember the sound. The howling. Long groans in the mist.'

There is a long pause. 'That is no beast. And that groan, as you describe it, is just the fog horn out in the estuary. So relax. You are safe here, Mr Sickert.'

9

The inside of Reid's car stank of fish and chips. Greene wondered briefly f Reid had just eaten or if it was always that way. There was too much in his mind to take the thought any further. From Charlotte Street they travelled west along Mortimer Street before eventually turning north past Broadcasting House, along Portland Place and Regents Park.

'Is this a kidnapping?' he asked eventually.

'That's your line of business, Sickert. Not mine.'

Angry that he hadn't thought the question through, Greene dismissed his own stupidity and got to the point.

'Let's get it out of the way then.'

Reid didn't reply until they had turned onto the busy Marylebone Road. 'What do you mean?'

'You want to ask me the same things you've been asking for the past quarter of a century, and even though I will tell you I don't have

God's Will

the answers you will continue to ask them until one of us dies. And you will do so because you know I have little choice.'

'Oh, you have a choice. You have plenty of choice. You're a free man now, Thomas.'

Greene pressed the middle fingers of both hands to his temples to release the pressure that was building there. 'No, I am not. Not by any stretch of the imagination.'

Despite Reid's best efforts, it had been nearly three decades since they had last met. Yet Greene had recognised Reid in an instant. The thin face, that lanky tall frame, the pale skin and ginger hair thinning to reveal a freckled, unnaturally large, domed head. He had looked old even in his thirties, at the time of Greene's arrest. He looked considerably older now, withered one might say, an old knight who had been crusading for far too long. But Don Quixote was without his trusty Sancho Panza.

'Whatever happened to Sergeant Calvert?'

'Have you had anything to eat?'

'So this is a date?'

Reid smiled and his eyelids dipped briefly, but he didn't answer. 'Nothing too extravagant, but I could stretch to a burger, if you like? Or maybe just a coffee?'

'Just ask me, Reid. Just do it so I can give you the usual reply and I can go...'

'Why would you never see me in prison?'

'Because I didn't have to. Besides there was nothing to say.'

'It may surprise you to know that I'm not here because of Lottie— not directly, anyhow.'

Intrigued, Greene studied Reid more closely. What drove a man to search for the remains of a body after thirty years? What difference did

God's Will

it make, other than to his own conscience. Did he believe he could have saved her? In a way, Reid was more haunted than he was.

Inspector Reid had been given extra time by the Home Office to interrogate him and Larry after their capture. Over the following four days he and his team had gone to work on the pair of them. They went too far. They were heavily beaten. If it hadn't been for the crimes there would have been an outcry. Reid had never given up trying to find out what happened to Lottie. He fell, abruptly, unceremoniously, into civil life not knowing, and here he was, long into retirement, still searching for the same answers. He had pestered Greene in prison with letters. So many letters. Greene almost felt sympathy for him. Almost, but not quite.

How many lives had Lottie's death affected? He was surprised Reid had found him so quickly. How many more would be looking for the answers, he wondered?

'I actually wanted to ask you some questions about the night that Larry died,' Reid announced finally.

Greene looked out through the windscreen as Reid slowed to let a group of young women cross the road. It looked like they had been drinking, and one of them stumbled in her high heels when she reached the pavement. The other girls laughed. Greene didn't know where he was now.

'He asked to see you and, per his request, you were taken from Brixton to see him at the hospice.'

Greene didn't speak for a couple of minutes and Reid seemed content enough to wait for an answer.

'He said nothing that would be of any interest to you.'

There was a glimmer of excitement on Reid's face. 'So he did say something?'

'Oh, he spoke all right. That's the whole problem...'

God's Will

'What do you mean by that?'

'If I tell you will you leave me alone?' Reid didn't say a word. 'He spoke but it made no sense. He blamed it all on God.'

'Blamed what?'

'His cancer, Lottie's death, life. I don't know.'

Although it was difficult to tell, Greene sensed Reid was disappointed. After that, his cross-examining was less intense. He even got the odd snippet of trivia about Soho and how it had changed in his absence. Nothing in particular grabbed Greene's attention, and he got the sense that his interrogator was playing a well-rehearsed part. Greene was more concerned with where he was being taken. He didn't question that he *was* being taken somewhere, though. He knew, even if Reid didn't sense it, that after a lifetime of incarceration there was very little fight left in him. He did what others decreed.

They had been driving for nearly half an hour when Reid guided the car into the curb of a residential road and turned off the engine. It was dark now, and other than a few lights at windows along the road and a line of glowing street lamps, Greene couldn't see very much.

'Did you know your former place of employment is no more? Milton's is a restaurant now. Russian, I think. Don't like the Russians. Too loud, no class. Most of them are criminals—wealthy ones, but criminals nevertheless. London isn't what it used to be.'

Greene didn't hear any of Reid's anti-Russian sentiment. The mention of Milton's had stirred a thousand memories.

'There was a mysterious fire a few months after you were sentenced,' Reid went on. 'Very odd. Nobody was injured but it seems —fortuitously—that Milton's was heavily insured.' He gave Greene a knowing smile. 'Has your friend Henderson been in touch with you at all?'

God's Will

'Henderson and I have nothing to say. We never had. I don't even know if he's still alive.'

Greene wiped away a film of condensation that had formed on the passenger window. The temperature inside the car had plummeted dramatically since they had stopped.

'Where the hell am I?'

Reid's hand pointed across the road. 'You're home, Thomas.'

Greene then realised with surprise that he was back at the B-and-B in Muswell Hill. Reid had simply approached the house from a different direction. It was cheap theatricals, but he had come to expect nothing less from his old adversary. Nevertheless, he had made his point.

I know where you are, Sickert, and I am watching you. And I will never stop until I find out what you and your sick friend did with that little girl.

10

Sickert wakes suddenly, choking, mumbling, sweat running from under his muddied hair across his brow like slushy, melting snow. A gentle hand wipes the residue from the soaked bandages across his eyes.

Sickert catches his breath but does not try to speak. The images in his brain are multiplying. Moments from his early life jostle for attention. Without sight, he struggles to hide from them. They form into some jellyfish-like creature in the dark recesses of his mind. Its dark form bobs gently on the periphery of his thinking, the terrible consequences of his actions dangling beneath it like tentacles. He only has to glance at it briefly to realise why this intense pain has been with

God's Will

him all along. It is because he, Thomas Sickert, committed a terrible crime a long, long time ago.

God forgive me. What have I done?

Footsteps, a creaking door, and a wheelchair approaching. It crunches on fallen ceiling plaster as it travels across the room and stops by the bed, on the side by the fire. The door closes. There is a brief staccato cough and then the questioning resumes. Sickert is only half listening.

Between each enquiry there is a long, measured silence, but all he can see is his distant past in his mind's eye. There are whispers in the air but he can't make out a word. Where is he? Who are these people? He wonders if *they* are responsible for his injuries. He quickly concludes they are not. If it's possible to define a human being from their voice, then this woman has goodness in her. What he *does* wonder is if this dire state of affairs is some type of retribution for what he has done in his life. He wants to cry, but the loud rumble of wood dropping into the hearth and a small announcement from the woman disturb his thoughts.

'My son Philip found you out on the estuary. You have been heavily beaten. He saw two men in the mist. I know who you are but not why you are here or why this has been done to you. I suspect it may have something to do with your infamy.'

Has she read his mind? Infamy?

'You are Thomas Sickert, of course—a man who, with Larry Solomon, was convicted of kidnapping and murdering a child many years ago.'

Of course. Larry. The man with the blond hair. And Lottie... I'm a killer!

'That is how I know who you are, despite your injuries. You are very recognisable. And now you wonder why we have not called a

God's Will

doctor or informed the authorities. We have not done so because we live in a remote place. There has been a crime, of course. But I have no intention of bringing danger to my door—or to you. No matter what you may have done in a former life, I certainly do not condone revenge. That only provokes more pain. We shall sit tight, for the moment. Is that what they say in films? You were once an actor, were you not? Is that the vocabulary of gangsters? Something you once were, also? My, what a colourful life you've led.'

'Please don't mock me,' Sickert mutters, with a sob. 'I don't remember what happened to the child or how I could have done it...'

'There are many theories on what happened. I wonder what the truth is?'

The fire suddenly catches and in the same moment the pain across Sickert's eyes throbs more intensely. He winces and places a hand on his brow.

'Your eyes are not good, your arm is broken and your shoulder was dislocated until Philip popped it back. Your ankle is also badly twisted. I suspect you have snapped tendons there. Your eyes are infected. I suspect it's the foxes. Their faeces gets into the mud on the esturary. It happened to Philip as a child. I nursed him back to health then and we will do the same with you. Just give it time.'

'What estuary?'

'The pain will pass, I promise. Do you remember where you live?'

'No. I want to leave here now. I appreciate what you have done.'

'We're snowed in. When the mist cleared, snow clouds took its place. It's been heavy for days. You're lucky you were found. The nearest town is twenty miles away. We don't have a car.'

'I remember *two* people finding me.'

Nothing, then after a long pause. 'You are mistaken. I have been bed-ridden this past year. Thomas was returning from town alone when

God's Will

he discovered you. Forgive me if this sounds a little melodramatic, but he saved your life.'

'You said your son saw two men.'

'Yes, of course. It was probably them who you saw.'

'I am thankful for what you have done, but why don't you contact the authorities now? Let them take the responsibility?'

There was a long intake of breath and then a bout of small coughs. 'We don't have a phone here, and if Philip goes I am in no position to defend you, alone.' She laughs, which sparks more coughing. 'There I go again. How very melodramatic. Thomas, you must know you are free. You have served your time. You must trust me.'

'Who were these men?'

'We don't know. But what they have done to you is monstrous. I will leave you now, but I will return later. Maybe you could tell me what you remember? If you need any assistance just ring.'

'Ring?'

Footsteps approach the bed and Philip places a small domed shaped object into his palm. He is too weak to even hold it. It drops and rolls off the bed onto the floor, its ring echoing around the room. A bell. Philip puts it back in Sickert's hand and gently closes his fingers around it. He hears the wheelchair moving away from the bed.

'Whenever you need assistance, Thomas.'

The woman's soothing, hypnotic voice seems to surround him, and sends him into a trance. He is falling into a deep, deep sleep, and no matter how hard he tries he cannot bring himself back.

11

God's Will

Osbert Maximilian Denby had come to the unavoidable and disturbing conclusion that the job of watching over Greene (he had decided to use his official title even when speaking with his new employer so as not to make a slip-up) was going to be considerably more difficult than he had been led to believe by Lamb, the mysterious figure who had gatecrashed his mundane life a week or so earlier. Putting the obvious perks aside, he realised he had been put into an incredibly dangerous position. Damn him! Damn him for knowing his past and damn him for his promises of riches—the man had him in the palm of his hand.

Nevertheless, his first day of employment had been simple enough—well, to start with, anyhow. Greene had proved to be a simple man, with a taste for the ordinary. A cafe, a bookshop and then an afternoon spent in a pub on Rathbone Place, luckily for Denby an area he knew well. It was later on that day that his surveillance capabilities were found wanting. Be it prearranged or by chance, Greene was picked up by a saloon car on Charlotte Street and whisked eastwards before Denby could flag down a taxi or get the registration. Lamb had provided him with a cheap mobile phone with two stored numbers for him to call when he needed to make contact. He called him straightaway with news of this development from outside The Marquis of Granby (it was here that he had previously watched Greene for over three hours) but was unable to contact his new employer until later that night.

Would today be any more fruitful? he wondered, watching his quarry across the kitchen table. Due to the position he found himself in, Denby was in a foul mood. Yet, through this fog of anger, he knew he must keep up the pretence. He hoped his reserves of will were enough for the task ahead, because if they weren't his future well-being was at risk.

God's Will

Today he resolved to try a different approach. He would stick with Greene, no matter what. Over breakfast he discovered his new *friend* was making another trip to the city, and he was ready and waiting when Greene walked out. No matter what Denby thought of Lamb he was right about one thing—he did need money. If only to get out of this hostel for the needy and away from Angie's dreadful cooking.

The front door had barely closed when Denby snatched it open and followed Greene out. 'How did you get on yesterday, old boy? Go anywhere nice?'

Greene didn't look round as they walked towards the high street. 'I just walked. I like to walk.'

Yes, you do, don't you, you selfish bastard! thought Denby as he considered his aching feet.

'And what are your plans for today?'

'Into London. There's a couple of things I need to do.'

'Mind if I share the trip in, Thomas? I say, you don't mind me calling you Thomas? Don't want you thinking I'm the pushy type.'

Getting no audible reply (he thought he saw a small nod) Denby took his place at Greene's side. The moisture in their breaths mingled in the cold air, forming a small patch of mist above their heads but the two strangers remained apart in every sense until they were aboard the bus.

'I'm meeting up with some old friends,' said Denby as they sat down towards the back. 'When I say "friends" they're more acquaintances, really. They have a certain regard for me. They see me as an inspirational figure, I suppose. I have some very highly placed connections. If I can help you in any way, Thomas, just say the word.'

Greene could not have been more uncommunicative. It worried Denby, and he considered the awful possibility that Greene may be onto him already. As the bus filled and slowly made its way to central London, he thought it through. For a full ten minutes he mentally

God's Will

retraced his steps from the previous day, but he was certain he hadn't been spotted. Then he wondered about his room. Had he left any incriminating documentation there that Greene could have seen? He had read up on him and Larry Solomon. What they had done was horrific, and it had turned his stomach to think that men could get pleasure from... *that*. He knew everything he needed to know about Greene and for the first time since his meeting with Lamb he felt he was redeeming himself in this work. He himself had been wrongly imprisoned. He wouldn't hurt a child. He liked children. Greene was the *beast*. He needed to be watched, and what if he was getting paid for it? Maybe Lamb was a grieving father. Maybe he was planning to hurt Greene? And what if he did? He deserved everything he got. The poor child.

Denby concluded with a resolute clearing of his throat that it was a no, it was not possible that the beast at his side could get the better of him. He was no professional by any means, but even without any surveillance experience he had done a fine piece of work to date. He would do this for the child and the money. Why not? But Greene was a clever one, and if old Denby was to achieve success in this enterprise he needed to tread carefully. It was like a game of chess and he had to be one move ahead always. When they arrived at Tottenham Court Road, Greene gave him a smile and wished him a good day. Denby was pleased as punch. A connection had been made at last. Giving Greene a wave he followed him off the bus and walked in the opposite direction. Within a minute, however, he was hurrying the other way, tailing his man once more.

Later that afternoon, as Denby shuffled down the Strand, his eyes glued to the back of Greene's head as it bobbed amongst the heads of tourists and commuters ahead of him, he was feeling pretty confident. He was already noticing a pattern to Greene's behaviour. This was

God's Will

good. After only two days, he had found a way of reading his personality. The younger man was without purpose; there was never a hurried step or a change in tempo. He would walk a hundred yards and stop and look in a window or stand quite still and look at the sky. After a long pause he would be off again. It infuriated Denby but at least it allowed him to keep up. They were both getting on, but Greene was ten years Denby's junior, and if he suddenly bolted or disappeared into a busy store Denby was certain he would lose him. But he never did. How did Lamb know that? When Denby was *offered* this work he had thought it would prove impossible; he had only gone along with it because of the money and the hidden threats, but now he was beginning to sense that Lamb understood Greene—and himself—a lot better than he realised.

Denby had bought himself a small notebook and from the beginning had jotted down notes and times concerning Greene's movements. So far that day it read, *8.12: Shared bus with Greene into central London—little conversation. 9.04: Book Bazaar—duration 8 mins. 10.12: Cafe Renault, Soho—no contact with anyone. 11.38: Left.*

To Denby's consternation, Greene had been walking ever since. The word Soho had been circled. He decided he would do this whenever Greene visited a new area. So far, with the exception of the bookshop, everywhere was new and had to be circled. There seemed no pattern to the geography of his movements, only to his behaviour. Denby hoped this would change. He was becoming increasingly concerned that he would have nothing to report back at the end of the week—Lamb was expecting a detailed report. Why he was worrying he wasn't sure. The only incident of note worth reporting, the previous day's meeting with the man in the car on Charlotte Street, had been greeted with little interest from Lamb when he did eventually track him down later that evening. The more Denby thought about it, the more his curiosity grew,

God's Will

not only in Lamb's interest in Greene, but in Lamb himself. It was the money that confused him. Who was he? Surely no grieving father, living a frugal existence in a drab apartment, would be able to offer that amount of money? Then it struck him. Something he remembered reading in one of the books about the case. *The Steiner Gold*. The ransom that—if the rumours were true—the kidnappers had hid and was never recovered. What if Lamb had discovered something? It didn't take a genius to work out that if Lamb was willing to offer Denby £50,000 he would clearly be making considerably more himself. Was that it? Was that why Greene was worth watching every hour of the day, or was it something more sinister? Whatever it was, Denby was determined to find out, if only to increase his own stake in Thomas Greene.

12

A couple of days later Sickert stirs from troubled dreams and is aware that someone is watching him from the door. It can't be Philip, he decides. He is outside chopping wood, a daily ritual and as regular as the twilight song of the robin at his window or the procession of rodents beneath his bed. Therefore it must be the old woman. Does she walk? Is the wheelchair merely a prop? There is, of course, another possibility—that there is a third person living in this house. What disturbs him most, perhaps, is that he can sense a presence in the room even when there is no aural evidence that anyone is there. Has his blindness given him a sixth sense? Whatever it is, it has warned him that he is not alone as he emerges into full wakefulness.

God's Will

He still lives in a painful limbo. One minute his eyes are stinging, red hot, seemingly inflamed to double their size; the next that sensation eases, only to be replaced by the throbbing pain in his ankle and splinted arm. Throughout it, the dark shape in his head increases in size until he can no longer ignore its meaning or his past—the early part of it, anyway. It shocks him that he can remember his early life in such vivid detail and yet remember nothing of his recent past. His childhood, his mother, his absent father, his teenage life, his brief time as an actor, even his early days in London are as clear to him as the pain of his broken body. What he can't contend with is that his recent life is a blank. Is it because of the attack, or is a part of him putting up the barriers, protecting him from some hell he is yet to face? Now he knows his suspicions must be real—that he is a killer.

And what of this place? How has he come to be in this remote backwater? Why does he trust so readily and without question the words of the old witch who tends him? He doesn't ponder on any of this for long as now he hears the wheelchair trundling towards his room. Other than Philip tending to his wounds and catering for his needs he has had no communication for days. Now she is back. Sickert feels calmer in the knowledge that she is coming. He can't explain it but he feels completely at ease in her company. The chair finally comes to a stop and as it does so Philip helps Sickert up onto his pillows. Why doesn't he speak? Is he simple-minded or just prudent? It's difficult to say. All he gets is this musty mixture of body odour and sweat. His breath isn't much better.

The old woman clears her throat and wishes him a good evening. A detailed update on his condition follows. Although the monologue is punctuated with coughs and splutters, there is purpose and assuredness in her tone. The image of a wrinkled spinster is fading, and another of an assertive yet kindly Miss Havisham type is taking its place. Sickert

God's Will

listens to it all patiently before asking her name. Again, as to all his enquiries, there is no instant response. She is thinking things through. But why?

'As a child I was known as Bepa.'

'Is that short for something?'

'Not that I'm aware of. Just a silly name for a silly girl. I lived in a dreamworld. My parents found it most unsettling.'

The chair again is a cacophony of creaks and clicks, and from this constant movement Sickert senses that she is as anxious as he is. He finds this strangely reassuring. He can't explain it but he feels the urge to talk to her, to explain in detail what he can remember. He has become so relaxed he almost asks her who was watching him from the door—herself or a third member of the household? He decides in the end to bide his time.

'Any more news of my attackers?'

'Thankfully, no. Philip has been out but there has been no one in the area recently. There are no new tracks and it hasn't snowed recently. He did, however, trap a few rabbits. He makes a fine stew.' There is a slight pause before she changes tack. 'You said you remember some of your past?'

The urge to talk to her, to pour out his heart, is strong but Sickert doesn't know why. Maybe she *is* a witch? Does she have a spell on him? Or is it in her voice? That peculiar yet comforting rasp that invites a response. He wants to remove the bandages and see her face.

'Yes, I remember some of my past in great detail now.'

'Why don't you tell me what you can remember? It may help.'

'Help? I can't be helped.'

'Why do you think that?'

'Because I feel great shame for something I can't remember doing.'

God's Will

'That makes sense. There must have been a happy time in your life, though?'

Sickert sighs, but after a moment or two he starts to reflect on his childhood. 'Not at the beginning. Not as a child. I recall being quite lonely. My father ran off with the woman next door when I was ten. Due to the reduced income we ended up on a council estate. I was bullied a lot. I found solace in TV shows and films. Imagination was my escape, but I knew it wouldn't be good enough in the end. I became a bit of a dreamer, like you. In my late teens I considered the possibility of a life elsewhere. I came to London in my early twenties. I had nothing. Not a penny. But I was free and I was content. Yes, I was happy then.'

'Tell me about it, Thomas. Tell me about that happy time.'

There is a long silence and internally Sickert sees his hand hovering above the broken pieces of a puzzle. Intent on making some sense of his life, he tentatively begins to place the pieces together.

* * *

As a teenager I struggled with a crippling lack of confidence and it was on the stage where I believed I could defeat this. And it worked, though it was less to do with the performances and more to do with the members of the opposite sex I met around that time. To my amazement I discovered that to some females self-consciousness in a young man was actually an appealing trait, especially if you had the looks—it may surprise you to know that I was quite a looker in my day. It was fun for a time, but it was clear that I was no actor. I really didn't have it in me —not for the theatre, anyway. I managed to get a job touring with a rather lecherous elderly director, I think I only got the job because he wanted to bed me. The performances were awful but I did my best.

God's Will

However, it was clear from the beginning that I was never going to make my fortune from acting.

A year or so into the job it was announced that we were to perform in Watford. Until then the company had only toured the North and the midlands. I suppose it was the town's proximity to London that excited me. For some undefined reason I was obsessed with a city I had never visited. Maybe it was from all the television I'd watched as a kid—*The Saint*, with the debonair Simon Templer, *The Avengers*, with Steed and his bowler hat and the umbrella that was also a sword—who knows? Anyhow, during the first week of the Watford run I packed my bag and took a train into London. To say I was unprepared for my great adventure in the capital would be understating the facts. I had nowhere to stay, or any real money for that matter, but I was young. All I cared about was making a name for myself. I wanted success in the place I had adored from afar. Whatever the reasons, I believed I was on the threshold of a great adventure when I arrived. After a week of sleeping on YMCA mattresses I managed to get a job working at a cabaret club called Milton's in Soho.

My boss was a man called Henderson. He was a really nasty individual who hated my guts from the very beginning. I was terrified of him, but I knew what I was getting into. It was hunger that forced me to take the job, not courage.

It was there that I met Charlie and Stella. Charlie was the general manager under Henderson and Stella the star act in the cabaret. She and I very quickly became lovers. She was different from every woman I had ever met until then. I had experienced numerous liaisons, with women of all ages, when I was acting, but they were from a different place. They were wholesome factory girls and smart shop assistants lived in a world where the only goal, it seemed, was finding a husband and having kids. I had even experienced the occasional cheap thrill on a

God's Will

Saturday night with married women whilst their husbands tanked themselves up down the local. I had, however, never met a woman with any kind of class. I had seen them in films and on television. Occasionally, I would see them at the weekends in the city centre in their expensive clothes. They never saw me, but I tried to imagine myself at their side. That, amongst other dreams, was why I came to London. I wanted to be part of that universe. For me, Stella was the first rung on the ladder to further success and excitement.

My immediate boss was Charlie Weston. Charlie was, in no small part, the life and soul of Milton's. During the day he was the caretaker, bottle-washer and general dogsbody for Henderson, but at night he was the compere and comic. In Charlie I found my first friend. A father-figure you might say, my own not having been present during my formative years. It was he who sorted out my accommodation, a small bedsit above the club with a view out onto an alleyway that was often littered with bins, blood, vomit and prostitutes. The bedsit was damp and had no redeeming features, other than it was free. I spent hardly any time in there, however, so it suited me just fine. Everything worked out pretty well until the end of the second week. It was then that I saw the reality of what I was getting into. It was a pivotal moment, and if I had had any sense I would have walked away and my life would have been different. But I didn't. I didn't apply an ounce of common sense and from that moment on I got deeper and deeper into a world I didn't understand.

Milton's had a nightly cabaret that was popular for the most part, but the sell-out night was always Saturday. During the early hours of one particular Sunday morning everyone had gone home and I was cleaning up behind the bar. Because I lived above the club I was often left with the responsibility of locking up. Around three that morning there was a knock at the main door. Presuming it was Henderson

God's Will

returning from one of his nights out, I rushed over and opened up, only to find a small fat man who could have been any age between twenty and sixty. He was bald, with grey eyes and grey skin—not a healthy-looking creature

'Where's Frankie?' he mumbled, wheezing heavily between breaths.

'Mr Henderson hasn't been in today,' I said.

This was the official response I was instructed to give whenever strangers called. The little man looked unwell and I said as much as I offered him a chair. His response was not what I expected.

'Fuck off! Who the fuck are you, anyway?'

Taken aback, I decided to tread carefully. 'I'm Sickert, the new barman.'

'New barman called Sickert?' the man growled, barging past me into the club. 'Yes, he did mention some northern scum had started.'

Dismissing his poor assessment of me, I tried to get rid of him. 'Well, I'll tell him you called.'

'Yes, you tell him, boy. Tell him Rimmer needs a word, urgently. Bexley's been on '

'Bexley?'

He frowned as if he had said too much and then directed his displeasure at me. 'Just give him the fucking message!'

I watched him go but said nothing more. Clearly he knew Henderson, and knowing how downright volatile the latter could be I left a short note and went to bed, hoping that was the end of it.

Some hope.

In a moment of intense horror I was dragged from my slumber and thrown against the wall by my bed an hour or so later. As I came to life I saw Henderson's face in front of my own. He was a stocky man with dark eyes and a thick neck bulging over his collar.

God's Will

'You stupid bastard!'

I couldn't speak. He was so close I could smell the alcohol on his breath and the stale reek of his aftershave. He was fuming. His pupils had shrunk to tiny dots, making him unable, it seemed, to focus on me. It was as if rage had taken over him completely, stopping him from functioning properly.

'If Rimmer ever leaves a message again you never, *ever*, leave a note. Never! You *tell* me. You just *tell* me. Do you understand? I don't like you, boy, and if you're not careful I'll do you...'

It was nothing personal. For men like Henderson an unnatural hatred for the world came pre-packaged.

'I didn't know. I don't know who or what Bexley is.'

'Bexley is nothing to do with you. Just forget about it.'

With these words the anger in him seemed to dissipate and he released me. I slid to the floor but I didn't take my eyes off him. I had a feeling there was more to come. But I was wrong. He just stood there, staring down at me. I realised then there was someone else at the door. I looked over and saw a very large man with cropped metal-grey hair, wearing a small smile, leaning against the frame of the door. He made an impressive figure, like a soldier or a gangster in a film. His name, I was to learn, was Levy. If anyone had told me in that moment that within two years I would rise to the top of one of London's largest criminal gangs and he would be my right-hand man, I would have laughed in their faces and probably carried on doing so for a number of days.

During that time Henderson turned my life into a living hell. But there was one thing that did temper the pain.

Stella.

God's Will

She was what my mother would call bonny. Not a classic beauty in the traditional sense—no doubt others wouldn't have seen the appeal—but to my eyes she was everything I found attractive in a woman. Stella had never had kids and even though she was in her late forties by the time we met gravity was yet to take its toll. She was insatiable. I had slept with quite a few women since I had left the north, but I had simply never met a woman like her. The majority of women I knew wanted a man to take control, but not her. She wanted to be satisfied and would do anything and suggest anything to make sure she was. My life at that time was a balancing act. Every day Henderson chipped away at my confidence, but at night Stella would build it back up again, and how. Our affair lasted for months. Nobody knew. Neither of us gave away our secret, but after hours, hidden in that little room, Stella and I found heaven. But it wasn't enough. Henderson was too much. He was turning me into a nervous wreck. It was at that point I very nearly got out and went back north. Then fate took a hand.

It was an early bright spring day, 8 March 1973, and the second year of the IRA's bombing campaign on mainland Britain. So far nobody had been killed. No one till then, that is. I was idly strolling by the Old Bailey when the concealed mechanisms inside two timed bombs, inside two separate cars, clicked into place and triggered two huge explosions. The combined blasts tore the cars into a thousand grotesque pieces. Paint was stripped from metal, leather from foam, rubber from steel, flesh from bone. They threw *me* twenty feet along the road.

It seemed that time itself had been forced out by the blast and that the world had been put on pause. For a short time afterwards nothing moved. Nothing, that is, other than a huge cloud of dust, which billowed away from the epicentre like a ripple on a still pond. After a few moments I saw a man rushing through the shattered remnants of

God's Will

the cars. Then I saw a woman's twisted body lying next to the mangled remnants of a car engine. At that moment the man who was running to her side didn't realise she was dead. But I did. I had landed in the doorway of a public house and my head was hanging back onto the pavement. The chaos was upside down, but I couldn't help but notice that the girl had been decapitated.

Amazingly, I didn't feel any pain at all. Other than intense shock, I was okay. I was then engulfed by the dust cloud that had been moving slowly along the road. In the same moment I saw a shape looming through the dust above me—a blond-haired male angel, it seemed. I wondered in that moment if I had gone to a better place. Then I noted his navy-blue suit and the shattered glass in the door. Apart from the dust that had settled on his suit the man seemed untouched by the chaos around us. In fact, I continued to suspect he was an angel right up until the moment an old man appeared at his side and also stared down at me. It wasn't until the old man stepped over me onto the street that I realised the man in the suit was trying to talk to me. There was a terrible ringing in my ears so I couldn't hear a word he was saying. Then he stopped talking and stepped through the shattered pub door and picked me up. The next thing I remember I was being dropped unceremoniously in a chair in the saloon. I think I lost consciousness for a while but when I came round the noise in my ears had reduced enough for me to hear the man speaking.

'Billy, give this young man a drink. He's had quite a shock.'

'So have I,' said the old man, reappearing at the door. 'I've got no windows!'

'Put it in perspective, Billy. That young lady out there doesn't have a head.'

I must have been trying to speak because he put his hand on my shoulder and smiled at me.

God's Will

'It's okay. No body parts missing. Just stay here until you feel stronger.'

As I checked my groin for reassurance, the old man joined us and handed me a large whisky. After I had drunk it in one the younger man took the empty glass from me and asked for another.

'Must go,' he then said with a cheery smile, patting me on the cheek. 'Take care, now. I'll send someone round to sort out the windows later, Billy.'

Then he was gone. Still in a state of shock I wandered out onto the street. By then there was police and army and ambulances. The girl now had a blanket over her, and in that moment I realised how fleeting life is. I knew then that I wasn't going home.

And the man with the blond hair? Larry.

13

The stench in the room was a combination of a number of things, body odour, cigarette smoke, damp and Vic vapour rub among them, but the abiding aroma was the previous night's meal—a half-eaten tray of chips and curry sauce that lay at the side of the unmade bed. Someone with a strong sense of smell might also have been able to define a faint trace of vomit that still hung in the air around the bathroom door. The occupant of this squalid little bedsit had been unwell. He had been unwell for many years, one way or another. At first it had been the rumblings of mild stomach discomfort and heartburn, but over time the pressures of his job and an unhealthy lifestyle had combined to magnify these issues until he could barely go through the day without spending

God's Will

hours on the toilet or retching at the gaseous bile that surged like lava in his throat.

Retired Chief Inspector Reid was not at all a well man.

Other than the bed, the room had a cooker, a sink and a small desk on which sat a computer monitor, keyboard and mouse. Illuminated, and seemingly mesmerised, by the glow of the screen, Reid stared at the words scrolling before his eyes, the only movement coming from a solitary finger as it slowly caressed the mouse wheel. The wall above the screen was papered with cuttings Reid had taken from newspapers, magazines and books. Further along, to the right of the desk, there was a large cork-backed noticeboard with photographs of people, locations, buildings and cars from the Steiner investigation. Above the cuttings there were two more photographs. The one on the left was a creased and faded black-and-white still of Lottie Steiner, aged three. It was the one given to him by the surviving relatives, which he had then used for door-to-door enquiries. In the end, like Caroline Hogg, Genette Tate, James Bulger and countless other victims of unimaginable violence, it had become the final representation of a lost life. The more recent photograph was of Sickert, or Greene as he now called himself, a day or so after his release. Reid had used a telephoto lens on his trusty old Pentax LX from the opened window of his car. He was happy with the result; it was grainy and maybe a little underexposed but despite the low light the image had no blurring at all.

The man Reid had despised for thirty years had changed little. Sickert was, of course, much older now, but although he had grown a beard, put on a few stone and was losing his hair, the eyes were exactly the same—dark and cold. Reid thought back to their conversation in the car and his comments about Solomon's final words.

He made some remark about God, did he? Lying bastard. He either said something relevant or nothing at all.

God's Will

Once upon a time there had been a metre of bare wallpaper below these photographs. But a recent flurry of coverage on the anniversary of the kidnapping had kept Reid busy with his scissors once more. The recent additions that filled this gap were in colour—but that, to Reid's frustration, was the only change. The press had nothing to add of any relevance to the child's disappearance.

Running to and from each of the photographs was a small length of string that led to a border of A4-sized pieces of paper. On each sheet large amounts of information had been typed out neatly. Reid no longer studied the photographs, or even the words he had written in such great detail. The cobweb of strings no longer served a purpose. He knew it all off by heart.

The only sound in the room came from the dust-coated computer tower at Reid's bare feet, where an ageing hard drive struggled with correspondence from a thousand amateur detectives, police reports he had smuggled out before his forced retirement, theories of his own, theories from retired celebrity detectives and hundreds of eyewitness reports who claimed to have seen Lottie Steiner in various parts of the UK on the night of her death. There was another list, Madeline McCann like, the geography here much more widespread, of places around the world she had supposedly been seen over the decades. With the advent of the internet the correspondence had increased, forcing the cooler fans within the computer to work harder and harder. If this hum was the soundtrack of Reid's life, the information stored therein *was* his life.

Reid had spent the evening poring across the many blogs he was subscribed to. They varied little but in name. *The Steiner Case*, *The Steiner Killings*, *Killers from Hell*—it went on and on. Who were these people? Where were they based? What was the fascination they all had for death? He had no choice in it, it had been his employment. If only

God's Will

he could go back in time and start again, become an architect, a doctor, an accountant, a roadsweeper—anything but this awful responsibility.

Each blog had links to others: *The Yorkshire Ripper, The Black Panther, The Moors Murderers, The Madeline McCann disappearance.* Death and horror. The uglier the ending, the more interest it drew. The more innocent the victim, the more hits. Somewhere along the line someone, somewhere, had suggested the guilty men had eaten Lottie—no doubt because her body was never found. It was groundless speculation, like a great deal of what had been rumoured over the years, but if Reid had learned anything about the human race it was that it had an extremely unhealthy fascination with murder. He sighed in despair and closed the page he was on before opening documents of his own. He transferred his attention to his own reports at the time of Lottie's disappearance. Fifteen minutes later, his mobile phone rang. He knew the tone instantly. He allocated tones to the few people he corresponded with. This one was one he rarely heard, such was the infrequent contact from his former sergeant. Instinctively he minimised the document he was looking at. The intrusion forced him back from a world of supposition and flawed evidence. He could hardly believe he was studying segments of his own investigation from thirty years before. Finding the phone in the bathroom, he answered with a low, empty voice and watched himself in the mirror as he spoke.

'Hello, Tony.'

'How's it going, boss?'

Even though he had expected to hear Calvert's voice at the other end of the line the sound of it triggered a series of tiny explosion in the pit of his stomach. He covered his mouth with his spare hand to stop himself from gagging. It was a moment before he could speak again.

'I've got something for you…'

Reid gave a long measured pause. 'You found him?'

God's Will

'I have,' said Calvert. 'For all the good it will do you. But this is the last time, Alan. I mean that. Are you home tomorrow evening?'

'I'm home most evenings,' he replied sullenly, ending the call.

He didn't move from the spot for some time. Instead he studied his reflection in the mirror. At some point a network of crimson-coloured veins had appeared and spread across his nose and cheeks. His eyes were bloodshot, too; he barely recognised himself. It occurred to him then that with a visitor coming the next day he should clean himself up, or at least his home. But he no longer listened to such thoughts. Appearance was as meaningless to him as a job or a relationship. So he walked back to the computer and opened the file that read simply, Inspector Bexley.

Thomas Greene was restless. He hadn't slept for days. He could no longer hold back the nightmares. Holes were appearing in the fabric of his mind and the past was seeping through. He could only think he had brought it on himself. He should never have bought the book from the little shop in Cecil Court, *The Steiner Murders*. The author's interpretation of his part in Lottie's death had left him numb. The night before, after Angie had gone to bed, he had caught a rerun of the documentary the girl in the bookshop had mentioned. In prison he had learnt to accept society's version of what had occurred, but thirty years on the untruths and huge inconsistencies screamed at him from page and screen.

Ten days on, the depression had evolved and the pain continued to deepen by the hour. Apart from meals and the occasional chat with Angie and Denby, he hadn't been out. Seemingly aware of this depression, Angie had begun to bring his food to his room. The pattern was always the same—a knock, a pause and a slow walk back along the

God's Will

landing to the stairs until the living room door closed and he was alone once more.

At the window Greene studied the overgrown garden in the strange bluish moonlight. He had a simple choice, he knew that. Give up completely or take this hell head-on. There was a knock at the door. It was heavier than Angie's, which could only mean one thing. *Denby.*

'Sorry to trouble you, old chap. Just wondered how you were getting on?'

'I'm fine, Denby,' Greene said, peering through the crack. 'I just need time on my own.'

'Well, you're wrong. Angie and I are worried about you. You can't hide yourself away, you know. You've got to get out. Become a citizen again. We've paid our debt to society, so sod 'em! Don't let the bastards grind you down!'

Wisdom was something Greene would never have attributed to Denby, but he knew he had a point. If he couldn't change society's perception of him he could at least learn to deal with his own pain.

'Let's hit Soho, Thomas! My treat. Let's blow away that depression with copious amounts of alcohol. For one evening let's forget about our pasts. Just you and I!'

The old man's laugh reminded Greene of Mister Punch. It was more like a squeal, and the rosy cheeks and ridiculous moustache only added to the pantomime. But he was right. What he needed right now was alcohol. And lots of it.

14

God's Will

'So you came to London to find wealth and success?' Bepa observes. 'A regular Dick Whittington.' She sounds remote, separated from the questions she is asking as if she already knows the answers. But how could she? She then makes a feminine enquiry. 'Did you love Stella?'

Without a second thought Sickert changes the subject. 'I'm hungry.'

'Rabbit stew's on its way. Stella? Did you love her?'

Did he? Does he still? And if he does, what the hell is it to her? The truth, even though he isn't going to share the fact, is that he doesn't know. He sees the colours of his life but doesn't feel the emotions.

'I don't know what love is. I never did. People who think they do are fools. It's a dream,' he grumbles. He still can't explain it but he is finding himself unduly compelled to share more and more of his past with this strange woman. There is also a sense of defending his actions. 'But I have felt strong emotions for people. You see, even killers have emotions. Do you know much of my life?'

'Some.'

What an odd situation this is, he tells himself. A woman he has never met knows more about his life than he does himself.

'How long was my sentence?'

'A quarter of a century I remember reading somewhere. It could have been longer. You don't recall prison?'

'Yes. No. I'm not sure.'

He wants to explain that although he has no fixed memories of places or people there are countless conflicting sensations within him. Other than the clear memories of his early days in the north with his mother in a little house at the end of a grubby little street and those early days in London, his mind is a vast alien landscape polluted with dense yellow fog. Just as he imagined walking through this strange house during those early comatose days after the attack, he now does the same with the past he is rediscovering. There are no landmarks, no

God's Will

roads, no distant mountains, no north, no south, but some unknown element of his being understands this world. It steers him away from areas of hidden darkness and untold horrors, helping his fragile, stuttering conscience back to life through tolerable memories of his former self.

After a surprisingly enjoyable meal of rabbit stew, potatoes, wholemeal bread and wine, which he is left to enjoy alone, Sickert relaxes on his bed and listens to the robin outside his window. There are other sounds, too. The house is alive with noise. Footsteps, voices, coughing, always coughing, and today, for the first time, music. It's difficult to define, too far away, but he thinks it is old music, from the war or even earlier.

Today Sickert feels less subdued. He grows more alive by the hour. He now wonders with hindsight if there really was someone at the door the previous day. Maybe it was just a dream, a remaining fragment of the nightmare, hovering briefly in his waking moments. How would he know? This is indeed a unique set of circumstances, enough to confound the brightest of minds.

The heavy meal and too much reminiscing has tired him out and soon he falls into a deep sleep. He dreams of London, of Milton's and Charlie and Stella, even Henderson. The dark lingering shapes of Lottie and Larry are still there, but somehow they are now diluted by newer images that cram into his mind.

Later he is woken by the loud splintering of wood out in the yard. Philip the wood chopper is at work once more. No wonder the estuary has no trees. But Bepa is back at his side. He hears her breathing and how it makes an odd whistle in her windpipe, as if something is blocking the way.

'What's wrong with your throat, Bepa?'

God's Will

There is a slight pop as her lips part. She inhales through her nose and the chair creaks. Sickert senses that she is trying to settle in a more dignified pose. He sees her in his mind in some faded nineteenth-century faded gown and white hair, and maybe a string of pearls around her neck—the Havisham comparison has stuck. He presumes she has been sleeping, too, and is bringing herself round before speaking. He is wrong. She is preparing herself for an announcement. She speaks softly and briefly.

'I'm dying.'

This shocking revelation forces Sickert's head weakly off the pillow and he stares sightlessly in her direction. 'Dying? How?'

'My throat, of course. A cancer. There's nothing to be done. I accept the path I have been given.'

For some reason her stoicism angers him. 'Is that what the specialist has said?'

'Of course, one of Harley Street's finest. There is nothing to be done.'

An awful sadness descends. All is silent now. The axeman is done for the day, and in the shared melancholy the two of them wait respectfully for the other's response.

Minutes pass until the stillness is broken by a blast of coughing from the old woman. Almost in the same moment Philip comes bounding up the stairs to her side. Sickert wants to help but he doesn't have the strength. He addresses Philip. Nothing. His silence frustrates Sickert and he yells at him as the coughing gets worse and Bepa moans with pain.

'You need a doctor. Get a doctor!'

'There's nothing to be done, Thomas,' Philip replies. 'Fate has shown its hand.'

God's Will

Sickert doesn't say another word as Philip takes his mother out. His mind is racing. So, the old woman's son Philip is no mute or simpleton. In a dozen words he has revealed himself to be a middle-aged man— eloquent, profound. And the tone of his voice is strangely familiar.

An hour later Philip brings his mother back into the room. She doesn't speak, but through her son she asks Sickert to continue with his story. He is at first reluctant, but a large glass of whisky loosens his tongue and defeats his reticence.

'I remember a career advisor once coming to my school and telling us all that if we were to avoid a life down the collieries or in the factories we needed to work hard. Nobody got anywhere in this world, he said, without diligence. It was industrious pioneers that shaped the world, made it a better place. And I believed him. I was no academic and left school with few qualifications, but I worked hard in the jobs I could find. Whatever I was, and whatever type of work I did, I always remembered that man's words, but I shouldn't have—because he was wrong. Spectacularly wrong. Success in life is down to two things only. Genetics and luck.'

Sickert awaits a response but there isn't one. No movement, not a cough, not a creak from the wheelchair. Even the rats keep their peace. He wonders if he is still dreaming and if the voice that has uttered these words are his own. Then a wheeze from Bepa's diseased throat signals their continued presence. Before he knows it words are gushing from him.

'Neither of my parents were what you might call good-looking, but I was. Sounds a little arrogant, doesn't it? But if you are to understand my story you must realise how important that is.'

God's Will

There is an odd gulping sound and in his mind's eye Sickert sees Bepa sipping some wine. Now all is still. The only sound is that of the fire.

* * *

Despite Henderson's thuggish approach to man-management I actually began to enjoy my time at Milton's. Seeing death up close that day by the Old Bailey had a distinctly positive effect on me. I was terrified of Henderson, but then he wasn't around much. Of course, Stella's contribution to my happiness was key. For the first time in my life I felt I belonged somewhere. Old Charlie was like a father to me and he made a big impression. To call him *old* is doing him a disservice. He was, according to Stella, forty-one, only a few years older than Henderson. But his face reflected a hard life. Brought up in Camberwell by Mr Barnado, he had had it tough from the beginning, yet in spite of this there was such a natural enthusiasm for life that shone from him you could almost see it.

The club was very popular with the criminal classes. It was owned by a man called Solomon, a reclusive and, from what I had heard, very shady figure who owned a great deal of property in London, particularly in Soho. After the confrontation in my room, I didn't see much of Henderson for a while. Then he appeared at the bar one afternoon and offered me what I can only describe as a strained reconciliation. He didn't speak for a while—he didn't even look at me, didn't even ask for a drink—but he didn't hit me or threaten to kill me, which I felt was quite a positive development in our relationship. What he did do was light up a cigarette and study his own image in the mirror behind the bar. It was then that he finally spoke.

'How you getting on?'

God's Will

I didn't respond for a moment because I thought he was talking to himself—after the abuse he had given me I had considered the possibility that he was psychotic. I gave a cautious remark about getting on fine. Then, to my amazement, he offered me a job. It was a managerial position in one of Solomon's sex shops in Soho. I could even keep my job at Milton's. Happy to increase my income and sensing that I had completed some sort of trial period, I took the job without a second thought. Next day I found myself on Broadwick Street, where I met an old bloke who showed me the ropes. Well, one rope. All I had to do was make it clear to anyone who called that I was the manager. There was a girl who worked the till and dealt with the day-to-day running of things, so there was very little to do. Just my kind of work.

This went on for weeks and I loved it, even though Rimmer—the obnoxious little man I had met at the club the night Henderson threatened me—appeared every night to collect the takings. The wage wasn't much, but on top of my income from the club it made a big difference. Then, one day at Milton's, I got chatting to Charlie and for some reason I brought up the question of the mysterious Bexley that Rimmer and Henderson had mentioned, whoever or whatever he was.

'Charlie? Who's Bexley?'

Charlie answered without taking his eyes from the glasses he was drying. 'Why do you ask?'

'Henderson brought it up. Told me not to mention it to anyone.'

'So why are you mentioning it to me?'

I shrugged my shoulders. 'Because I don't want him threatening me again.' He knew about the midnight confrontation in my room. 'I need to know what's going on. Don't want to put my foot in it.'

God's Will

Making sure there was no one to overhear us, Charlie waved me close. 'Bexley is a policeman. A detective inspector, to be precise, who happens to be one of the most corrupt men in the Met.'

'I see.'

'Do you?'

I was naive but not stupid. I had overheard plenty at the bar, and a lot of it was about corrupt coppers. Plenty actually drank there. There was an odd camaraderie between the law and criminals generally, often in plain view.

'Well,' I said with a swagger, 'I presume Henderson is lining Bexley's pockets to turn his head the other way regarding his ongoing concerns.'

Charlie scoffed at the comment. 'Hark at *Pinky*. You'll be running the place soon.'

'I learn quick, Charlie. I don't want to stay a barman all my life.'

His tone changed. 'What, like me?'

'I didn't mean that.'

He laughed again. 'You're so green you could hide on a lawn.'

'Green?'

He leant against the bar he had been wiping and looked at me. 'What's your job in the sex shop?'

'Manager.'

He shook his head with disappointment. 'Wrong. You are the *man in the chair*.'

He found much satisfaction in the confusion on my face. 'Man in the chair?'

'It's a term. When the boys in blue come calling, you, being the manager and all, will be carted away for selling illegal films and magazines. You will spend a few months inside while the real manager…'

God's Will

Henderson. The penny dropped. Charlie grinned and I felt a bloody fool.

'While Henderson is free to employ another *manager*.'

Charlie went on to inform me that Bexley would try and warn Henderson about raids, but not always. I had disappointed Charlie. He had seen something good in me, but had been disappointed in my eagerness to make money. I felt bad but I knew it wouldn't alter the path I had taken. I was angry as hell that I had been cheated by Henderson. All because I had been so willing to accept anything he offered me, for the sake of the money—but mostly because I was afraid of him.

I soon got my own back, however. That little chat with Charlie had come just in time.

A few days later I took a phone call at the shop. It was a man. He was looking for Henderson. There was something about his tone that led me to think he had authority of some kind. Call it instinct, but I had a feeling he was a copper.

'Is that Mr Bexley?'

'Who's asking?'

My mind raced. 'Rimmer.'

Due to an asthmatic childhood I was pretty good on wheezes. I only hoped my East End accent was as convincing. There was a long pause and it occurred to me that Bexley might never have met Rimmer. It was a massive gamble, but it paid off.

'It's time to clear the decks, my asthmatic friend.'

The line had no sooner gone dead than I sent the young girl home and locked up. Witnessing the police raid from a cafe across the road five minutes later, I began to understand that if I was to get anywhere—and make any money—I needed to wise up and broaden my horizons.

God's Will

15

In his hour of need Denby had turned out to be a generous friend to Thomas Greene. And, if it was required, a shoulder a cry on. Thanks to him, the evening in the city was a fairly pleasant experience. They visited so many pubs they blurred into one and by nine that evening Greene had no recollection of leaving any of them. Why he had avoided all contact with Denby he didn't know. The old soak was the perfect drinking companion. He just didn't stop. Not only drinking—it was his anecdotes and the general *joie de vivre* that burst from him, stoked, seemingly, by the huge amounts of brandy he consumed that truly impressed Greene. He himself was no drinker and felt out of his depth, but he found the drowning sensation strangely satisfying.

Around ten that night they found themselves on Rathbone Place, the place where Greene had encountered Reid that night. Unknown to Denby, Greene had negotiated their path. In his drunken stupor he had become all maudlin and felt the urge to find some connection to happier times. He hoped to find it in the Wheatsheaf, a haunt once of such literary giants as Julian McClaren Ross and Dylan Thomas, and one of Larry's favourite pubs. He was to be disappointed. The place had changed and he found the interior not unlike a thousand pubs in the capital. Fruit machines, jukeboxes and, horror of all horrors, a television installed, he presumed, to satisfy men who didn't talk to their wives *or* anyone else. Drunk as he was, Greene considered complaining to the landlord on the injustice of it all, but he thought better of it and turned back to Denby, only to be cross-examined again.

'Do you ever shut up, Denby?'

'Sorry, old boy, didn't mean to go on.'

God's Will

'You remind me of someone I once knew.'

'That's nice. An old friend?'

Greene laughed scornfully. 'Not a friend. A criminal solicitor called Fenton. You sound just like him, so do me a favour and shut up.'

To his surprise he found that Denby had already done as requested. And he wasn't the only one. There had been a sudden lull in the bar's din. Looking around to find the cause, he discovered everyone staring towards the main entrance.

Through blurred vision Greene followed the collective gaze to see a middle-aged man and woman standing at the door. They were dressed completely in shades of grey and black and were staring into the bar with the same intensity everyone was giving them. They seemed like two spirits, eyes empty, faces drawn, a chilly quality hovering about them. At first Greene thought they were dark-skinned, Mediterranean possibly, but as they came further into the bar he could see that their complexion had more to do with grime than pigment. Their skin had an oily reddish tint and their hair was shiny and lank in the manner typical of people living in life's gutter. The woman's hair was long and dark, greying in parts. She was the taller of the two, and to Greene's eyes the perfect embodiment of a witch. It was an observation that worried him greatly when she fixed her eyes on his and walked towards him.

'The Ghouls...' he heard Denby whisper in his ear. 'For God's sake, don't buy anything!'

Greene heard what he said but didn't take it in. The woman was so close to him now he could see the black flush of blocked pores on her nose and cheeks. He could also see the emptiness in her eyes.

'Buy,' she said, pushing a handful of photographs towards him.

Without thinking, Greene took them from her. Denby gave a long, painful sigh.

'Buy,' she repeated.

God's Will

Looking down at the merchandise, Greene realised very quickly there wasn't much to buy. The small Instamatic prints were of nothing in particular, just a selection of blurry images of buildings and streets, littered with the occasional shot of greenery. He was at a complete loss. Everyone was looking at him and the woman now, at this possible trade that seemed to have as much bearing on them as it did on himself. Lost for words and out of money he looked at Denby in desperation.

'You buy,' she said again, but when Greene looked back at her he realised her attention had switched from him to his drinking partner.

'Now look here...' said Denby, scowling. 'I've got enough of your damn pictures to decorate me room!'

'You buy,' she said again. Her voice was almost that of a man's, throaty and hoarse.

Denby was caught, and it was clear that it wasn't so much the pressure from this odd couple he was under, but of every drinker in the building. If he gave in, they were safe, but if he didn't the Ghouls would move onto another victim.

'Oh, sod it!' Denby growled, taking out his wallet. 'Here you are, you swine. Now, this is the last time. In future, leave me be!'

Snatching a fiver from his hand the pair turned in unison and made for the door. There was an instant collective sigh of relief and giggles from around the room. Walking over to the window, Greene watched as they moved off towards Oxford Street, pushing, unless he was hallucinating in his drunken state, a cumbersome, old-fashioned, baby's pram.

Denby was struggling to put his wallet away as Greene turned to apologise.

'I just didn't know what to say,' he mumbled.

'It's all right, old boy. Not your fault. Blame it on the cowardly landlord!' he shouted over to the bar. 'Never around when he's needed!'

God's Will

'Who were they?'

'The Ghouls, as I say.'

'Well, they scared the life out of me.'

'It's actually more to do with the fact they only come out at night. They haunt Soho like…'

'Ghouls?'

'Quite. You can keep them,' Denby added, pointing to the photos. 'A coming-out present from the spirit world, if you will.' The thought of this made him laugh, which in turn made him think of alcohol. 'Another drink, old boy?'

'They were pushing a pram. Don't tell me they've got a kid?'

'The story goes they had a child that died in tragic circumstances. Sent the pair of them doolally, by all accounts. And on the evidence available, I would say the basis of that legend has more than a little credibility. My round, I do believe.'

As Denby went to the bar, Greene stuffed the photos into his jacket pocket and returned to the window. The Ghouls were almost at Oxford Street now and, silhouetted against the gaudy lights, they looked out of place and time. He decided the Ghouls was an apt name. The seemed like two spirits that had somehow slipped into a world alien to them and were unable to go back. A little like himself. He thought back a few moments to the woman's mesmerising stare and, despite the stuffy heat of the bar, felt a cold shudder along his spine.

16

Sickert asks for a drink and Philip, always on hand to cater for both of his patients, walks from the fireplace where he seems to spend most of

God's Will

his time. As he passes Sickert a glass of red wine—his reminiscences are becoming more and more drink-fuelled—and the patient takes a large mouthful, Bepa makes an observation.

'You talk of genetics and fate as if they were pillars of success. Surely there is more to achievement than mere luck and a pretty face?'

'Not in my experience. Maybe in yours? I expect there's not much call for beauty in such a desolate place.'

'I haven't always lived here,' the wold woman replies before coughing again and releasing a loud sigh. 'Now, if you are to tell us more about your life, I think we need more drink. A bottle of Bourdeaux from the cellar, Philip, but not the '59. We're running low there.'

'Please do,' Sickert mutters. 'It's very soothing on the throat…'

There is an awkward pause, throat being a no-no area of conversation, but not for Bepa. She laughs and wheels the chair closer to the bed.

'Tell me more Thomas. I'm intrigued. It's a little like a bedtime story.'

Sickert frowns at the flippant remark. She is tougher than he first suspected, but she's also dying, so he lets it go and continues.

* * *

Other than my sudden move to London I had been very cautious in my life. And I decided the sooner I changed that the better. Inspired by Henderson's bullying and Charlie's patronising tone, I decided to show them all by running off with the club's takings.

God knows where I got the idea, possibly from the stacks I used to see Henderson counting in his office at the end of each day. Henderson was lax, especially when he had been at the ale. What I needed was a

God's Will

night when he was out of the way and Charlie was busy. By that time he was allowing me to take the takings up to Henderson's office. I think I decided on a Wednesday night when Solomon, my elusive boss, organised a meet with Henderson and his boys at one of his other clubs.

I had it all planned. At the end of the night I would take up the takings as usual, but instead of placing them in the wall safe I would stick them in a bag, which I had on a rope hanging out of the window at the back of the club. All I had to do was wait until the end of the night. Fate, however, had other ideas—fate not disguised and subtle as we always imagine it is, but like a big neon arrow throbbing in the night, pointing to the spot.

There was a regular at the club called Skelton, an ageing drunk with wiry ginger hair and a colourful array of put-downs. On the night of the robbery he was very drunk, which made his observations all the more acerbic. As well as the bar staff, he decided to extend his circle of insults to the dancers and musicians from the show. If Henderson had been around he would have toned it down or said nothing at all, but as he wasn't the old man got a little too cocky for his own good. Apparently some joker had told him Henderson had gone away for a few days. This false assumption would cost Skelton, and me, a great deal.

Unwisely he decided to get a little too familiar with one of the dancers during the break. There was a small troupe who supported Stella in all her numbers. This particular girl had come to collect drinks for the girls, only to find Skelton in full flow on his usual bar stool, his sack-like belly resting on his thighs. She told him where to go and he responded with some choice remark about the size of her arse, which, to be honest, was pretty accurate. This was Milton's, remember, not Las Vegas. The real trouble started when Henderson walked through the door an hour later, surprising the hell out of both me and Skelton. My

God's Will

plan may only have been put on hold, but for Skelton the end of the world was nigh.

The dancer, it turned out, was one of Henderson's favourite girls and it didn't take long for him to hear what Skelton had said. More out of wickedness than a sense of gallantry he decided Skelton needed to be taught a lesson. Unfortunately for the old man, Henderson had returned with Levy, the man with the cropped hair I had first seen the night I was dragged from my bed.

I was watching from the bar when Henderson was told. His immediate reaction was curious. I realised I was seeing a man mulling over the options available to him. High above the dance floor the rotating mirrored ball cast bands of light across his face, and in that glittering light I think I saw true evil for the first time. I've thought about that moment often over the years, mostly because I could never understand how somebody could come to a conclusion the way Henderson did. You see, instead of dragging Skelton out, instead of barring him, instead of adopting a natural conclusion, he ordered one of his finest champagnes and invited the old man to his table. There, he and Levy got the old man drunk. They were up for a bit of fun. All night they plied their victim with the finest liquor, waiting patiently until everyone had gone.

At three the following morning I was cleaning behind the bar and silently bemoaning my lost opportunity when Henderson told me to go to bed. I explained there was still work to do, but he insisted. And when Henderson insisted, you tended to listen. As I walked to the stairs and heard him mutter to Levy to lock up, a chill ran through me. I didn't know exactly what they were going to do to Skelton, but I knew it wouldn't be pleasant. To be honest, I couldn't stand the old bugger. His nightly sarcasm had been a thorn in my side ever since I started, but not liking him didn't mean I wanted him hurt.

God's Will

Lying on my bed, listening to the stifled cries and pleas echoing along the corridor from the ballroom, I tried to tell myself it was nothing to do with me. Turning out the light as if the darkness would shut out the noise, I tried to close myself off, but all it did was intensify the crying, the anguish and the laughter. All the time my one thought was not of what the old man was going through, or why I did nothing to help him. No. It was of Henderson sitting in the circling light of the ballroom, deciding in a calm and rational way what form of punishment he was going to give the old man. That I couldn't understand. That I still can't understand, which is quite something coming from a murderer, I know.

I've seen fights and I've seen bullying—it's always the same. People do nothing as the crime slowly plays out in front of them. It only takes one of us to speak out and turn the tables, but few of us have the courage, and that night I was, as I had always been, in the majority. Eventually the cries died away and shortly afterwards I fell asleep. Not surprisingly, Skelton never returned to the club. I saw him a few weeks later scurrying through Soho, his head bowed, his face blistered and haunted. He saw me, I'm sure, but I learned then that even fools have their pride. I had none, however, just shame and a certain amount of relief in knowing my cowardice had not led to his death. I learnt something else, too. If one is to flourish in life one must be prepared to get over setbacks instantly and learn from the experience. My instant reaction was to get out of Soho and find a steady job, but I had learnt a lot in my short time. There was money to be made, and if men like Henderson could do it, I knew there was an opportunity for a good-looking, single, white male like me. It was just a matter of finding it.

A couple of weeks after Skelton's beating, we had a VIP visit the club. Henderson was keen to make a good impression and it was made clear to us all that nothing, repeat nothing, was to be allowed to ruin his

God's Will

night of pleasure. With that, he took Charlie to one side and as they talked I studied Henderson once more. This time I saw something different in him. Was it simply his disturbing sense of excitement, or was it something more intense. Ambition, perhaps?

The night was a success. According to Charlie, the man was a German dignitary, who by all accounts had a great time, which was something that couldn't be said of his dour wife...

* * *

'Are you all right, Thomas? What's *wrong*?'

Sickert has let go of the empty wine glass he has been holding and it rolls off the bed and smashes on the hard dusty floorboards. Rats scurry away and Philip moves forward. He stops and Sickert knows it is Bepa who has stopped him; he can see her in his mind's eye, watching him intently.

'You've remembered something. Something important?'

Sickert nods and then continues to speak as if he hadn't stopped at all.

'The man's wife, the dour one, was heavily pregnant. She looked as if she wanted to be anywhere in the world but a seedy Soho nightclub. I didn't know it then, but Lottie Steiner, the child who would change my life forever, was only a few weeks away from entering the world.'

Bepa does not speak again for a while. She seems to be allowing Sickert time to absorb and understand these memories as they surface. Then she insists that he continue. She sounds fascinated with his relationship with Larry in particular. Again, Sickert can't explain it, but he feels the urge to do as he is told. Soon he is back in time, the old woman listening as before.

God's Will

* * *

I continued to front the sex shops in Soho, but I was getting the jitters every time the phone rang. I needed to get out of there, and soon. My plan to rob the club was still in my mind, but this time I decided I would do it on a Saturday night in order to take full advantage of the largest take of the week. It meant a longer wait, with the added risk of getting done for fronting the Soho shops, but I believed it was worth the gamble.

Before any of that could take place, though, I was given another job in the Solomon empire. It started one Friday night with Henderson throwing myself and a couple of the girls into his car and taking us over to the Rotella, a casino in Mayfair owned by Solomon. There had been a series of conferences somewhere and the delegates, who were staying in a nearby hotel, had descended on the casino. Consequently the casino was short-staffed.

I walked in and found myself in a dream. Apart from the brightly coloured clientele, maroon and gold were the predominant colours beneath rows of huge chandeliers. It was a remarkable place, the kind of thing I had only seen in movies or on TV. I almost expected to see Simon Templar or Bond at one of the tables. It was all so glamorous. Not that there was much time to appreciate it. Within minutes I was thrown into a maelstrom of activity. This was a very different clientele from Milton's. Before he left, Henderson took me to one side and told me, in his own inimitable style, that he wanted me back to help Charlie clean up when I was done. I was near the bar when he left and as I turned to go back to my duties I was aware of a young man staring at me. He was tall, blond-haired, dressed in a tuxedo and strikingly good-looking. It was Larry, of course. He didn't say anything at first, but just

God's Will

watched me. I was filling a tray with glasses of champagne and was very conscious of him.

'Was that your boss?'

'Mr Henderson, yes.'

'Looks the nasty type.'

'He's fine. I can handle him, anyway,' I said confidently.

He replied with a frown. 'I seriously doubt that.'

He looked very at ease with himself but, curiously, I also had a sense he was somehow separate to everything in that place. As if in some strange way he was above it all and didn't really want to be there. I got that straightaway.

'I suppose I should be offended,' he said, with a grunt.

'Offended?'

'You don't remember me, do you?'

'Should I?'

He laughed. 'There's gratitude for you. Maybe it was the bang on the head—or the blast.'

Then the penny dropped.

'Jesus, sorry! I didn't get a chance to thank you.'

'You can do it now. I'll have a double bourbon. What's your name?'

'Tom Sickert.'

His eyes narrowed and for a moment I could see his mind was searching for something. It turned out to be my surname that had caught his attention.

'Sickert? No relation to Walter Sickert, the painter?'

'Don't think so. Never heard of him.'

He chuckled and took a cigarette from a silver case as I placed the drink on the bar. 'An intriguing character, a painter who took a great deal of interest in the crimes of Jack the Ripper. He actually believed he had lodged in a room used by the infamous whore-killer. He did a

God's Will

painting of the room and entitled it, not surprisingly. "Jack the Ripper's Bedroom".'

'Gloomy bugger. I prefer I nice landscape myself.'

He threw his head back and laughed out loud at that. This drew the attention of the head barman, who could see me but not the man in the tuxedo.

'What are you doing here? Get out with that champagne or I'll–' He stopped mid-sentence and I looked up to see it was because of Larry.

'Mr Sickert and I are having a conversation,' Larry said, calmly, firmly, lighting up a cigarette.

The man looked horrified. 'I'm sorry, Mr Solomon, I didn't realise. I'm so sorry.'

As the head barman sloped off, Larry introduced himself. So this was Solomon's son. That surprised me, because Larry was so well-spoken. I had presumed Solomon was like Henderson, a rough-around-the-edges thug. But Larry was the coolest-looking man I had ever met, a little like Robert Redford in his youth with his blond hair, blue eyes and tanned skin. His voice was like honey.

'So where do you normally hide yourself away?'

'Milton's.'

He frowned. 'That hole? Do we still own that? Recently I have tried to educate my father on his businesses. Less is more I find. We really need to move upmarket.'

For the next half an hour he asked me all about my life, never once mentioning his own. Occasionally he would interject some idea or theory on something I had said. I can't explain it, but from the very first moment I felt I had found someone like myself. A kindred spirit, if you will.

'So here's what I am thinking,' he said as I served another customer. 'You and I get out of this place and have a night on the town.'

God's Will

'But I can't. My boss, Henderson...'

'I outrank Henderson. Take the night off.'

I didn't. I made my excuses, mostly because I didn't feel prepared, if that makes any sense. I did agree to his invitation for lunch one day. What he saw in me I don't know, but there was a mutual understanding of each other. We just clicked. But I wasn't thinking of friendship. As I made my way back to Milton's I reflected upon the important connection I had just made.

When I got back to the club I was surprised to find Henderson and Levy playing cards in one of the booths. I was no sooner inside than Henderson shouted over for more drink. Nervously I hurried over to take away the empties and returned with more of the same. As I turned to go, however, Levy spoke to me for the first time.

'Where's your manners, boy?'

I'd seen him at the club a dozen times or more, but never drunk, and rarely so talkative. He was an imposing figure when he didn't say anything, but in this state he was even more frightening than Henderson.

'I'm sorry,' I replied, my voice an octave higher than usual.

'You will be unless you fill my glass.'

I looked to Henderson in the vain hope that he would calm the situation, but he was enjoying my humiliation too much for that. I topped up Levy's glass and was about to do the same to Henderson's when my boss suddenly moved it away, forcing me to spill it over the back of his hand. He didn't say anything as he got up. He just gave me that inhuman glare all thugs adopt just before an attack. I knew what was coming. I know bullies. I know how they work. I was shaking, not with anger I'm sorry to say, but with complete fear. Slowly raising his hand, he placed it in front of my face.

'Lick it clean.'

God's Will

'What?'

'Lick—it—clean.'

My spirit poured from me like sand, and nothing I could think or do would stop it. Apart from the fear, I was empty. It blurred my vision and thoughts. I compared this horrendous moment to the happy one I had experienced only an hour before with Larry. The contrast made it worse.

Up until that point I had never shown any sort of courage in my life. I had always been afraid of the bully. And what I felt in that moment showed me that type of fear does not weaken with age. I couldn't breathe and could barely stand, but I knew the only way out for a coward was to do as he was asked. Telling myself there was no one of merit to see my humiliation was small recompense, but it was all I needed.

Slowly I moved my head forward, but before I could even shame myself, his hand was on the back of my head forcing it down hard onto the table, over and over. It was so effortless for him. Then it was Levy's turn. Christ, how many times my face hit that table… when he eventually removed his hand all that remained was darkness and a thin shrill filling my ears.

Half blind, I staggered back to the bar and sank my throbbing face in the small sink, which was filled with dirty water. My nose and jaw throbbed and my lips were so swollen I couldn't close my mouth to stop the mixture of water, beer and cigarette ash entering it. The taste of it made me wretch, which my tormentors found incredibly funny. Falling back onto the floor, I wiped the blood from my face with some beer-soaked towels and cried. I heard them mocking me, and I wanted to hurt them both so much. But the truth of it was, I couldn't. I didn't have the physical or mental strength.

God's Will

Next day there was no sign of either of them so I set to work clearing the bar for opening time. Around nine Charlie turned up. As soon as he saw my face he wanted to know what had gone on. As much I wanted to tell him I just couldn't find the words. Although he was angry he didn't pursue it any further, but he knew. I guessed from his subdued reaction that I hadn't been the first to suffer at the hands of Henderson and his pals. Later that morning, as we were about to open up, he took me to one side.

'Look, if you want to get out of here, don't let any of us hold you back. I've got money. I could help you out. Stella and I won't think any less of you.'

After our disagreement a few weeks before I wasn't expecting that. I don't know what I was about to say to his suggestion because in that moment the door opened and there, to my amazement, stood Larry Solomon. He walked in like a cat. He didn't make a sound. He was wearing a t-shirt and trousers and had a casual manner that seemed elevated at the same time. He stopped and looked at my face.

'What happened to you?'

I searched for a convenient lie. 'A couple of drunks did me on the way back last night.'

I could see from the look in his eye he wasn't convinced. 'Is that right, Charlie?'

I was surprised to find they were on first name terms. Even so, it was clear from Charlie's reaction that he wasn't keen on Larry.

'Apparently so…'

'I'm fine,' I insisted.

'Well, let me take some of the pain away from you by letting you know I'm promoting you. I've got work for you elsewhere. If that's okay with you, Charlie?'

God's Will

'It leaves us one short. And he won't be easy to replace. He's a grafter. Henderson won't be happy.'

'Henderson is an employee. If he doesn't like it he can always leave. If I find out he did this, he won't be on the payroll much longer, anyway.'

More than anything I wanted to tell Larry what had really happened, but it was more than success I wanted from life. I wanted respect too. And you don't get that by snitching or having other people fighting your battles. I decided I would have my revenge on Henderson and Levy soon enough.

I didn't know what the work would be, but I was pretty certain it couldn't be any worse than working behind the bar at Milton's or fronting a sex shop. Happily, I was right.

'So what's this job you have for me?' I asked as I followed Larry out to his car.

I tried to sound as nonchalant as I could, but inside my stomach was churning. It wasn't due only to this potential improvement in my living standards, but because of Larry—he just had such class and style; I felt completely out of my depth in his company.

'It's a job I've made for you,' he responded once we were moving. 'Nature has blessed you with good bone structure and dark eyes. Do you have a girlfriend?'

I briefly thought of Stella who was technically my other half, but heard myself say no all the same. He grinned to himself; in a way I felt he was laughing at me, but I didn't care.

'Good. I heard on the grapevine that you acted for a time.'

'That's right. Mostly theatre. I don't know what you heard, but Olivier I ain't.'

God's Will

'I'm not looking for an Oscar-winning performance, and I'm not sure on the length of the engagement, but I would like you to act for me.'

'I see—and the part?'

'A playboy would describe the character rather well. You do like women, I take it?'

'I'm not gay, if that's what you mean.'

He ignored the comment. 'I want you to flirt with as many women as you can at the Rotella. Walk the floor, charm them with witty observations, disarm them with smouldering looks—that sort of thing.'

'And that's a job?'

He laughed. 'No, the job is persuading these women, who by the way tend to be very wealthy and in need of companionship, to spend as much money as they can at the tables. Officially you don't work for us, of course. You will even be provided with a decent-sized stake so you can play the part effectively.'

'Sounds good.'

'There is a drawback, of course. No job is without its risks.'

'And that is?'

'These women tend to be very ugly.'

We laughed. For decent money I would have seduced a monkey back then.

'And the wage?'

'There isn't one.'

Now I wasn't laughing. I flashed a glance at him in time to see him stifle a teasing smile.

'Your income, young Thomas, is a percentage of the ladies' losses on the tables and all the moolah they spend at the bar. You will be surprised how wealthy these old dears are—and how gullible.'

God's Will

My mind was racing. I was drunk with excitement. We were travelling along Fleet Street at the time, past the Daily Express building towards St Paul's. I could almost see myself in a scene from a film, a dashing young male and his co-star, shooting by historical sites in a white convertible jaguar with the wind in our hair and the sun shining down on us. I had already forgotten the previous night's beating.

Larry took this moment of quiet reflection as a lack of interest or possibly fear, I think, because after a few moments he continued. 'You won't get a better offer.'

'I know,' I said, matching his coolness. 'I'll take the job.'

He nodded but said nothing and continued to do so for a very long time, but as we crossed Tower Bridge onto the South Bank he made a very curious enquiry. 'Do you believe in fate, Tom?'

'I've never really thought about it,' I replied. 'You?'

'I've thought about it a little too much.' I got a feeling from his heavy tone that he really had. 'There is an old French proverb that says fate is often met on the road you take to avoid it.'

Thinking back, I realise he might have been talking to himself as much as to me. I didn't see it at the time because I didn't know about his life or what was going on in his head. After another long silence he braked sharply and turned towards Lambeth.

'Does Lady Soho mean anything to you?'

'It isn't a sex shop, is it?'

He laughed so much he nearly ran over a cyclist. 'Maybe it was a little before your time. Her real name was Veronica Wood. A remarkable woman, who once upon a time had been one part of a musical hall knife-throwing act, the other half being her drunken and somewhat violent husband, Leo. She endured years of abuse. Then one night, after a particularly heavy drunken assault, Veronica decided enough was enough and took one of the knives from the show to the

God's Will

sleeping Leo. It was said that his intoxicated state was such that he didn't even wake as she slipped the blade in and out of his belly. Despite her years of suffering, the court showed no mercy and Veronica was given a life sentence. There the story would have ended were it not for her friends, who decided that her story should not go untold. For years they brought her case to the attention of the press, organised charity events and raised money for her release, and in doing so found friends in high places. It was the tabloids that gave her the title Lady Soho. She was a familiar face in that area and performed there often. When her case was finally reviewed, in the mid-sixties, it was decided Veronica Wood had suffered enough and she was released. Overnight she became a champion of the oppressed. From the funds raised by her friends she invested in a public house in her beloved Soho.'

'That's quite a story. Is she still in Soho?'

'No,' he said with a growl, putting his foot down to overtake a lorry. 'She was forced out. She has another place now. A pub called The Duke of Cumberland.'

'So you're saying what? That was her fate?'

'Fate?' he replied, pulling the car to a stop by the kerb. 'Who said anything about fate?'

'But you–'

'I just thought you'd like to know all about her before you met her.'

I looked up to see we had pulled up outside a pub, The Duke of Cumberland. With the story of Lady Soho fresh in my mind I went inside to find a party atmosphere, even though it was still early afternoon. The place was packed out with familiar faces—Ronnie Barker, David Frost, Marty Feldman. Amazingly they all knew Larry by name. As Larry was surrounded by friends, someone called out his name and I looked over to the bar to see a tall auburn-haired beauty

God's Will

waving over to us. Larry made his apologies and pulled me through the throng.

'Veronica, my darling!'

As we reached the bar she leaned across and gave him a huge hug. 'Where have you been hiding! I've missed you!' She let go of him when she noticed me and narrowed her eyes. 'Are you the cause of my Larry's distraction?'

In a beat she had gone from beauty to witch. I didn't know what to say. Instead I looked at Larry. Then they both burst out laughing.

Larry and I spent a great deal of time with Veronica. Although she was in her mid-forties, almost twenty years Larry's senior, she was very much like him. I will never forget that day in The Duke. The atmosphere was unlike any I had experienced in my life. It was friendly, welcoming, everything a public house should be. Growing up in a grimy northern city I really wasn't used to that. But more than anything, I learnt a lot about Larry Solomon. Far from the arrogant, brash thug I had expected Solomon junior to be, I had found a sensitive, art-loving romantic.

Who would have guessed it?

Later that night, Larry took me to his apartment in Fitzrovia. He'd given me the night off, anyway, and suggested staying at his place. We got a takeaway and watched a film, a bizarre Lindsay Anderson flick called *Oh Lucky Man*. It's about a young salesman who must abandon his principles if he is to succeed in life. I wasn't sure if Larry was trying to tell me something, but as I didn't have many principles to abandon it really didn't bother me in the slightest. I wanted success and frankly I didn't give a damn how I got it.

We talked long into the night and when I had no energy for that, Larry read to me. I didn't mind; he was very good. He could have read the Yellow Pages and still make it sound interesting. I always believed

God's Will

he would make a much better actor than me. He mostly read prose, as often as not Dickens. He would do all of the voices and had a real talent.

Next morning I woke early. There was no sign of Larry so I made a coffee and showered before touring his huge apartment. It was a little like going back in time. The apartment was extensive and on two floors. It was a mixture of seventies chic and classic style. Terence Conran would have made a few bob there, as would the many antique shops in that area back then; it was a sumptuous fusion and I think Larry was one of the very few people who could have pulled it off. On the top floor I was surprised to find an artist's studio. When I opened the door I was nearly struck blind. The sun shone down through a line of skylights into a room with white-painted walls. Dozens of paintings were stacked against them, although there were maybe half a dozen or so hanging. Narrowing my eyes against the light I walked in. In the very centre of the room was a huge canvas on a large easel covered with a paint-dotted sheet. It was clearly a work in progress and, therefore, something I presumed Larry was working on himself. I had to have a look. I was about to pull back the sheet when I heard a noise behind me.

'And what do you think you are doing?'

Startled, I let go of the sheet and spun round to find Larry, shirtless, leaning against the door frame, drink in hand, his blond hair flopping onto his forehead

'I was looking for the toilet...'

Christ knows why I said that. Possibly from the look on his face. He was angry as hell.

'Well, I don't think you will find it under there, do you?'

'Sorry, I just wondered what it was.'

God's Will

'It's a work in progress,' he said walking into the room, 'and none of your damned business.'

'Did you do all these?' I asked, gesturing behind him.

He nodded and took a sip from his cup. 'I dabble. I'm no painter.'

'I'm no actor.'

'But you understand what it is to play a part, to perform? Therefore, you are an actor.'

'And if you get satisfaction from painting, you are therefore a painter.'

I made the observation because to my untrained eyes his ability was considerable. And varied.

He circled me, padding softly. 'What brought you to London?'

I thought for a moment. Now I had discovered a deeper side to Larry I didn't want to disappoint him with some flippant remark.

'Ever since I saw London in films and on TV as a kid I've been drawn to it. I don't know. Maybe I think it takes a great city to bring the greatness out of a man.'

It was pseudo-philosophical bullshit and I know Larry saw straight through it, but to his credit he gave me my moment.

'That's very profound. London is the most remarkable of cities. It surprises me daily. There is much of London I can show you, though there is a great deal I hope you never find.'

17

Tony Calvert knocked on the door and stared down the stairwell he had just climbed. He was a little breathless and realised he was getting out of shape. He tried to hide the fact by tapping his breast pocket to see if

God's Will

he had brought the wedding anniversary invite. He had, but it was a waste of time. Alan Reid didn't do parties. His wife had insisted and he smiled at her kind nature. When had they all last met, he wondered? He didn't get a chance to pursue the thought any further as the door opened to reveal his one-time colleague and friend. Calvert had been Reid's sergeant for more than five years. Together they had dealt with many cases They were a good team. That was, until the kidnapping of Lottie Steiner.

'Tony, thanks for coming.'

The door had been snatched open and Reid, or rather his condition, shocked Calvert Exhibiting an appearance most tramps would be ashamed of, the former chief inspector was a ghost of his former self. Calvert walked in and closed the door behind him. The stench inside was a most unbearable. He hadn't seen Reid for over three years, and his physical appearance had deteriorated massively in that time. The man was a wreck.

'Could I get you a drink?' Calvert waved a negative with an open palm. Sorry about the mess,' Reid added, noticing the tray of cold food by his bed for the first time and quickly depositing it in a bin under the sink. 'Not been feeling too good lately.'

'You need someone to keep an eye on you. Do you not keep in contact with your sister?'

'Moved to Norfolk a couple of years ago,' Reid replied before coughing violently.

'Christ, Alan, you need to see a doctor.'

'I'm fine. It'll pass.'

Reid hurriedly made the bed and gestured for his guest to sit. Calvert didn't respond. His eye had been drawn to the mosaic of paper clippings and photographs above the computer. For a moment he was back in 1976. Newspaper images of Lottie's father, Marcus Steiner; of

God's Will

Larry Solomon and his father and of their huge family home in Kent; Larry's white E-type Jaguar with a young police officer standing guard forlornly on a lonely country lane; Thomas Sickert at various ages; Lottie's nanny, Olga Holtz, Bexley; and, above them all, like an angel staring down in bemused silence on a world of misadventure, Lottie Steiner. Next to that was a picture of a bearded man Calvert vaguely recognised as a much older Sickert. The wall was like a tribute and he was reminded of one of those roadside memorials to crash victims. He looked away and found another photograph by the bed, of another child. He sighed inwardly and got to the point of his visit.

'Bexley's been located.'

'Where?'

'Spain. Valencia.'

'How?'

'How did he get there or how did I find out?'

'Both.'

'He got there on a false passport, I presume. Any copper worth his salt knows where to get a decent fake in London, especially back then. I suspect he got out of the country after he left the force—it was only a month or so before the kidnapping. He would have known that investigators would find out the full extent of his involvement with Solomon. I don't agree he was involved with the kidnapping, though; he was corrupt but he wasn't stupid.'

As if on cue, the computer woke from its idle state, the hard drive wearily struggling to life. Calvert glanced across as the screen lit up, then grunted an almost mocking laugh as he read the title of the blog Reid had been reading. *The Mystery of the Steiner Gold.*

'Or maybe he managed to sneak out the Steiner gold in his underpants.'

'And how did you find out?'

God's Will

Calvert stretched and rubbed his eyes. 'Some reporter tracked him down. Laughable, isn't it? The combined efforts of the Met can't even get a sniff of him and some lowly hack with a nose for a story locates him thirty years later. Although I suspect there wasn't much enthusiasm to hunt down one of their own. They had a lot on their plate back then. He's living quite openly in a luxurious part of town. He's married. It'll be all over the newspapers soon enough. The Spanish want him out. A new administration has swept into power and they've declared war on corruption, and that includes corrupt elderly coppers. It'll look good for them, but not so good for the British government. It'll be Ronnie Biggs all over again.'

'I must see him.'

'Be my guest. He's living under the name of Culbertson. I'll have the address tomorrow.'

Reid looked at him for moment or two before his eyes narrowed and he stepped forward, reticently.

'There's something else?'

Calvert sighed. 'I don't know why I'm doing this. Okay. The security business I started up around the last time we met has really taken off and Jackie and I are moving out to the sticks. I'm no spring chicken. And neither are you. Maybe you should see my doctor. He's very good–'

'What do you have for me, Tony?'

It was wasted breath. Reid only wanted to know what nugget he had tucked away.

'I know I said I wouldn't help, but that's easier said than done. Against my own better judgement I've spoken to a lot of people, but as you may imagine there isn't much to tell. Anything of note has already been documented or,' he added, pointing to the computer screen, 'dissected by cranks on a thousand websites. The problem is it was all so long ago you can't rely on people's testimonies now. I hope for your sake her body is found one day so you can move on.'

'If her body is ever found it will be no thanks to anyone but me.'

Calvert sighed again, despairing. 'Over the past couple of years I've contacted a lot of coppers. Some still serving.'

'And?'

'And? I didn't get anywhere. But, as I say, the business is taking off and I'm taking on a lot of staff. I always hire retired coppers if I can.' He stared at Reid, unsure whether to continue with this potential bombshell. It was too late now, he realised. Reid had the scent. 'A few weeks ago I took on an ex-copper called Brown. He served in the Kent County Constabulary. We got chatting and he remembered me from the Steiner case. Then he dropped a bombshell. He was on duty on the night of the kidnapping. He remembers the night vividly. It was his first night on patrol and there had been a road fatality. A woman had hit a deer at speed. It was a right mess. The woman was killed outright and there was car and venison all over the place. So much so, they closed the road. Ten minutes later an E-type Jaguar shot around the road block on the wrong side of the road. A convertible.'

'Did no one get the registration?'

'The car was coated in mud. They were unable to see either plate. They only knew it was white because of the bonnet.'

'Larry Solomon's E-type convertible was white... and coated in mud.'

'Not that much.'

'It wasn't found for forty-eight hours. It had rained. How many were in the car?'

'It was dark but he believes one.'

'Lottie could have been in the back or the boot. So that confirms my theory that she was taken to Radstone House, the Solomon family

God's Will

home, and buried somewhere in the grounds. They are extensive, to say the least.' Reid rushed over to a pile of papers on the floor next to the computer. 'I have a diagram somewhere. Why the hell didn't he come forward with this information before?'

'Because, Alan,' Calvert replied, frowning, 'this was nowhere near Radstone House. It was the A2, Dartford way.'

Reid's eyes flicked from side to side, his brain crunching stored information for small detail. 'Dartford. The A2? That's Kent? That's miles away.'

Reid's body may have been deteriorating, Calvert mused, but his mind was as sharp as ever.

'I know.'

Reid stood up, papers dangling from his fingertips. 'But I don't understand…'

'It might not mean a thing. It could be coincidence. But if it was Solomon's Jag it could mean one of them took Lottie somewhere and then rushed back. I think that she was already dead at that point and they had buried her. That's why the car was coated in mud—maybe a field or a wood. Maybe that was why they were rushing. Who knows? What I'm trying to tell you is that they could have buried her anywhere. You're never going to find her body now.'

Reid looked like he had been dropped from a great height and had crashed through the ceiling then been stunned to find himself still living. He looked devastated and yet ecstatic all at the same time. Reid repeated the words "the car was coated in mud" a dozen times and stared distractedly at the newspaper cuttings on the wall. His former sergeant watched him closely and sensed a growing bitterness, as if somehow every face, every clue, every piece of evidence, every counter-claim on that wall had deceived him, deliberately. Calvert knew how this small detail of geography would have rocked his

God's Will

theories. For more than a minute he tried to speak to him. As a friend he felt a loyalty to a good man, and even though he knew it was impossible, he wanted to end this lifelong obsession.

'There must be someone else involved,' Reid said, and Calvert knew he hadn't listened to a word. 'This opens up so many other avenues. This could mean she didn't die that night.' He suddenly looked back at Calvert, who was now sitting on the end of the bed, his head bowed in defeat. 'It could even mean...'

'Don't! Don't do this, to yourself or me. Hasn't this fucked your life up enough? Look at you. Living like a drunk. You were one of the most able coppers I ever worked under. The whole business is cursed. It wrecked your marriage and nearly mine, too. At one point I was worrying more about a German kid I had never met and her whereabouts more than my own two.' He stood up and paced along the small gap between the sink and the bed. 'For months I was doing what you've continued to do. I was actually feeling guilt because we couldn't save her. Those bastards murder her and dump her and don't show an ounce of remorse and *I'm* feeling guilt? That was the day I decided to move on. And after thirty years you should, too.'

'I owe it to her...'

Was Reid right in his belief that Lottie's body could be found? Calvert glanced at the screen again. Or was there more to it? Did the legend of the Steiner gold have some basis? He groaned inwardly and gave himself a brief, stern talking-to. His contribution of information over the years had fed this fire of self-destruction; he couldn't put it out now but he could at least stop throwing fuel on the flames.

'You owe Lottie nothing, Alan. You did nothing wrong. And what difference would finding her body make now? She isn't suffering any more—you are.' They were standing before one another now, the

God's Will

obvious truth of Calvert's words hanging between them. 'Alan, we both know what this is about.'

Reid tried to pass him but Calvert grabbed him by the shoulders and turned him so he was facing the bed.

'Even if you were to find Lottie's body, it wouldn't change a thing. It won't bring *her* back.' Calvert had let go with one hand and was pointing at the picture next to the bed. 'It won't bring back Becky. Look at her, Alan. Leukaemia killed her. It's bloody unfair and it's awful, but it happened and I am so sorry you went through that. All you're doing is shifting the pain from your daughter to a kid you never met. You feel guilt because you couldn't help either, but you shouldn't.'

Reid screwed up his eyes and Calvert could feel the tension rippling through his body. In the same moment Reid pulled himself free and walked to the door.

'I don't need your cheap psychology,' he snarled, wrenching the door open. It took him half a minute of deep breaths before he could speak again. 'There are some things I've discovered that could change everything about the case. Did you know that Larry asked to see Sickert the night he died?'

'They were a couple of gays!' Calvert was shouting, angry to be ignored. 'He probably wanted to express his undying love for him. So what? I don't care. If you want to haunt yourself for the rest of your life that's your business.'

Calvert walked out, and every step he took felt like he was wading through mud. Before he could descend the staircase, however, Reid called out his name. He turned to see his former colleague at the door, his expression empty, his eyes revealing uncertainty. He was clearly going to speak, but Calvert had had enough.

'Whatever you find, and whatever you take from what I've just given you, is your own business now. It's over for me.'

God's Will

Calvert reached into his pocket and took out the invite. 'It's our wedding anniversary. Jackie thought it would be nice to see you again. I was going to tell her it would be a waste of time, but she's a bit like you—full of hope, always seeing possibilities when there aren't any. But in her case that's healthy.'

He tossed the invite at Reid's feet and carried on down. He didn't look back, but he could feel Reid's eyes burning into the back of his head. Those reproachful, bloodshot eyes so full of sorrow.

18

Bepa clears her throat and Philip clears away the remnants of the meal Sickert has half eaten: more rabbit stew, some heavily buttered stale bread and some batons of half-cooked carrots. Outside, a storm rages. It surrounds the lonely house and in the turbulence the tree taps fervently at the window. Crows call out to one another across the marsh, as if for reassurance. Winter is in full swing.

'Do you think Larry was warning you?'

'In what way?'

'With his remark about the darker side of London?'

Sickert considers the question but with only half a memory he can only give half an answer. 'I presume so, but I guess at the time I didn't know what he was warning me against.'

'Do you know now?'

Yes, Sickert thinks. Yes, I think I do now. The holes in his memory are filling, day by day. He's afraid.

'My eyes no longer hurt.'

God's Will

'But they are still infected.' Her tone is that of a stern matron, but in a breath it softens. She is now a young nurse treating a sickly infant. 'This job you took. Did it turn out to be all you had hoped?'

'If you mean did I feel a sense of shame for taking advantage of wealthy old women, I'm afraid to say I did not. I enjoyed the work. It suited my talents perfectly.'

She seems either deaf to the sarcasm that rises in him from time to time, or indifferent. She is always considerate and obligingly open. None of this makes sense to Sickert, but he feels cocooned by her presence and her hypnotic voice.

'So you and Larry became good friends?'

'Very much so. But I took no heed of his warning. I was enjoying myself too much.'

'Tell me more...'

* * *

The day after I met Veronica I started my new job at the Rotella. It was as if I had been born for the part. I soon discovered wealthy woman aren't that different from poor ones. They have the same needs; they simply pursue them with clipped consonants and better-designed clothes. Naked, they thrust and gasp and demand just the same. In most cases they have stripped their (mostly disloyal) husbands of most of their assets and throw themselves into a world of sexual liberty, towards men like me. Larry was a very perceptive businessman. He had watched these women flaunt themselves and seen a business opportunity. There was a regular called Deborah. Larry called her Madam Moneypot. She could easily lose a couple of grand a night and think nothing of it. Mostly because I was on her arm. She had a large belly—a particular anathema to me—and bad breath. Yet despite these

God's Will

unfortunate flaws, I seduced her on a regular basis. I played the part to perfection. In the first couple of months I earned Solomon senior £30,000 from Deborah alone. My cut gave me more than I had earned the previous year as a real actor. It was a wonderful time.

Larry had been wrong about one thing, though. The old dears weren't all ugly, with halitosis; some were breathtaking. Especially the Mediterranean and middle-eastern types. And they weren't all divorced. One particular lady was married to a government official and it was her, and a little bit of pillow talk, that really changed the course of things for me.

One night after a heavy session at the Rotella, and an even heavier one in her bed, this particular lady told me about some shady land deal in Cyprus that her husband was involved in. He had got wind of it because he worked for the Foreign Office, and if he hadn't been fucking his secretary I would never have found out. I fed this back to Larry straightaway. He in turn told his father. I later discovered it made Solomon a great deal of money.

I got a good payout from it, too, and as my bank balance grew I started to behave differently. I found there was a new confidence about me. It affected the way I acted. There was a swagger to the boy now. I wasn't aware of it at the time, but I was letting go of my past. Maybe that was why I was in London after all, to reinvent myself, to free myself of all the sadness and disappointments of my youth. I even started to lose my northern accent. I was now the one with the clipped consonants. As the months passed, I was spending less and less time at my place above Milton's. I was still seeing Stella, but her novelty value was wearing off. I experienced a higher level of satisfaction from the more appealing, wealthier types I met at the Rotella. She had become surplus to requirements. It was time to move on, but I didn't feel it that important to inform her just yet.

God's Will

With my promotion my life changed beyond all recognition. My reputation as a bringer of steady income to the Solomon empire earmarked me for special interest from the big man himself. Not that I heard that directly from him. Amazingly, even though I had worked for him for six months, four at Milton's and two at the Rotella, I was yet to meet him. Our first encounter came the day Larry shocked me with the news that I was to lose my job.

It was midweek, some time in the morning, and the casino was deserted. Or so I thought. I was at the bar having an early-morning refresher—I had found a taste for bourbon and rye—when in walked Larry. He was wearing a light cotton suit and white shirt open to the navel—this was the seventies, don't forget, and class had taken a back seat. He was very tanned. I hadn't seen him around for a week or so and presumed he had been on holiday. We drank and chatted, but he was subdued for some reason. It was clear there was something troubling him. I had only seen him like that once before, that day at his flat when I tried to peek at the canvas in the upstairs studio. Then he just said that my work at the club was over. I asked why and he gave me a simple explanation.

'Why do you think? Women talk. When they find out you've been doing half the old dears in London they will either cut off your balls or call in the Old Bill—either way not a positive outcome for you, or me. And don't think for a minute that I would do a thing to defend you.'

'But I thought I was doing well…'

'Don't worry, there's other things we can find for you.'

On that he got up and walked out. I was so pissed off. For the first time in my life I was in a groove and making myself good money in the process. Knocking back my drink in one go, I slammed the glass down on the bar.

'Don't let it get you down, son.'

God's Will

The voice came from above my head and I looked up to see a dimly lit shape staring down at me from the shadows of the balcony above the bar. There was something in the man's voice that genuinely scared me.

'Who's that?'

I heard a laugh and then footsteps and watched as two figures descended the stairs next to the bar. As they approached, the smaller man went behind the bar and fixed himself a drink. He was heavily built, with big arms that stretched the black jacket he was wearing.

'As Larry said, plenty more jobs in the company. You must be Mr Sickert. You made me a pretty packet on that Cyprus business. I've heard a lot of good things.'

Eddie Solomon was the opposite of his son in every way. His face was pockmarked and greasy, a legacy of teenage acne, and his accent was very broad—I guessed south London. Simply from the way he held himself I knew he had no class. Well, not like Larry. As he took a sip of his drink I glanced at the other man, the *heavy* leaning on the end of the bar. I should have known it would only be a matter of time before I saw Levy again.

'What do you think of the club then?' Solomon asked.

I nodded with admiration. 'It's impressive.'

'It grabs you, doesn't it? And that's what it's all about. As you have no doubt discovered. In such a place, people feel almost obliged to spend. Especially the old tarts, eh?'

He took my empty glass and topped it up with my favourite tipple. I looked at him quizzically.

'Bourbon and rye? Know what people like, Tom. Understand their passions as well as their weaknesses and it might surprise you what doors it can open. Larry has spoken highly of you, and my son is a good judge of character.' He handed me the drink and looked directly at me. 'Tell me. What's the most important thing in the world?'

God's Will

What a random question. What could I say? I went for the most obvious.

'Money?'

He smiled and shook his head in disappointment. 'No, the most important thing in the world is loyalty. Especially in my line of business. For instance, I have recently learned of an employee who is planning a way out of my organisation—which is fine. I just object to him leaving with my money.'

I felt a huge sense of fear and wondered if I had inadvertently let slip my plans to steal the Milton's takings to Stella. I glanced nervously at Levy, to find him staring back at me. Just then Larry reappeared and studied us all, cautiously.

'Take young Tom with you,' Solomon said.

'Are you sure?' Larry replied, shocked by the suggestion.

'It will be good experience for him.'

'I'm not sure this is for him.'

'Take him.' It was less of a request, more a direct order. 'If he isn't up for it he can get another job.'

I wasn't sure if I was happy to be ignored, but when I realised I wasn't the thief he was talking about I decided I would put up with it. I followed Larry and Levy out into a deserted alleyway at the back of the club. Parked up in the shadows of the summer sun was a gorgeous maroon Rover P5B saloon. I recalled the queen had one so I felt quite proud to ride in it. We didn't drive for long and as soon as we got into Soho I knew we were going to Milton's. I just didn't know why. Inside we found Charlie and Stella chatting at the bar. I could tell from their surprised reactions that we were not expected.

When Larry spoke he sounded completely different. He was in work mode. 'Where is he?'

'In his office,' Charlie muttered, a confused tone to his voice.

God's Will

We went up and I felt a huge rush of excitement as Levy opened the door. Henderson was counting money as we went in, which seemed quite ironic in a way. But he wasn't alone. Sitting across from him was a man I didn't recognise. Awkwardness hung in the air until Larry spoke up, in a very matter-of-fact way.

'If you'll excuse us, Inspector Bexley.'

'Of course, Larry,' said the man, tapping a rhythm nonchalantly on the arm of the chair and getting up. I could see he was trying to work out what was going on. 'Looks like you gentlemen have got a bit of business. Give my regards to your father, Larry.'

'Give them yourself. He wants a word.'

'Ah. Well, he knows where to find me.'

'You find him,' Larry replied, stepping aside to let him out. 'If you don't, it will be Margate for your hols this year.'

Bexley smiled faintly at Levy and me and went out. The door closed. Nobody said a word. God knows how, but Henderson seemed to understand everything. My presence must have only added to his humiliation. My move up the ladder had proved to be a fast one, and I could see from the disbelief on his face how clearly he realised the tables had turned. I remembered then Larry's comments on fate and wondered if I had any control over my own path.

'Time to go,' Larry said.

If Henderson was about to deny any wrongdoing the look on Larry's face stopped him in a heartbeat. 'I'm sorry, Larry. I just got a bit short. I wasn't doing a runner. It wasn't that much. Come on, I've worked hard for your dad. I even looked after you when you were a nipper.'

Larry wasn't listening. 'Where is it?'

'In the safe,' he said dejectedly.

God's Will

Levy collected all of the money from the table and what was in the safe and stuck it in a bag he had brought.

'Is there any more?' Larry asked. 'Think about the reply, carefully.'

Henderson gave a huge sigh of resignation and I wondered what was going on in his head. In mine there was an image of him in the ballroom and the flickering light across his face the day he and Levy beat old Skelton to a pulp. How safe he must have felt then.

Larry led us out, with Henderson between Levy and me. I glanced briefly at Charlie and Stella, who looked on in dumb silence. At the door I gave Stella a wink. As we reached the top of the steps onto the street we met Rimmer. He stared open-mouthed as Henderson was stuffed into the back of the car.

'Looks like you might be out of a job, little man.' I said it with such assurance, and it felt good.

We drove for a while and then stopped on some waste ground by the Thames at Rotherhithe. We all got out and Henderson was placed up against the car. Larry looked at him for a moment and then called me over.

'Hit him.'

'What?' I gasped.

'Hit him. Hurt him the way he hurt you. You did, didn't you, Frankie?'

'It was Levy too!' he scowled, attempting to save himself.

'Is that true?' Larry asked.

Technically it *was* Levy who had smashed my face against the table that night, but it wasn't Levy who had stolen from Solomon. I knew where my loyalties lay. In any case Levy's evil stare was powerful enough for me to shake my head and walk to Henderson.

The only punch I had ever thrown in my life was in the playground as a fifteen-year-old, and then not very convincingly. I was appalled. I

115

God's Will

should have felt confidence, knowing I could have revenge on a man who wouldn't fight back, but in a way that made it even more difficult. The pressure was on and I knew I had to do it. I drew my arm back and caught him with a lacklustre jab across his cheekbone. I think it hurt me more than it did him.

'Not like that,' Larry grunted, with a scowl. 'Levy, show him.'

Levy pulled his one-time friend away from the car and headbutted him in the middle of the face. Blood spilled into the air the way mine had. With one hand still on his lapel, Levy then jabbed him with his right, three times. Henderson sagged in his mighty paw. There was no emotion from Levy or Larry; they had clearly experienced this a hundred times. Henderson collapsed onto the dry dirt with force and a mushroom cloud of dust billowed above the devastation. Larry stepped forward and pulled him up a little. He was still conscious. The violence under the blistering midday sun made it look like something from a cowboy film. Henderson was being run out of town.

'If I ever see you again I will kill you,' said Larry. 'And you know me well enough to know that's not idle chit-chat, do you not?'

Henderson gurgled a positive and I should have felt good, for all the pain he had caused me over those months, but the simple fact was I felt nothing but sympathy for him. I had promised myself revenge but it just wasn't in me. I was revisited by that horrible sensation I felt the night they beat me. That helplessness, that aching pain deep within, because you know you can't do a thing to defend yourself. I thought of Skelton, too, and the haunted look on his face when I saw him weeks later. Would I see that in Henderson when I saw him next, I wondered? I would never find out, because I never saw him again.

As we drove off I realised that Levy had been reporting back to Solomon over the months I had seen him there. Even the weekend they had beaten me. Now I understood what Solomon meant by loyalty.

God's Will

I spent that night with Stella in my room back at Milton's. As it turned out, it was the last time I would ever stay there and the last time Stella and I would share any intimacy. I was moving on, and I would be looking for a better class of woman. As she slept with her head on my chest, I relived the day I had been through. I felt fear for the first time about what I was getting involved in, but it was only briefly felt before being washed away by a rush of exhilaration for what was to come.

19

Try as he might, Greene couldn't stop his mind drifting back to his time at Milton's, the beginning of it all. Ever since his release he had been afraid of that presence in the darkness; he became more fearful of it as the days passed and he knew soon it would be impossible to hold it back. The only way to defeat it, he finally decided, was to face it, head-on. Make a connection to his past. Speak to someone. Someone who was there. Why it would help him, he didn't know, but there was a strong sensation within him telling him it was the only way to move on. He had to find the people he was closest to at that time. That meant Charlie and Stella, people he genuinely cared for, and the sooner he started the better.

He got up early and took the thirty-seven into London. Denby tried to latch onto him on the way out, but he made his excuses and hurried on without him. As before, he got off at Tottenham Court Road. Like a tour guide without a crowd, he walked from pub to pub, cafe to cafe, mumbling to himself each time some visual trigger stirred a memory. They were all around him. At ground level much had changed, but up above little had. There, in the shadows above the garish shopfronts, the

God's Will

architecture retained its original form. This was where a great deal of the population lived. Bedrooms and attics were homes to the moths drawn to the big lights of London. The more he walked, the more the memories returned, and the more he thought of them the more the monster stirred. There was nothing he could do to stop it other than to keep moving.

But there was no one left. Even in the places that had maintained the original fixtures and fittings he recognised no one and none of the staff or patrons knew anyone from that time. He was contemplating returning home when a half-forgotten memory surfaced. There was another place he and Larry visited regularly, although it was not in central London. As far as he could remember neither Stella or Charlie ever went near the place, but it was all he had left. He flagged down a cab and directed the driver south of the river.

Greene's arrival coincided with a darkening sky and heavy salt and pepper sleet. Under this cloak of semi-darkness he crossed a busy dual carriageway and stared at an ageing door with large bulbous windows on either side. From a distance it seemed like a face watching him. The sign above the door had letters missing, and the painted image was weathered, but his memories of The Duke of Cumberland were as rich as ever. Other than a barmaid texting blithely and a scruffy twenty-something eyeing him from a bar stool, the place was empty. For an odd moment he was sure he could hear the ghostly echoes of music and laughter, but it disappeared when the girl asked what he wanted to drink. He ordered a whisky on the rocks and sat down far enough away from the bar to avoid conversation. The girl had her head down, staring into the screen, and for a moment he couldn't stop himself from imagining Veronica, or Lady Soho as she liked to be called. Whatever happened to her? What happened to all of them?

God's Will

There was a noise to the right of the bar as a stocky man waddled with difficulty into the room from the direction of the toilet. Straightaway there was something familiar about him. It would be a minute before Greene realised it, but the answer to at least one of his questions was now sitting in the room with him. The fat man coughed and wheezed, and some sensation within Greene told him that he knew this person, even though all he could see from where he sat was a silhouetted head before a window. He put down his glass and his eyes narrowed. Hidden in the gloom of that face, eyes were studying his own, dull eyes in a face like a landscape in the midst of winter—grey and bare to the world. It was a face he remembered well. Then came that noise again, that wheeze as air was forced into ageing lungs.

Rimmer.

Greene was unable to move. Before him was a direct link to a world he had concluded no longer existed. He had thought he would be lucky if he found a friend of a friend, or maybe an old lag who vaguely remembered his involvement with Solomon. But Rimmer? There was no love lost between them. Rimmer was the gopher, rarely away from Henderson and Solomon's side. No job was too small for him. If there was money to be had, his would be the open hand. His greed would turn any crooked errand into a life-enhancing moment. And he hated Greene because he had done what he could never do, find his way into the affections of Solomon, one of London's most powerful men. Yet he had to be careful. It was possible that Rimmer was aware of Charlie and Stella's whereabouts.

Like a wild animal, Rimmer studied Greene from the shadows and, although he was small, the younger man was filled with unease. He took a deep breath then walked over and sat before him, an element of his former life resonating within him. He emptied the whisky glass and gripped it tightly.

God's Will

'Well, I never…' Rimmer muttered between breaths. 'You've got some front.' Raising his pint to his lips he shook his head, slowly. 'If I was you I'd go abroad somewhere. Hide away from my shame. When did they let you out?'

'It's nice to know I've been missed,' Greene replied, his voice without emotion.

'You didn't waste any time. Things have changed, Tommy boy.' Putting down the pint, Rimmer suddenly cackled loudly as if the comment had triggered some thought in his old wrinkled head. Greene watched as it bobbed in and out of the shadows. The old man had lost weight, but not enough to take the pressure off his ailing lungs. 'Yeah, that's very true, Tommy boy. Very true. They've changed more than you realise!'

'But not you, eh? You always did keep your ear to the ground, Rimmer.'

'I don't miss much. I've got a good view of the world. I see things clear enough.'

'Maybe only appearances change, though?'

'We'll see, Tommy boy. We'll see.'

Even though Greene didn't show it, the comment troubled him. It was clear Rimmer knew something he didn't. Masking it with a smile, Greene pursued his prepared line of questioning. It didn't matter that it was Rimmer.

'Thought you were an East End boy.'

'The old girl left me her house. Moved here a few years after…'

Greene knew he was about to say *the killings*, but even for Rimmer it was hard to say. Was it so horrendous? Even to men like him?

'Sorry to hear about your mum.'

'Cancer.'

'There's a lot of it about,' Greene grunted.

God's Will

'Yes. Heard about Larry... couldn't have happened to a nicer boy.' Rimmer's smile gave way and there was sudden aggression in his tone. 'What did you do to that little girl, you bastards? Animals, that's what you are!' The girl looked over and Rimmer reined back his anger. 'Not long now, though. One down, one to go.'

His smile was like fire in the darkness. He had touched a nerve and Greene could almost sense the joy.

'What became of Charlie and Stella?' He asked the question nonchalantly, as if he was asking about the weather, or where he could find a good barber. He disguised the fact that a negative response might tip him into depression completely.

'Charlie and Stella? From Milton's?' Rimmer was smiling again. That wasn't a good sign, and Greene knew it. 'They were old friends of yours, weren't they? Well, let me see, old Charlie died a couple of years back, up north somewhere.' Greene's heart sank, and did so again as Rimmer's smile widened. 'And old Stella... gone, too, I'm afraid. Dead. Back in the eighties. Isle of Wight, Isle of Man, one of 'em.'

The pain ran through Greene like a powerful wave, clearing his mind of everything except their faces. Again he didn't let it show. He wasn't going to give Rimmer that pleasure.

'Looks like you got nobody left, Tommy boy... but then what would you expect after what you did? I'm surprised they let you out.'

The pain within Greene eased and moved beyond him, leaving not fear but hatred and a rage strong enough for him to kill again... but things were different now. Now he could control the anger and match Rimmer's sneering hatred. A little bit of the Thomas Sickert of old had returned.

'Who's running things now, Rimmer?'

'If you're here to find out if you're safe or not, I'm happy to say you are not!' An almost evangelical raising of the arms showed Greene

God's Will

the real measure of the old man's joy. 'You done a bad thing to a powerful man. A man with powerful friends, men that do not forget easy! I'm surprised no one done you in Brixton.'

He had a point there, Greene conceded. He had made a lot of enemies before his arrest, and when he realised he was doing the last stretch of his sentence in London he had feared the worst. It never happened. In fact, the lack of attention he had received had suggested an element of untouchability that had put fear into the other cons and earned respect from them and screws alike, something that under normal circumstances would be unheard of for a man involved in a child murder. It was as if he was being protected, but he always had a sense he was being saved for a later date, not being saved *per se*.

'So who *are* you running for now?'

'I'm me own man!'

It was Greene's turn to touch a nerve or two. 'I seriously doubt that. Now, who?'

Rimmer got up, a fat finger waggling like a dagger before him. He swayed before Greene. 'Someone who don't like you! Who don't like you one little bit!'

For a moment Greene was at a loss. He had made a lot of enemies. By his own admission he had been a little too flash for his own good towards the end. That had been his downfall. But he really couldn't see who would go out of their way to keep an eye on him for a quarter of a century.

'You don't know, do ya?'

He didn't. All he could do was watch Rimmer's finger cutting the air before his face and wait. And when it came he shouldn't have been surprised at all.

'Frankie! Frankie Henderson!'

God's Will

It was a double blow, a shock to the system that couldn't be concealed. Greene walked out in a daze, Rimmer's mocking laugh following him through the door. Outside, the darkening skies hung low and the sleet had turned to rain. He leant against the wet wall and caught his breath. The traffic hurried by, unaware of him and his pain. For the first time since his release he wanted to be back in his tiny cell. He longed for that isolation. Where were his walls of safety now?

Henderson. He would never have expected that. But events had led to a murderous vacuum into which anyone might prevail, he reminded himself. After the kidnapping there would have been an all-out gang war across London. With Solomon gone, his throne would have been up from grabs. It would have been the quickest to react who would come out on top, a brutal man a little smarter than the rest. That, he conceded, was Henderson in a nutshell. After his beating he had disappeared but, if Rimmer was right, he was back—and the little man was spot on… Henderson had a score to settle.

There was a break in the flow of traffic and in the lull something occurred to Greene. He and Larry had changed Henderson's fortunes. Without their actions he would have remained a no-one, hiding in the shadows. Surely even Henderson would realise that? He had served his time, Larry was dead and Solomon long gone. What the hell did Rimmer know, anyway? Maybe he was worrying for no reason.

Greene looked to the sky and laughed to himself because he knew better than most that life just doesn't work that way. Even as the small club manager, Henderson had illusions of greatness. Yes, he had good reason to fear Rimmer's words. Despite his temperament, Henderson had pride and he would remember that day by the Thames in Rotherhithe where, under a blazing sun, he was so convincingly humiliated. Greene knew it would only be a matter of time before he came calling.

God's Will

Making his way back to Muswell Hill, colder than he had imagined possible, all Greene could think about was Stella and Charlie. Rimmer could have been wrong, of course, but he doubted it. Men like that forged a reputation and a living from information. So he had lost them both. Now there was no one.

Later that evening Greene watched as Angie did the dishes unaware, it seemed, of the shadow that had fallen on him. As she worked she sang, and in her voice he found a little of Stella. Stella would have been twenty years her senior if she had lived, but their character was very similar. In his head he reran those contented early days at Milton's.

Suddenly he was aware the room had fallen silent and he looked up to see her staring down at him.

'Are you all right, love?'

It was odd how the lonely see loneliness in others. Greene smiled at Angie and she smiled back, and from that he found he knew her a little better. The lost wander alone together, as they say.

Just then there was a commotion in the hall and after a scowl the door flew open to reveal Denby, giggling uncontrollably with a bottle of booze in each hand.

'Felicitations to one and all!' he said, his rotund frame swaying in the doorway. 'Shall we have a party?' Getting no reply he stared at their somewhat dour expressions. 'What's happened here then? Somebody die?'

The snow that had fallen heavily on his release was gone now and in its place a grey depression consistent with the time of year set in, dimming the city's vibrancy. Occasionally the sun shone, but the raw northerly wind took away its richness, giving the streets a sombre tone, reflected in the skeletal trees and colourless parks and gardens.

God's Will

Mindless of the conditions, Greene walked the streets of London aimlessly for weeks. He was without purpose now he knew Charlie and Stella were gone. The small sense of curiosity and hope freedom had given him on his release had become muddied by uncertainty and self-loathing, and he withdrew from the world. In prison he had found strategies to survive, but in a world of freedom he was a leaf tossing in a storm. Drink was now his only escape. The all-consuming bouts of heavy drinking with Denby continued, and they were now spilling into the day. His life became one long blur of bars and hangovers. And he was a haunted figure in more ways than one. The presence of the Ghouls, that strange couple he had met first in Soho, had become a constant in his life. Every night he encountered them, either in pubs or walking the streets of central London. There was something unnerving about them, something that troubled him deeply. In a way they mirrored the void within him.

One night there was no sign of Denby so Greene went out alone. It was the usual night of excess but as he stumbled drunkenly through the cold on the way home, he discovered some kind of altercation involving a group of teenagers on Hampstead Road, near Euston Station. Knowing better than to get involved, he walked into the road to get past, but as he got level he realised the cause of the commotion was in fact the Ghouls. They had been circled by a group of teenagers who were jeering and mocking them; one was even spraying water from a plastic bottle at them. The man and woman were clearly afraid but seemed either incapable of or unwilling to defend themselves.

'Leave them be!' To his surprise, Sickert realised it was him who had shouted.

'Or what?' said a lanky boy with a baseball hat.

'Just leave them,' he repeated, wondering why the hell he had got involved. 'Let them go.'

God's Will

The water sprayer at the back continued and hit the woman in the side of the head. She bent forward to protect the contents of the pram and Sickert felt anger grow more intensely inside him. He stepped forward and headbutted the kid, but before the lad had even hit the ground he was pounced upon and beaten to the ground. He tried to get up but a flurry of kicks and punches knocked him down again and again. He curled into a ball, foetus-like on the cold tarmac. Through it all he got a glimpse of the Ghouls walking off at speed, without so much as a backward glance.

It took him hours to get to Muswell Hill. In his condition, no taxi driver seemed willing to pick him up—even without a torn jacket and bloodied face he was looking more and more like a tramp, anyway. He hadn't shaved for weeks and was still in possession of only one change of clothes, and that was yet to be laundered. Somehow in the fracas he had lost his key. Angie's initial anger at being woken in the early hours disappeared when she saw the state of him.

'Mr Greene, what's happened to you? Come in out of the cold.'

She tended to his wounds and ran him a bath in her part of the house. The hot soapy water took away some of the pain from the many grazes and bruises, and a large mug of sweet tea topped with whisky gave him just enough energy to stay awake. After fifteen minutes, the bathroom door opened slowly and through half-open eyelids he saw Angie dressed in a short satin baby-doll dressing gown and red fluffy wedge slippers. She looked like a character from a bedroom farce, and he knew what she wanted.

'I thought I'd slip into something more comfortable,' she whispered, kneeling by the bath.

Taking a mouthful of tea from the mug she leant forward and passed it to him through her lips. He accepted the gift and gulped it down. She brushed his cheek and he heard her breath shudder as she exhaled.

God's Will

'Such a handsome man. Such dark eyes and a manly chest. Maybe I should shave off that beard. There's a strong handsome chin under there, I bet. I've met a lot of men in this house over the years, but there's something about you I find irresistible. Let me wash you, Mr Greene. Let Angie wash away your pain.' She placed a hand on his chest and he closed his eyes. Slowly the hand slid across his torso and beneath the bubbles. 'I don't want to know what you have been to prison for. It doesn't interest me. I believe every man deserves a second chance. But there's something inside me that tells me you are a good man. And a woman's intuition is rarely wrong.'

Greene glared at her. 'Well, it's wrong this time. And as for washing away my troubles, that's beyond anyone's abilities. Particularly with what you've got in your hand—because that isn't the soap.'

20

Sickert has slept. How long for he can't calculate. The clock ticks, the rats scurry, the fire crackles, yet there is a distinct change in the atmosphere. Is it in the room or his head? The storm has passed and the branch taps at the glass only gently. No sign of his red-breasted friend today.

When Bepa eventually speaks her voice is faint, as if her spirit is fading. 'I didn't take you to be a religious man, Thomas.'

He is puzzled by the remark and thinks back to all he has told her. As far as he can gather there has been no mention of anything even vaguely ecclesiastical.

'I'm not... not in the slightest.'

'It's possible I misheard you.'

God's Will

'When?'

'Whilst you slept. You were talking. You said that it was God's will.'

'God's will?'

The phrase musters up some vague memory, but too vague. It doesn't connect to anything solid.

'I want to take off the bandages,' Sickert mutters, pushing himself up awkwardly. 'It doesn't hurt like it did.'

'Give it another couple of days. The cream and antibiotics are doing their work. We have the infection on the run.'

Sickert is puzzled. 'Antibiotics?'

'I have Philip crush them up and put them in your wine.'

He laughs at her audacity. 'You could have just asked.'

'Men rarely do as their told.'

Sickert finds this comical, considering her son doesn't do anything without her say-so. He enquires about her own life. It's the first time, and he doesn't know what to expect. To his surprise she is open about her emotions, decidedly philosophical, just sketchy on detail.

She has never married. Philip's father was a career man and died shortly before he was born. The house was formerly the property of wealthy landowners who sold up and emigrated to Australia in the early sixties. The house is extensive, with a courtyard and stables. Sadly, it has become too much for them both and when she has gone she has instructed her legal representative in London to sell up and create a financial portfolio for her Philip.

The old woman promises that when he is well enough Philip will show him round. A few minutes later she is hanging on his every word, as he is himself. He is, of course, the main player in his own narrative.

* * *

God's Will

Henderson's demise became the catalyst for my success. Within a week of his disappearance I moved into one of Solomon's plush apartments in Fitzrovia (just around the corner from Larry). I was in receipt of a significant wage and had been invited to one of Solomon's monthly get-togethers at the family home near Lambourne End in Essex.

I got the sense that Larry was not happy about the invite from his father but said nothing on the way. It was a hot summer evening and the sky in the west was a crimson red as we sped along the A113 towards Abridge, within the Lambourne parish. A couple of miles before the town, Larry turned off onto a minor road. Shortly after that we joined a long winding gravel drive that led, snake-like, through rows of foreboding giant oaks. In the twilight they seemed like huge monsters staring down at us as we sped along. I felt a pang of trepidation, but it was outweighed by excitement. We finally arrived in front of a huge house, where Larry threw the car into a large braking arc on the drive. Breathlessly I stared up at the imposing building. I was awestruck. Larry had never mentioned this place. Why, I couldn't understand. It was so impressive. I got out of the car in a daze. To some, a row of thirty-foot columns wouldn't mean a great deal, but to a kid from the north, one who knew nothing of grandeur and pomp, it had the intended effect.

It grabs you and that's what it's all about. Solomon's words echoed in my mind.

All the time I had existed in a humble two-up two-down, Larry had lived in this magical place. I felt shame for my own background and I was determined to rid myself of it. Below the columns, in staid replication, four footmen waited solemnly, clearly unimpressed by Larry's driving skills. Tossing the keys to one of them he welcomed me to Radstone House. I later discovered that Solomon had picked the

God's Will

place up for next to nothing thanks to a crooked official in the planning department of the local council. Amazingly, he had even received funding to put it back to its former glory. Very quickly I was discovering how corrupt the world was, especially Solomon's world.

I was so overwhelmed by everything around me it was a moment or two before I realised Larry had disappeared. I presumed he had gone into the party I could see across the grand reception area. I tried to follow him, but due to the constant flow of waiters bearing crates of champagne and trays stacked high with canapés and hors d'oeuvres it was simply impossible. Then I heard his voice. From nowhere he had appeared at the bottom of the stairs on the far side with a magnum of Champagne and a tray of canapés.

'Come on then!' he shouted.

'What about the party?' I asked.

'Plenty of time for that. It's still early. Come on, I'll show you round.'

After an hour of drinking and eating in his huge bedroom, we showered and dressed. Thankfully we were roughly the same size and I didn't have to wear the dreadful suit I had bought in a panic at the charity shop earlier that afternoon. The suit he gave me was hand-made and I felt I was cheating somehow as I put it on, as if I'd suddenly found myself on a podium accepting an award that wasn't rightly mine.

As we left the room Larry put his hand on my shoulder and looked at me. I could see that he was troubled and needed to say something; I just didn't know which Larry would speak. Would it be the one who had become such a good friend to me—a caring man who could quote Shakespeare and read Dickens into the night—or the thug who had threatened to kill Henderson and had probably killed before? It turned out to be neither. His face suddenly drained of colour and he spoke without emotion.

God's Will

'You still have a choice in your life, Tom.'

I knew he was talking about my former life and a criminal future, but I played dumb. 'What do you mean?'

'You are about to meet people who can and will influence your life. I didn't have choice in mine. By the time I was old enough to think for myself I was already part of that world. You can still walk away now. You have a chance.'

I laughed. 'You're a funny one.'

I was so close to him I could see his pupils contract. My response had angered him, and I could see he was debating with himself. It went on for half a minute or so then, finally, he sniggered, nodded to himself and turned. A moment later we were descending the stairs. Once we were amongst the throng I watched how he changed again. It was as if he was preprogrammed to alter his personality depending on the circumstances. A minute before he had been a friend, with my welfare uppermost in his mind, but the moment he walked into that roomful of people he had become another man, Mr Charm. He could change that quickly. Nevertheless, it was quite something to see him glow in the adoration of others. I would see it again and again as the years passed, the attention and the admiration fusing to make his existence more worthwhile. Of course, I was lost in the crowd, hidden in his shadow, but it was all worth it just to see him working the crowd.

Finding myself alone, I surveyed the scene. The room was huge, similar in size and design to the Rotella. Chandeliers, with long drapes, vast mirrors and massive paintings. But where the colours of the casino mirrored its rich activity with gold and reds, Radstone's subtle hues attempted to emulate a more refined lifestyle. It was beautiful but confusing. Solomon was a thug from south London. I suspected a woman's influence.

God's Will

On one side of the room there was a small jazz quartet playing pop hits of the day. I got myself a drink and wandered about. There must have been over a hundred people and in the party atmosphere everybody seemed to be free of any inhibitions. The closer I looked and the harder I listened to the accents and conversations the more I realised these were not your run-of-the-mill hoodlums. These were people with money and influence. I realised then what Larry was warning me against. The pull here was strong. He understood me well enough.

'I know you, don't I?'

The man who had appeared before me had a round pleasant face and brown mousy hair, greying at the temples. His suit was well cut but plain. He looked out of place, physically speaking. He didn't have the style others seemed to carry with ease, but he had something, an authority of a kind. Then I remembered. Inspector Bexley.

'You work at Milton's.'

'Not anymore,' I muttered with a new-found confidence.

'Coming up in the world? I better keep my eye on you,' he said with a wink.

In the same moment I heard another voice and turned to see Solomon striding towards me.

'Tom, I wondered where you'd got to. Where's that boy of mine?'

Although he stank of alcohol, he wasn't drunk. Solomon was always in control.

'Around somewhere.'

'Shall I put out an all-points bulletin?' Bexley enquired.

'I see you've met the inspector? Always nice to have a policeman in the vicinity. You never know when it's going to turn ugly.' They laughed as Solomon took me by the arm. 'Come on then, Tom. I'd like you to meet the wife.'

God's Will

Knowingly, Bexley watched us over his drink as Solomon dragged me away. His eagle-eyed stare remained on me as we approached some huge patio doors on the far side of the room. As if Solomon was emitting some potent electrical charge the crowd parted and there, like a Greek statuette at the end of an avenue of plane trees, stood the most beautiful thing I had ever seen in my life.

'Tom, this is Julia.'

Now, if Solomon's wife had been a big-titted blonde I would have been prepared. But this I would never have expected in a million years. Julia was dark-haired and elf-like, and reminded me a little of Hepburn in her prime. She didn't speak at all that first night, except with her eyes. And what eyes. As Solomon spoke and I tried my best to listen, I found little Julia talking to me the way a wife shouldn't, especially to her son-in-law's best friend. She was, as I was to discover later, not Larry's mother at all. His real mother had died years before. Not that I learned this from him; on the subject of parentage, Larry was decidedly reticent.

Finally, thankfully, Solomon took me away. As we walked off I could sense Julia's eyes burning into the back of me. The sensation was still with me as we walked out onto the balcony, but it faded as Solomon showed me what he was and what I was not. He didn't do it directly, not in an arrogant showy way, but by the tone of his voice when he told me how he had risen from abject poverty to these dizzy heights, where he was surrounded by the powerful friends he had made. I saw through it, of course, but in the glow of that magnificent house, surrounded by its huge estate, I was a child on the first day of school having a one-to-one with the headmaster.

Solomon had a way with people, a very different way to men like Henderson. Solomon listened to everything you said and could, I'm sure, have repeated every word if required. But that was all part of the

God's Will

trick, because although he was listening intently, he was also wrapping an invisible web around you, and in most cases—including my own—you didn't realise it until it was too late. Nevertheless, that night at Radstone was a special moment for me. The darkness and horror of my association with Solomon would come later. If only I could have known.

Into the early hours of that night I drank and joked with powerful men and beautiful woman—men of finance, the judiciary, pop stars, MPs, models and, of course, a corrupt Metropolitan police inspector. It was a cocktail that I could barely take in, so overpowering and evocative was its taste. There I was, the little boy from the north, suddenly at the heart of everything I felt important.

By three the following morning, and with no sign of the party letting up, I was aware that the staff had gone and some people were drifting off to various other parts of the house. I went for a tour and found Solomon in a small room talking with a man who seemed familiar to me. I'm good with faces but I just couldn't place this one. I walked out to get some fresh air and found activity in what looked like a summerhouse in a small copse beyond the glow of the main building. I was a child in a sweetshop and there was nothing I didn't want to savour. Yet I had barely got onto the lawn when I felt a hand on my shoulder.

'Time for bed.' Silhouetted against the house Larry's wavy blond hair shone like a halo.

'I was just following the party.'

'The party's dead,' he said solemnly, his head now tilted up to the stars. 'Anyway, I've got an old friend I'd like you to meet.'

I followed Larry to the house, yet as I glanced back to the summerhouse and the flickering pale light at its windows I couldn't help but feel he was trying to stop me from seeing something. To be

God's Will

honest, I didn't think too much of it as we went upstairs. My mind was more concerned with whom I was going to meet. Opening the wardrobe, Larry took out a bottle of whisky and tossed it to me.

'I ll get the glasses.'

'I thought I was meeting somebody?'

'You already have!' he yelled, throwing his jacket on the floor.

I suddenly got the joke. His *old friend* was a rare bottle of single malt. I poured him a drink but he didn't reappear so I walked into the bathroom, to find him staring at himself in the mirror.

'Are you okay, Larry?'

'No, Thomas, Larry is not okay,' he said slowly and in a whisper.

I was shocked to see him that way. I didn't want to leave him, but having seen what he was capable of that day with Henderson I certainly didn't want to upset him any more than he already was. Hiding my shock the best way I could, I went to my own room along the passage.

Later on, still nursing the whisky, I heard footsteps and raised voices below my balcony. I peered down to see Solomon and the man I had seen earlier. In the still of the night I could hear quite clearly. The other man was foreign. It then dawned on me where I had seen him before. He was the VIP from Milton's, the German diplomat, Lottie's father. There was another man, too, a very overweight character in an ill-fitting dinner suit. His name was Fenton, and he was Solomon's legal advisor. He was a man of dubious character and as crooked as he was fat, and that was very. The argument was about a debt Steiner owed Solomon, and the latter was not at all happy. Fenton, unusually for him, was playing peacemaker.

'Eddie, calm down. I am sure Mr Steiner has every intention of adhering to his financial responsibilities.'

Solomon was fuming. 'He better. I've been patient enough.'

God's Will

Despite having Solomon in his face, Steiner was the epitome of calm. 'Mr Solomon, as I have explained, the money can be raised. You must please put things into perspective.'

Solomon stuttered with anger. 'Put things in perspective? I'll put you in a fucking hospital in a minute, you smug kraut!'

Fenton parted the two men with a limp-wristed wave of the hand. His faux upper-class accent jarred on my northern ears. 'Herr Steiner is right. Now, why don't we all calm down and toddle over to the House of Fun and relieve ourselves of this pointless stress. If you could excuse us for a moment, Herr Steiner. Maybe warm up a blonde for us all—the younger the better.'

Steiner bowed grandly before walking off across the lawn to the copse. The House of Fun was clearly the summerhouse. Neither Solomon nor Fenton spoke until the German was halfway across the grass. Then I heard Solomon make a reference to a part of Steiner's lower anatomy and what he might do with it when he'd cut it off. I very nearly went into my room to control the sudden belly laugh the comment provoked. I was glad I didn't, because if I had I wouldn't have heard what Fenton said next.

'I have guided you through the legal minefield for over a decade, Eddie, and at times we have sailed very close to the wind, but I have kept the law away from your door.'

Solomon was still full of anger and consequently not in the mood for a lecture. 'Your point being?'

'Be careful with Steiner. If you push him too far he may disappear and you will lose everything he owes you or, worst-case scenario, he could turn the tables and take things to a higher level and the law could come down on you. Don't forget the man was recently widowed.'

God's Will

'I don't give a fuck. I've done nothing wrong. It's a gambling debt he's run up! Anyway, he wouldn't fucking dare! I got connections, too, you know? If he messes with me, I'll crush him!'

Fenton looked around and up. Luckily I was quick enough to pull my head back into the shadows.

'Slowly, slowly, catchy monkey. His wife died earlier this year in childbirth. Sympathise with him. Explain that you appreciate that he's under a lot of pressure. He'll have his skeletons, too. Everyone has. If he hasn't we'll create a few for him. For instance, what is he doing right now?'

'What—birds? Get some photos of him in action, you mean?'

'Possibly. Not here, though. That would be incriminating yourself.'

'And you, too,' observed Solomon to Fenton's obvious discomfort. 'So let me get this right. You want me to blackmail him to get the money he owes me legally?'

'No. Currently he is in a bad situation, but if you turn the screw you could quadruple that debt.'

Solomon nodded with glee. 'I see your point, Fenton. What a greedy little mind you have.'

'I try my best, Eddie, I try my best,' he smirked with an oily laugh.

'Where's Bexley? He can give me some advice on this.'

'Bexley is where Bexley always is, engaging in some physical activity across the lawn.'

'Typical. You can never find a copper when you need one.'

Fenton laughed again. 'Shall we join them?'

Placing an arm around Solomon's shoulders, Fenton led him off towards the flicker of light across the lawn. No sooner had they left when I noticed a silhouetted shape near one of the trees that had been out of view to the trio of men. It wasn't until Solomon and Fenton had been swallowed up by the darkness that the figure morphed. I recognised him instantly. They had been wrong: Inspector Bexley was *not* where they had presumed him to be. I was not the only one within earshot, it seemed. He was clearly as aware of me as I was of him but, amazingly, he didn't seem to care. As our eyes met fully for the first time he raised his glass to me and then sauntered off along the path, whistling a happy tune.

21

Greene awoke in a great deal of pain—and not only the physical type. Sure, there was much of that. The side of his head, his right collar-bone and the very tip of his nose ached at varying degrees, but it was as he re-ran the previous night's excesses that he felt the real agony. The memory of being beaten up by a group of kids was bad, as was the thought of the Ghouls leaving him for dead, but it was the memory of his moment of failed intimacy with Angie that hit home hardest.

'Maybe tomorrow?' Angie had said as he rose from the bath, his manhood clearly unaffected by her touch.

'I don't think so,' he had replied. 'I'm not interested.'

The look on her face had genuinely scared him, especially when she looked down at his flaccid cock. 'You're not gay, are you?'

'I'm just not interested,' he repeated, picking up his clothes and walking out into the living room.

A woman scorned was one thing but Angie had reinvented the phrase and taken it to a whole new level.

'What do you mean "you're not interested"? Who do you think you are? Do you think I throw myself at every man who steps through my door?'

God's Will

'I don't know and I don't really care.'

Before he knew it she was hitting him with a large cushion. There he was, a notorious felon dripping bathwater all over cheap shagpile and being attacked with soft furnishings by a woman he hardly knew. The moment had been both ridiculous and strangely comic, but inside he was hurting. He wanted her, he wanted to be a man again, but torment from his past still cast long shadows over him.

He rolled onto his side and opened his eyes. The first thing he saw was himself—a young, bold, virile Thomas Sickert mocking him from the front of the book lying on the carpet. He had read it three times. What a contrast to the pale, bearded old man on the bed. Larry smiled back from the cover, too, and Greene knew he could never hate him, no matter what.

He heard footsteps on the stairs and feared the worst, but all he got was a gentle knock on his door. Maybe Angie had regretted her outburst and was waiting at the door with an apology and a cup of tea? He quickly dressed and looked out. No Angie, no tea, just a letter at his feet. He picked it up and closed the door. It was addressed to him, but with the Needham House address crossed out and that of his current abode written above it. He had already received correspondence from the Home Office, but this was clearly not an official reminder that he had just left prison. His tired eyes ran along the return address on the back. He could barely believe what he saw.

Fenton Solicitors.

Even though Denny was dressed for the cold winter weather he simply couldn't keep the chill at bay. The morning sun shone but it did little to raise the temperature. He shuffled along the road, rubbing his hands together as he did so, towards the building he had visited for the first time a month before. The meeting had been agreed over the phone.

God's Will

Lamb had said it would be a good way of focusing their efforts, and Denby relished it as much as he did the freezing weather. If he had a choice he would be anywhere else in the world but there. Lamb scared the hell out of him, but unless he could find something incriminating about him he would be dancing to his tune a little while longer. He had discovered one nugget of information that could possibly come in handy, and that was regarding Lamb's interest in Greene.

The disappearance of Lottie Steiner and the manner of the murders of the three other victims had earmarked it as one of the most gruesome crimes of the twentieth century. However, a recent discovery in Germany suggested that the ransom for Lottie, something that was long believed to have been unpaid, had indeed gone ahead. Rumours had circulated for years suggesting the British and German governments had consistently lied over the full extent of the kidnapping. Now, a German historian trawling through thousands of newly released documents had stumbled upon details of a transfer of gold bullion worth, at the time, one million Deutschemarks. Documentation detailing the shipment by air to Stanstead airport from Munich in August 1976 (the year and month of the kidnapping) on the then state-owned carrier Lufthansa, had been popping up on various websites over the past few days. He had heard this by chance in the pub one night, and although there was a lifetime of evidence to prove the contrary, he always paid heed to omens and hunches. This information, he believed, would arm him in his war against Lamb. Joining a nearby library, he located a website detailing the recent discoveries, not to mention eyewitness around Europe who claimed to have been involved with the transfer. The same website had numerous theories on what had happened to the gold and where Lottie's body might be buried. With this new information Denby was about to prove he was more than capable of fighting his own corner.

God's Will

The cold followed him up the staircase and stayed with him as he knocked on the door. Memories of the previous meeting ran in his head like a horror show. It got colder as the door opened and the tall outline of Lamb stood motionless in the shadows.

'Won't you come in?'

Denby walked into the living room as before, but decided this time not to sit. He wouldn't let Lamb have him at a disadvantage as on the previous occasion.

'Before we go any further, let me first explain that I know all about the gold bullion and unless we renegotiate the terms of this so-called financial agreement, I will contact the relevant authorities and report you!'

It was a rousing, stoic speech and Denby was proud of himself. That feeling was short-lived. Leaping forward with the agility of a man half his age, Lamb grabbed him by the collar and threw him like a rag doll onto the armchair. Pinning his shoulders back against the leather he peered deep into the old man's eyes.

'What are you doing, man? Let me go!' Denby squealed.

Tears filled his eyes and he wished himself back a minute in time to unsay what he had said. There was such anger in Lamb's tired, bloodshot eyes it was a full minute before he released him and another five before he spoke again. He stood at the window with his back to Denby and the old man could almost see the tension rippling across his shoulders.

'Forgive me, Denby,' he whispered in a detached tone at last. 'I have had a difficult few weeks. Let me get you a brandy.'

Denby's whimpers faded to sighs of relief. 'That's good of you. I'm sorry. I don't know what I was thinking of.'

'It's no matter,' Lamb replied, holding out the glass. 'And, on reflection, I think you are right.'

God's Will

He gulped. 'You do?'

'Of course. I've been unfair. I realise now you are taking just as much of a risk as I am, if not even more, having to live with the man.'

Denby sat up and straightened his clothes before taking a very large mouthful of the fiery liquid. This sudden change was unexpected.

'In fact, that's one of the things I wanted to discuss. From your detailed reports it seems to me that Sickert has no focus.'

'That's right. He has no friends, no purpose in life. Forgive me for questioning your thinking, but do you really believe he is planning to find a hoard of missing loot?'

'There has been a development. Thanks to your good work I've realised that Sickert is prepared to bide his time. Wherever the gold is hidden—and, yes, I know for a fact it is—I don't think he is in any hurry to get at it. He's waited almost thirty years; I'm sure he can wait another five, maybe ten. Either way, too long for you and I, Denby.'

'So what do we do?'

'We light a fire.'

Denby screwed up his mouth. 'I don't follow, old boy.'

'What do people do when their house is burning?'

'Run like hell?'

Lamb said nothing and in the silence the penny dropped for Denby.

'Or, rather, run to their valuables!'

'Exactly.'

'My, you're a clever one!' Denby emptied the glass then frowned. 'But how do we do that?'

'Leave that to me,' Lamb said softly. He was back at the window staring down at the street below.

'You said "one of the reasons".'

The observation didn't stir any reaction at first and Denby didn't dare push his luck any more than he had. The depressed figure before

God's Will

him was a stark contrast to the one he had met earlier in the month. Even during their phone conversations, Lamb had appeared confident and menacing. He wondered if it was the gold. It would make sense. Now everyone knew, the game had changed.

'Reasons?' Lamb said eventually.

'You said there was more than one reason you invited me here.'

'Ah, yes.' Shaking his head as if to clear whatever had settled internally, Lamb walked to a chest of drawers by the door and took out an envelope. 'In here you will find the address of a hotel and enough money to tide you over for the day. A reservation is already made. There you will be contacted and given a parcel.'

'What sort of parcel?'

'That is not your concern. This man could arrive at any time, so sit tight. Meals will be brought to your room. Everything has been arranged.'

'When do I leave?'

'First thing in the morning.'

'For the whole day?'

'It's a five-star hotel.'

'Oh, well, if it's important I will of course make every sacrifice,' Denby spouted, smacking his lips and finishing his brandy.

It happened in a supermarket of all places. Reid had called in to buy some milk of magnesia or equivalent for his heartburn. He was queuing at one of the tills, wishing for the old woman in front of him to shut up about the price of bread so he could neck down the medicine that had fast become as necessary to him as the whisky he guzzled daily by the bottle. He called it a Gaviscon chaser.

But he never reached the end of the till. The old woman was still talking as he felt the intense pain in his chest (a very different pain than

God's Will

before). In fact she didn't stop until he hit the floor, the bottle smashing at his side in almost the same moment. Not that he was aware of any of that.

'It was a type of heart attack,' said the man in the white jacket.

He was very dark. Central Africa, Reid suspected. Uganda, Kenya or maybe Tanzania. He didn't do accents but he was sure he was right. During his time as a military policemen in Kenya he had had a bellyful of Africans. This African was leaning over him, checking his pupils with a light. The man's face was uncomfortably close to his own; he could taste his breath. He hated that. There was another one on the other side, a black female nurse with monstrous breasts who was fussing over him. If he had had the energy he'd have bashed them with his bedpan—if they still used such things. The last time he been in a hospital was to say goodbye to his dying daughter, thirty odd years before.

'Are you a heavy drinker, Mr Reid?' No reply. 'From your silence I take it you are. I have run tests anyhow and I *know* you are.'

Uganda, Reid decided. Definitely. One big bugger had nearly knocked him out with a single blow when he tried to break up a bar fight in Kampala during his first year of employment. When was that, he wondered—sixty-four, sixty-five?

'What you have, I believe, is cardiomyopathy, a condition in which the heart muscle weakens; the early signs are heart rhythm abnormalities. Heavy drinkers are very susceptible… do you feel faint at times?'

'Where am I?' Reid asked, frowning at an elderly man in the opposite bed who was doing his level best to listen in to their discussion.

'St Thomas's, by the Thames. You even have a river view. You're a lucky man.'

God's Will

'I wouldn't call that particularly lucky.'

'I meant, to be alive, Mr Reid.'

Reid slept, kind of. Whilst an undercover officer he had napped in various positions in many locations, but as far as he could recall never in a hospital bed. He lay motionless, a matrix of sensors and drips looped across his torso and arms, linking him to a machine by his bed. He wasn't sure what it did but he found he came to rely on its steady beep and occasional whirring. He trusted it. It told him he was with the living.

It was now morning and as the sun crept along the ward, inch by inch, bed to bed, he watched closely, speculating whether death had visited this room of the almost-dead. The nosey old man in the bed opposite was staring at him still, his eyes fixed on his own. Reid was too weary to speak so he looked away. Outside the window a type of darkness had descended and the hope of a bright day was already fading with the light. In the quiet and stillness of this early hour his mind was unusually clear. He wondered if that was due to the ambience or the life-enhancing drugs. He certainly didn't feel that aching urge for booze. If it wasn't any of that, it might be fear. Death had always been a part of his life. He dealt with it on a daily basis, but it was always someone else's. His own mortality was rarely considered.

He thought back to his meeting with Calvert. A lot of what he had said had remained with him—words and various strong emotions on a constant loop in his head. He hated Calvert, hated the very thought of him for reminding him of how his marriage had fallen apart and of how his daughter, Becky had suffered. *Damn you, Calvert.*

So Bexley was in Spain. What could *he* tell him? What could a crooked copper tell him that would change anything now? And what could he do himself? A man with a weak heart and limited resources... He closed his eyes tight and felt a surge of emotion build inside him. A

God's Will

low yelp escaped from his throat and he started to sob. He heard footsteps and wiped away the tears. When the person got closer he looked up to see the fat nurse who had fussed over him the night before. She was yawning at the end of the old man's bed, her huge breasts pushing out towards the window. Then she suddenly stopped, mid-yawn, and hurried to the old man's side. She was no longer languorous; something in the bed had triggered her obligation to care. Her hands were now a blur on the staring man and on the buttons beside his bed. Then she was gone. Reid then understood why she had reacted so. The old man would never eavesdrop again. Death had indeed visited them. The proof of it was to be found in his stare.

It's getting closer, Reidy. Keep on your toes, mate. It's just a matter of time now.

An hour later Alan Reid signed himself out of St Thomas's Hospital, by the Thames. Defying a strongly worded plea from a first-year Ugandan student doctor that it could be the death of him, Reid explained that he was feeling much, much better.

22

Sickert's eyes are itchy and he wants to get at them. It's an odd sensation but he hopes a positive one. They say the urge to scratch a wound is always a good sign. Now his energy levels are growing he is getting fidgety. Other than on the guided trips to the toilet, when he hobbles along on a pair of wooden crutches, he's not using any of this new-found energy. His ankle aches terribly—Bepa suspects torn ligaments and he thinks she's spot-on. He's frustrated and consequently struggles to sleep. In the silence of his room the noises from the house

God's Will

surrounding him are magnified. One constant is Philip talking in another part of the house. Away from his patient, he talks and talks, his voice soft and tuneful. Sickert realises now that it isn't his voice he recognises but someone who sounds like him.

His new-found energy leads to frustration but his imagination comes to his rescue. High above him he imagines a cloudless sky, while the warmth from the hearth is that of the morning sun. He doesn't hear the rats any longer, their noisy feet are those of deer springing across meadows and hillsides. For the first time ever he doesn't live for what is to come but how he connects to the world now. The recounting of his past—even though he knows the pain is yet to come—is strangely therapeutic.

Philip is at the door. He has recognised his footsteps. No chair? No Bepa? Philip tidies away the empty plates from the bedside and puffs up his pillow.

'Today Thomas, today we go on a journey.'

Sickert is fearful. Even though he knows there is another life elsewhere—a home, maybe a wife—this stinking bed in this decrepit house is, for the time being, his only world.

The journey Philip has in mind is not a long one. They follow the same path to the toilet, past it, along a hallway, up a short staircase and then stop without a word. Outside the warmth of his bed the cold bites at Sickert's bare skin and he shivers as he shivered on his arrival. Philip holds him close and knocks on a door with his spare hand. Three raps.

A rent man's knock, Sickert remembers his mother saying.

Bepa beckons them in with a regal 'Come.'

This room is warmer than Sickert's and carpeted. A living room? Bedroom? Philip guides him in and sits him down in a cushioned velvety wooden chair, then the door closes and he is alone with her.

God's Will

'Forgive me for not visiting you. I fear you must do the honours from now on. I don't have the strength.' She readjusts herself in the bed and the springs protest briefly but then settle. 'Now, how are you feeling today, Thomas? Stronger, I hope?'

Bepa is in front of him. A hurried appraisal of his new environment tells Sickert that there is an open fire off to his left. He feels the warmth and recognises the hum of burning fuel. The loud click of a clock sets the pace. The noise comes from what he imagines is a dusty mantlepiece above the hearth. Bepa's scent is stronger here and somehow familiar. A perfume once used by an old girlfriend, perhaps?

'I am feeling better by the day, thank you,' he replies. 'The question is, how are you feeling?'

'I'm dying, Thomas,' she whispers matter-of-factly and changes the subject. 'Is Philip a good nurse?'

'He is, and I am thankful.'

'Shall we talk?'

'Why do you take such interest in my past? None of it is good.'

'I disagree. I have found your past fascinating.'

'Oh, it's that, all right. I'm a convicted murderer...'

There is a delicate silence, which is shattered a second later by Bepa laughing out loud. This is followed by a weak cough. Sickert recognises the pattern. There is a longer silence before she enquires about society's view of him.

'The world has made its judgement on me,' he tells her. 'And the world is correct. I am a killer and I have done much wrong in my life.'

'But there is goodness in you. I sense that, despite my years, or maybe because of them. I know that much.'

Sickert finds her astuteness moving, knowing she is dying and her energies should be directed elsewhere. Despite that unworldly husky

God's Will

voice, she is no witch, no sorceress: she is wise, a philosopher and a compassionate one at that.

'It's all relative, I suppose,' he concedes. 'I cared for Larry once, as Philip cares for me now. But that was at the end. After Lottie.'

This final comment has thickened the air There is silence for a while. They both know what these words mean.

'So you remember?' she asks.

'Yes, I do. The recent stuff is missing, but that time until our arrest, yes, I remember all of that. Every little bit of it.'

* * *

Yes, there was a time when I cared for Larry, because although he hid it away, Larry was very, very sick.

For the following couple of years after meeting Solomon my life became one endless round of excitement and excess. It was sprinkled with violence and corruption as well, but I knew what I was getting in to. During that time Larry and I became like brothers. He allowed me in because I complemented his extremes. Like him I could be just as happy walking around a gallery or laying out the law to those on the *manor* It was a life that suited me. I don't know why. Maybe because of the ack of structure or because it was so varied. Or maybe because I spent it with Larry. Every day was an adventure. One night we would be dining at the Ivy and the next day we were flying over to Europe for a holiday. Solomon allowed this; he even encouraged it. But there was always one constant, The Duke of Cumberland. Larry was obsessed with the place. I think it was the artists he met there. He loved actors and would love to hear anecdotes from the theatre. I remember one evening Peter Ustinov, the renowned actor and raconteur, was there and the place was rammed. Veronica, always on hand to enhance the

God's Will

enjoyment for her punters (and her profits) sent out to a local restaurant and had food delivered. Before long the gathering had turned into a huge party. There was a small stage and people got up and performed little scenes: Shakespeare, poetry, comedy sketches. It was an amazing place. I never did anything but often Larry would sing a funny song or recite a touching poem. But over that first year together I began to notice a change in him. And I wasn't the only one who saw it.

The morning after the party at Radstone, the one when I met Julia for the first time, I went down to find the house deserted. Whilst I'd slept, the staff had been busy tidying away the remnants of the festivities, and in the morning sun the house was even more impressive. Years later, as I flicked through an old copy of *Country Life* in my cell at Brixton I would discover to my shock that Radstone had become a retirement home. I decided then I would never return. But that morning in the late summer of seventy-three I was blissfully unaware of the future and how it would unfold.

Where I had talked with Solomon and met his beautiful wife a table was set out with food and drink. Inspecting the small silver platters, I found eggs, bacon, chops and kippers. Feeling rather sensitive after the night's excesses, I decided on yoghurt and a juice and sat on the patio where Solomon and I had talked. It was still early and the sun had yet to pitch above the trees of the copse, but it was warm and pleasant in the summer breeze. Birds sang and rabbits played on the huge lawn. In the stillness of the morning I thought about the conversation I had overheard the night before. Fenton's suggestion about blackmailing Steiner was clever. For Solomon it was all about increased revenue, no matter how. Knowledge is power, and the more you know about your opponent the more leverage you have. I had been given a free tutorial on how to succeed and decided it would not be wasted. I also thought about Larry's comment. *No, Larry is not all right.* What the hell did

God's Will

that mean? In the end I just put it down to the booze. Finally, I thought of Bexley's contented smile and wondered what he was up to.

After a short while a dour butler appeared from the house and served me coffee. When I enquired where everyone was, he informed me that Solomon and Larry had returned to London. I was so angry that Larry had just gone and left me. Angry that he hadn't taken the trouble to tell me what was going on.

'Is there a bus into town or a train station nearby?'

'There'll be no need for that,' said a voice. Turning I saw Julia in the doorway. 'I can take you back.'

As the old man went inside, she made her way over to me. At that point she was in her mid-thirties, but dressed in a violet summer frock in the fresh morning light she could have been half that age. I wished her a good morning and got to my feet. It was an impulsive thing and I was a little embarrassed. I'd never stood for a woman before. I think I must have got it from Larry. His good manners were rubbing off. She told me that Larry had sent his apologies and that something important had come up in London. I knew she was lying. He had disappeared, just upped and gone. It was becoming a regular thing. Over breakfast I tried to find out as much as I could about Julia. She was well-spoken, and the tone of her voice was relaxed, with only a hint of an accent—one I could not define.

'Did you sleep well, Tom?'

'Yes, thank you.'

'You don't mind me calling you Tom, do you? Thomas seems so… I don't know. Maybe it's the connection to the bible? Are you the doubting type?'

Sipping my coffee, I smiled. 'I've never really thought about it. But no, Tom's fine.'

God's Will

She then asked me what I thought of Radstone. I replied that I thought it was incredible. She agreed and glanced back at it as if she'd forgotten how it looked, or how impressive it really was.

'I suppose it is. I've never really thought about it. I suppose it's a little like living near the sea. After a while it loses its magic.'

Her words seemed empty, as if they were falling from her lips and she wasn't in control of them. For a few moments she seemed lost and I didn't know what to do. I realise now she was thinking of Larry. I remember trying to come up with some profound reply when she suddenly sighed and grinned.

'Look,' she said, 'I can take you back. I need to go into London myself, so why don't I give you a lift? Just let me know when you are ready.'

'You don't mind?'

'Why should I? More coffee?'

I was in heaven. This was everything I ever wanted. I had somehow found myself in a world that I thought only existed in magazines or television and films. Julia was the most beautiful woman I had ever seen, and as she talked about her life with Solomon and Larry I was convinced I would be part of their world before long. After breakfast I borrowed some of Larry's clothes and packed the little I had, then went out to explore the grounds. I knew where I was going. If I've been anything in life it's a little too inquisitive. Going round the side of the house, I made my way across the lawn to the copse and the summerhouse lurking in its shadows. At some point it had been a ruin, but instead of returning it to its former glory it had been modernised to accommodate a long conservatory. It looked to my untrained eyes as Scandinavian in style. The door was locked and I was forced to settle for a view through the windows. An open fire dominated the centre of the room, with a suspended flue reaching up to the aluminium ceiling.

God's Will

Surrounding it was an array of sofas and armchairs. There wasn't any light to speak of, but in the little there was I was sure I could make out the shape of a projector on a small table.

'Lovely, isn't it?' I'd been so absorbed with the interior I wasn't aware that Julia had crossed the lawn to collect me. 'I find it a lovely place to go when the world gets a little too much. Everyone should have a place, don't you think?' I watched her for a moment. How the sun glinted in her auburn hair, how her knowing smile told me that she understood that I felt a little out of my depth and that it was all right. 'Shall we go?'

In a cherry red Lotus convertible, Julia and I returned to London. I was happy to be with her, happy to be seen with a woman so beautiful. I don't know if it was her smile or the way she played with her hair, but there was always a sense of youthfulness about her. By that, I mean she always seemed to be carefree, even reckless. In time I would discover it was reflected in everything she did. Even driving. I must have aged at least ten years on that journey back to London. She was no driver.

As the green of the countryside gave way to the red sprawl of suburbia I felt sad that we would be parting. By the time we reached London the talking had stopped and in the silence that descended we seemed to understand each other a little better. And there was a reason for that. In time I would discover that Julia and I had come from very similar backgrounds. But that didn't matter to me: it was simply another proof that it could be done.

I think I told Julia some stupid story about meeting a friend and asked her to drop me off on St John's Wood High Street. Ridiculous, really, because apart from Larry I really didn't have any friends. From there I walked back towards my new flat in Fitzrovia through Regent's Park. It was late summer and the park must have been alive with colour, but I was unaware of everything, my head dizzy with

God's Will

possibilities. I was nearly at the flat when I decided to divert to Soho and call in at Milton's. I was moving onwards and upwards, away, regrettably, from the likes of Charlie and Stella.

'How's things, Charlie?' I managed to convince myself that I was calling in the club to say goodbye to him, but the truth was I wanted to show off. I wanted him to appreciate how well I was doing. I was already becoming a little too big for my boots, and nobody saw it clearer than Charlie.

Putting down the crate of beer he was carrying he looked across at me and smiled. 'Young Tommy. How are you?'

Of course, I could do little else than tell him exactly how I was. I told him all about the party and my meeting with Solomon and, of course, my new job. Then I broached the subject of Henderson's humiliation that day at Rotherhithe. To my surprise, however, Charlie didn't see any humour in what I had to say or what had happened to his former boss.

'Be careful. Henderson's no fool. Don't think he didn't fight back because he was scared of Larry. It's Solomon senior people are afraid of, not his son. And you'd do well to remember Solomon only has loyalty to the people who are of use to him. Like I said, be careful.'

I knew he was right, but I was young and growing in confidence and just didn't see how his words could ever affect me.

It was a great time. I was making so much money it was laughable. I even bought a motor, a nineteen sixty-two Austin-Healey, a nippy little number and great for attracting the girls. I was, what they call now, living the dream. Yet working for Solomon was remarkably simple. I was mostly making cash collections from all his going concerns, everything from protection to prostitution. We even had an excellent cat burglar, aptly named Tigger, whom the infamous Peter Scott (possibly

God's Will

the greatest British thief) had recommended to Solomon. He would thieve to order up and down the country and, if required, occasionally on the continent. Bits of information would come in from all over and I would take a look. If it looked a goer, I would feed it back to Solomon and he would send our man down. It's surprising how many people don't trust banks. On top of that I had my own band of Lotharios I had employed to take over my job at the casinos. The Rotella continued to attract bored heiresses and rich widows, and my money-making from the same line of work had elevated me to the post of their boss. I would move them around—Solomon had a couple of smaller casinos—and then *get rid* when their face became too familiar. At school I was atrocious at mathematics, but it's remarkable how one can improve in such matters when a great deal of money is to be earned.

For the rest of that year I spent virtually every weekend at Radstone House. Slowly I was becoming part of the family. Each day in London I did my work conscientiously and to the point of obsession until the early hours of Saturday morning, when Larry and I would travel beneath the stars to Radstone. Julia never asked what I did, but she knew, I'm sure. I don't think I have ever been happier in my life than during the summer of seventy-three.

But as the end of the year approached I was aware of something unsettling growing inside me. Despite the luxurious lifestyle and the money I was making, I was beginning to find the whole experience troubling. To my surprise, I had discovered an element of myself that would simply not complete the cycle. Maybe because it was running up to Christmas and I was reminded of my past. A part of me was still that little boy up north, looking at the world so innocently. It dawned on me that I loved those TV shows and movies back then because the protagonist was the good guy fighting the baddies. I was now the baddie. I don't know why, but it played on my mind. I was torn

God's Will

between what I was and what I wanted to be. That was, until one night between Christmas and New Year when it all came to a head.

It had been a very cold day and Larry and I had spent the whole evening at the Rotella. We were already well into Sunday morning and slightly the worse for wear, sitting at one of the abandoned gaming tables. From time to time Larry would appear at the club and, more out of fun than a sense of loyalty to his father, he would fleece some poor old dear for everything she had. Due to the cold we just couldn't raise ourselves to make the journey to Radstone that night, so instead we hovered around the casino, drinking too much champagne. Larry had attracted a rich widow, an Egyptian woman. She was, let us say, of mature years—not that she was letting that hold her back. Despite her age it was clear she had been an attractive woman at some point in her distant past. She still was, I suppose. At that time of the morning I was just too tired to consider such things. Larry had done well. She was clearly dripping with wealth and, through a combination of alcohol and limitless charm, he had enticed her into a thoroughly charitable frame of mind. It was an impressive sight. How much champagne she had ordered I couldn't say, but that night the bar must have outdone the tables. You could almost feel the family empire swelling.

Sitting together they looked like mother and son, and briefly I saw myself in Larry's place. It wasn't a pleasant image. Was this what I had reached for? Was this the pinnacle of all my dreams? I was disgusted. But like witnessing a spider devouring a fly, I felt compelled to watch. When the woman began to run her bony brown fingers through Larry's soft golden hair, however, I decided enough was enough and made my way to the door.

'Where are you going?' Larry called after me.

'I'm tired,' I said, glancing across the green baize of the card table. 'Time for my bed, I think.'

God's Will

Just then the old woman whispered in Larry's ear before emitting a loud, empty laugh. Larry simply smiled as he walked towards me.

'Don't go.'

'Larry, I'm tired. I want to go to bed.'

'Me, too. But why don't we have a bit of fun at the same time.'

At first I wasn't sure I'd heard him correctly. Pretending I hadn't, I started to leave again. 'It looks like you've got your hands full—you enjoy yourself.'

Suddenly there was that flash of anger. 'What the hell is your problem? It's just a bit of fun, for God's sake! What's wrong with you at the moment? You know the job. Take them for what you can and then give them what they want. Haven't you got it yet? You and I are the same.

Up close, I could see the reflection of the red lights above the tables in his eyes, turning them from a tranquil blue to something darker and altogether more threatening. But it didn't matter, because I knew in that moment I loved him. I have never felt a physical attraction for any man before or since, but I felt that for him, intensely.

'Life is very short. Enjoy every moment. We both want the same things. Let the rest have the tedium. We're special. Forget your background. This is something deep inside us both. I saw it in you the first day I met you, and don't deny you didn't see it in me.'

I realised after a moment or two that I was simply rooted to the spot, my gaze fixed on his. His words were in stark contrast to what he had said at Radstone when he I felt he was telling me to avoid working with his father. But this was the first time he had ever spoken about our relationship. As we looked at one another I recalled Charlie's words about Solomon and I could still remember the conclusion I'd reached. It wasn't Solomon's world I wanted to be part of—it was Larry's.

God's Will

Glancing across at the woman as she leant back, her shawl falling from her bare shoulders and exposing her bulging cleavage, I realised he was right. I wanted it all, everything there was to have, but more than that I wanted to share it all with him. In that moment I realised how far I would go to stay with him.

One of Solomon's men drove us back to Larry's flat and there, surrounded by antique furniture and paintings, the old woman took us both. At first I was embarrassed and couldn't rise to the occasion. But watching her at work, naked but for a black satin slip, her golden skin, freckled and firm despite her years, taking Larry in her mouth I was soon filled with fire. She offered him to me and I took him as she had and it felt the most natural thing in the world. I had crossed a line, but then I had been crossing a lot of those.

Despite the conclusions I had reached, I woke next morning filled with shame. Beneath the sheets, Larry and the woman were pressed together, fast asleep. I studied them for a while. Through the thinning blur of foundation I could see the imperfection in the woman's skin—I never learnt her name—and, comparing them as they slept, I saw the contrast of age. In the stillness of the morning I saw more femininity in Larry than in that old lizard. In sleep her mystery was gone, and in the cold light of day I couldn't imagine how I had seen it there in the first place. Taking the opportunity to avoid any embarrassing conversation, I dressed and made myself some breakfast. Over coffee I considered Larry's comments again. He was right, of course. I had known all along. I had just needed confirmation from another place, from someone whom I cared for and admired greatly. I was certain then that, with him in my life, there was a very good chance my future would be brighter. It was then that I remembered the painting in his studio. Making sure he and the old girl was still sleeping, I went up. It was the first time in months I had had the opportunity to wander alone.

God's Will

I opened the door and there it was—the huge canvas in the centre of the room still covered by the white dust sheet. Almost fearfully I tugged at the seam. As it fell to the floor my heart stopped. What I found shocked me. It was a self-portrait. But instead of a handsome, blue-eyed Larry, I found a haunted, ageing figure staring back at me. He had painted himself in another time, the nineteenth century, in a jacket and matching waistcoat somewhere between dark brown and black. The face was dark, too, with blacks and greys, and eyes that stared back at me, unnerving me completely. Was this how Larry saw himself? Was this the way he was inside? I didn't know what it meant then, and I still don't now, but I will never forget the tormented gaze that forced me out of that room.

* * *

There is an odd type of silence. The air is empty of words, but their meaning hangs between them, shading the atmosphere darkly. 'You said Larry taught you a lot. What did you mean?'

Sickert has Bepa's rapt attention. It's like Frost and Nixon without the cameras and the anticipated admission. His interviewer is learning as she goes. He knows this but doesn't care. He wants to talk.

'Shortly after I moved into the flat I started to receive parcels. Each one was a neatly packaged book.'

'What type of books?'

'There was no pattern. Just books.'

'How did you know they were from Larry?'

'I knew. It was just the way he did things. And he was a huge Dickens fan. There were quite a few of those.'

'Did you read them?'

God's Will

'Yes, I did, but not Dickens—too heavy for me. I could never understand why he just couldn't get to the point. It wasn't all fiction. Occasionally I would receive something on the history of London, a book of poetry, or something odd, like garden birds. I had a little garden at the back of the flat. One day he sent a book about painters—but not your everyday sort of book. It was called *Notorious Artists*. Do you remember what Larry told me about Sickert, my namesake?'

'That he had some fascination with Jack the Ripper?'

'That's right. And he did. So I would read. Unless I was learning lines, I rarely read as an actor, but with Larry I began to absorb information and to read novels I would never have considered before. I think in his own way he was trying to educate me, but in a way that made sense to me. We would often read to one another. He had a remarkable voice. I remember the first time I heard him recite poetry was in the Duke itself. It was by Dickens. Up until then I hadn't realised he had written any poetry. It was called "Lucy's Poem". It was quite a sombre piece. Halfway through I glanced over at Veronica at the bar; she had tears in her eyes. It amazes me even now to think that a man who had the ability to bring great pain to people who crossed him also had such a rich vein of warmth running through him.'

The old woman says nothing to this, and Sickert, too, lapses into silence. It feels like they are sharing the stillness of a forest clearing or the invigorating properties of an oasis in the desert, something he did not expect when he embarked with her on this journey. The question is, what effect will the journey's end have on him—and on this woman who bears testimony to his revelations?

23

God's Will

Angie Roberts opened the door to find a tall, sickly-looking man standing on her doorstep. He wore a tired overcoat and scuffed black brogues; she surmised he was in his late sixties. He looked hungover and poor. He had to be a friend of Denby's. They all shared with him the same weary, frayed-at-the-edges demeanour. Until Greene had arrived there had been a steady number of Denby's Soho buddies calling at inconvenient hours. Then, for some reason, it had all stopped. Angie was about to close the door on him when he fixed her with a hard stare.

His voice was low but there was authority in it. 'I wonder if I might speak with Mr Greene?'

'Could I say who is calling?'

'An old acquaintance.'

Angie felt nervous but couldn't explain why. A car slowed on the road and the passenger, a man, looked up at the house, but she was too distracted by this man on her doorstep to take any real notice. She was used to officials calling round—years ago, when the house was full of former felons—uniformed coppers were regulars at her door, but this man was different. There was a type of gravitas she did not recognise. She found herself stepping back, allowing him in.

'Mr Greene has gone out.'

'Do you mind if I wait?'

'Well, no, but it could be hours,' she said, leading him through to the living room.

'I'll give it an hour,' he said, 'if that's okay with you?'

Angie found herself quite unable to resist his request. Leaning against the sideboard, she watched as he sat down and looked around the room. It was then that she saw how tired he *really* looked, poorly almost. His skin was grey and his cheeks were flecked with red dots as

God's Will

if someone had flicked red paint at him. Drink, she decided. It was a moment before she realised he was staring at the painting on the wall.

'I remember having that on my living room wall many years ago. When I was married.'

'It's a print. Nothing special.'

'I like it. Don't know why.' The man then changed the subject dramatically, although the tone did not. 'Did you know that this man Greene is actually Thomas Sickert, the notorious child-killer?'

Angie felt her heart sink. Thomas Sickert? That butcher? Who hadn't heard of Sickert and Solomon and the Steiner kidnapping? Then she gathered her thoughts. 'Hang on. I deal with low-category ex-cons. Who the hell are you?'

'Maybe I should have said I was more of an adversary that an acquaintance. My name is Reid. I was the investigating officer at that time. I'm now retired.' His open admission of obsession with the child's disappearance hung in the air and struck a chord deep within her. 'You know the child's body was never found?'

Angie felt her skin crawl. What hit her the hardest was the moment of failed intimacy the night before. She was shaken by the revelation and at her reaction. She couldn't hold the shock back and felt her knees give. She sat down on the sofa across from the visitor. 'Are you sure?'

'Very.'

'I knew there was something about him. How could they do that to a child? I had no idea.'

'Don't be hard on yourself. You do a fine job.'

'But why has he been sent here?'

'Well, think about it. He's a notorious killer. He's been given a new identity. They would have to send him somewhere. His appearance has changed quite a lot. So why not here? You didn't suspect him, so why would anyone else? It was organised by the Home Office, I presume?'

God's Will

'That's right. A gentleman called Malory. He was the one that got me the funding to start up again the other month. A nice man.'

Reid took out a card from his inside jacket pocket. 'It may interest you to know that there are some who still search for her to this day. It would be of great interest to me to know who he communicates with.'

'You think she's still alive?'

'No.' His gaze drifted from hers. 'No, I don't. All I'm saying is that it would help me a great deal if you would be willing?'

In all the time she had done this work Angie had always promised herself that she would be impartial and stick to the rules. Feelings and judgement would never play a part in the work she did. This was different. She could still remember where she was and what she was doing on the day she heard of the kidnapping and the murders. The papers said they had done unspeakable things to the little girl before disposing of her body. The whole business had had the nation rapt for months, but there never had been a conclusion. Everyone knew she was dead. The only compensation was that she had no parents to mourn her. Yes, of course she would help.

'Yesterday he received a letter from a solicitor.'

Reid sat forward eagerly in his seat. 'Did you get the name?'

'Yes, I did. I've got a good memory for names. Fenton. Somewhere in Southwark, I recall.'

The man's eyes narrowed and the flush of red across his nose and cheeks seemed to glow like lava.

Fenton Solicitors were on Lant Street in Southwark. Greene found the place easily enough. He knew the address well, and Willie Fenton even better. Larry had once said he hadn't so much been born than found in a sewer. Greene smiled and nodded in acknowledgement at the memory. It was impossible to imagine Fenton as a child. Children possess

God's Will

innocence and honesty, qualities that eluded Fenton and the company he kept. His calling to the bar had been a moment of madness that the legal profession had surely regretted ever since. He was as crooked as they came and was, without a doubt, the reason Solomon had chosen him for representation. Greene had visited the firm hundreds of times over his three-year period of employment with Solomon, most of those visits concentrating in the final few months before his arrest. On each trip he was a courier. Towards the end that is what he had become, Solomon's delivery boy in everything but name.

On Lant Street Greene followed his path like a man possessed. Going inside, he found nothing had changed. He entered a bare, unwelcoming entrance hall with a lift directly across from the main door. Automatically, he walked towards it and closed the door then pressed the button. It was shocking that nothing had changed. As if to intensify his feeling of helplessness the lift swayed and creaked around him as it carried him up to the second floor.

Welcome back, Thomas Sickert.

Why was he there? What good could come of this? The lift slowed to a stop and as the door opened another opened in his mind. It was a mirror image. Nothing had changed at all. Not the musty smell of the wood-panelled walls, nor the hypnotic patterns in the hand-tiled wooden floor that once fascinated him. But he had changed, even if this place hadn't—even his name. A quarter of a century on his view had narrowed with bitterness and age; he saw nothing more than a floor.

Stepping warily down the corridor, its odours evoking memories ever more intensely in his mind, he approached the door he knew well. 'Come at your earliest convenience,' the girl had said on the phone, 'and bring some form of identification.' He had done all of this, but still didn't know why he was there.

God's Will

Suddenly the door opened and he stood face to face with a young woman of twenty or so. Although her frame was small her hips were large, a fact she seemed to be denying in an overtight black skirt, with bulging buttons holding it all in. Around her neck she wore a pearl necklace, clearly fake. She was also wearing too much make-up. Despite this it was still possible to see her prettiness beneath the tacky appearance.

'Oh, shit!' she said, with a start. She was down-to-earth as well—Greene liked her more by the second. 'Sorry, you gave me a fright.'

As she caught her breath, Greene gazed at her loveliness. After weeks studying Angie it was refreshing to be close to a fresh-faced female like this—even if she was young enough to be his granddaughter.

'My name is Greene, Thomas Greene.'

'That's right, I spoke to you on the phone. I'm Miss Hawkins, Mr Fenton's secretary,' she said with a smile, her composure recovered. 'Mr Fenton is just out at the moment. He shouldn't be long. He'll be very happy to have found you. We've been sent from post to pillar. Or is it pillar to post? I always get it mixed up. Anyway, Mr Fenton will explain. Would you like a coffee?' He declined and looked away. 'I'll make one, anyway. Mr Fenton loves his coffee. Just take a seat and I'll be back in a sec.'

Sitting down in the small seating area beyond Miss Hawkins' desk, Greene read the gold lettering of Willie Fenton's name and title on the opened door. It reminded him of the unjust structure of the world. Like many of his clients, Fenton had become wealthy exploiting the innocence of others. Transferring his gaze elsewhere, he found himself looking at a painting by the window. Something told him it was Dutch. A small smile washed across his lips as he remembered the many hours he and Larry had spent in galleries. He had learnt so much from him.

God's Will

He got up to walk over and study the intense colour and the use of light. It wasn't a landscape, but he liked it. Not that Fenton would have been aware of any of this. It would probably have come to him as part-payment of a legal fee or as a thank-you from Solomon or someone equally corrupt. One thing was for certain—someone somewhere would be missing it.

After a short time there were footsteps out in the corridor, heavier than the girl's, but faster than Fenton's. The door opened.

'Mr Greene?' said a man's voice.

He turned to face the newcomer, a man he had never seen before in his life.

'Yes?'

'Peter Fenton.'

This Fenton had prematurely grey hair and was very tall. His face was pale, with thin lips that could only manage the weakest of smiles. Thrusting a bony hand out of the sleeve of a badly fashioned, shiny suit, he looked at Greene with weary eyes. For a moment Greene couldn't move. He glanced at the lettering on the door. Fenton nodded at his confusion.

'Never got round to changing the name on the door.'

Fenton junior? *Old Fenton had offspring?* So there was such a thing as cross-species procreation. He hoped for the woman's sake the moment had been brief. Fenton was still staring at him and he realised in the silence that he had spoken again.

'I'm sorry?' muttered Greene.

'I said, I believe you knew my father? Would you like to follow me?'

The past tense? Greene was smiling inside. Things were looking up. It occurred to him that even the most banal of replies would have

God's Will

revealed far too much emotion, so he said nothing as he followed him through the door.

The room was smaller than he expected. Then he remembered that originally it had been used for storage. The larger room, the one where he'd met the girl with the hips, had been his father's office. On one side of the room, just to the right of his desk, was a smallish window, with a view towards the Thames. Not that he could see it. All there was were rooftops, lots of rooftops. But, like the tiled corridor floor, the form and pattern was familiar. Other than an abundance of satellite dishes the view had hardly changed at all. It was so familiar to Greene, in fact, that he wasn't even looking at it really. His eyes were open and his gaze was fixed, but he was seeing it in his mind's eye, through a lens suddenly opened once more. Willie Fenton would have him wait in that room for hours sometimes. A lot of the information for Tigger the cat burglar came from Fenton. As a solicitor to wealthy clients he often knew what items were insured and for how much and, more often than not, where they were kept.

'Not very inspiring, I must admit,' Fenton said, noticing him staring out. Greene turned to face him and for the first time Fenton seemed to read the suspicion on his face. 'It's not unusual for me to receive looks like that, Mr Greene. I am under no illusion what my father was and how much he was despised.' It was a comment intended to defuse any tension before it arose, and Greene hadn't been expecting it at all. 'You've served your sentence, but I have no intention of serving one for my father.'

It was a short but impressive disquisition and no doubt perfected over the years to disarm the people his father had crossed. There was a crash in the next room, followed by a muffled expletive from Miss Hawkins. Fenton, who had just picked up a file from his desk, closed his eyes and sighed.

God's Will

'Oh God,' he muttered to himself.

The door flew open and there stood Miss Fenton with a perplexed look on her face. 'Sorry, Mr Fenton—that was that coffee pot thing. Shall I nip out and get another?'

'Miss Hawkins... when I am with a client, you must remember to knock.'

'Sorry, Mr Fenton, I keep forgetting. Shall I then?'

'Shall you what?'

'Get another coffeetiere.'

'A cafetiere?'

'That's the fella.'

He nodded and the door closed. He looked up at Greene. 'Are you looking for work?'

'Why do you ask?'

'There may be a secretarial position coming up in the near future. Now...' He frowned and his tone changed. 'For obvious reasons I have had a great deal of difficulty locating you. The name change was a particular issue, but after lengthy discussions with the parole board—I have signed the Official Secrets Act, incidentally—all parties are now satisfied that things can proceed.'

Greene scratched his beard and leant forward. 'What can proceed?'

Fenton coughed but didn't look at him. 'It has been my responsibility to trace you and inform you of a certain... endowment, a one-off donation. In short, a sum of money to be made available to you on your release. But you are to understand that it is a request of your benefactor that their identity remain a secret. If you don't or can't agree with the terms of the request, I have the authority to revoke the offer. Do you wish to make any comments at this point?'

Greene chose not to say anything—not until he had heard the catch, which was surely in the next sentence.

God's Will

'Before you do, it may interest you to know that this sum of money is currently running at a total of £161,043,25.'

Greene couldn't have spoken then if he had wanted to. He felt dizzy. His breathing became irregular. The best he could do was stare at Fenton with a half-opened mouth. It was as if he hadn't come through the door, or got in the lift or even got out of bed. Surely he was still asleep in Muswell Hill?

Seemingly aware of his shock, Fenton glanced over the crossword he had almost completed and as he did so Greene came to the conclusion that this was Larry at work. Who else could it be? He had the finances and, despite the state of their relationship at the end, it was he who had cared for him before their arrest. Even the anonymity smacked of his old friend. Before his troubles, his acts of philanthropy were legendary. Well, if it was Larry, he still didn't like it. There was still a sense that he was profiting from the past. And what good was a hundred and sixty grand to a condemned man?

'And what else can you tell me?' Greene muttered almost in a whisper.

'Other than the financial package?' Fenton said abruptly, answering the final crossword clue. 'Nothing.'

'But you have to tell me something…'

'I don't have to do anything, Mr Greene,' he snapped. 'I'm sorry if I sound dogmatic, but I must abide by the rules set down by my client.'

There was something in the tone of his voice when he uttered the word *client* that struck Greene. It was as if he had given something away. He could see it in his eyes, and he knew then how different he was from his father. Honesty was alive and well inside Fenton junior.

'Do you agree to the terms?' he reiterated firmly, as if to cover his slip.

God's Will

Greene didn't answer. He just couldn't clear his head to think. Instead he got up and started to leave, but something stopped him on the way to the door.

'Can I ask a question?'

'You can ask,' Fenton replied, hiding his eyes from him by folding up the newspaper.

'Is my... benefactor living?'

Fenton looked up and thought for a moment.

'I suppose it does no harm to tell you that they are.'

Greene didn't actually remember walking out of Fenton's office, or even going outside. The only thing he would recall later that day was accepting the deal and signing the paperwork before he left. The rest was a blur, a drink-fuelled one mostly. The only time the day made any sort of sense was through the bottom of a glass. He was finding it impossible to deal with the contrasts. This sudden change of fortune should have made the future clearer, but instead confusion surrounded him like a fist.

London was the problem. It lived, it breathed, it carried him along with its energy until he couldn't remember why he was back or what he intended to find out. Hidden away in his little room in Muswell Hill he could pretend he was in control, but every time he stepped outside the door he couldn't. No matter how hard he tried, he couldn't deny the existence of the city's power. London had him before he had even left the North. That little boy in the two-up two-down had about as much chance of escaping it as he had of escaping his past when he walked out of Brixton.

It took him hours to get back to Muswell Hill, but he had all the time in the world. He was stuck on automatic and aware of nothing around him at all; his focus was internal. So if it wasn't Larry, who

God's Will

could it be? He considered everyone he had been close to before his conviction. Stella, Charlie and Solomon were dead, and Levy had disappeared in the early eighties and must be presumed dead, too. He even considered Julia. Then he remembered something Charlie had said to him the day after his beating by Henderson and Levy.

'I've got money,' he had said. 'If you want to get away, Stella and I won't think any less of you.'

Could it be that Rimmer was wrong and that Charlie was still alive? It was possible. Oh, yes, it was. After today he concluded anything was possible. And there was more of the same when he arrived home. He had no sooner taken a step inside when he heard a voice from the landing. Denby was talking on the public phone situated between the two upstairs rooms. For some reason there was something in the tone of the old man's voice that made him push the door to but not close it. He listened. The old man was angry about something, and because he was trying to speak quietly at the same time it made him sound a little like Punch. Greene smiled and was about to take the keys out of the lock and close the door when Denby spoke again.

'Well, I spent the whole day and no one turned up! This is too much like hard work. Do you hear me? What? The phone? I had no choice! I used up all the credit on the mobile leaving messages for you all day! I'm beginning to think this is a wild goose chase. I've spent the whole day waiting for a man who didn't turn up. And if that was a five-star hotel, I'm a black man! The rest of the time I have to spend my days with the prophet of doom. He's doing nothing but drinking me dry and depressing the hell out me.' A long pause. 'So you say... well, I hope it's worth the wait... no, no, he's out somewhere. Probably back in his beloved Soho. What? Tomorrow? Really? The same hotel?' A long pause. 'Well, if you're sure!'

God's Will

As Denby slammed the phone down and Greene closed the door, the living room door opened. There stood Angie. The two of them stared at one another along the hall. There was something in her eyes, a look of fear or possibly anger. He presumed it was due to the bathroom incident but he was in too much shock from what he had just heard to think about it now. He took out the keys and closed the door.

To his surprise, Angie smiled at him. 'Hello, Tom.'

Greene didn't reply because he was suddenly aware of a shape in the shadows at the top of the stairs. He looked up to see Denby staring down at them both with an awkward grin.

'Ah, hello all! Thomas, old boy! How are you?'

Greene gave him a weak smile. He really wanted to say something, but his mind was working overtime. Was this it? Was this Henderson at work? Had he been watching over him since the very beginning? He was so angry he could taste it—an acidic rush that made him want to spew anger at Denby. But something stopped him. A sudden sense of calm he had not felt for some time. A voice of his own murmured in his head.

Play dumb, Tommy boy. Bring them out of the shadows.

'Right then, gentlemen,' said Angie. 'I'll say good night.'

'A nightcap, Thomas?' said Denby, clearly flustered.

'Not for me.'

'Maybe at the weekend? I've missed your company today.'

'Been away?'

'What? Ah, no. Day out. Called on an old friend. What about it then? Tomorrow night?'

'Maybe, Denby. Maybe.'

For a moment Greene was afraid his tone had given too much away. Had he revealed, in a reckless way, some of the anger he was feeling inside? If Denby had any inkling that he had heard any of his

God's Will

conversation, though, Greene never got the chance to find out. Because within weeks Denby, his old drinking partner, his Soho buddy, was dead.

24

Greene had hardly slept. There was simply too much going on in his mind. In the few periods of sleep his mind allowed him he had found only grotesque unreality. He dreamt he was back at the Old Bailey, and Angie was a witness for the prosecution. Wearing the nightdress with the slit and smoking a cigarette, she cackled as she revealed to the court his sexual shortcomings. The crowd laughed and he hoped his defence would calm the situation. The problem there was that his barrister was Peter Fenton's secretary, Miss Hawkins, who made a bumbling malapropos appeal to the court that only made everyone laugh all the more. The nightmare ran through the night until he was woken in the early hours by an insistent, gentle knock at his door. Angie.

Her voice was muffled through the wood but it was upbeat when she said there was someone to see him. He didn't know what had brought about the change in her but he was thankful of it all the same. He needed affection more than he would ever admit. He dressed and dragged a comb through his hair before going down. From the staircase he could make out a familiar voice in the living room. Suddenly the door opened and there he found Angie wearing a face he had never seen before. It was the sort his mother wore when the vicar came round.

'Oh there you are. We're in here, Tom.'

Ignoring her false warmth, Greene walked cautiously into the living room.

God's Will

'Mr Verecker...'

'Good morning, Tom. Now, what did I tell you? It's Brian now. Just thought I'd call round to see how you were getting on.'

When Angie eventually went out, leaving them alone, Greene told Verecker everything that had happened since he had left Needham House. From his meeting with Rimmer and all he had discovered about Henderson to the news of his windfall and Denby's conversation on the phone the previous day. As he did so it made Greene not happy exactly, but strangely fulfilled. That came as a shock to him. He talked for some time, about his fears and suspicions, but ultimately he wanted to get across to Verecker, a man of learning and compassion, that he needed to come to terms with what he had done all those years ago. For the first time since his conviction it seemed important to him for someone to understand the guilt he felt.

Judging by his gentle smile, Verecker clearly sensed this and there was a long silence after Greene stopped talking. It was as if the other man was choosing his words very carefully. He was a friend in a way, but still a man who had once held power over him, albeit in an official capacity. Greene sensed it was this neutrality that allowed Verecker to see a possibility he hadn't considered.

'You don't think this money could be from this Henderson character, do you?'

It was such a staggering remark that Greene thought he was joking. It then dawned on him that, having spent a lifetime with crooks, Verecker must have built up a certain kind of shrewdness when it came to sob stories. The comment surprised him so much he didn't even answer.

'If you do have something that might benefit him,' Verecker went on, 'and he has gone, as you say, to great lengths to have this Denby

God's Will

character watch over you, it might be another way of forcing your hand.'

'Yes, but—a hundred and sixty-thousand pounds?'

'He may think what you know is worth a lot more than that. Maybe it has something to do with your relationship with Larry? This is a dangerous situation, Tom, and you really shouldn't be telling me. What you do is your affair, but please be careful.'

None of this had occurred to Greene. He had a feeling Verecker only saw it because he was unlike him. With a sigh, Verecker put down the empty teacup he'd been nursing for nearly an hour and mustered a smile.

'Listen to me,' he said, dislodging himself from the sofa. 'I sound like a copper. My mother always said I was in the wrong profession.'

Greene stared at him. He had been so caught up in his troubles he had forgotten all about Verecker's.

'Your mum, how is she?'

There was a long pause, followed by a deep sigh and a forlorn smile. 'She passed away a couple of days ago.'

'I'm sorry, I...'

'You weren't to know,' he said stoically, walking to the front door. 'At least she isn't suffering anymore.'

Greene felt guilt-ridden and followed him out onto the porch. He wanted to connect with him somehow. 'I'm so sorry. We must meet for a drink. Listen, keep this to yourself, but I'm moving on.'

'Well, I suppose you have the resources now.'

'You think I should use them?'

'It's legally yours. Maybe it's time to move out of London once and for all?'

'I couldn't. Too old for that. But at least I can now get a place of my own.'

God's Will

'It's your own life,' Verecker conceded, wrapping himself up in a long scarf. 'Just be careful, Tom. I've got a bad feeling about his Henderson character. Take care and yes, we'll have that drink one day.'

On that he walked out. As Greene watched him walk wearily up the road he couldn't, despite the man's woes and warnings about Henderson, stop a selfish smile finding it's way onto his lips. Within twenty-four hours his life had mostly definitely changed for the better.

Outside Seven Trees Golf and Country Club near Sevenoaks, lines of luxurious saloons and four-by-fours stood proudly, like horses waiting for their riders. Reid parked his donkey of a Ford in front of a couple of Range Rovers and a Porsche, blocking them in. He wouldn't be staying long.

It was early evening and cold, and the sound of muffled pop music blared across the car park. It got louder as he opened the main door. Walking among the smartly dressed guests, he felt out of place, their easy found happiness from a glass was something he never understood. He only drank to suppress pain. Golf trophies and photos of past champions with smiling buddies only added to his isolation. There was even one of Calvert, a golf fanatic even as a young sergeant.

'You never did understand my fascination for little white balls, did you?'

Reid turned to find Calvert, hands in his suit pockets, at his side.

'I was never much of a friend to you, was I?' Reid admitted.

'You are what you are. Don't beat yourself up about it. You didn't bring a present?'

Reid swayed nervously, unsure how to explain his reasons for being there. 'I was going to, I just…'

'It's okay, Alan. I know you're not here to wish us well. You got my message?'

God's Will

He nodded 'Something else. It's just a question. Fenton, the solicitor?'

Calvert sucked his teeth and shook his head. 'Corrupt as the day's long, as you well know. Died back in the nineties. His son runs things now. From all accounts the opposite of his father in every way.'

'Creene had an appointment there this morning.'

Calvert grinned. 'What do you think, then? Have they been looking after the gold for him all this time?'

Reid shook his head and gave an empty laugh. 'You know there's no gold. There never was. Well, not that it was ever shipped over to the UK. Everything you said... I know you're right, but I have to go on.'

'I know you do,' Calvert acknowledged with a sympathetic nod. He took a small piece of folded paper from his wallet and held it out. 'I've heard on the grapevine that Rimmer's been shouting his mouth off about Sickert coming to him for help. He does a tour of gangland London out of Soho, if you want to see him. I don't believe it myself. He may well have gone to see him for something else, though.'

Cautiously, Reid took the paper from him. A part of Reid wanted to reach out to him. To thank him? Maybe to apologise in some way for treating him like a dogsbody over the years? To plead for forgiveness for selfishly keeping him from his family on a lost cause? At the very least he wanted to tell him he was unwell and the likelihood was they would never meet again. In the end he didn't rise to any of these notions: he just gave him a smile, this one warmer for an old friend, and then watched as he walked off towards his wife and friends. Alan Reid felt the urge to cry again for the second time in a week when he unfolded the paper and read the address in southern Spain for one John Culbertson, formerly known as Gerald Bexley.

God's Will

25

The stuttering click of a magpie sounds out across the marsh. It echoes through the cobbled yard Sickert is yet to see and into his room. He finds himself visualising the bird, sitting high in one of the three trees he saw on the marsh. He no longer wonders who beat him. Does it really matter, he asks himself? In a way he's glad it happened and that he found this odd place. Or maybe it found him. Even after all their conversations, he is still unable to sever himself from the strange hold this place, and Bepa, has on him.

'You talked about Larry's problems. How did they manifest themselves?'

Philip brings him food and drink. A bowl of dried figs and nuts and some more of the brandy. He adjusts himself in the chair and thinks back in time.

* * *

How did Larry's problems reveal themselves? In lots of ways. One day, for instance, he took me to the British Museum. We'd been quite a few times by then, but that particular day we had gone to see an exhibition. Alexander the Great, I think. Larry was the perfect guide. He knew so much about everything, but never made me feel bad because I didn't. After a couple of hours we decided to go for lunch at a nearby restaurant, but as we went out of the main entrance we found a mob on the steps outside. It took us a minute or so to get out, but when we did we discovered a copper attempting to dislodge a drunken tramp. As we watched and the crowd laughed and jeered, Larry suddenly went wild. Pushing his way through the bodies he demanded the man be left alone.

God's Will

When the copper asked why, Larry said because the tramp was a friend of his. The comment sent the crowd into hysterics; even I was laughing. But then I saw Larry's face as he turned on the crowd. He was incredibly angry and he said something in Latin. Latin, for Christ's sake! I don't to this day know what he said, but what got me was the way it was said. He was like a witch casting a curse. It was a weird moment but it had the desired effect. In a minute the crowd had dispersed and we were alone with the tramp. Even he seemed in awe of Larry. He took his hand, thanking him profusely for his kindness. I thought that was it, until Larry invited him to lunch. For a while I wasn't quite sure what the hell was going on, but sure enough, ten minutes later, we were in a top restaurant, eating and drinking to excess, despite the tramp's attire and smell. Afterwards Larry stood on a chair and asked for silence from the rest of the diners while he recited a poem. I was astonished, not only because they had allowed him but by Larry's behaviour. Of course, I knew why Larry was given a wide birth, but what I couldn't gauge was his temperament. One day he was drinking and gambling to excess in Mayfair, the next he was handing out food parcels to tramps at a local hostel. He had a particular soft spot for tramps did our Larry. He seemed fascinated by the vulnerable. Maybe that was why he had so much time for me.

What I feared most was that he would be unable to keep the two worlds apart. At what point would the walls break, and which side of him would take control? We were in tandem, both changing at the same speed but going in opposite directions. We seemed to arrive at similar crossroads in the summer of seventy-four.

By then I was spending less time at my apartment and more and more at Radstone. Week after week Larry and I would spend our time there, walking the extensive grounds and talking of everything from music to philosophy, from women to ecology. It was as if I was having

God's Will

a second childhood. There was nothing we couldn't do. Often we would picnic beneath a huge willow tree by the River Roding, which skirted the estate. Like young princes unaware of the pressures of responsibility, we drank and ate, sheltered from the hot sun. We would make love, swim and afterwards skim stones across the cool dark waters, our young naked bodies glistening in the sun. We became closer than ever. I was also becoming closer to Julia. Often all three of us would go out in her Lotus with a picnic and find some wonderfully remote spot where we could drink and laugh and talk. It was a careless existence. It didn't take me long to rid myself of the label outsider. I had made the transformation. I had peeled off the pupa skin; I was spreading my wings and preparing to fly. But as I became freer mentally, Larry, of course, was not. He was a prisoner to his father's ambitions.

While I spent more time at Radstone, Larry was spending more and more time in London running the organisation, and being involved in all the violence and corruption that went with it. We still had our fun, and he didn't seem to mind that I was living it up whilst he was serving his apprenticeship. I realise now why that was. He knew—if I didn't—that it couldn't go on. What we had was very special, but eventually it would have to end. The trouble was, I was far too busy enjoying life to see it.

One day at Radstone I woke to find myself alone. By then I was getting used to that. It was a hot summer's day so, grabbing a couple of bottles of wine and a picnic, I made for the river. The lawn at the rear of the house had just been cut and I was overwhelmed by the smell of freshly cut grass. It was so hot—too hot almost. I needed somewhere cool, and I knew just the spot. Beneath the huge willow tree, the water-cooled breeze wafted over me and for over an hour I ate and drank, watching house martins as they skimmed the surface. Solomon had this

God's Will

wonderful old cook called Jeanie who could conjure up a feast in no time. She adored Larry, and any friend of his was a friend of hers. Needless to say, she did me proud that day: smoked salmon, cheeses, oatcakes, quail's eggs, roast beef and Italian salami. It was far too much, but in those days I could eat like a horse without putting on an ounce. Eventually I felt very sleepy and started drifting off, only to be interrupted by the sound of a woman's voice.

'How innocent we all seem in sleep.' Julia had been away for a few days. I would like to think she had come to find me but I doubt it. Either way, there she was in all her beauty. 'Anything left for me? I'm amazed none of us have died of heart disease. Eddie's doctor is always warning him of the horrors of rich food. The truth is—I think he's too afraid to get rid of Jeanie.'

'Eddie afraid? I didn't think that was possible.'

Smoothing her short coffee-coloured skirt against her equally coffee-coloured legs, she looked at the river moving slowly, quietly, past us.

'We're all afraid of something, I suppose. We all have our little demons.'

'And what about you?' I said, trying to catch her gaze.

It was odd but I actually think the question angered her. It was as if somehow I had inadvertently found a chink in her well-manicured shell.

'I imagine my fears are pretty similar to your own...'

With youthful arrogance I nodded knowingly, not really understanding what she meant. But now I do. We came from similar backgrounds. Neither of us was going to risk what we'd found by rocking the boat. Somewhere along the line, maybe that day she drove me back to London, we had reached a silent understanding. We didn't need to talk about what we were or where we came from. Neither did

God's Will

we have to speak of our attraction for one another. It was as if some celestial clerk had done all the hard work for us, leaving us to enjoy the outcome. I remember we talked and drank into the early afternoon. Later we walked along the riverbank, barefoot, giggling beneath the scorching sun. Nature was in full bloom. It gave us all its magnificence, its colour and scent and drama. Eventually we discovered a small alcove where kingfishers dipped beneath the surface for sticklebacks. As we dangled our feet in the cold water and Julia rested her head on my shoulder, I glanced back at Radstone, gleaming in the distance. The view was stunning. How far I had travelled in just over a year.

As we talked, Julia explained that one of the main reasons Solomon had bought Radstone was its proximity to the river. He was a keen fisherman and a member of the local hunt. The thought made me smile. He had made his son a gentleman but, no matter how hard he tried, he'd never pull it off himself. No matter how many antiques he bought, or how many earls and barons he surrounded himself with—and no matter how much fly-fishing he could slip in between terrorising half of London—there was no way Solomon would ever have a trace of his son's class.

'Does Larry have a girlfriend?' Julia asked. 'He won't tell me. But I'm sure he has someone special tucked away. I can tell…'

I found the comment very odd because a few months before Larry had said something very curious in his apartment one night. We had been drinking heavily and as we lay on his bed, Larry had muttered drunkenly that he had met someone who had changed his life. He was looking directly at me when he said it, and as I looked a little deeper into his eyes he clammed up. For once the words deserted him, and I'm afraid to say I felt an incredible sense of joy. Not because I had seen a flaw in this remarkable man but because I felt he was talking about me. Yes, how conceited. I thought he was talking about little old me.

God's Will

Pathetic really, especially when I realised that day with Julia that it was actually someone else.

Then I remembered something odd that had happened a few weeks earlier. As I say, Larry was a huge fan of Dickens and he had talked me into going to a place called Gad's Hill near Rochester. Dickens had bought a house there called Gad's Hill Place. It took ages to find it, and when we did we found it had become a school, so we couldn't get in. Instead we spent the day in nearby Rochester. On the second day there was a literary festival in the town and Larry suggested he went on his own. That suited me fine and I went to a local pub for lunch. Because of the festival the place was packed and all I could find was a tiny upstairs table by a window. The wait for my food was a long one, made even longer due to an American tourist intent on explaining all of Dickens' motivations and extraordinary capacity for creating characters. I really wasn't listening and didn't hide the fact as I stared out of the window. It was then that I spotted Larry sitting outside a cafe. Presuming he had nipped out for lunch himself I was about to go down and join him when a woman appeared from a side street and they embraced. I couldn't see her face but she was tall and stylishly dressed in a summer frock, heels and a wide-brimmed hat. They talked briefly and then walked off. Clearly Larry had arranged to meet this woman. I didn't know if it had been done before we arrived or whilst we were there. I didn't mention it to him later. Like Julia, I had no intention of rocking the boat. But did Julia know about this woman? Or was she as confused as me? Was that why she was asking, to gauge my reaction? I did wonder at the time if it was because she was becoming envious of what Larry and I had. Well, she could spend as much time as she liked trying to find out, just as long as she did it with me.

* * *

God's Will

Later, Sickert is alone in his own room. Eight days into his containment/hospitalisation he is feeling much more like his old self—whatever that may have been. A great deal of his past is now clear to see. The alien landscape has gone and been replaced with people and places, a kaleidoscope of emotions growing from them, evoking memories happy, sad and every place between. There is still mist and shadow at the edges but it is quickly dwindling and soon he knows he will be staring at all the lurid horror of Lottie's kidnapping. *No, not yet, I'm not ready yet.* As he recounts his story he knows he is getting closer and closer to that moment.

Outside the wind is strong and it howls down the chimney, blowing smoke back into the room. He can taste it in his mouth. He sits up and for the first time finds the numbness in his arm and ankle receding. He pushes himself to the end of the bed and gingerly puts some pressure on his ankle. The pain is still intense but manageable. If he is to make an escape he needs a little longer yet. As he sits back something else occurs to him. Now the pain in his eyes has reduced, too, is he able to see once more?

He slides his fingers under the bandages at the back of his ear and tries to pull off the dressing in one go. It comes away, but also takes with it the scabs that have formed over his eyes. It is the original stabbing pain again, but magnified a thousand times. His torso twists half off the bed and his head smashes against the floorboards. Rats scuttle around his head and shoulders and he opens his mouth to scream, but the only sound he can make is a hollow yelp like a dying animal.

He writhes with agony, his ankle and arm too weak for him to pull himself up onto the bed. He yelps again and the haunting sound emanating from his lungs stirs activity elsewhere in the house. Voices, shouts, footsteps—two pairs of footsteps. Despite his torment, he wonders how. How is it that two people run simultaneously in a house where only one is capable of running?

The pain increases; it stabs at his eyeballs and the bleeding, bloated lids. It is so intense he wretches, the stomach-knotting pain doubling him over. Vomit fills his mouth, but he is upside down and his only useful arm is trapped in the bedclothes. He is choking to death. In that place where this life ends and the next world is fleetingly glimpsed, recent memories—until that moment hidden deep within his soul—rush into his brain. The agony is all-consuming. A moment later his body falls limp and silence fills the void.

26

Mohammed Mian was not a happy man. Alan Reid had been his tenant for many years and one he could rely on. Not only would he be losing peace of mind over one of his many ongoing concerns, he would also be losing a regular source of income. No matter how much he increased the rent, Reid always paid, and without a word of argument. If only all his tenants could be so understanding. It wasn't easy being a landlord; they never stopped complaining. But not Mr Reid. Reid was the perfect tenant.

'So what is it, Mr Reid? Are you winning the lottery?' he mused, trying to peer into a room he hadn't seen for years.

Reid was at the door, blocking his view. Mohammed wondered what state it was in. Knowing Mr Reid, though, he guessed it would have been well kept.

'No, I'm moving on.'

God's Will

'You need somewhere to keep your things? My brother has a storage depot in Romford, very reasonable rates. You don't look too good, Mr Reid. Looks like you should be in hospital.' Reid's red eye lids closed briefly and for a moment Mohammed thought he was about to topple over. He raised his voice to stir him. He didn't have time to look after sick tenants, especially one who was on his way. 'You keeping that nice flat good, Mr Reid? 'Cos cleaning take me a lot of time. Mohammed a busy man. It cost money…'

Reid produced a roll of twenty-pound notes. 'Keep the deposit. And I would appreciate it that if anyone comes calling you haven't seen me, ever.'

That produced a greedy smile and a theatrical wink. 'I understand, Mr Reid. I am renowned for my secretive ways! You are not the only one who applies such undercover behaviour–'

'I'll keep my things here,' Reid said impatiently. 'I'm paid up for another month. So keep out.'

The sound of hard leather against stone distracted Mohammed sufficiently for him to look down the stairwell to see a man he had encountered a number of times on his visits. Reid was a good tenant but he was also an oddball—not that that was a problem for Mohammed. He just didn't like the peculiar characters he attracted. It dawned on him then that he didn't know what Reid actually did. He never mentioned work, and he was always in when he called. So how did he generate income? Maybe something shady was going on? There was certainly something shady about the character climbing the stairs. Decidedly crooked.

Decidedly crooked, thought Mifty. Asian landlords. He waited until the man had left, with a nod and a smile as he passed and no doubt a knife in his belt for those not forthcoming with the rent. *Paki scum.*

God's Will

'Mr R.'

'Mifty,' Reid acknowledged, allowing him into the room.

'You don't look too good.'

'So people keep telling me.'

Reid had drawn on Mifty's knowledge of the streets for a long time and he had made many visits to Reid's flat over the years. It was normally a pigsty. This time, however, the room was the tidiest he had ever seen it. By the door were bags and bags of shredded paper, and another pile of kitchen utensils, packets of unopened food, and other miscellaneous household implements. In the centre of the bed was a small navy blue hold-all, the type people used for hand luggage on planes. Mifty had relieved enough tourists of luggage over the years to know that, no matter the size, a lot could be crammed into even the smallest case. He wondered what was in this one and where Reid was going. So he was departing. He had heard the Asian mispronounce 'Bon voyage' as he left.

There was something else. The room was silent. In all his visits the old computer had always been on, churning away. All that remained where it had stood was a thicket of fluff and screwed-up balls of paper. The biggest change of all, though, was the empty wall above the desk. The Steiner case montage was no more. That had been there so long there was a darkened outline of dust surrounding the vanished slips of paper with typed detailed information and the many photographs. Mifty had made so many visits, often pointless, fruitless, forays for information on the Steiner Murders, he could almost still see them stuck up there. The two images he remembered most clearly were of the two girls. One of the Steiner kid herself at the zenith of the pyramid of photos and newspaper cuttings, and another by the bed. That, in time, he had discovered was Reid's own daughter, who had died at a

God's Will

young age. Mifty had grown up hating coppers, but because of Reid's torment he had changed that view—and that was why he was here now.

'Moving home, Mr R?'

'Never you mind, you nosey little fucker.' A smile flickered across Reid's lips. 'You found him?'

'You know me. I don't mess about.'

'Where is he?'

'Marylebone. Very nice place. Top floor flat. Sumptuous.'

How is it that the corrupt always land on their feet? Reid mused. He took out the roll of twenties again and peeled off ten notes. He was about to hand them to the little wiry man with the stoop and toothy smile when he reached into his pocket and took out a piece of paper. 'I've got another job for you.'

'I'm a busy man at the moment. I'm thinking of going legit. I've been offered a job.'

'A job? You? Don't be ludicrous. Now, I want you to track down a man called Brian Verecker, a former prison officer. I discovered today that he is possibly working in the probation service or in a bail hostel but don't know where.'

'Retired screw, eh?' Mifty scratched his stubbly chin and chuckled. 'Yes, I'm up for that. Usual terms?'

'Usual terms,' Reid agreed, opening the door.

'Where *are* you going, Mr R?'

Directing his visitor out into the stairwell, Reid considered his reply carefully before replying. 'To find a man I should have killed a long time ago.'

Within days of the money transferring into his bank account, Thomas Greene moved into a top-floor flat on New Cavendish Street in Marylebone. He had been lucky. A short time after his visit to Muswell

God's Will

Hill, Verecker had called to inform him of an up-coming property. His nephew, a successful graphic designer, had been offered lucrative work in Rio on a twelve-month contract and was looking to rent out the apartment for a very reasonable rate. He would be more of a caretaker than a tenant. Greene took it with glee. He longed for the freedom of solitude. It was a new beginning, but his old life wouldn't let go.

Try as he might, he couldn't get Denby out of his head. It sickened him to think the man had been tailing him, watching over him and ultimately reporting back to some mysterious figure ever since his release. But who was this individual? The more he thought about the overheard phone conversation, the more he thought about Henderson. Verecker was right. There was no doubt it was him who was behind the money. That was what Henderson did. He was a great persuader. He knew people, understood how they worked, and he knew a fool when he met one. Greene had met a lot inside. They had a desperate look in their eyes.

It was midweek and early evening, and Greene knew Denby would be looking for him, probably in Soho. It was time to turn the tables; Greene would find him instead. He was preparing to go out when there was a knock at the door. He presumed it was Verecker as no one else knew he was there. He opened the door to find a tall figure standing there, but it wasn't Verecker.

'Good evening,' said Reid. He looked paler than Greene thought possible for a living creature. 'Going out?'

'What the fuck do you want?'

'A chat.'

'I've told you I have nothing to say. And how did you find out where I lived?'

God's Will

'I have my means,' Reid said lightly, peering over his head. 'Nice place. Had some ill-gotten gains hidden away somewhere, did we?'

'Go to hell...'

'I will, and probably sooner than you think. But for the time being maybe you could help me? You went to see Fenton, I believe?'

Greene tried to reel in his anger and mimicked mock outrage. 'Are you following me, Mr Reid? I could get the police onto you, you know?'

'Don't taunt me, Sickert.'

'It's Greene, actually. The government has gone to great lengths to change my identity and you could get in a great deal of trouble if it was discovered you had given that away.'

'You know, if you disappeared now, nobody would any the wiser...'

Greene was tired of this. This long-standing hatred was draining. He picked up his keys and pulled the door to. On the way down the five flights of stairs Reid talked continuously and exclusively about the night of Larry's death. It wasn't until they reached the pavement that he changed the subject and uttered the name Gerald Bexley.

Greene stopped as he was about to cross the road and turned to face Reid. 'What about Bexley?'

'He's been located in Spain.'

'I didn't know he was missing,' Greene lied.

'Yes, you did. I'm going to see him and I'm going to find out all he knows, and then I'll be back to see you. So don't get too comfortable in your little bachelor pad, will you?'

Getting a cab and losing Reid in the process, Greene began an exploration of Soho for his old drinking buddy. Thoughts of Bexley the bent copper would have to wait. Where the hell did Reid find the energy?

God's Will

After a hurried search of Denby's usual drinking holes he returned to the first, the Wheatsheaf on Rathbone Place. There he found Denby holding court at the bar, a large brandy yo-yoing to his moustached mouth. Greene lost him briefly as he went in and made his way to the bar, but a vacant seat, and a side door suddenly opening revealed he had been rumbled. Denby was so attached to his drink he had carried it out with him as he rushed into the street. Greene, slowed by the flotsam of regulars at the door, was four or five seconds behind but got out in time to see him darting by The Marquis of Granby onto Rathbone Street slurping brandy as he went. He was going in the right direction, anyway, for Greene's purposes. He planned to take Denby back to the flat and get the truth out of him, even if it took all night. But when Greene reached Rathbone Street, Denby was nowhere to be seen. He simply couldn't work it out. He walked forward slowly, eyes darting from side to side, expecting to find his quarry hiding in a doorway. But no. There was no sign of him.

Crash! He turned, attracted by the sound of breaking glass, but for a moment couldn't work out where it had come from. Then he saw it—a walkway between another pub and a restaurant, a passageway he remembered using years before. He remembered its name—Newman Passage. Then he heard a shout. Was that Denby? Its pantomimic urgency hurried Greene forward. Entering the shadows of the passageway he had a genuine sense he had somehow gone back in time, which was perhaps not the best place to be then when encountering the Ghouls They appeared from nowhere and it was pure chance he didn't crash into them and their pram. Face to face in the dim light of the passage he could just about make out the faint flicker of light in their empty eyes, reflecting that coming from the old light fitting above. A chill ran through Greene. Were they the reason for Denby's shriek? Something caught his eye and he glanced down to see the remnants of

God's Will

Denby's broken brandy glass. He wanted to run on and find the old crook, but he was held in the hypnotic draw of this oddest of couples. They seemed just skin and bone, wrapped up in the most bizarre collection of clothes, like characters from a Dickens novel.

Greene was about to push past them when he thought he recognised something in the man's eyes. It was a look of familiarity, a sense that he had seen him somewhere before. It only lasted for a moment, but it stayed with him. Something else occurred to him as well. What was in the pram? And why did they insist on pushing it everywhere? In that moment, as if they had read his mind, the pair shot forward, almost knocking him down, and headed towards Rathbone Street. Then they were gone, leaving Greene to wonder fleetingly where on earth they came from and what they did each night.

The way clear, he rushed forward onto Newman Street, but by then Denby was nowhere to be found. Disappointed that his search for the truth was to be further delayed, Greene walked back to the flat, a mild headache finding a home between his eyes. He cursed under his breath but then slowed, an unsettling sensation of depression forming in his mind. There was another sense, too. It had been with him since meeting the Ghouls and in the cold wind it only intensified—a feeling that he was being followed. More than once he stopped and looked back, only to find the street empty but for litter caught up in the blustery wind. At first he suspected it was Denby, back to shadowing him again. But no, he would be too cowardly to tail him after such a close encounter. The Ghouls, possibly? Well, if it was, they had abandoned their squeaking pram. It could, of course, be Reid. He would never give up searching, because that was all he had left. It was the obvious conclusion, but he just knew it was someone else.

Henderson.

God's Will

Where was he? And at what point would he realise that Denby was as useful to him as a fork in a sugar bowl. Surely then he would come for Greene himself?

Due to the evening rush hour it took Reid much longer than he expected to locate Needham House. He couldn't find any spaces nearby so he ended up parking at a bus stop. He no longer cared about parking tickets and such like. He was in a hurry. He was booked on the two-thirty a.m. flight to Malaga. After leaving Greene he had actually been on his way to Heathrow when the call came through from Mifty. *I got your man.* He was good. Reid was never sure how he did it—it probably wasn't legal—but he always came up with the goods. It could take days, or, like now, he came straight back with a result.

The interior of Needham House reminded Reid of the dozens of hostels he had visited as a young copper. It was a painful fact that down-and-outs were always the focus of the authorities when an incident occurred in the vicinity. These types of places always had the same smell of disinfectant, and glancing at the ragged crowd milling about the foyer he understood why it was so liberally used.

'Can I help you?' asked a tall man coming down the corridor towards him.

'I'm looking for Brian Verecker.'

'I'm Verecker,' the man grunted cautiously.

'Is there any chance we could talk privately?'

'That depends who you are and what you want...'

Reid decided to use the same approach he had used with Stockwell. In fact, the mention of his name might allow him even better access. What did he have to lose?

'My name is Reid. I'm a former Met inspector. I got your name from a former colleague, Robbie Stockwell.'

God's Will

Verecker's tough exterior mellowed at these words. 'Robbie Stockwell? That name brings back some memories.'

Bingo.

'He sends his best. Would we be able to talk?'

'Of course. Follow me, Mr Reid. Looks like you need something to warm you through.'

Reid sat before a desk and studied Verecker's tidy little office as the other man produced a bottle of Bells from a filing cabinet. As he splashed a couple of fingers into some mugs Reid noticed that Verecker was in the process of completing the cryptic crossword in *The Times*. He angled his head to read the remaining clue.

Omnipotent care in an overpriced oven.

'You look rather pale,' Verecker observed, passing him a cup and sitting down.

Getting a little tired of people's observations on his sickly state, Reid transferred his focus from the newspaper to the whisky and made his standard response. 'I've not been too good recently, health-wise.' He knew he shouldn't touch the whisky; his ulcer had been abused enough, but maybe Verecker was right and he needed something. He took a sip. After the niceties were out of the way Reid got to the point of his visit. 'According to Stockwell, you were the two men who escorted Thomas Sickert to Branston hospice the night Laurence Solomon died?'

'That's right,' Verecker said matter-of-factly. 'Sickert was actually cuffed to me. I sat by the bed with him the whole night. Solomon had asked to see him.'

Verecker had a strong Yorkshire accent and reminded Reid of a sergeant he once knew from up north. It relaxed him even more. 'How long had Sickert been in Brixton at that point?'

God's Will

'I would say nearly a decade. He was one of the most well-known cons we had, due of course to the notorious nature of the crime. Has some new material come to light? You are *the* Alan Reid, after all.'

Reid squirmed in his seat. He was not comfortable with his fame or with the lie he was about to tell. 'No, it's actually for a book I'm writing.'

'A book?' Verecker seemed impressed. 'Will I be mentioned?'

'Not unless you feel comfortable about that.'

'I don't know how I feel, but then I don't know what you want to know yet.'

'Of course, forgive me. You must be aware of the rumours and theories about what happened to the child–'

'The German girl? Lottie, wasn't it?'

Reid's throat became dry and he reached for the whisky once more. Fire shot through him. When it hit his stomach he wanted to retch, but he fought it off.

'Yes, Lottie. I have only discovered the details of the hospice visit recently and I wondered if Solomon said anything to Sickert before he died.'

Verecker's eyes opened wide. 'Well, if he did I would know. But I'm sorry to say he didn't, not by my recollection.'

'Were you conscious through the whole of the night? You may have nodded off briefly'

Verecker stiffened, clearly offended by the implication that he was a slacker. He sat up and adjusted his cuffs. All the backtracking in the world wasn't going to change the fact that Reid had affected the mood, negatively. Sensing his slip Reid changed tack and enquired about everything but notorious felons. It was a device he had used a hundred times in interrogation. It worked, and he pretended to listen as Verecker talked about his mother who had recently passed away. But he wasn't

God's Will

really listening, because he didn't really care. He was just happy he had won back the man's trust so he could return to the subject of Sickert and Solomon.

'I believe you got to know Sickert quite well at Brixton. Do you recall that time?'

'Yes, quite clearly, but I must say, and this may sound odd to you of all people, but I found him of decent character. He was a big reader. I often engaged in conversation with him about literature.'

Reid fought off his disgust at the comment. 'Did either men ever meet during their time inside?'

'Not that I'm aware of. Solomon spent most of his time at Rampton, Ashworth and Broadmoor at the end. All high-security psychiatric hospitals, as you will know. He was not what you might call of sound mind.'

'Did you ever come across him?'

'Never, other than the night of his death, of course.'

Reid didn't know why, but something jarred within him at the phrase *the night of his death*. No doubt it had something to do with his regret at losing one half of a possible explanation. That left only one direct link now. 'And Sickert? Ever have any trouble with him?'

'No. I'll say it again. A model felon. Ironic, isn't it? They did such terrible things and yet had more manners and civility than men of lesser crimes.'

It was Reid's turn to stiffen, this time at this description of a couple of cold-hearted killers. Was it that or was there something else in the way Verecker spoke about Sickert and Solomon? 'And how do you reach that conclusion? About Solomon's *civility*, I mean? He spent the rest of his life in a nuthouse...'

God's Will

Verecker pulled at his cuffs again and leaned forward. 'I am, of course, speaking of my own experiences with Sickert, but from all accounts they were both very similar.'

'I see. Did Sickert ever talk about what happened? Did he ever give a reason for what they did?'

'Never, and I didn't ask. Odd, though. Prisons are full of men who claim they were stitched up, but never him. I will admit that I got rather close to him; he seemed a decent man, despite his crime. No, I believe he was resigned to the fact that for him life was over.'

'Sickert came here on his release, I believe?'

'Not sure how you would know that as his whereabouts come under the Official Secrets Act. If he was here though he's not here now.' Verecker smiled softly and his big brown eyes seemed to grow wider. 'You're not writing a book at all, are you?' Reid was embarrassed and impressed equally at the man's perceptiveness. 'You have to let it go, Mr Reid. I can only imagine how much hatred you must feel for him, but he's served his time now. We can't go back. Let it go.'

Reid wanted to say a great deal but resisted the temptation. He got up. 'Providence...'

'Is that how you see life?' Verecker asked, looking up at him quizzically. 'Because I don't. I believe every man—'

'The remaining clue,' Reid interrupted. 'Omnipotent care in an overpriced oven. It's providence. The last two words are an anagram.'

As Verecker looked down at the paper Reid made his way out.

Nothing here. Move on, Reidy.

There was only one more possibility left—a recent addition. A one-time friend and colleague called Bexley. Reid's only thought now was his journey to Heathrow and his early morning flight to the south of Spain.

God's Will

On the way back from Soho and his aborted hunt for Denby, Greene stopped at an off-licence and picked up a litre bottle of Scotch. Once home, he dragged a chair over to the window so he could study the world below. It was just after midnight but New Cavendish Street was still bustling with cars and people.

No matter how bold his intentions were to resolve his problems he was still afraid. The small amount of confidence within him was balancing on a knife edge. His nerves were shot to hell and it took all the strength he had to find the energy to keep going from day to day.

In the early hours of the next morning he woke with a throbbing head and intense pain in his left arm—he had slept on his side and the blood flow had been restricted. After a couple of Ibuprofen, a shower and two large cups of coffee he felt a little more human. He knew he really should have gone back to bed and slept, but instead he watched the dawn rise through the window, thoughts of Henderson and Denby milling about in his head. The waking world below remained entirely unaware of him and his concerns.

Try as he might he could not hate Denby. The old sod didn't stand a chance. On his release he would have had nothing to live on. He didn't have a job, and you don't drink brandy at that rate on the national pension. No, Henderson was clever. He would have discovered from a crooked official that Greene was bound for Angie's happy home in Muswell Hill and then made an approach to the only occupant, one Osbert Maximilian Denby. There would have been an invitation and the old fool would have been plied with brandy, then he would have been presented with a package filled with wonderful opportunity. The type the likes of Denby could never resist. The only question was, what was Henderson looking for? There was obviously something Greene had forgotten, something from long ago that made his survival essential. Was that why he had survived for so long inside? The problem was, he

God's Will

didn't have a clue what it was. It couldn't be the gold. Could it? Despite the nonsense spouted in the press and on the internet it didn't exist. He knew that because he was there, he saw it all unfold, and the longer he kept that to himself the better.

27

Sickert mumbles in his bed. Somehow he is back in it and his eye dressing has been replaced. The pain has reduced but he feels awful. Philip fiddles around the bed. The tangy smell of vomit hangs in the air.

'I need to see your mother.' The only response he receives is stillness. Philip has stopped moving and is close to his side. 'Do you hear me? I need to see Bepa!'

'Neither of you are well enough. She's been bad, like you. You should have left the bandages alone.'

'Look, I think I know why I'm here, and it's important I tell her. You could all be in danger. Please take me to her.'

A few minutes later he is reluctantly led to Bepa's room. He asks them both some general questions about where he was found and the men Philip saw—their appearance, their age. Then he asks where the house is situated. 'I have had some type of understanding,' he declares. 'Memories. Recent memories. I understand. I know why I'm here. You have to know that you are in danger having me here.'

'We shall take our chances, Thomas.'

'How can you be so calm?' he yells. 'I need to leave.'

'You have taken off the scabs from your eyes a little too soon and I'm sure you felt it.' He knows her light tone hides a large degree of

God's Will

motherly concern. 'There's blood, and there will be more scabbing, but I think you should be fine to leave in a couple of days.'

'And for that I am thankful,' he says with a sigh. The earlier collapse and recent outburst has taken it out of him and his body flops in the chair. He fiddles with the belt of his dressing gown and prepares himself for a declaration of his own. 'Do you remember when I spoke in my sleep? What did I say again?'

'You said "God's will".'

Determined to rid himself of confusion, Sickert presses his fingers to his temples and speaks slowly, deliberately.

'Eighteen months before my release Larry was diagnosed with lung cancer. By then he was in Broadmoor on the Isle of Wight. As I've explained to you, Larry had many mental issues that got worse and worse, but that didn't explain why he did what he did. Lottie's body was never found. If it had, my future would have been so much easier to contend with. You see, I didn't kill Lottie. I put her murder down to Larry's illness and what he had gone through in his life. But I don't know what happened to Lottie. I was determined to find out, though.'

'So you are an innocent man?'

'No, Bepa, I am far from that... I just didn't kill Lottie.' He heard her mouth open to speak but nothing came. 'As the cancer spread and his condition deteriorated he was moved to a hospice on the mainland. He had only been there a few days when I was woken one night and informed that Larry had asked to see me. I knew it was the end. It was also my last chance.'

'Last chance?'

'To find out what he did with Lottie. Whilst one officer guarded the door out in the corridor I sat at Larry's deathbed, handcuffed to another. More than once I was convinced I had lost Larry, but then his eyelids would flicker or his chest would rise, unexpectedly. Finally, in the early

God's Will

hours of that morning, as the officer dozed at my side, I was stirred by a haunting sound. Laurence Solomon was calling my name. His voice was hoarse and faint, but I heard it in the silence of that room. Even though I was still handcuffed, I got up and stooped over the bed, my chained wrist hanging back behind me.'

'D dn't this officer...'

'Verecker.'

A long coughing bout delayed her response. 'Didn't Verecker not wake?'

'No, I'm sure of it. I glanced back at him a couple of times. I knew Larry was very close to the end, but I had to find out. I said my name and there was a sudden glimmer of light. I could see that he recognised me. He whispered something. I'm sure it was my name. Bending even lower, I put my head close to his ear and asked the question I had imagined asking so many times alone in my cell. *What happened to her, Larry? What happened to Lottie? Where did you take her?* The answer came back to me like a sudden cold breath of wind in the darkness. It was barely audible, but I was certain I heard him say "God's will".'

'God's will? He said that?' There was another long silence. 'Was he religious?'

'No, and never had been. I repeated the question over and over because I knew he was at the very end of life. It's impossible to say at what point he died or if anything I said made any sense to him, but as I stood up and stared down at his lifeless body, I knew it was all over. A minute later I heard a noise and turned to see Verecker coming to life. He got up and looked at Larry. He knew. In the intensity of the moment I had forgotten I was handcuffed to him or that he was even there. He asked me if Larry had said anything. Of course, he had, but in my thinking he had said nothing at all. It was just the ramblings of a dying man. I walked to the door but stopped as I felt the pull of the handcuffs.

God's Will

I turned to see Verecker staring down at the corpse. *It's all over*, I said. *It's all over now.*'

'Why would Verecker be so affected by this? He was just a prison officer after all.'

'I don't know, really. Maybe because, despite our crimes, he knew we cared for one another. He seemed touched by what he'd seen. He was that type of man. I was just feeling too much anger to sense any other emotion. Why Larry had given in to the naivety of religion at the end I will never know. He was the one who had shown me that there was no great mystery, no spirits guiding us, no master plan, nothing but what lay before our eyes. As I returned to Brixton that night all I wanted was to die, to end my life and the pain that would exist knowing he no longer existed in the world.'

'How strange it all is. But if you weren't part of the kidnapping and weren't responsible for her death, why do you torture yourself so?'

'Because I was part of the kidnapping. And I am a killer.' He starts to sob and the salt from his tears sting his bleeding eyes.

'Tell me the rest, Thomas. Let's finish this before we both go.'

* * *

Larry's problems were there all along. I was just so caught up in my own ambition I didn't see it. On top of his disappearances he was getting violent, too violent even for gangland London. And he was enjoying it.

A year into my new job I had progressed from running Solomon's going concerns. I was operating under my own steam, making decisions, signing cheques, I had learned so much in such a short space of time it gave me amazing amounts of confidence. It was a criminal life, and I knew I could never go back. Away from Julia and Radstone,

God's Will

this was what Solomon did. And because Larry was his son, it was what I did too.

What I enjoyed was the power. Purely because of my association with Larry I became one of Solomon's boys. Wherever I went, I knew people would say *Here's Tommy Sickert, he's one of Solomon's.* That was all that was required. Showing my face meant Solomon was watching. At the beginning, Larry and I did it together but after he met that mysterious female, I hardly saw him. I didn't question him about it, for one very simple reason. His mood swings had become more and more spectacular. What I'd seen outside the museum with the tramp was just the tip of the iceberg. After Rochester it got worse. He was becoming difficult to be around. One day he was the epitome of reserve, the next day downright evil. I didn't question it. I didn't try to get to the bottom of it because I didn't want to burn my bridges. I was on Solomon's payroll, sure, but one falling-out, one word from his son, and I knew he would drop me like a stone.

One part of the job had me chauffeuring Julia to and from Radstone. A few weeks after that day by the river with her, she was entertaining a few of her female friends. God knows where Larry was. On the Saturday night Julia asked if we would like to join them. Of course, I was more than willing to eat well, surrounded by beautiful, wealthy women. Halfway through the meal one of the old girls, a large blonde by the name of Honor, who had had a little too much claret, started teasing me about being alone with them. She then drunkenly said something about Julia and I having an affair. It was a very embarrassing moment that was sensed by everybody, except old, thick-skinned Honor. Then something dawned on me. Was it Julia I had seen in Rochester? Was it her I had seen in the square? The thought shocked me to the core. If Larry and Julia were having an affair, there would be extremely good reasons to keep it secret. Stepmother and stepson? I

God's Will

couldn't believe it. I was also incredibly jealous. Mind you, of which one I couldn't say. I was also angry, because if it was true it was being carried on behind my back. But my anger was the least of their concerns. If Solomon ever found out there would be hell to pay.

That night as I lay in my bed I thought about Julia and Larry. By then I think I loved them equally. Although I had barely touched Julia, I found her presence almost too much sometimes. I could still remember that day by the river when she had rested her head on my shoulder. If that was all the love she could give me, then I would die a contented man. Yes, I think I'm right in saying I loved Julia very much indeed, but it didn't stop me turning Honor away when she slipped into my room that night. Standing beside my bed, she insisted I fuck her the way I fucked Julia. I didn't say a thing, but in the darkness I did to her what I imagined I would do to Julia if the moment ever arose.

I didn't see Larry again for a while but when he did come back it was as if nothing had happened. We lived our usual lives to excess and without compunction, but even then I knew things had changed forever for us. One day I got a call from him. He explained he'd just had delivery of a beautiful red Porsche but was caught up in another part of London and couldn't get back to pick it up. Could I bring it over to the Rotella? It was outside his apartment and the keys were in it.

Only living round the corner I rushed out, keen to drive such a car. Now, I should have thought it odd that a salesman would just leave a new car on the street with the keys in it, but I was dealing with Larry here, don't forget. He could be very persuasive. I was driving for twenty minutes before I was stopped and arrested. If I had bothered to look up as I got in the car, I would have seen Larry at his window watching me. From there he had watched the idiot owner park the car and leave the keys in the ignition. To him it was just a bit of fun. The old Larry would have paid my bail and taken me out for a slap-up

God's Will

lunch. Then Fenton senior would have got me off on a technicality. In time it would be a moment we would look back on and laugh. To make things worse, Solomon was in the States and it took me over a day to track Fenton down. I was forgotten. On top of that, I now had a police record. What upset me most was that Larry had picked me out for humiliation above all others.

On Christmas Eve 1974 Larry went over the edge completely and it shocked everyone. Solomon had organised a seasonal get-together for his boys in a Soho restaurant, and I was happy to see Larry in good form. He was sitting next to a guy called Rogers. He was like me, a lieutenant, and did a similar job. I was at the other end of the table so don't know how it started but suddenly I heard a scream and looked up to see Rogers with a steak knife sticking out of his chest. I then saw that Levy was holding Larry up against the wall. It was madness, and Rogers was lucky to survive.

Larry ran out. I eventually found him sitting on a doorstep on Frith Street, just around the corner.

'I was wrong about you,' his said suddenly. He wasn't looking at me. His head was bowed, almost in defeat.

'What do you mean?'

'You're no better than the rest. Well, Thomas, old chap, you're welcome to it all. I don't want it... do you understand me? I just don't want it.'

I couldn't quite believe what I was seeing, but to my utter amazement Larry Solomon was crying. Tears were running down his face, tears painted blue and green and red from the flashing lights of the sex shops along the road.

'What is it, Larry? What's wrong?' I drew the conclusion that this odd behaviour stemmed from his troubled relationship with his father. 'Look, why don't we just go away? Just you and me?'

God's Will

He started laughing uncontrollably. There he was, sitting on the step, drawing attention from passers-by with his head back and his hands clasped together across his legs, laughing his head off. It wasn't forced in any way; it just seemed that there was something in his head he found terribly funny. Then, as soon as it had started, it stopped and he got up to face me. His mood had changed again and I didn't know what to do. He was four or five feet away and smiling at me.

'Have you seen my steak knife? I put it down somewhere. I think Rogers may have it...'

He said it so matter-of-factly, without any emotion, I just lost my temper.

'Larry, what the fuck is going on? You nearly killed him.'

'I hear there is a rather decent dog track not far from here.'

'Larry, talk to me...'

'Or we could just get a taxi and find ourselves a good old-fashioned East End pub. Cor blimey, governor! What do you think?'

'Will you talk sense, for Christ's sake!'

Rushing forward, he grabbed me around my chest, forcing us both onto the road.

'And what good would that do, dear Thomas?' he yelled. He was so close to me I could feel the warmth of his breath on my face. 'You're incapable of listening. You're blind, my friend, and whatever happens now is your own affair. Do you understand me, Tommy boy?'

Inside I was terrified of what I was seeing and of what he'd become. Then, after staring deep into my eyes for what seemed like an eternity, he nodded and stepped back. I stared back at him. I didn't recognise what I saw. It was as if his remarkable spirit had left him and all that remained was something very ordinary. I sensed then that our lives had gone full circle, that I was more like him than he was himself. But there was something more. I realised that with him or without him, I would do anything not to return to my old life.

I was so troubled by Larry's behaviour I decided to take a trip to see Veronica at the Duke the next day. To my amazement the place had changed beyond all recognition and Veronica was gone. God knows when she left. Due to Larry's absence I hadn't been for months. In the place of photographs of actors and writers was an array of broken-nosed boxers and minor cabaret acts. I later discovered that Solomon was buying up a lot of property in areas where he had heard big business was showing an interest. The plan was to hold out as long as he could and then make a killing. It was easy for him. Even if the owners refused, Solomon would convince them it was a good idea.

I also discovered that Larry had only found the Duke by chance after Solomon had sent him down to check out the area. Somehow he must have convinced his father it wasn't worth the trouble, but in the end Solomon always had his way. At what point Veronica was approached I don't know, but after she sold up I never saw her again. What must have made Larry particularly bitter was knowing that whatever he did, wherever he went, he couldn't escape his father.

28

Reid was not a good flyer. The symptoms were nothing out of the ordinary: sweaty palms, mild headache, increased blood pressure, but now he was conscious of his weakened heart these relatively mild conditions magnified and made a hypochondriac out of him. Every slight pain or cough filled him with terror. That was possibly why he rushed from the plane as soon as it landed at Malaga airport. His

God's Will

anxiety only increased at passport control, where lackadaisical officials chatted with one another, blithely unaware of the snaking queue of frustrated Brits. The tension stayed with him during the taxi journey into Aquadulce just along the coast from Almeria, right up to the moment it stopped outside Bexley's villa on Paseo Maritimo, overlooking the Mediterranean. There it quadrupled.

He knocked and waited, then waited some more. All the time he was eyed curiously by a local man trimming hedges along the road. After five minutes Reid went over. The man looked fearful.

'Culbertson?' Reid enquired, giving Bexley's pseudonym and pointing to the villa on the corner.

'Reporter?' The man was bald, small and a local. A large tuft of greying black chest hair poked out of his overalls like a small mammal.

'What?' Reid replied, putting his thin leather briefcase under his arm and gesticulating with both arms.

'You English reporter? Tabloid?'

It suddenly dawned on Reid that now the news was out about Bexley's crooked past there was probably a regular stream of reporters appearing at his door. That explained why he wasn't home. It also explained why he might not be home for quite some time. If the locals were all expats (and a lot of them crooked) it was very possible that his enquiries about Bexley's whereabouts might fall on conveniently deaf ears. It was time to apply some trickery. Taking out a false warrant card he used for such occasions Reid flashed it at the wiry man, muttering the word *Interpol*. Whether the gardener was a law-abiding citizen or hadn't done his tax returns for a number of years Reid couldn't know, but no sooner had he pocketed the little red wallet than the man began babbling like a scolded child.

'Nevada!' he said, pointing towards the sea.

'He's gone to America?'

God's Will

'No! *Nevada.* Yate!'

The man was gesturing and jabbering for more than a minute before it registered with Reid that he wasn't talking about the New World but attempting to explain that Señor Bexley was down at Puerto Deportivo, Aquadulce, aboard his yacht the *Nevada*.

On his way from Bexley's villa Reid took the advice of the taxi driver and booked a room at a small hotel. Happy in the knowledge he had a bed for the night he continued on his way to the port. As marinas go, the one at Aquadulce was of medium size and pleasant-looking enough. It was crowded with boats of various kinds—yachts, cruisers and, in the distance, a couple of megayachts that Reid could quite easily have confused for ships. He was no sailor. The *Nevada* was an elegant cruiser and in superb condition. Bexley had clearly invested his crooked money well. Conveniently for Reid, it was moored near an Irish bar in a busy little shopping area. The place was filled with loud holidaymakers wearing even louder clothes. He found a table and did his best to ignore them by keeping his eye on the yacht thirty feet away from him.

Feeling a little tight-chested, he took one of the tablets he had been prescribed by the hospital. He was hungry and thirsty, too, so followed it with a large plate of chips, three San Miguels and a double whisky. He checked his watch and saw that it was past seven in the evening. It had taken him most of the day, but he had found what he had come for. In the hot evening air he studied the activity aboard the boat. Doing his best to shut out the blaring pop music and raucous behaviour of his fellow countrymen, he placed himself back in surveillance mode.

He could make out three people—a short, skinny, dark-haired woman reading a magazine in the shadows of the open-back pilot house, a tall Mediterranean youth mopping the open deck and Bexley

God's Will

himself at the stern, gesticulating erratically with a mobile phone at his ear. He was fatter, greyer and browner, but Reid would never forget his old boss in a million years.

Especially as he had had a two-year affair with Mrs Reid.

He finished his second double whisky and made his way over. The boy stopped scrubbing the deck as he approached.

'Hey, boss! Visitor,' the boy called out, leaning on the mop handle.

Bexley was now silhouetted in the pilot house but didn't move until he had ended the phone call. The woman got up and went down into the galley as Bexley walked forward into the sunlight.

Reid sat on a metal mooring post on the dock and wiped sweat from his forehead. 'Evening, Gerry.'

'Do I know you?'

'You should do,' he responded, his confidence bolstered by too much booze. 'You spent enough time fucking my wife.'

Tension hung in the hot fuel-scented air and an elderly couple, enjoying the sunset, looked outraged but continued walking along the quayside, just a little quicker. Reid laughed lightly, fanning himself with the thin briefcase. 'Don't worry, I'm too old to play the outraged husband. And I'm not well enough to knock you out.'

'Alan Reid…'

'You remembered,' he said, grinning.

Still Bexley played the cautious hand. 'What do you want?'

'Invite me aboard and fix me a drink and I'll tell you all about it.'

There was no response at first and Reid wondered if he had played *his* hand the wrong way. A moment later, though, Bexley flicked his head back, indicating for him to come aboard. He ordered the mop boy to bring beers then retreated apprehensively into the shadowy recesses of the *Nevada,* followed by an eager and slightly tipsy Reid.

God's Will

The boy produced a tub and filled it with ice and bottled beers. The two men sat around it in the shadows of the pilot house, though it was still too hot for Reid. He plunged a hand into the bucket as much to feel the cold ice against his skin as to get a drink. Other than make his arm uncomfortably cold it didn't do a thing.

Despite their palpable hatred for one another the pair chatted amiably for some time on other things—Bexley's potential extradition; London; the Met; the criminals they had known, befriended, and convicted; the gutter press; house prices in the UK… It took them a while, and a dozen beers, but eventually the subject of Bexley's affair with Reid's wife came to the fore.

'There was no love, you know, Alan,' Bexley said, almost cordially.

'There rarely is with affairs, I would imagine. The attraction is the danger. When it all becomes respectable the magic disappears. Not that I have ever found any magic in it. Love is just another word for security, convenience. It occurs between two people who happen to get along and have similar interests.'

'Michelle loved you.'

'She had a funny way of showing it,' Reid scoffed, staring up at the light of the sunset on the surrounding curtain of cliff, turning the oyster-brown rock to red velvet. 'Whatever Michelle and I had, I killed. You probably gave her more pleasure in your brief, sordid sessions than I ever did in twenty years of marriage. When Becky died, when she needed me the most, I abandoned her for work. I'm tempted to say don't feel bad about me finding out, but I suspect you don't anyway.'

'Reid the philosopher. Never imagined that,' Bexley grunted as he called out to the boy for more beer. 'So why are you here? Have they sent you to get me? Am I to be treated like a murderer? I'm not a criminal. Do they realise how many collars I made over the years? Back then we had to collude with crooks to find out what they were

God's Will

scheming. Fucking liberal media. Makes you sick. Human rights this, human rights that. Oh dear, that poor child-murderer can't get the Disney Channel in his cell, let's fund his case to the European Court of Civil Rights! Makes you want to vomit. Boy, where's that beer?'

When the boy still didn't appear, Reid took out a handful of ice cubes from the tub and wrapped them in a handkerchief. Dabbing it on the nape of his neck, he crossed his legs and sat back in the canvas chair.

'Speaking of child-murderers, you were close to Eddie Solomon, weren't you? What do you know about the kidnapping?'

Bexley puffed out his cheeks and shook his head. 'Is that why you're here?'

He got up and walked out into the sun, looking up at the cloudless sky. In the same moment Reid heard the clinking of glasses behind him. Presuming it was the boy with more beer, he didn't look round. Then, mid-yawn, Bexley spoke again.

'There's nothing to tell, Alan. I explained everything at the time. I was close to Solomon, that's true. I knew them all. Larry, Sickert, Fenton the crooked brief... I even dined out with Steiner and Solomon a few times. Steiner was in a lot of debt to Solomon. Gambling debts. But I was told the debt was paid and the problem resolved. Maybe that was where Larry and Sickert got the idea of the kidnapping from; maybe they thought there was easy money to be had. It never did make any sense to me. I mean, why kidnap a kid and then kill her without the payout? Madness.'

'You must know something! Somebody from that time must have some information!' Reid was on his feet, pleading, overheating, wiping the sweat from his face with the dripping wet handkerchief.

God's Will

Bexley shook his head again, this time with profound disappointment. 'I'm sorry, but that's the truth. We can't tell you anything you don't already know. Can we, love?'

Reid glanced round to see the silhouetted shape of the female he had seen earlier. It wasn't until she got close that he found something strangely familiar about her. He wouldn't have recognised her if he had passed her on the street—she was never under suspicion at the time so he had never taken a great deal of interest in her. It was only because they were talking of that time and of those terrible events that Alan Reid recognised the beautiful woman before him.

Eddie Solomon's widow, Julia.

29

'How does it feel to know there is an end to the pain?'

Sickert has asked this question with his head tilted towards the right of the bed. He presumes it's where Bepa's head is. It's a calculated guess. She hasn't spoken for so long he wonders where her face is and as she hasn't coughed for some time he also considers the possibility that she has fallen asleep. It doesn't really matter now. These memories, the telling of his distant life is no longer for her. He is reminding himself of what brought him to this particular part of the universe. The spell she cast upon him days ago is irrelevant now. He retells this life of contrast for his own education, for his *own* end.

'It is strangely comforting.' He jolts at her words and repositions the blanket Philip placed across his shoulder an hour or so before. 'I do fear for... Philip. He is a sensitive man. Like his father, he worries far too much about a world he doesn't understand. I have made provision

God's Will

for him. I wonder what happened to your friend Larry after that night in Soho? You loved him very much, I can hear that in your voice.'

'Did I? I loved nobody but me, I think. I betrayed him, Bepa. Now, in hindsight, I recall my Luke: *Before a rooster crows today, you will deny Me three times. And Peter went out and wept bitterly.* I wouldn't deny Larry in that sense, but I would give up on him and for that I have wept bitterly for my disloyalty many, many times.'

* * *

I spent the Christmas of seventy-four with Julia at Radstone and sensed, not only from her subdued manner but also from the uncomfortable atmosphere, that both she and Solomon had been aware of Larry's problems much longer than I had. During that time Solomon had been taking me with him wherever he went. Yet over that Christmas, and through the first half of the following year, I didn't see him at all. As long as I was amongst the wealth and in Julia's company, I didn't care. Occasionally she would disappear, and I was convinced it was to see Larry. I didn't know where he was or what he was doing, but by then I was past caring. I was just happy I was still needed and still getting paid.

The following summer—July of seventy-five—Solomon asked me to organise another of the parties he held from time to time. To be honest, I'd only experienced one of them—the night Larry introduced me to Radstone—but I was more than happy to be given such an important task.

The parties were very big occasions, the highlight of the Lambourne calendar; which was laughable in itself. If the local population had known what deviants attended Solomon's parties they would have been horrified. It was a real rogues' gallery. Not that they all looked like

God's Will

crooks. A lot of them were very wealthy and highly respected and gave no indication of what they were really about. Only a select few, including Larry and me, knew that, but with Solomon there was a reason for everything. I suppose I may have been aware that I was being tested, that Solomon was trying to find out if I had any talent in that area. Communicating effectively with the powerful and the corrupt was an indispensable talent in Solomon's organisation. In the end, though, it was a pretty simple thing to organise. Solomon supplied me with the guest list and all I had to do was arrange the catering and the music. All in all, it only took me a couple of days.

On the night of the party itself, Solomon was his usual charming self and Julia his doting wife. The evening mirrored the one I had experienced the year before, when I first met Julia. A lot had happened since then. One year on we were very close. As I looked for her later on that night, I inadvertently walked into the library to find Solomon, Fenton and Steiner, Lottie's father; the man with the gambling debts Fenton and Solomon had discussed. That night, however, the atmosphere between the three men was considerably more relaxed. Clearly they had resolved their differences.

Leaving them to talk, I went upstairs to find Julia. She wasn't about, but as I made my way downstairs I heard the noise of activity from one of the many bedrooms. It was pretty obvious what was happening inside. I couldn't help but sneak a peek. Opening the door, I discovered to my horror Julia on all fours hooked up to a young black guy. She tried to say something to me, but it was clear from her expression that the moment was far too intense to be interrupted.

Rushing downstairs, I very nearly ran to the library to tell Solomon. But I quickly thought better of it and rushed outside instead. The night was cloudless and quite cool for the time of year. Across the lawn I could see the lights from the summerhouse. I tried to force the image of

God's Will

Julia being fucked out of her head out of my head and walked over. I think I knew what I was going to find even before I opened the door. What surprised me was the cordial atmosphere. In the middle of the room a fire glowed beneath the huge brass flue. In its glow I could see naked bodies on all sides. On the far side was a cine-projector and a large screen showing a colour 16mm movie; although I couldn't see what was playing, I could hear the soundtrack of grunts and screams. God knows who had organised it all, maybe Julia herself.

There were bodies draped across sofas and armchairs, everywhere. I inadvertently walked in front of the screen and saw, around the silhouette of my head, images of a threesome, doing what any three naked people might do given the time and encouragement. It recalled the image of Julia on the bed at the house, but even before I could dismiss it there was a shout for me to move. Crossing to the fire, I surveyed the scene. Looking on as a bystander, it all seemed so cheap and ridiculous, this type of throwaway passion. Guilt and affection had been left at the door, and everything was reduced to a sordid game. On one sofa a young Asian girl was in the throes of passion with three old men. And I mean *old*. I was shocked, disgusted, embarrassed almost—not for me, but for her. Then I felt anger at the knowledge that she was enjoying it. I couldn't understand how she could relish the attention of a trio of overweight elderly men, men who under different circumstances wouldn't get within a mile of an attractive woman like her. But because they were wealthy, because they had influence and power, they could do what they liked with her.

I went back to the house feeling disgusted with the world. Disgusted that Julia was part of it as well. In my bed I listened to the laughter through the noise of the wind in the trees. The more I listened the more the images expanded in my mind. As they increased, so did my disgust, because deep down inside I knew I wanted to join in, too.

God's Will

I know Julia was embarrassed that I had found her like that because through all of July and August I didn't see her once. Until the end of summer I spent most of my time alone at Radstone. I should have been happy, but I wasn't.

Late one night Solomon appeared without warning and asked me to join him in the drawing room. As we drank I took the opportunity of mentioning Larry's absence. It had been eight months since I had seen him last, on the night of Rogers' knifing in Soho. Solomon was a difficult man to read and I was taking a real chance asking such a sensitive question, but to my surprise his reaction was one of a concerned father than a psychotic.

'As you've probably noticed, Larry's not been himself recently. So I've sent him away for a while.'

With a drink in his hand, looking out into the darkness, I thought I'd seen another side to Solomon. I was genuinely touched.

'When will he be back?'

'I'm not sure,' he said, frowning and walking over to the drinks cabinet 'You're close to my boy, aren't you?' There was something in his voice that troubled me. I understood the implication, and I understood Solomon. What I said next was pivotal.

'He's the closest friend I've ever had.'

I don't know what meaning he took from the words, but it seemed to put him at ease.

'Let's change the subject, eh?' Pouring a glass of my favourite tipple, he passed it over and sat down across from me. 'You're a good lad, Tom. You're a grafter, and so am I. There are too many lazy fuckers in the world. When I ask you to do something, you do it and, what's more, you don't complain when you do. I like that. But more than that, you're a bright lad. With Larry out of the way for a while I'm missing my right-hand man.' He pursed his lips and sighed. 'Larry was

God's Will

starting his apprenticeship, you might say. I've been thinking that you would be the ideal replacement. You and Larry have worked closely, you know the set-up. It'll be easy for you.'

I tried not to show emotion, but inside I was bursting with unadulterated fervour. I should have been afraid. With such a high-profile position within a criminal set-up I would become well known to the authorities. But I didn't give a damn. Ambition and greed outweighed the fear. Money was the deciding factor, not conscience, not fear of arrest—money.

'What do you think?'

I smiled a greedy, heartless smile. It was a very good moment that, very intense and incredibly exhilarating. At the heart of it there was no Larry, no Stella, no Charlie, just the money and Julia and me. Despite her peccadilloes I needed her.

He didn't wait for the answer. He could see the seed of ambition in my eyes bursting into life. Solomon had a talent for people. 'You help me out on this, Tommy boy, and I'll look after you.'

Yes, it was a very good moment indeed.

So there I was, Solomon's second-in-command. In a couple of years I had outgrown my narrow view of the world and was moving forward at such a rate I could feel the wind of change around me. At first I approached the work tentatively, but as I saw the fear Solomon's name generated I grew in confidence. From keeping an eye on the businesses, I began starting up my own. I had such clarity of thought. I had so many ideas. I was young; I knew what kids enjoyed and, on the strength of this, I started a nightclub. I hired dancers and booked a couple of up-and-coming bands. I sent invites out to every celebrity I could. It was a huge success and on the back of it I set up two more,

God's Will

which did even better. Despite Larry's absence, Solomon was a happy man, and with good reason—I was making him a lot of money.

Thinking back now, I wonder what Solomon had seen in the eyes of that young man. Was it just greed, or did he also see how little I cared for his son? My only friend was in trouble, but I didn't give a damn. Power had changed me completely. I didn't know where he was or what was wrong, but as long as it didn't affect me, I didn't care.

Within a couple months of the party I had completely forgiven Julia. With her it was impossible not to. After the chat with Solomon I hardly saw him. On the odd occasion that I did, we rarely spoke. Away from the parties and social gatherings he was a very private man. A paradox, you might say. Despite the fear he instilled in people and the power he got from it, it was as if he was at a loss with what to do with it. Often I would see him just wandering round Radstone, his mind elsewhere. Then at night I would hear him and Julia arguing. It was the usual soundtrack to an unhappy marriage: the screaming, shouting and sobbing, which all seemed so bloody unfair, because when Julia and I were together we were so contented. Solomon had filled Radstone with rare and expensive furnishings and it looked, to the newcomer at least, the home of a man with taste and reserve. But I knew he didn't have an ounce of love for Radstone, or anything in it. Just owning it all was enough for him. Knowing that other people were envious of what he had was all he needed. It was Julia who had painstakingly decorated each room. I can still remember the pride in her eyes when she described how she had trawled the libraries and bookshops to discover its past and bring it back to its former glory.

But even Julia's feminine touch couldn't hide the emptiness. I think even she sensed that. There was simply no love. No little feet had jumped on the Edwardian carver chairs, no sticky fingers had dirtied the Regency rosewood tables. It was a museum, a sanitised world populated briefly by us all. The only time it ever came to life was during the parties—if you can call that living.

Solomon's absence was a blessing to me. It meant I could spend my time with Julia. Each day we would picnic by the river or drive to a special place a few miles away called Baker's Hill. One day after a little too much wine we climbed to the top and lay side by side on the grassy slope. It was very hot and the sun was our blanket. As we lay side by side, her back against my chest, I was aware that our breathing was in sync. Silly, I know, but at the time it seemed to mean something, as if we were destined to be together. Propping myself up on an elbow I allowed my other arm to trace the contours of her slim body beneath the crisp cotton white dress. I was very nervous but continued because she didn't resist. Then I understood why. She had fallen asleep. I had to smile.

Julia and I were together in every sense of the word, and what I felt for her was as strong as anything I felt for Larry. Did I miss him? In a way, yes, but I was also aware that with his absence I had become what I had always wanted. I was practically living at Radstone by then, and running so many of Solomon's outfits I was virtually in charge. Power is a wonderful thing. It can liberate and focus you. It gave me the ability to forget my past completely. Now the picture was complete. As if someone had sucked all the fog out of my head the world was clear and simple to understand. I could see that people I had once despised—the wealthy, the business types—were the true innovators. The risks they took made the world a place worth living in, and their arrogance was merely a result of the risks they took. I tried to wipe away all that reminded me of my past, even my recent past. And that, of course, meant Milton's and Charlie and Stella. As time went by, my principles dispersed into nothing, until finally I felt so complete I could take on the world.

God's Will

Then, in February of seventy-six, as we celebrated Solomon's birthday at the Rotella, everything fell into place for me. It had been the usual night of excess and Julia, Solomon and I had had a great time. It was a very wet night and we left through the entrance *en masse*, huddled beneath umbrellas. Levy always led the way with a couple of men on either side until Solomon was in the car. I was somewhere towards the back. As I walked out and Solomon's two cars came to a stop at the curb, a man ran out from behind one of the huge columns at the front of the casino screaming at Solomon. He was drunk and wild about some money Solomon had taken from him. Solomon waved him away and walked to the car, but as he reached the opened door the man pulled a sawn-off shotgun out from under his long raincoat. Time stood still for a moment. As if fixed by the flash from a camera, I could see everything so clearly. Shock does that. It freezes the image, condenses time, allowing you to study every detail. Solomon had his head half-turned in disbelief. I can still see it, his expression a mixture of anger and helplessness. There was this little man who had decided to fight back, and you could see in Solomon's eyes he hadn't thought it possible. At his side Julia was also looking back, although she was bending down to get in the car. Even terrified she looked beautiful. And all around them I could see Solomon's men, Caesar's bodyguard, stuck in the moment, not sure who to save—themselves or their boss. The only thing that seemed to be moving in the madness was the rain. Like tiny dots of silver it fell onto the scene, binding it and cleansing it in a constant steady flow. I saw all of this clearly because of what I'd become. I didn't feel a thing anymore. No fear, no adrenaline, nothing.

Levy was the closest to the man, but even he seemed defenceless. As I watched his face I remembered that night at Milton's again, the night I was beaten and they mocked me. I felt the urge to laugh, but it didn't last long. Because this moment was not good for me. It wasn't

God's Will

Larry I needed to worry about now, it was his father. Without him I was nothing. He held the key to my continued success; with him alive I had wealth, I had power and I had Julia. What I did next was probably driven by all of this, but I also like to think it was because I wanted to do the opposite of what I'd done that night at Milton's. I wasn't aware of it, but as the man screamed at Solomon I had manoeuvred my way down the steps behind him. I'd come out last and as he ran out I had a clear view of everything from the top of the steps. Levy was yelling at him to put the gun down, but the man was also yelling back, which only intensified the moment. Then, mid-sentence, the man fired, and in a second Solomon was on the ground. The man walked forward and pointed the gun at Solomon's head, ready to empty the second barrel, but by that point I had skirted the cars and come out between them. I was on the pavement a matter of feet away. I don't remember hitting him or how, but I knew I had put him out of the equation with a single blow. The yelling and the horror only lasted seconds, but in that moment I had secured my future. Solomon had been shot in the hip and by the time we got him to hospital he'd lost a lot of blood. But he survived. He was out of action for months, but he got through it. And it was all thanks to me.

As I drove Julia home later that night, I felt I could have got out and raced her back. I was on such a high I was sure I could take on anything, any problem, any cause and still come out smiling. I was the hero of the hour. I'd won the Derby, the hundred metres and the bloody lottery. At the beginning I'd put my good fortune down to luck, but that night I sensed something more powerful was playing its part. Destiny.

As if sensing my glory and not wanting to ruin my moment the rain receded, allowing the moon to shine through the breaking cloud. As we entered the grounds at Radstone, the burning torches on either side of the drive (lit for Solomon's birthday) seemed to glow a little brighter

God's Will

for the returning hero. Even the forest of oaks, normally so proud and somber, appeared to bow to my achievements. Finally I was the complete package. I'd done it all and there I was, alone with Julia. We both knew what was coming, but we were also aware there was no need to hurry to it.

As the sun rose that morning we touched for the first time. Julia was different from Stella in every way. Her breasts were smaller, but nonetheless round and full, and her perpetually suntanned skin had an almost powdery softness that reminded me of the very first girl I kissed. It was difficult to believe she was ten years older than me. As her tongue danced with mine I remembered that day by the river and that hot afternoon on Baker's Hill. On both occasions I had dreamt of making love to her, never once believing it would ever happen. As we kissed I couldn't help but open my eyes for a brief second to admire her —even that close I couldn't see a flaw. Her hair, a dark sweeping flow that framed her elf-like face and brushed her bronzed narrow shoulders, smelt of jasmine and spices, and for a moment I was that little boy again, dreaming of being the hero on the screen. I could see it all again as surely as I could feel the warmth of her skin. I realised then that as a child I had drawn an invisible line to a point in the future, a point I'd been trying to reach ever since. I was touching her hair as she opened her eyes and whispered.

'Fix me another drink.'

After a few minutes she reappeared at the door in a long fur coat. For a moment I nearly laughed. It was huge, and all that I could see, other than dead mink, was her tiny head and a pair of strapless high heels. Then she showed me the prize. I knew I'd won it that day by the river, but the excitement I felt right then made the long wait well worth it. Her waist was narrower than I'd imagined possible, and the rest of her figure was equally stunning. I walked over to her and confidently passed her the drink.

'Not here,' she murmured, smiling. 'Not here.' She crossed the room and walked out onto the balcony, inviting me to follow. The temperature had dropped considerably through the night and the huge lawn had been transformed into a vast frosted lake. The cold didn't touch us. Nothing could. We were cocooned from everything. Taking the drink from me she nuzzled against my chest and together we drank and watched the sun as it rose. 'What do you want, Tom?'

'I want it all,' I said, taking in the fresh morning air. 'And I want you.'

'Yes,' she said, almost indifferently and looking out across the white shimmering expanse. 'I rather thought you did.'

Hand in hand, her head on my shoulder, we wandered to the copse on the far side. When we reaching the spot where we had talked for the first time almost a year before, we stopped and studied each other's faces. It was a bizarre, hurried union, one characterised by the circumstances we suddenly found ourselves in after the long period of restraint we had both endured. Instead of tiredness, there was desire, and where guilt should have blunted our passion, the same emotion defined the moment. We made love long into the morning until we lay hot and breathless beneath Julia's huge mink coat, the coal fire in the centre of the room keeping the winter cold at the door. Outside I could see the servants in the house going about their business, but I was under no illusion that they had been put under strict orders not to venture anywhere near the conservatory in the copse.

As we slept side by side I dreamt I was Alexander the Great and Julia was Roxana, his wife, and together we would travel to the ends of the earth, conquering and strengthening our kingdom. Then, when I awoke later on I became distressed as I remembered how Alexander

God's Will

had died, alone and incredibly young, unable to enjoy the fruits of his labour. Telling myself I didn't want to conquer the world, just my little bit of it, I got dressed, leaving Julia sleeping beneath the fur. There was a lot to do.

I knew even by that point in the day the news of Solomon's attack would be common knowledge. But I had learned a lot from my employer, and I knew exactly what to do to keep the empire together.

30

There were a number of empty whisky bottles by Greene's chair by the window. They increased by the day. From unscrewing the cap to the moment the intense pain in his head woke him the next morning, he could not recall a conscious moment between. His nightmares were the only real thing in his life. Each night was the same and had been for some time. The same dream repeated over and over. It was an alcohol-fuelled hallucination that had increased in definition and horror since its beginning weeks before. It was the one of the house, with the flowers and the blood-stained body of the man he knows. Over and over it played until morning time. Nothing, it seemed, could stop it. Alcohol only intensified the pain.

Some days he was certain he saw Lottie staring up at him from the road, or from the windows of the Georgian townhouse opposite. Her dark hair was combed straight and she was wearing the summer frock he remembered she wore on the day he last saw her, the white one with the red polka dots and the white socks and the polished black shoes. Alcohol did help there: it numbed his senses and he slumbered in a nether world of disjointed thoughts. Yet he knew that before long a

God's Will

bottle a day would no longer do the trick. The hell was so intense he was terrified of even going out. Instead he had his groceries delivered from a local store, and two or three times a week a middle-eastern boy would appear with his order and stare fearfully up at what he had become. On top of the drinking, he was eating very little and somewhere along the line he'd stopped trimming his beard. He knew the child to be the owner's small son. One day he came with another boy. Having seen them from the window, he went to the door to wait and overheard them talking outside. He knew the odd word of Arabic from his time in prison—a man he knew had become a Muslim, not because he was overly religious but because the Muslims had an altogether better diet. He had suffered from Tourette's. The word the Muslim's had used when mocking this man was *majnun*. It was the Arabic word for madness. And that was the word he overheard the young boy muttering to his friend when describing Thomas Greene.

English majnun...

'Señor, there is someone at reception who wishes to speak with you.'

Reid had settled up at the small hotel in Aquadulce and was preparing to leave when a fat-faced porter appeared at his door. He followed the man down, convinced there had been a misunderstanding as there were plenty of other English in the hotel; it was more than possible that there was another Reid in the place. As he glanced down into the small marble lobby, however, he realised then there had been no mix-up. Julia had come to call.

At the marina she and Bexley had explained how they had first met by chance again at a party in Malaga. Julia was escaping, like Bexley, only she was guilty of nothing more than being married to a gangland thug and stepmother to a child-killer. Reid had repeated his questions

God's Will

about the night of the kidnapping but Bexley had repeated his claims that he knew nothing. Julia, however, had remained silent throughout.

As Reid reached the bottom of the stairs, she stepped forward, her head hung down. 'I have some information for you. It won't take long.'

They found a table by the window in the deserted dining room opposite the reception. She wore baggy black trousers and a tight white t-shirt. Reid only had his grey suit and white shirt, only today he didn't wear the jacket. She wore Chanel 5, while he reeked of stale body odour. He ordered a whisky, she lemon tea. In the mid-afternoon sun Reid could for the first time see tiny flaws in her loveliness; a millimetre or two of grey at the roots of her hair, small lines around the eyes and dark patches below them, both thinly submerged beneath foundation. She had tended to her tiny imperfections as best she could.

'You've caught the sun...' she observed, noting his uncomfortable red nose, cheeks and scalp.

He ignored the observation with cold reserve. 'What do you want?'

She bit her lip and spoke plainly. 'My husband told you he doesn't know anything about the night of the kidnapping.'

He frowned and sat back. 'And you're here to tell me he's lying?'

'No.' she whispered, her eyes on the busy little road outside, 'I'm here to tell you that there is someone who knows a great deal about that night. Because he was there.'

Reid picked a beer mat up off the table and tapped it subconsciously on the marble top. 'Who?'

She stared at him for what seemed like an age, as if she didn't have the courage to say it out loud. In the end she said it with her eyes turned away from his. 'Levy.'

Levy had been no more than a name in Reid's head, and a pretty hazy one at that, until that moment. It was that way because Jack Levy had been presumed dead for years.

God's Will

Reid's face was a caricature of dismay. 'Levy? Solomon's henchman? Alive?'

Julia was still looking away from him but now searching in her pretty little purse for a cigarette. She looked lost and relieved all at the same time. 'Gerry doesn't know. And I would rather him not find out it came from me–'

'Where?'

He now had her full attention. She was staring at him, pleading. 'Please keep this to yourself–'

'How can I possibly keep it to myself? Why even tell me if that's what you want? Christ, you're naive.'

'Because Levy's not well. Not well at all.'

'There's a lot of it about,' Reid observed, without emotion. She seemed hesitant to speak again, so he pressed her. 'Where?'

'Here in southern Spain. He arrived in the early eighties and needed help. I found him a home and send him money from time to time. He has a wife and daughter.'

Reid shook his head in consternation. As if being alive wasn't astonishing in itself, psychotic Jack Levy was married with children?

Julia reached in her bag again and took out a piece of paper with an address sprawled in biro. 'He lives in a small fishing village called Corazona.'

'When was the last time you saw him?'

'A couple of weeks ago. I call round to see how he is from time to time. His wife, Maria, doesn't want me near the place.'

'Good judge of character that one.'

Julia told him all she knew and described the house in detail then, without ceremony, got up and left. She had just pulled away in her shiny red Peugeot when Reid became aware of someone at his shoulder. It was the fat waiter with the meaty jowls.

God's Will

'More drinks, señor?'

Reid shook his head and got up. 'Just a taxi, me old mate.'

Denby was a frightened man. Since their phone conversation before Greene disappeared from Muswell Hill he had not heard from Lamb at all. Two days on the trot he had been sent to a deplorably bad hotel in Brent Hill to wait for a delivery that never came. In a desperate attempt to find out what was happening, he went to Lamb's flat. To his increasing concern there was no reply to his knocking. Nobody, not the current tenants nor the rather unsavoury Asian landlord, had seen Lamb or, even more worryingly, ever heard of a Mr Lamb. Then there was the business with Greene. He knew from the look of anger on his face the night he tracked him down in the Wheatsheaf that he was onto him. It had to have been that night on the phone. He must have overheard his conversation with Lamb. *What a mess, what an almighty bloody mess! When will you learn, you stupid old fool?*

How had this all happened? Because Lamb had seen weakness in him? Because he knew that Greene would be coming to Muswell Hill? And how did he know that? That sort of thing was only known by the probation service. Did Lamb have friends on the inside? Or was he part of the establishment himself?

Denby was in the Star Tavern in Belgravia, a pub he knew well. He had a talent for remembering trivia on each pub he visited. It often got him a free drink. The Star was where Bruce Reynolds and his boys fleshed out their plan for the Great Train Robbery. Any other day Denby would have been happy to share that fact with any of his fellow drinkers in the hope of a free brandy—but not today. That magic was lost to him. Today it was just a building full of strangers, where he could no longer hide from the world. In his depressed state he felt his crimes were as evident and as clear as his own fear of Greene and

God's Will

Lamb. He wasn't in control, and he now realised he never had been. His life was a conveyor belt of misery. He had merely hidden that fact away and lived in the moment, concealed in a hazy brandy-filled stupor.

A group of men laughed over at the bar but Denby wasn't in the mood to join them and sensed he never would be again. The awful truth of his life was that he was a weak man and had fallen for the temptations the easy life afforded. Booze, women, parties… kids…

Oh, my God—children…

So many images of them in horrific states of despair. What had drawn him to that hell? Why had he downloaded them? *Why, why?*

Semi-muted sobs escaped his moustachioed lip and he pushed his thumbs into his eye sockets as if to purge himself of the horror show. It lasted all of five or six minutes and then it stopped, leaving him with a clarity that had evaded him for a lifetime. It is a fearful thing to face yourself, he thought. And the fear was there because he had discovered some part of himself that was not corrupt. Lamb had no right to put him in this situation, and Greene was in no position to make him feel guilt for his own indiscretions. So his answer was simple. Play one off against the other. Get them both off his back in a single move. Find Greene and explain exactly what Lamb was up to. The blackmailer would surely do nothing to him if he knew his quarry was onto him. Denby still had plenty of expenses left, and the latest payment had just gone into his account. He still had time. He could move on, sod the probation board. Start afresh. Change his name. Greene's mistake was returning to the same area. That was stupid. *I won't do that. I could move to a new place, begin a new life away from the likes of Lamb.*

So there it was. There was a way. First he had to track down Greene, wherever he was. Explain it all from the beginning. Sure, he would be angry, but he would appreciate his help, he was certain of

God's Will

that. There may even be money in it. Not gold—even if it did exist—but a financial snifter. A goodbye thank-you for coming clean.

Yes, that was the way. That was the only answer to his problems now.

31

Sickert has eaten and Philip has joined them, although he sits a distance away. It is night now and Bepa asks if Sickert would like to return to his room to rest. He turns down the offer, and wonders how long she has left. He wonders too why his attackers have not visited the house. For that, and for Bepa, he will go on and finish what he has begun. He takes a mouthful of wine and tells them both a bedtime story.

* * *

Instead of letting things cool off, I stepped up collections from all Solomon's going concerns. I made sure the boys made their presence known and spread the word that Solomon's reign was far from over. I wanted to find Solomon's attacker. He had escaped in the chaos somehow. I wanted to impress my boss by tracking him down and blowing his brains out, but Levy told me that Bexley had been in touch and wanted me to calm things down. So I did, and focused on the business instead. I thought I was doing it for myself, that staying at the helm would bring me more wealth—but it wasn't about money anymore; it was the power. I liked what I'd become. The respect and influence the job allowed me was too damn intoxicating to ever let go. Once you have a taste of that you never want to go back.

God's Will

For three weeks I was at the peak of my life. I had the power to do anything I wanted, to anyone and anything. And of course I had Julia. On the third day of this glorious, but brief, reign, I woke late at Radstone to find Julia had organised a picnic. Driving to Baker's Hill, we ate beneath the sun and drank into the early afternoon. Afterwards she led me down the hillside along the river and into a wood that surrounded the hill. There we followed an old track to the very centre of the wood and, in a secluded spot below the remnants of a giant oak, we made love. Apart from the faint breathless sighs of joy, it was the most soundless place I have ever known. For those three weeks we always found time to visit that special place. It was a type of heaven for us.

Then, as I knew it would, it ended with Solomon's return. Whilst he was in hospital I made sure he knew what was going on with the business. The last thing I wanted him to think was that I was taking over—although the idea had crossed my mind a number of times. After weeks in one of London's more expensive private hospitals, my employer came home. With Julia's help I had made a list of his closest friends and arranged a welcoming home party. He was so happy, he cried. I was quite emotional myself, but not for him. Pride's a terrible thing, but if I wasn't going to be proud of me, who was?

By midnight Solomon was feeling tired and everyone decided to go so he could rest. I'd organised a bed to be put in one of the small downstairs rooms looking out onto the balcony. Even during my brief time with them all, I knew their tastes and their pleasures. I knew waking up in that room and looking out across the beautiful estate would give Solomon a feeling of calm after weeks in a stuffy hospital, but I also knew he would think of me and the trouble I had gone to in order to make his recuperation that bit more pleasurable. I had planned all of this without a glimmer of guilt, even though I knew as he slept

God's Will

downstairs I would be sleeping with his wife upstairs. Julia didn't care a jot; in fact that night we had the best sex we'd ever had. She got a real kick out of taking risks, like she did with the black guy at the previous party. I still felt that demanding to be fucked over the upstairs balcony was pushing things a little too far. I should have been more aware of her dangerous side, mainly because it brought out the recklessness in me. In a way that night was the beginning of my downfall. All along I'd understood there were limits and why they were there. It was occasionally okay to cross them, but with success swelling my ego I had trampled over them until I didn't know where they were anymore.

Next day at breakfast Solomon announced that he and Julia would be going away. Then came an embarrassing eulogy, so unique to us working-class types, about loyalty and strength of character. They were going to the States for a while. Apparently, Larry was getting more like his old self and they were to meet him there. It was a horrible moment, and the sadness was clear to see in Julia's eyes. My feelings for her by then almost surpassed what I felt for Larry. That relationship was built on admiration; what Julia and I had was structured more on the understanding of where we'd both come from. Our success was due to our association with Larry and Solomon. We had betrayed father and son alike.

Within days I was running the family business alone. To be honest, there was little to do. Criminal empires require little nurturing. Pruning would be a more accurate verb. Each season the plant must flower—preferably more so than the previous year—and to do that one must be ruthless. Solomon had explained to me how important it was to cut away the dead wood that weakens the structure. Have the strength to do that, he had said, and never be afraid of the outcome, and your success is assured. Yes, I had learned a lot from Solomon.

God's Will

It had all been so easy. Within a few of years I had gone from down and out, to the head of one of London's biggest criminal networks. Acknowledging this was half my problem, I suppose. Being alone to consider the enormity of what I'd done was the very thing that undermined my success. I missed Julia from the very first day. And knowing she was with Solomon only contributed to my sense of isolation. Over the weeks and months my self-belief and arrogance, fuelled by alcohol, spiralled out of control, like planets destined to collide. Sober, I began to revert to what I was; drunk, I was the worst I could be. I tried to spend as little time as I could at Radstone. It was too big and reminded me too much of the people who truly belonged there. London was my problem. Within the grip of its overwhelming power, I saw myself for what I was, a little man unable to deal with the power at my fingertips. God knows why, maybe for a sense of security, I moved into Larry's old apartment. It was probably the worst thing I could have done.

Larry's expensive colognes and pungent Turkish cigarettes combined to remind me of what we had shared. In the living room I was reminded of him every day by the huge self-portrait he had now completed and hung on the wall in the living room. There had been some adjustment to the eyes, and somehow he had constructed a weak smile from the former grimace. He no longer looked haunted. A few blobs of paint and a swirl of a brush had turned him into a tormentor. He mocked me day and night, laughing the way he had when I saw the madness in him the first time, that night in Soho when we fought like children in the road. I could still remember his words.

You're blind now, my friend, and whatever happens is your own affair.

How I wanted in that moment to be that nobody again, dreaming naively about TV shows and rich women.

God's Will

Somehow, on the periphery at least, I managed to keep myself together, but without Julia all I had was a vacuous existence. Instead of watching the gambling tables, I was soon playing them. In a perpetually drunken blur, I drifted from one Solomon house to another until eventually I found myself at the Rotella. There I would really gamble. As the drinking got out of control, so did the stakes. I was falling apart. And without Larry and Charlie or even Stella and Julia, there was no one to put me back together. Solomon's men—and that's what they were after all—had conceived a collective hatred for me ever since the night of the shooting. Solomon had rewarded me well for what I had done, but thanks to that moment, that moment of opportunism, they despised me. They may well have been a set of dumb bastards, but they saw through me. And none of them saw it clearer than Levy. I was far too full of myself for my own good. One night, after a particularly bad loss at poker, I caught his eye across the table. The look was one of delight. He could see the end even if I couldn't.

Each day the misery repeated, but somehow I just kept going. I kept telling myself that it would sort itself out, but the denial was more harmful than anything. Despite the front I put on so much had happened to me in such a short period of time, I had become splintered. I didn't operate in the normal way. I wasn't in control. Someone else had taken over and didn't understand the mechanisms that made me what I was. The structure was cracking under the strain of someone who didn't know what was important. It was a type of depression, I suppose. When it got bad I would hide away in Larry's apartment, but when it lifted I was a terrifying version of everything I had once despised. I would be chauffeur driven from place to place, immaculate in Pierre Cardin suits, Barkers brogues and Saville Row ties. I looked good—there was no denying that—but if you looked close, really close, it must have been possible for anyone to see the confusion and the

235

God's Will

loneliness. *We live to learn*, Charlie once told me. But I didn't listen. I gave up on him, and I remember with shame our final meeting at Milton's one hot spring day in seventy-six.

Why I was there I wasn't sure. I told myself I wanted to show him he was wrong about me. But my old self would have realised what I was really going for. Not to show myself off, but to ask him for help. It had really got that bad. It was late morning when I arrived and Soho was bustling with life. It was jeans and t-shirt weather, summer was on the way, but I didn't do that anymore. I was now a suit-and-shades man. God knows what I must have looked like to the punters as I got out and rearranged my tie. Maybe they saw me as I had first seen Henderson, as a prick in a suit.

Telling the driver I didn't need him until later, I walked in. The smell of disinfectant and cigarette smoke mingled to remind me of my days behind the bar. For a brief moment I felt a warm sense of happiness as I recalled those nights with my old pals. How happy we had been back then. But, like a smudge on a window in my mind, I wiped the memory away and sat down. I rearranged my cuffs and heard Charlie before I saw him. There was always the sound of activity with him, either the clanging of a mop bucket or the whine of a Hoover, invariably accompanied by a happy song or a whistle. And suddenly there he was, his old face ridiculous and wonderful all at the same time. A part of me wanted to hug him, but another part—the new, unrecognisable part—wanted something different.

'Can I help?' he asked, with his back to me.

'That depends, Charlie,' I said. The tone of my voice didn't reflect my feelings. I sounded arrogant, brash. It scared me.

'Well, well, well,' he muttered, 'and what can we do for you, young Thomas, on this fine day?'

God's Will

His tone was part mocking, part indifferent. He'd seen it all before. After the initial look of recognition, his attention had gone back to his work as he mopped behind the bar. That angered me more than the confusion I felt. It also forced my mood from one of need to an altogether darker one.

'I just came to see how you're doing.'

'Oh, we get by.'

'How's Stella?'

'She's fine. We're all fine.' I could hear it all in his voice. The detached tone, so different from the one he had used before, when I was under his wing.

'Takings are up, I hear?'

'Yes, we've been doing a comedy night. It brings the punters in.'

'What's the matter, Charlie?'

'Don't get you, son.'

'Come on, it's me. What is it with you? I've done well for myself. Why can't you be happy for me?'

He didn't reply at first. He didn't even look up from his mopping. 'Is that why you're here? Felt the need to show me how well you've done? Is that it?'

'I just came to see how you're all getting on. To see if I could do anything for you.'

I tried to look at him, but his eyes were focused on the swirls of beer-coloured, soapy water. Round and round they went and as I watched I think I felt hatred for him. I didn't show it, though. I played my hand carefully, just like Solomon.

'Is there anything I can get you? More staff?'

'We manage fine with what we got.'

'Will you fucking stop it?'

'Don't get ya, son,' he said. But still he didn't look up.

God's Will

'You're all the fucking same, you know that? Solomon was right. He said, Tom, there are only two kind of people in the world, leaders and followers. And I didn't believe him. But he was right. You're just a follower, Charlie.' For a moment the mop stopped and I watched as a line of water ran off along the length of the bar. Then he put down the mop and started to walk away. 'That's right, walk off. Walk away. You're a waste of fuckin' time! I once asked you why you worked behind a bar, do you remember that? Do you remember what you said? You said because I'm already a rich man. And do you know what? I actually believed you. But the truth of it is, you mop floors because you are a follower, a gutless arse-licker. You're no better than Rimmer. But at least Rimmer knows what's good for him. He knows how to better himself. He hangs around Solomon because he knows it'll benefit him. And I'd rather be like Solomon than you any day of the week.'

I knew I'd hurt him and I was angry with myself because it hadn't been my original intention. He'd only got as far as the end of the bar, but when I'd finished my rant he stopped and walked back towards me. He then spoke softly and slowly, as he always did. 'I understand you, Tommy, and I know what men like Solomon do. He's lulled you in and cut out all the goodness. You've no idea. A boy in a man's world, that's what you are. I told you to steer clear of Larry and Solomon but you didn't listen... because if you had you wouldn't be sat there like a fool.'

His huge hands were on top of the bar and I felt afraid—not because of his size, but of what he said. Most of it was right, but he was wrong on one point. I wasn't a boy anymore. Over those three years in London, I had become a man—and a dangerous one at that.

'Fuck you, old man! Fuck you! That's just what I'd expect you to say. If you want to work in this shit hole, if you want to waste your life cleaning up after people less capable than yourself, that's fine by me. Just don't make me feel bad because I don't. I've done well. You

God's Will

should be proud of me!' My voice was shaking with anger and shame. He heard it and understood why, but he didn't say a thing. He just stared at me across the bar. His silence was infuriating. 'Who the hell do you think you are, anyway? Fuck you! Fuck you!'

There was a small tower of glass ashtrays in the middle of the bar and before I knew it I'd swiped them across at him. They smashed into him with such force he was knocked back against the counter. One of them had hit him on the side of the head and blood trickled from the cut through his white hair. At first I thought he was going to fall but, steadying himself, he just looked back at me. I couldn't look at him, though. Not directly—not into his eyes, so I watched the blood staining his pure white hair. In a moment like that it isn't just hatred you feel. Even for the most twisted of minds. There's also a sense of disgust in what you've done. It sits alongside all the other emotions your actions have brought into play. Guilt, shame, pity. The thing is, I'd reached such a point I didn't choose to acknowledge such emotions anymore. Conscience was something I'd learned to live without; I found it took more than it gave. As if carried back by the tension of the moment, I thought of the first day we met. I had seen then a sense of pride in Charlie, and I understood it came from how he saw himself in the world, but in that moment as we faced one another I saw a different kind of pride. The type that is found in knowing your instincts were right all along.

God knows what he saw in my eyes. It's possible, I suppose, he could see the shame I denied myself. I never did find out. I would only see Charlie one more time before my arrest, but I realise now it's what we shared in that final encounter that changed his view of me.

I stormed out in a rage and walked towards Shaftesbury Avenue. Half of me wanted to go back and face Charlie again, but there was still enough of the old me to keep me going away from Milton's; some

God's Will

rational thinking was still possible. After a few minutes I decided the best thing to do was get a taxi to the Rotella and sleep it off in one of the upstairs rooms. I didn't want to go back to Larry's flat (by then I had given up my own); it was too depressing and not a place to be when sober.

Any other day I would have waved down a taxi and been at the casino in a matter of minutes, but for some reason that morning I couldn't find a taxi. When I did see one I jumped in front of it to stop it. It wasn't until it passed with a blare of the horn that I saw it already had a fare, not that it didn't stop me screaming abuse in its wake.

'You could always get a bus,' said a female voice from the pavement. I was preparing to transfer my venom from the taxi to the newcomer, when the horn of an oncoming bus forced me to dive onto the pavement. 'Unless, of course, you're run down by one,' she added, smiling down at me.

It was Stella. I hadn't seen her for a couple of years, even longer than Charlie, but unlike my relationship with him, our relationship hadn't so much ended as faded into nothing. That's if you could call it a relationship. It was just sex after all.

'Come on, I'm too old to pick you up. What is it then, your chauffeur's day off?'

I brushed myself down. 'Stella. How are you?'

'Ah, you know me. Getting old but getting by. Anyway, never mind about me, you're the talk of the town. Solomon's favourite boy, I hear?'

'Save it, eh?' Somehow I managed to say this with a smile.

'You been to see Charlie then?'

We were just around the corner and I guess she had put two and two together. I tried to ignore the question by having another go at flagging down a taxi, but then I would have done anything to hide the shame burning inside. It occurred to me then that if I had got a taxi

God's Will

straightaway, or turned along another road, I wouldn't have even see her and she would have seen Charlie in that state. I tried to tell myself it meant something. That it was a moment of kismet. Anything other than what it was, a simple coincidence that would have a terrible outcome.

'Well, better get to work…'

'Don't go,' I said suddenly. I had to stop her. I didn't want her to find Charlie the way I'd left him. I had to redeem myself. 'Why don't you take the day off and come out with me?'

'How can I take a bloody day off?'

'Because I'm your boss and I say so.'

She was genuinely surprised, but I could tell by her bashful smile she was flattered. I would like to think it was because of my charm, but I admit it was more to do with my success. Slipping a ton into her hand I winked and suggested she should pamper herself.

'Tommy, I can't…'

'Yes, you can. I'll organise a replacement, don't worry about that. Now go on. I'll pick you up at seven.'

'Are you sure?'

'Of course I'm sure. Now go home. I want you looking beautiful,' I said, eventually flagging down a taxi.

As it stopped, I kissed her on the cheek. She got inside and, even as it pulled away, I knew I was merely putting off the inevitable. The truth was, I didn't want to take her out, any more than I wanted to be running Solomon's organisation. I just didn't want her to hate me as well. The only way I seemed to be able to control my life was by being one step ahead of the hurt I was causing. I couldn't stop what I was doing anymore. With Solomon it was natural. He had perfected the art of manipulating the outcome so nothing touched him. But I didn't have that skill. I couldn't even control my own emotions, let alone anyone else's. The long and short of it was that even though I had changed, I

God's Will

still had some conscience left. Not much, but enough to make me worthless in Solomon's world. Things were moving too fast and the best I could do was hurriedly remove the obstacles before the impact came.

I remember very little of that afternoon. I may have bathed or watched television. All I do remember is thinking the last thing I wanted to do in the world was have a meal with the loud and brash Stella T. I nearly got one of the boys to go round and tell her something had come up, but in the end I got the same man to collect her and take her to The Ivy. That would at least be an hour less in her company. As I went out I caught a glimpse of myself in the mirror. I was surprised how well I looked, considering what I'd put myself through. I was still only twenty-six and at that age the body and mind can take so much more stress and strain. I felt a lot more energised after a restful afternoon and there was a spring in my step as I emerged into the sunset. Maybe things weren't as bad as I thought. Maybe the storm was over and I was at last entering calmer waters.

It was a warm London night and the city was bathed in a red glow from the melting sun. I could smell spices from the curry houses, coffee from the thousands of cafés, and even the fragrance from the flower stalls over at Covent Garden. I was stimulated by the mixture. I could see Stella's blonde curls from behind the menu as I entered the room. The headwaiter, André, saw me straightaway and took me over to the table personally. I apologised for my lateness and kissed Stella quickly on her cheek. I got a powdery film of foundation on my lips. I disdainfully wiped it off with a napkin as she glanced back at the menu, then ordered a bottle of Dom Perignon and a whisky chaser and chatted briefly with André. She loved it all.

'Do you know him?' she whispered.

God's Will

'André? Of course.' The look of admiration in her eyes was quite moving. It was strange to see my advancement reflected in someone who had known me from the beginning of my London adventure. 'Now, have you ordered?'

'If I could understand it I would. It's all in bleedin' French!'

I laughed. 'You look fantastic.'

'Thank you. You don't look too bad yourself. Well, better than this afternoon, anyway.'

To my surprise we had a great night. Presumably mellowed by my success, Stella behaved differently that night. Almost like a young woman on a first date. We laughed and joked as before, and after months with Julia it was nice to relax with a woman I didn't care that much for. We talked about everything—Milton's, the regulars, acts from the show and, finally, our sessions in the club after hours. No doubt it was that recollection that made her touch my hand over coffee.

'Tommy, I won't forget this.'

The comment really shook me. I'd only invited her out so she wouldn't see Charlie as I'd left him but, of course, she didn't know that. To her it meant something. 'Where now then?'

'Back to mine?' she said before noticing my raised eyebrow. 'For a drink, you saucy sod! Just a drink. I realised today that you've never seen my flat. I'd like you to see it.'

I spoke softly. 'I would love to.'

Collecting another couple of bottles of champagne we went across the city to her flat. The outside of it reminded me of my home up north. It had that same blackened red brick, stained by decades of lead and soot. Even the windows had a look of sadness about them—a look of resentment as if the house had found itself in the wrong part of town. Inside, the staircase was broad, with bare steps that echoed every step and sigh. Once it was home to a family with servants—a place where

God's Will

love and happiness filled the air, a place where children would have run from room to room, a place where those same children could mature in a safe environment. But over the years it had been carved up into boxes. There were no longer living rooms or bedrooms or dining rooms, but individual worlds where lonely people waited for their luck to change, or to qualify for work that would take them elsewhere.

Stella's little world was on the second floor.

She giggled as she fumbled with the lock and as I watched her I knew I wanted her again. The way it had been before I met Larry; no-strings-attached fun for two. The flat was small yet tidy, with the scent of lavender. Not real lavender, but the type you get from a can, an imitation that lessens the original by association. Everything in Stella's home was a cheap reproduction of something, not in itself worth having. She was like my mother in lots of ways, trying to make her existence a little better by copying what she felt was stylish on as little money as possible. Christ, I hated that. It really got my back up. But I didn't let it show. I wasn't going to ruin my chances of a bit of slap and tickle because of a dislike for chintz.

Stella put on some music and, with an easy charm, swayed as she fixed the drinks. I don't actually recall who was talking or what the subject was, but I remember I wasn't contributing very much. I was thinking too much of what I wanted to do to her. She had her back to me as I approached. There was that wonderful rush as I placed my hands on her hips and slid them round to her flat belly. Her dress was made of polyester or something equally cheap, but it was just that cheapness I'd missed. She was different from Julia and her friends. Stella's commonness felt more appealing for some reason.

'I thought we were just having a drink,' she said, and I could feel the tension in her body. 'Come on, let's just have a drink.' I shrugged

God's Will

the remark off and kissed her neck. It only forced a laugh from her. 'Tommy! You sod. Get off.'

'Come on, Stella, we used to be great together.'

'I know,' she said, her tone still light. 'But things are different now. Besides, I'm *up*.'

Up was her way of saying she was having her period. But as I felt her large breasts through the smoothness of her cheap dress, I knew even that wouldn't stop me.

'Get off me!' The tone was still light, diluted by a little laugh, but there was also an element of caution, fear almost.

I could feel her semi-hard nipples through her bra, and I hoped from that she was just playing hard to get. It's what men like to think. Suddenly the resistance stopped and, as she twisted to face me, I kissed her.

She stiffened. 'Is this what *she* likes? A bit of rough?'

'Who?' I murmured, nuzzling her neck.

'Who? You know who.'

She was serious now, and so was I. 'Who?'

'Julia. Your lover.'

The comment had the desired effect. 'What did you say?'

'You heard me. You're a bloody fool, Tommy. It's common knowledge. The only person who doesn't know is Solomon. You think you're so clever, don't you? I decided to come out with you not because I think you're God's gift, but because I like you. In a way I feel partially responsible. Tonight was just about warning you. You have to watch yourself, Tommy. Solomon's a nasty bastard. You think Henderson was bad? You wait until you see Solomon go off on one. He's mad… as mad as his son. And that's common knowledge as well!'

'Shut up.'

'He's in a mental hospital in the States because he's gone loopy.'

God's Will

'Shut up.'

'Do you know why he's loopy? Because he's just like you, weak at heart, but still trying to give it the big I am!'

'Shut up!'

'And as for your beloved Julia. You think she's so classy? Did you know she was a whore until Solomon took her off the streets? Half of London's been through her!'

'Shut the fuck up!' Gripping her arm with my left hand I slapped her hard across her face. She started to laugh but tears were in her eyes and soon she was sobbing, but it didn't stop her.

'Charlie was wrong about you. You're not worth saving! You're just a little boy trying to play it tough in a man's world.' The words were like wasps, intent on damage. Individually I could deal with them, but in a swarm they were impossible to deflect. 'Charlie said we should help you, but not now.'

I was reeling. I despised her and I wanted more than anything to show her I *was* a man and she was wrong. I pushed her back against the ridiculous small drinks bar she had against one wall. As she went back she twisted to her side and I took the opportunity to complete the turn by forcing her head down, knocking the drinks onto the floor. She was screaming for me to get off. But my blood was up and I wanted to silence her. Pulling up her dress I grabbed the top of her knickers and ripped them down as far as her knees. She tried to force herself up, but I was too strong for her. She had given me the strength. I forced her down again and made myself ready, while noticing the deep scarlet stain in the pad in her little azure knickers lying on the floor. I didn't see it as a distraction.

I don't remember entering her but I was aware afterwards how unnatural it felt to be inside a woman during her time. Holding her hands down I went through the motions of love. But this was as far as

God's Will

you could get from love. This was an empty gesture, one that would taint us both and affect our view of love and passion always. It didn't last long, but a second after I'd finished I am sure, even to this day, that I have never felt so empty. With her blood coating me I fell back onto the sofa and watched her still draped across the bar. In my empty state she was no longer desirable. She was almost like a child. The defiance had been replaced by a sobbing that came from a place deep within her, undiscovered until that moment.

With shaking hands she pushed herself up, then straightened her dress and stumbled to the bedroom. All of this was done with her back to me, and done with all the dignity she could muster.

* * *

Bepa is silent. She has listened without interruption. Barely a cough has passed her dying lips. She breathes, she sighs, yet she passes no judgement on him, and for that he is beholden.

She is my confessor. Forgive me, for I have sinned.

32

To his frustration, Reid found the journey to Corazona much longer than anticipated. This was mostly due to the young taxi driver who was not familiar with the village and needed to ask directions along the way. After an hour Reid believed he had been hoodwinked—never trust the whore wife of a crooked copper, he told himself. And then, success. An old woman selling fruit at the roadside gave the skinny driver with the greased-back hair direct instructions that he seemed to understand.

God's Will

'Remote!' he announced, jumping back in the car, clearly disgusted at the village forefathers' choice of location. 'Far off the well-travelled road!'

As well as the colloquial chatter and colourful music from the radio, a thousand questions screamed in Reid's head. Why now? Why at the end of his life had he found things he had searched for so long? Could he not have stumbled across these revelations, these witnesses, when he was younger, before he had had time to push all that he loved and needed through the shredder?

Hold your horses, Reidy. You haven't discovered a thing yet.

He felt his heart racing as the taxi pulled off the main road to Almeria. It was followed by a sudden stabbing pain in the centre of his chest. He gulped down a white tablet the hospital had given him for such moments and loosened his shirt collar.

A few minutes later the pain subsided and in quiet repose he watched as the driver slowly steered the car around the hillside and down towards the calming turquoise sea. He could already see the small cluster of brightly coloured buildings along the shoreline below. Corazona beckoned.

Unknowingly, Reid overpaid the driver and made directly for a taverna by the water's edge. He wanted a drink; he wanted to calm himself. Mostly he wanted to be ready when the moment came. Julia had informed him of Levy's alias—Señor Seagrove, the man from Corazona—and described the white house with the pretty terracotta roof up the hill, the one with the redundant bleached-white concrete swimming pool and the partially dead, partially horizontal olive tree at the front.

After a difficult climb up a relatively easy slope he found his objective as described and rested against the wide trunk of the half-dead tree. The smells of olive and eucalyptus filled his nostrils and he

God's Will

was briefly reminded of his honeymoon in Malta decades before. The pain in his chest made a sudden return so he took another tablet before walking to the door. Halfway there a tall, dark-haired girl walked out. They stared at one another for a moment before she enquired in Spanish if she could help him. He replied in English that he hoped that she could.

'I am looking for a man called Seagrove.'

The girl's smile was a brief one. Her eyes narrowed and she backed towards the door. Then she was gone. A moment later another woman appeared, this one older. Reid knew it to be Maria. Julia had talked of her simple beauty and greying black hair. There was a detached, cautious look on her face. She was studying him. If she didn't trust Julia, what would she make of a man who threatened to bring disruption into her life?

Reid repeated that he was looking for Seagrove. Maria's reply was brief and her accent strong, guttural and low. 'He used to live here but not anymore, señor.'

'I was informed that he is still here. He was seen just a couple of weeks ago.'

'You are wrong. He is not anymore, now please go.'

'Maybe if I told you who gave me this information you may think differently.'

'I doubt that.'

'Does the name Julia Culbertson mean anything to you?' Nothing. 'Once known as Julia Solomon.'

A look of disgust spread across her proud brown features. Reid was certain she was about to spit out venom in response to the name, but before she could do a thing there was a terrible howl from inside the white house with the pretty terracotta roof. Reid pushed past her and went inside.

God's Will

The inside of the house was tidy but dark. Reid hurried along the hall and found himself in a spacious living room. At first glance it appeared empty, but then, on the far side of the room, silhouetted against a wide window, he made out a large wicker chair with its back to him. As his eyes became accustomed to the dim light he discerned a hand drooping over one arm of the chair, trembling. Reid moved towards it quickly but cautiously as Maria and her daughter entered the hallway behind him. Maybe because he already knew it was Levy, a hardened criminal with a history of violent crime, he gave the chair a wide berth, arriving face to face with the occupant with his back to the window. Maria entered the room at the same time.

Levy was bearded and thin and his face was ashen, but Reid recognised him in an instant. In the light of the window he registered the man's vacant stare. Saliva ran from his blue lips, down his white whiskers and onto a heavily scarred bare chest. Now Maria and the girl was stationary at his side, Reid could hear the whimper of a man in a great deal of pain. He wasn't sure what he was expecting, but it wasn't this. Julia had told him the truth.

'So you have found him, what now?' asked Maria, squatting by the chair and wiping away the dribble from Levy's chin. 'You bury him in England instead of here? What is the difference?'

'My name is Reid. I just want to talk to him.'

'Like that whore, Julia?' She took out a small bottle from a pocket in her apron and daubed a little of the contents on Levy's lips. This triggered an instant response and the corpse rose, its eyes fixed on the other man. Reid braced and prepared for an imminent attack. But it never came. A moment later Levy fell back into the chair, exhausted and coated in sweat.

Maria choked back tears. 'Why don't you all leave him alone? Hasn't he gone through enough in his life?' Reid, angered by the

God's Will

comment and aware that Levy was in no condition to be questioned, slowly made for the door. Maria stopped him with more words, this time a plea. 'Don't go, Señor Reid.'

He looked back from the hallway, wondering at her sudden change of attitude. 'Why?'

She rose slowly. 'I know who you are. I hate you. I hate you all, but he needs you. He will never say it but he needs you as much as you need him.'

33

The next day Sickert is led to Bepa's room. They talk generally about everything, from their respective childhoods, London, even the weather, but she never makes comment on the previous night's revelations. Then Bepa rings a little bell, similar to Sickert's own, and Philip appears, his heavy feet thumping across the floorboards to the bedside. There is a clatter of cutlery, plates and glass. A small meal of cold rabbit, eggs, dry bread and wine is consumed in silence. It is warmer now and Sickert knows the weather has changed for the better; he can feel shafts of winter sunlight caressing his bare ankles. Nothing is said, not a word. He suspects Bepa will say nothing until he has told her everything. She is hanging onto life, reserving her failing spirit for his revelation. There is something in the air, something profound and boundless, that tells him that there is a compelling reason for their supposedly chance meeting.

And once again he goes back.

* * *

God's Will

From Stella's flat I wandered out into the darkest part of the night. It hid me beneath its cloak for a short time, until the dawn came and the sun revealed me to the world. By then I was at the Thames. I wasn't thinking of suicide, though. I was too much of a coward for that. It had something to do with the eternal repetition of ebb and flow, the pull of the moon, the cycles of time. The dark waters reminded me of what had gone before, and what may soon follow. It was around seven in the morning when I eventually walked into the Rotella. There I found them waiting for me. But not for the reasons I first thought. I'd got it into my head that Stella would have screamed blue murder after I'd gone and that Levy and the boys would use it as a reason for getting rid of me. But I was wrong again.

'Where the fuck have you been?' Levy was part of a large group of the boys around the bar. 'We got trouble. Lemmy Bones is dead.'

Lemmy Bones was a doddery old gay who ran one of Solomon's fruit machine arcades in Soho. He wasn't actually called Bones; it was a nickname given to him on account of him once being a rag-and-bone man and also the skinniest man in London. I didn't show any emotion at this. My mind was elsewhere. I fixed myself a drink as Levy gave me the details. At some point during the previous evening a group of men from a rival gang run by a Greek called Nicholas Jannaidos had walked into the arcade, robbed it, smashed it up and shot old Lemmy dead. I was hearing all this, but because of recent events I wasn't really taking it in. It wasn't until I had finished my drink and poured another that I was aware that everything had gone quiet.

'Well?' said Levy.

'Well what?' I muttered.

'What do we do?'

God's Will

In that moment it occurred to me that this was all a pack of lies. Maybe I was being set up, or at least tested. They hated my guts and wanted me out of the way. After a moment I quickly concluded that that sort of scheming was way beyond men like Levy. I stared at them all for a moment. Then suddenly I saw Stella in my mind's eye. She was right, of course. They all knew.

If it had happened at any other time, I don't know what I would have done. But stained as I was because of my actions, I felt the urge to redeem myself again, to do the opposite of what I'd done the day before to my old friends. I had no feelings for old Lemmy whatsoever. It was all about redressing the balance and showing that roomful of scum there was more to me than just fucking my boss's wife.

'So you think its Nicki the Greek?' I said, my gaze fixed somewhere beyond the room.

'I'm sure of it,' Levy replied. 'What do we do? We need to move quickly. Too much time has gone already…'

I was hoping he would stop there. But he didn't. He just kept repeating the same points over and over. *We need to move… What are we going to do?.. How are we going to do it?* He just wouldn't shut up. I wanted to smash the glass in his face, anything just to stop him talking. I could feel a rush of pressure running through me, from my feet to my chest, and although I wasn't aware of it the feeling forced the glass from my hand. As it smashed on the far wall the sound was flat and empty. Then I turned slowly and said, a little too calmly for my own comfort, 'Let's go then.'

It took us most of the day to track him down. Nicki the Greek owned a lot of scrapyards around London, but in the end it was his flash Rolls that gave him away. The day was very hot and sticky and around lunchtime we stopped for a drink somewhere in the East End. We'd only been there for about ten minutes when the car rolled by,

God's Will

along Barking Road. Rushing back to the cars, we caught up with him and stayed close until he pulled into one of his sex shops in Soho, another of his sidelines. We went in mob-handed but in a calm and orderly fashion—if we gangsters have anything, it's style. As we piled in, one by one, I remember thinking how proud Solomon would have been. I could never be him completely, but no one could accuse me of not having a little of his panache.

Once inside the Greek's office it soon became clear it would be a tight fit for all of us but, not wanting to be left out, everybody forced themselves in anyway. The room was even hotter than outside; there was nowhere for the heat to escape—no windows, no vents. Instead there were just lots and lots of shelves with files and journals in conservative colours, navy blues and racing greens. Nothing gaudy, and nothing out of place, except for us, that is. As we pressed in Nicki didn't speak for a moment or two. He just looked up at us all; and in that silence I watched him. He seemed surprised, but he didn't show an ounce of fear. What really surprised me was his age. I'd seen him about, but up close I realised he was a lot younger than I thought.

'What's this then? Avon calling?' he said, with a cheery smile.

Levy, never one for witty retorts, kept the conversation to a minimum by throwing the desk out of our way. Then, after straightening his tie, he forced Nicki up against the wall. Just above his head there was a picture of the Queen and Prince Philip, which, when I considered the Greek connection made me smile, despite the situation.

'You're not gonna sell many cosmetics with that approach, boys,' he said.

'Shut up!' Levy screamed, but still the Greek smiled. He smiled as he was given the reasons for our visit, and even as he discovered we were far from happy about his involvement in Lemmy Bones' death. I

God's Will

must admit, I was impressed. He was like Solomon in a way—he had flair.

'Look, why would I trouble Mr Solomon? Especially after all his problems recently, what with his hip trouble and his boy's mental state?'

'Be quiet,' said Levy, slapping him on the side of the head.

'No, I mean it. I wouldn't dare. Especially with the mighty Tommy Sickert in charge.'

I had liked him right up until that moment. He was laughing at me and I couldn't help but think that unless I did something quickly the rest of them would be, too.

'What do we do with him?' said Levy.

If this was a fit-up, or if in some way I was being tested, everything had been set up for that moment. The focus was on me; my reply would be everything. What I said in that moment would affect the rest of my life.

'He ain't gonna do nothing.' Nicki grinned. 'He's a lover not a fighter. Ain't that right, sonny boy? You only have to ask Solomon's other half to know that.'

The sardonic smile, the look of ridicule, all that he gave me in that moment would force my hand and finalise a chapter in both of our lives. I was at the peak, staring down the long winding road to hell. If only I hadn't turned onto that road and seen Stella. If only Lemmy Bones had had a day off. If only. In my head Stella's words were repeating over and over: *everybody knows but Solomon.*

'Kill him,' I said.

Two words. Just that. But they were words powerful enough to garner the respect I had wanted all my life. I didn't look at their faces. I didn't have to. I had in a moment secured their reverence.

Show time.

God's Will

'What?' said Levy, with an inflection I hadn't thought possible. It was a good moment that—a clear and special one. It revealed to me the type of fear I had shown to him the night he had beaten me at Milton's. 'You can't kill without Solomon's say-so,' he said almost in disbelief.

'Yes, I can. Kill him.'

'We can't kill him, Tommy!'

Fucking hell-fire. Tommy. He actually called me Tommy. That was it. 'Give me the gun.'

I wasn't panicking or shaking or lost in a corrupt world. I was calm, reasonable. I was making my point. This was no Aristotle. This Greek would never see his part in the complexity of life. All he understood was the game, and now so did I. He was still smiling because he believed he was safe. His pasty, unshaven face and glib smile didn't help his case either. By then I simply didn't like him.

'You can't kill me...' he said, his grin broadening.

But he was wrong. Reaching into Levy's jacket I took out his old Webley and shot the smile off Nicki's face. The noise was louder than I had expected. When it faded it was replaced by the deepest silence I had ever known. Nothing could have prepared me for that moment. Blood was never so dark, emptiness so wide and loneliness so complete. More than anything I wanted to show them what I was all about; I wanted to prove myself when the moment came. Now the moment was gone and the pain was eternal.

I don't remember going out and I don't remember giving up the gun, but both things occurred in the few minutes afterwards. The next thing I actually remember was holding my hands firmly on the frame of the car door outside. I was gripping with everything I had, stopping the others pushing me inside. I don't know why. Maybe because I thought they would then do to me what I had done to Nicki. I put my strength down to the adrenaline rising through me like helium. It was the

God's Will

opposite of what I expected to feel. I was so high I felt I could fly. Somehow I freed myself from their grip and ran along the busy street. For a while I could hear footsteps behind, but soon all I could hear were my own. I was young, don't forget, just twenty-six, and guilty as hell.

I wandered through the streets for most of that day and thought about many things. Most were too painful to dwell on, especially those that dealt with recent events. I tried to take myself back to my childhood. How I would have gladly exchanged one moment there for that nightmarish day in the heat of the city. Dusk came with a thick strip of heavy cloud that skirted the capital, flirting with the prospect of rain. Oddly it didn't touch the horizon, and beneath its lowest part it was possible to see a narrow gleam of orange sky. I was crossing Tower Bridge when it happened. I remember thinking that if I had been at any other part of the city at that point, I would have appreciated little of its majesty I wasn't the only one aware of the impending magic, either; although many continued their journey home, there were still some who found the beauty too irresistible to ignore. We all knew it was coming, and when it came and the sun dipped from the cloud into the breach the moment was spectacular. Beneath the curtain of cloud the air was clear, and the sun, bright and proud, warmed my face like never before. Then it was gone, and with it I became aware of the crowd going past. The people who passed me that day didn't see me. They saw the shell of what I had become. They saw the hand-made suit and manicured hands of a successful man, but what they didn't see, and couldn't see, was the dying man inside. I heard a voice in my head. Charlie. A snippet of wisdom that had stayed with me. *If all you know about a man is what he tells you, you know nothing about him at all.* How right he was. I had convinced Solomon I was something special, but I was nothing. A dreamer, nothing more.

God's Will

Concealed by the gloom of dusk, I made my way north towards Soho and Milton's. I wasn't in control. It was the landscape and the thoughts in my head that governed my path. I saw this as clearly as I saw the dead Greek lying at my feet.

From the street I could hear music. It was a Wednesday—mid-week cabaret. As I descended the steps I felt the first drop of rain. Naively I tried to forget all that had happened and cast my mind back to a simpler time, of starting my shift behind the bar. All I wanted was Charlie to talk to. He would know what to do. He would have the answer, but as I entered the building, I died once more as I heard Stella's voice from the stage.

It was as if I was travelling through the tables on a conveyor belt. People drank and talked unaware of my presence, but I wasn't looking down. My focus was fixed on something higher. Stella had just started. I knew this because she was singing 'Cheek to cheek'. She had told me it was an easy song to start with. The dance floor was empty and I crossed it slowly, trance-like. She saw me, I'm sure, but didn't look down at me once. She just sang, her gaze lost in the cloud of smoke above the tables. As I reached the stage her voice faded away, quickly followed by the band as each instrument fell silent. It didn't stop me, though. Nothing would. I climbed the steps behind her, but she didn't look round. Apart from the noise of my feet on the wooden stage and the occasional clink of glass there was silence throughout the club. As I approached her from behind, I suddenly tripped on the cable from her microphone. There was a gasp from the audience, but somehow I managed to stay on my feet. Still Stella didn't look round. As I reached her I saw her eyes were closed and she was holding the microphone tight against her breast. Drunkenly I fell onto her and held her tight. Tears were rolling down my cheeks and I was pleading with her to forgive me. How long I held onto her I don't know, but when I felt an

God's Will

arm on mine, I looked up to see the lights in the club on and Charlie by my side.

'It's okay, son,' he said softly. 'It's okay now.'

As I descended from the stage I could see figures standing at the periphery of the dance floor. It wasn't until I got close I saw who they were. The news of my downfall had travelled far. Staring at me with varying degrees of contempt were Solomon and Larry.

As I was led out there was a feeling that I find almost impossible to describe now. But I'll put it like this. Imagine every moment of joy and despair in your life, all their intensity and pain fused together so completely there is no way of pulling it apart, no way to separate the good from the bad. You pull at it until your fingers bleed, but it can't be done, because the white heat of your actions has bonded them together forever. If you can imagine that, then you are halfway to understanding what I went through from that day on. There was so much of it, I couldn't think clearly. It formed inside me another layer of myself. Eventually I would find a way of controlling it, but that was all it was. It didn't die; it got stronger. The problem is, I never realised the extent of the damage until now.

34

Maria made them a weak sangria and served up a small selection of tapas before apologising for the unusually hot temperature for the time of year and smearing Reid's sunburnt face and scalp with aloe vera, which grew naturally in the garden. The soft touch from another human being made for an uncomfortable experience, but the soothing results were much appreciated.

God's Will

The light lunch sat between them on a low table in the little garden at the back of the house, like a peace offering. A gentle smile had found its way to Maria's lips as she prepared the food and reminisced about the area and her childhood. Reid took some of it in but found Levy's comatose state through the window too compelling. Even ravaged by illness it still seemed possible (to Reid at least) that this eternal warrior could be placed on any battlefield and he would rise to the challenge. From the many photographs he had in his collection, he estimated that the man had lost three or four stone but he was still tall and heavy-boned and he hoped for his own sake that Maria was correct when she said he was not the violent man who had terrorised London all those years ago.

Reid complemented Maria on the well-maintained garden—a complete contrast to the one at the front—and delicious food before asking her how it was possible Levy was still alive. Her explanation seemed well-rehearsed, but he realised the concise answer was as much to do with her own peace of mind as anything else.

After Solomon's death Levy had been a man without a purpose. He had never worked legally in his life and therefore had never paid tax or national insurance. The only official documents that proved he existed at all were his birth certificate and his school records, and they were destroyed in the Blitz. Amazingly, considering he had had chosen a criminal life, he had never been arrested. Thanks to men like Solomon and Bexley he had avoided the courts. Officially, Jack Levy didn't exist.

After drifting from job to job—working as a doorman, debt collector, bare-knuckle fighter—he had finally found himself in the employ of one of Thatcher's young entrepreneurs, a young drug dealer who got out of his depth before he had even started. One winter's night in eighty-one Levy and his youthful employer were ambushed by a

God's Will

group of axe-wielding competitors. Levy was of the old school and loyalty came with the hours, even for drug dealers who didn't give a damn for anyone. The kid was no fighter and he was hacked to pieces —cue Levy's last stand. He was badly cut up and bleeding profusely, but somehow he got away. Calling in some old debts, he had located a doctor (a recently struck-off individual who had become a little too well-known in the abortion racket), a passport and, after a quick phone call to his old friend and lover Julia, a plane ticket to sunny Spain. Julia had met him at Malaga airport. The rest, Maria said, was history.

Reid asked no questions. He listened in silence, sipping at his sangria and picking chorizo from his teeth, but mostly he studied the man in the window. Everything around him, including this remarkable señora was alien to him, but he felt at peace here in this foreign place full of revelation.

'Julia and Jack were lovers in England,' Maria explained. 'I don't know when. He talks to me about everything. He is a haunted man. He is a dying man.'

'Dying from what?'

'He got a taste for cocaine in London, no doubt from his drug-dealing boss. I was a nurse for many years in Malaga. I met him at a centre for sufferers of HIV. He had progressed from cocaine to heroin. Dirty needles, I am afraid, is the sad explanation.'

'Jack Levy is dying of Aids?' Reid shook his head in dismay. Another revelation—how many more? 'Your daughter?'

'From my first marriage. She knows very little of his past and I would like it to remains so.'

'Does he still have feelings for her? Julia, I mean. Is that why you hate her?'

She leaned forward and placed her crossed arms on her mocha-coloured knees. 'No, I am not jealous. She just reminds him of the past.

God's Will

That unhappy past. I will never understand why you British have to live your lives to such excess.'

'Put it down to the climate,' he joked, but without a smile. There was a very long pause before he spoke again. 'Was he there that night? The night of the kidnapping? Does he know what really happened?'

'Yes,' she said, as if it was a great relief to share it with him. 'And it has haunted him ever since.'

The more Greene drinks and the more potent the liquor, the more vivid the nightmare becomes. The dream has changed. Instead of waking at the discovery of the bludgeoned man at the door, he is now unbound and able to travel inside the house. The staircase is open before him, offering itself to him. He knows what he has to do and where to go. His vision flashes with fear and panic but he climbs to the top as he had planned. Finding the nursery, he hesitates at the door. Hoping to find her alone with her doll he opens the door, only to discover it partially blocked from the other side. He knows what it is and what he is about to see, but there is this tiny glimmer of hope deep inside giving him the belief that this time it may be different. He forces the door fully open— only to find nothing has changed. There he finds another body, this time a woman. Like the man, her head is so battered her long blonde hair is mottled with flesh and blood. He knows in that moment that all his plans are wasted. He is too late. This is hell and he has found death. He hears a car outside. He runs to the door but steps on the woman's hair. In the moonlight he can see blood on his shoe. He knows what this means and that he should be thinking of his own survival, but instead he is appalled at how disrespectful he is being.

Greene wakes to find himself in the chair before the window in his flat, tears on his face, his seat sodden with urine. His head is aching and his dehydrated body is consumed with cramps and aches. This hell is in

God's Will

his head for a reason. It will stay there because this is worse than a nightmare... this is a memory.

Mid-afternoon, Greene went to Muswell Hill. Enough was enough. If he couldn't change the past and if there was no possible way of ending his nightmare he would do the only thing that was open to him. Changing into the remaining set of spare clothes he had, he got a bus from Tottenham Court Road, though not before quickly consuming a couple of espressos at a small cafe on New Portland Street. People in the queue stared at him and didn't come too close. He didn't care. He thought of the Ghouls and laughed aloud. The space around him grew larger.

An hour later he was back at his former residence. At first there was no response. Then, as he glanced across at the main window, he noticed a twitch of the curtain. He banged again and again until finally Angie appeared and opened the door on the chain.

'What do you want?'

'Derby.'

'He's not here.'

'Angie, I don't have the energy. I need to see him.'

'He's not here.'

'When will he be back?'

'He won't. He's gone. About a week ago. I don't know where he is.'

'I don't believe you.'

'Don't matter to me, you evil bastard!'

She must have seen it in his eyes as he drew his head back—the storm within him, an imminent explosion of anger that was about to spew. She slammed the door and retreated through the hall. He was seconds behind her, his shoulder smashing the door open, sending splinters and broken security chain in all directions as he crashed to the

God's Will

floor. He climbed to his feet breathlessly, wild eyes telling her that it was pointless reasoning with him. She stepped back as he rushed upstairs, clenched fists at his sides. Finding Denby's room empty, he screamed in despair then searched his own room and the adjoining bathroom before coming back down, this time more hurriedly. Denby's absence determined his next move. Angie was in the living room now. In a moment he had her by the hair up against the wall beneath the painting of the Mediterranean woman.

'Where is he?' he snarled, saliva dripping down his beard.

'Don't hurt me! I don't know. Really I don't. Please don't hurt me.'

Like a man waking from a dark and confusing dream, Greene slowly released her as his temper died. Then he was gone.

An hour later he was back in central London. Soho, Marylebone, Fitzrovia—one pub after another. In his drunken, mazy state he was lost, an echo of himself, a victim of his past. The only thing in his mind was Denby. Where was he? Feverishly he pursued his former housemate, but Denby was nowhere to be found.

Where the hell was he?

It was late afternoon but now a bank of cinnamon-coloured cumulus was crossing the city, cornering the sun into the western horizon. It still shone in places, but not on Greene. He walked for another hour until he realised he was lost. He got it into his head that he was near the British Museum, but he couldn't find his way. He was tired and cold and wanted to go home. As he reached a street corner, the sun suddenly appeared through the clouds and he slowed to appreciate the moment. It was only then that he realised where he was. Bloomsbury, near a place that was very special to Larry.

48 Doughty Street was the home of Charles Dickens for only a couple of years, but by the time he had moved on he had become

God's Will

famous throughout the world. In the early part of the twentieth century the house was converted into a museum. Once again, Greene knew this because of Larry. Within minutes he was at the door and going in. Inside, the house was exactly as it was all those years ago. A longish passageway led to a small cashier's desk surrounded by everything Dickensian—postcards, bookmarks, mugs, pictures, DVDs, audio tapes and, of course, books. Behind the small wooden counter sat a young woman armed with the empty smile so consistent with shopkeepers and waiters. Due to Greene's filthy state and smell she was at first hesitant to allow him access, but when he threw a handful of five-pound notes on the desk she realised she had little choice. As she counted out the change Greene glanced at a photograph of Dickens in later life. Studying his old whiskered face, he wondered what he would have made of the incident.

Each room was made out as it was when Dickens lived there with his young family. When he first visited, Larry gave him the tour. Now he did it alone, quite literally as it turned out; it was nearly closing time and he was the only visitor. Wandering from room to room, he could imagine the family going about their business. The smell of the place, not to mention its creaks and character, combined to give him an escape from the world and for a while he felt free. For half an hour he was lost within its timeless shell, each room reminding him a little more of Larry and those happy years they spent together. In the basement a video of Dickens' life played on a loop in a darkened room. He found a seat and watched it for a while. At the end, inevitably, the narrator described Dickens' death at Gad's Hill Place near Rochester. Greene wasn't listening; he was too haunted by his own past.

By early evening he was near his new home in Marylebone. It was a week day, but even then the pubs were teeming with business types treating themselves to some 'Dutch courage' before boarding the

God's Will

Marylebone and Euston trains home. Studying the small huddles of businessmen around the bar, he imagined what they did and what they made of the wild-looking man in the oversized coat (given to him by Angie) who came to join them. He wondered if his former landlady had contacted the police, probation board and Malory. Dismissing the probable answer, he finished another drink. And what about Denby? His disappearance confused him. Greene knew Denby would be looking for him. Henderson would be having kittens knowing he'd lost him. But why had Denby just disappeared like that? He ordered another brandy (damning Denby again) and tried not to sound drunk, which he was, considerably.

The landlady served him. Her look triggered something in him. She was mid-sixties, with long greying hair, and was wearing a green dress with a huge amount of jewellery. But it was the dress that caught his eye. There was something about it that reminded of him of someone a long time ago.

The sun was setting and in the faint light the glowing Telecom Tower seemed like a moon orbiting the city, its gravitational pull holding him in, forcing Greene to stay. Warmed by the brandy and longing for his bed, he stumbled across Euston Street and along Portland Place. On the other side of the road he spotted a man squatting on the pavement outside the Chinese Embassy. Then he remembered it was a silent protest against the ban on the Falun Gong religion in China. Each day there would be somebody there reminding the Chinese regime that despite torture and brutality they would not give in. Not that the Chinese took any notice, but there was the protestor anyhow. Greene watched for a moment or two as commuters hurried by, mindless of the little man at their feet. He really felt for him. It seemed such a pointless demonstration. Then he remembered Veronica Wood, the woman who was given a life sentence for killing her violent

God's Will

husband. How effective had her friends been in a similarly pointless protest? It was then that he realised whom the barmaid had reminded him of. Where, he wondered, was Veronica now?

As he was about to turn onto New Cavendish Street Greene became aware of an altercation on the corner. He knew London well enough not to get involved and walked on until a high-pitched wail stopped him in his tracks. It was a man, a man who sounded a little like Punch. In seconds he was at the scene, pushing his way through the small crowd of teens who had gathered. He couldn't believe his eyes. There was his elusive pal Denby, jumping up and down and screaming at the top of his voice. And the reason for his dismay? The Ghouls.

'Go away... damn you! Leave me alone!'

Denby was very, very drunk and springing up and down like a jack-in-the-box. But it was a moment before Greene realised why everyone was laughing. Denby had jumped up and down so vigorously he had impaled himself (his jacket anyhow) on a row of low railings directly behind him. What made it even funnier was that the Ghouls were unaware of this, and were awaiting payment for the scattered photographs under Denby's feet. Greene smiled at the farcical situation, but it was only funny for a second. Once he isolated himself from the moment, forgot the crowd and blanked out Denby's piercing voice he sensed the coldness of the two odd people, who seemed to live only for the night. They were as unaware of the crowd as they were of Greene, and for a worrying moment he was convinced that it was only him and Denby who could see them.

Angered by the baying crowd and eager to deal with his old pal, Greene stepped forward and stuffed a fiver in the male Ghoul's hand. As the man slowly turned to give him yet another handful of photos, Greene saw that lock of familiarity in his eyes again. What was it that stirred within him; where had he seen him before? Stuffing the photos

God's Will

into his pocket, he unhooked Denby from the railings and watched as he dropped onto the ground in a drunken heap. The show was over and in seconds the crowd and the Ghouls were gone. All that Greene could hear now was the squeaking of the pram as they disappeared into the night.

Denby, clearly not recognising his former housemate, scowled up at him. 'Not another one! What do you want?' He was as drunk as Greene and struggled to focus on his face. Then his eyes narrowed and a small smile washed across his lips. 'Thomas, you old scoundrel!' he spluttered, climbing to his knees. 'I didn't recognise you! I've been looking for you everywhere. How could you leave old Denby without saying goodbye?'

'I'm saying goodbye now.'

'Eh? What's that?'

'Get up.' Although Greene said it calmly, he was burning with rage.

'Did you pay 'em, Thomas? Did you pay the Ghouls?'

Greene didn't answer. He was too busy trying to decide whether to kick Denby in the head or not. Realising it would serve no purpose, he pulled him to his feet.

'That's very kind of you, old chap,' Denby responded. 'Are we going on somewhere?'

'You could say that, old boy,' Greene replied. 'You could say that.'

It wasn't far to go—just along the road—but as they walked a lot of thoughts busied themselves in Greene's mind. Was it coincidence that Denby was on Portland Place when the Ghouls cornered him? If it wasn't, it meant only one thing—Henderson knew where he lived. It was a bad few minutes for old Denby, because in that short time Greene came to a lot of conclusions, none of which put the drunk in a favourable light. It scared Greene what he was going to do, but he'd put up with enough. He just wanted to know what they wanted of him.

God's Will

Why couldn't they just leave him alone? Denby was mumbling something as they walked and at first Greene didn't listen. Rage had made him deaf to his rambling.

'I've got news for you, Thomas. Important news. You have to listen. Will you listen?'

'Oh, I'll listen. And you will talk.'

'I want to talk I want to tell you everything.'

Reaching the main entrance, Greene propped him against the wall and searched for his keys, but he never once took his eyes of Denby. Now he really did despise him, and soon the old bastard would know why. As they reached the second floor Greene noticed the light on his landing above was out, though he thought nothing of it as he hauled Denby up the next three flights. It was difficult to make progress as Denby kept stopping to hug him. And that just made Greene even angrier.

Then they were there. Greene's room was at the very end of the top floor corridor, which was almost impossible to make out in the darkness. Above the noise of Denby's gasping, Greene heard a noise ahead of them. He stopped and peered into the gloom. Something was wrong; he sensed it deeply. His fear was realised a second later when a dark shape rushed towards them out of the blackness. The sudden pain from a blow to the centre of his forehead sent him crashing to the floor. Whoever it was had considerable strength because no matter how much he tried, he couldn't get up. Sober he may have stood a chance, but with seven or eight brandies washing around inside him it was an impossible task. So instead he lay still in the darkness, listening to Denby's pleas for help as he was dragged down the stairs and out onto the street.

God's Will

35

Sickert isn't sure if Philip is still in the room or if Bepa is even awake anymore. It doesn't matter now. This is for him. He needs to justify the pain he feels. It is there for a reason.

* * *

After the scene on the stage with Stella, I was led from Milton's in the capable hands of Levy and another man who had been with me at Nicki the Greek's end. Solomon and Larry went in another car. It was late and we drove along deserted streets polished by the rain. I stared blankly at the passing buildings and pondered my obsession with the city. Why did I love it so? Why do I still love it?

At Regent's Park the golden dome of the mosque glowed in the rain like a midnight sun. The city seemed still and contented, unaware of my insanity. As I thought of this I came to the conclusion that it was life's failures that made London what it was. To every successful story there were a thousand like mine—great acts of desperation and wickedness that we all have the ability to perform and which combine to expand the fabric. To my surprise, we didn't go to the Rotella as I had suspected but continued out to the suburbs. Would it just be a bullet to the head? Regardless of what I had done for Solomon over those months, it would be much simpler for him to get rid of me.

After half an hour without a stop, I realised where we were going and I sat back and slept. I hadn't had any rest for over twenty-four hours. I woke as the cars pulled onto the gravel drive of Radstone House and glided between the towering oaks. I wondered what

God's Will

Solomon had told Julia and what she may have told him. And the thought of her reminded me of the night I had saved his life.

Once inside I was taken to a part of the house I had never visited. The room overlooked the rear of the house, away from the summerhouse. Levy put me in and locked the door and, apart from the servants, he would be the last person I would see for over a week. I didn't see Larry for even longer.

From time to time I would hear Solomon barking out orders to his lieutenants from another part of that huge catacomb of a house. What I didn't know at the time was that in killing the Greek I had caused an all-out war across London. People died because of what I did. I would later discover that Solomon had returned at just the right time. Another day and I would have been dead myself. But why had I been saved? What was the purpose? Had Julia or Larry had a hand in my survival? Whatever the reason, I was thankful. Maybe I was adopting the type of loyalty Levy had to Solomon. I was like them now.

Like everything at Radstone, my new home was large. I had a bathroom, a living room and even a small balcony that was watched night and day. But they had nothing to fear from me. I wasn't going anywhere. Each day food was brought to my room on a silver platter, cooked to perfection and accompanied by a well-balanced claret. Then, one week later, Solomon himself appeared at my door. He entered the room like a ship on its maiden voyage. He was almost shining. He'd lost weight and it suited him. He wore a type of suit he would never have worn before, a pinstriped affair in a style that was big at the time. He looked younger and somehow more energised. There was also a glint of something in his eye that at first I couldn't decipher. He was impressive—but then, to me he always had been. He was carrying a bottle of single malt and a couple of glasses and I knew before he sat down he had it all worked out. No matter what I said he would agree.

God's Will

He would do it with that same fatherly smile and he would listen, as he always did. No matter what I said he would show me a better way. I was defenceless.

'I'm sorry for everything I've done,' I muttered like a child. 'I never planned for it to be like this...'

'Hush,' he said, which smacked more of nanny than gangster. 'It's okay. Here... drink this. I'm sorry for all that's happened, too, son. You've been through a lot. And in a way I feel responsible. I should never have left you alone.'

Over the next half an hour his performance ranged from benevolent family member to social worker. Now, I'd worked with some good actors in my brief time on stage, but he was good. I say this with hindsight because at the time I was too terrified to notice anything, which I suppose was part of his plan. I didn't feel the hook. I didn't even see it coming. It was all in the detail. How I'd been put under too much pressure too soon. How the shooting and Larry's problems had confused the situation. I had to realise that killing Nicki had caused a lot of problems. Good people had lost a lot because of what I'd done. Then he finished with the old chestnut about standing by me the way I had stood by him that night outside the casino. It almost made me vomit.

It was clear when he'd finished. It was a performance, after all, and once you've acted for a while you become aware of the sort of heavy lull that descends when it's all over.

'How's Larry?' I said, aware of my cue.

'He's a lot better. Not that you'll be seeing much of each other. I've had very good people looking at him. He's really come on. I think the best for both of you is that you get on with your work. Get your heads down, get back on your feet as it were.'

God's Will

For a moment I saw the veneer peel away. His tone changed briefly, and underneath I caught a glimpse of utter ruthlessness. As he stood up the charm returned, and then I understood what I had first seen in his eyes. Power. It had been with him the first day we met at the Rotella, but as Larry's illness had affected them both it had faded until the night of the shooting when he lay wounded in the rain. There I was sure it had died, but, ironically, that moment had been a catalyst and he had returned to London no longer the worn-out heavyweight, but a lean contender hungry for the title again. I'd done him a favour. I'd broken myself and killed another man doing it, but in the end I had done him a favour. There was no mention of Julia and, to be honest, I didn't see anything significant in that, but I'm sure now that as he spoke words of comfort to me that night he knew everything that had gone on and that it was only a matter of time before he dealt with me.

Shortly after our *tête-à-tête* I started to make the occasional trip back into London. The war was over but the peace was a fragile one. It simply didn't make sense to rock the boat. Levy was my chaperone on each trip and I sensed in him a certain amount of respect. It could have been pity, though—it was difficult to tell with Levy. He was never the most communicative of people. On the odd occasion he did say anything I always found it something of a disappointment, as if the detail couldn't live up to the billing. I think he was aware of it, too. That was why he was the way he was.

Solomon told me to immerse myself in my work. And it was over those weeks that I found out what that work was. My fall had been a great one. Gone were the trappings of success and, with them, the power that had made me unrecognisable to myself. I was to be a general dogsbody or, to put it into even simpler terms, a common crook. One day I was delivering packages, the next collecting the takings from the network of brothels and arcades he had all over the

God's Will

city. Solomon also 'inherited' a few of Nicki's scrap metal yards and I spent a lot of my time grafting in them. Ironic, I think you'll agree. It was hard, filthy work but I valued my time there. Hard work is a type of therapy and I enjoyed being a working man again. Anything I could do to distance myself from the gangster image was fine by me. Every day I would get a call from one of Solomon's boys and off I would go to deliver or collect, never once questioning my instructions. Why didn't I run? Well, where could I go? What could I do? I had no one. Any ties I had to my past were severed. All that remained were memories, the glow from the occasional flicker in the darkness. Besides, London was, as it always has been, my life. And even with my change of fortune I was still making money. It was a way of living, and I was happy to be alive.

It was during this time that my strong association with Fenton was established. He didn't like me from the beginning, and the feeling was mutual. He had all of Solomon's immorality and none of his charm. He was devoid of any goodness for the world, and didn't care one jot for anyone. He lived for profit and the theatre of the court. I suppose his dislike for me came from knowing I knew all of this, that he was just as corrupt as any of his clients. Each day at his offices in Southwark I would wait in the little storeroom until he appeared with 'the mail', as he liked to call it. I didn't know exactly what was in the packages, but I was pretty sure it wasn't legal.

This numbing existence continued in an ever-repeating cycle until summer, that hot summer of seventy-six, when I was moved from Radstone to the Rotella. God knows what happened to all of my things in Larry's flat, but at that point I wasn't really in a position to complain. After the opulence I'd become accustomed to it was quite a shock, but it was at least comfortable and free—although I use the word 'free' advisedly. Whilst at the Rotella I was accessible and they could keep an

God's Will

eye on me. Solomon knew I wasn't going anywhere. As I've said, he was a fine judge of character and he read me very well indeed. I didn't see much of Larry during that time. Occasionally he would turn up at the Rosella and for a second I would remember the happy times, then reality would kick in and the pain would worsen. I can still recall the moment I first saw him after I'd moved into the casino.

It was mid-week and I was sat at a table near the bar. He strolled in with that casual indifference I thought I would never see again. He, too, was reborn and, like his father, slimmer and more together than I thought possible. As I watched him prowl the long line of tables, wearing elegance like a cloak, I was happy to see he was back together again. I made sure he didn't see me. I didn't want to be the one to remind him of what he'd gone through. I came to the conclusion—and still feel this strongly after all these years—that if we had never met things would have been different for him. He had issues—that was clear—but without my interference I'm sure he would have dealt with them and evolved into someone strong. Someone who would be able to transform the wealth Solomon had secured, into something legitimate and worthwhile. I'd come into his life at the wrong time and disrupted the transformation. The chrysalis had evolved out of cycle.

We wouldn't actually speak for another month but as I watched him that night I realised how much I cared for him still. Even though I was sure the disappointment I had caused would have changed his feelings towards me, I still loved him completely.

Shortly before we did finally speak I was summoned to his father's office. I'd been left alone for weeks but I knew it wouldn't last. What I didn't know—what none of us could have known—was that something was stirring far off that would change all of our lives forever, a storm so powerful and destructive it would break us all. What pulled us towards it was Solomon's greed. His new-found energy was making him over-

God's Will

confident and for the very first time he was taking huge risks. The world around him was changing. The framework he had based his success on was cracking beneath him. Gone were the faces and firms he had controlled for so long. Gone, too, was the respect. The new kids on the block had little regard for the old structure. They had seen the Great Train Robbers get huge sentences with only moderate violence and decided they may as well be hung for a sheep as a lamb. Consequently, the world was becoming more and more violent. Even for a man like Solomon.

There was also a new approach to policing, which had quite an effect on how Solomon operated. During his time hundreds of corrupt police officers were relieved of their posts because of their links to organised crime. Overnight most of Solomon's contacts in the Met were gone. They were men he had nurtured since the beginning of their careers, patiently waiting until they reached a position that would be beneficial to him. Very few had the courage to say no. Most of them were happy to have past indiscretions forgotten for the occasional blind eye and a regular payment. These were the things that allowed Solomon to progress; without them he was forced into a world he didn't know, trying to hold on the best way he could. I think he was well aware of all of this, but he was blinded by arrogance and greed. In spite of his new image, he was still like a punch-drunk fighter, convincing himself he could go on forever. But the next fight would overshadow anything that had gone before and, of course, I would be central to his plans.

I sensed my time had come when Levy came to collect me one day from the bar. I spent every day there so I was easily found. Normally it was a phone call and I would go up to see Solomon. But that day Levy came in person, with a look in his eye I had only seen once before... that day in Nicki's office. After that our relationship had changed. It

God's Will

was as if he understood what I was going through, and although he wasn't going to risk what he had to help me he had sympathy for me. Maybe it came from knowing that he knew what would happen to me eventually. I don't know. But from his gaze that night at the Rotella, I felt a genuine sense of comradeship.

Silently I followed him to the upper gallery, past the private rooms the wealthier clients used for Solomon's girls, along the network of corridors to the top of the club until we arrived at the foot of the staircase that led to Solomon's office. The building had originally been a theatre and in some of its more remote corners there was always a feeling of timelessness, a sensation that figures from the past might suddenly reappear from the shadows. And the feeling was no stronger than at the foot of those stairs. They went from dim light to none at all. Solomon always did have a sense of theatre, and it had the desired effect on me. Oddly, Levy didn't leave straightaway. He watched me as I disappeared into the shadows of the narrow staircase. I thought it was to make sure I didn't run. But as I waited at the door and looked down at him, I knew it was something much more. In that short time I think I understood what it was like for men who lack the strength to go all the way to the top, men who must exist as little more than bodyguards to men who have. I even considered the possibility that he may have thought that under different circumstances it could just as easily have been him standing at that door instead of me. I hoped in that moment he was aware of how much pain he had caused in his life.

As if at an invisible signal from Solomon, Levy then turned and walked along the corridor, leaving me alone in the darkness. With a cautious knock I waited until I heard a muffled grunt. Taking it as a cue to enter, I opened the door. I knew the room well. Don't forget, during my brief time as gangster number one, I had spent a lot of time there. There was a large oak desk over to the left and, above that, a row of

God's Will

three small windows that revealed St Paul's Dome in neat square segments. To the right of the desk, beyond a dark leather sofa, stood a cheap-looking bar similar to the one I'd seen at Stella's. Unlike hers, though, this looked even cheaper amongst the many antiques Solomon had crammed into the room. I didn't see him immediately. Apart from a small lamp on the bar it was pretty gloomy in there, but as I closed the door, I saw him. He was relaxing in an armchair, his feet resting on a small glass coffee table and on one arm of the chair I could see smoke rising from one of his fat cigars in an ashtray. It wasn't until I walked towards him that I actually saw his face. Surprisingly he was without his usual look of assurance. Instead I found a distant, almost troubled man—one, it seemed, who had suddenly discovered a great weight upon his shoulders. As I stopped before him I realised he wasn't looking at me. His focus was far off, as if the problem had taken his mind elsewhere. I'd never seen him like this and I didn't know what to make of it. He muttered my name and thanked me for coming—as if I'd had a choice in it. His focus was now on me. It was then that I realised, to my astonishment, that he was drunk. It wasn't too obvious and he wasn't over-articulating his words, but it was clear enough from his delivery that he had consumed more than usual. Finding him like this actually gave me a feeling of confidence and I sat down without invitation. Once I was settled he leant forward to pick up a piece of paper lying on the table.

'Thirty-seven thousand, five hundred and twenty pounds exactly,' he said before sitting back again. 'Quite a total.'

I knew what it was. My gambling debt. I knew he'd use it when he needed to. 'I thought it was more,' I said. 'I'm more conservative than I realised.'

He grinned confidently. 'Despite your knowledge of the tables you weren't very sensible when it came to my money.'

God's Will

'You were away. I got bored.' I'd had a long time to prepare my defence, but even then I was surprised at my arrogance. Pulling at the reins, I added that it had something to do with the pressure I was under at the time.

'Pressure?' he said, picking up the cigar and sitting forward again. 'Pressure, you say? Yes, I suppose you were under a lot of that. What with fucking my wife and all, it must have been a difficult time worrying I might find out or not.' Even though I'd known he'd find out one day, I was still shocked to hear him say it. To my surprise he was still smiling. 'So what to do, Tom? I mean, how do we resolve a situation like this?'

I wanted to say something meaningful, something that would show that I was more than a fool who'd blown it all. I said something about working the debt off. It was greeted with a laugh. He didn't need to say a word, but he did anyway.

'Oh, you'll work it off, son.' He chuckled, the smoke circling his head. 'One way or another, you'll do that. But how? How?' He stressed the word with a bark, his breath piercing a hole in the thin billowy cloud of cigar smoke.

The sombre atmosphere of the staircase had somehow stayed with me and for a moment I saw him as more sinister than ever before. I wouldn't have been the first to feel fear in that room. For only the second time since I had killed a man, I genuinely feared for my life. I'd never seen him like this, and it made me more afraid than ever—not of his violence but of something I couldn't see or touch, something that came from him and scurried away into the dark corners of that darkest of rooms.

With all of these thoughts spinning in my head, I watched him watching me. It should have given me ample opportunity to prepare a caustic reply when the moment came, but Solomon was anything but

God's Will

predictable, and when the moment did come, it was different from anything I could have ever imagined.

'I've met a lot of different types of people in my life, Tom. Some small and insignificant who want nothing more from life than reputation. My dad was like that. He worked in a factory making basins... metal basins for the army. He did that day in, day out. Got up of a morning, went to work, came home, went down the pub, came home, beat his wife, then went to bed, before starting it all over again next day. God bless him. Now there are other people, like my Uncle Vinnie, for instance. Now, he was a nobody like my dad, but unlike him he wanted to be anything but insignificant and would do almost anything to reach for his dream. And what was his dream? Well, that was my old mum.'

A faint smile washed across his lips, but there was little warmth in it.

'One night when my dad was tanking himself up down the pub, Uncle Vinnie was with my mum. There they were, calmly sitting at the kitchen table making plans to end her misery. They had it all worked out. When my dad was tucking away at his supper at the kitchen table, in preparation for his nightly violence with my mother, old Uncle Vinnie was going to do him good and proper with a hammer.'

With this revelation he leant forward again and stared at me without emotion. 'But they didn't reckon on me listening on the stairs, did they? Listening to their sordid little plot. And, what's more, they didn't imagine that little seven-year-old running out into the cold night to warn his old dad.' Sitting back, he looked up at the ceiling and smiled as if the recollection was of a family holiday or Christmas morning itself. 'Uncle Vinnie didn't stand a chance. Neither did my old mum. Only trouble was... I lost my dad as well.' Tilting his head to one side and sticking out his tongue he gave a clear indication of his father's

God's Will

end. 'Now, ever since that day, I have always put people into those two categories. Uncle Vinnie or good old dad. And with you I find you are definitely an Uncle Vinnie.'

'I'm honoured,' I said, deciding playing safe was pointless. Not that he was aware of my bravado.

'You see, you want to be somebody, but there's a little voice inside always holding you back. I didn't see it at first, but now I know. As I got older I realised that some people simply can't be put in those two categories. Some characters are too complex, or too powerful to recognise their...' he stared at the tip of the cigar as he searched for a suitable noun, '...their consequences. Is that the right word? Consequences? Yes, I think it is. The consequences of their actions. Good, that. I should write that down,' he nodded, his face brighter having spelt out his thoughts. 'Does all this make any sort of sense to you, Tom? You see what I am trying to say is that people are of interest to me. Not only those that I come up against, or ones that owe me money—obviously that concerns me—but it's finding out what people are all about that fascinates me. I'm a fisherman, as you know, and from it I have acquired a certain type of tolerance. You see, you can't go thrashing around in the water. You have to be patient and read the flow of the river. Understand its depths and currents. Only then can you really appreciate its possibilities. Now, I can do that with people, Tom. I've done it all my life. I did it with you. I just reeled you in. And, you see, once they're in the pot, as it were, I like to find out what flavour I'm gonna get. See, with you, I know exactly what I'm getting. You are, and don't take this the wrong way, ten-a-penny. But sometimes a big fish comes swimming my way—a beautiful exotic thing, unseen in the cold waters where I fish normally. One day there he is, and I gotta reel him in and, if I'm lucky, I might discover something wonderful to my advantage. But this fish won't make a noise—no, he won't make a

281

God's Will

noise at all. In fact, if he wants to go back into the water alive he knows he has to show me all the wonder he holds, because that's the only way he'll get amongst those warm currents that'll take him home again. Are you following any of this, Tom?'

'Perfectly.'

He clicked his fingers and laughed. 'You see, that's what I've liked about you from the beginning. Your penetrating insight.' Getting up, he walked across to the bar. 'Fancy a drink?'

Oh, yes, I wanted a drink. I was just a little too afraid of what he'd add to it.

'I've got a lovely sherry you might like. Very pleasant, very soft on the palate,' he added, his eyes suddenly revealing an element of loathing.

'No, really, I'm fine.'

'Please yourself. For instance, I know of a man, a very important man, a diplomat, believe it or not, who thought he was above me. Thought he was dealing with an amateur. But not only was he out of his depth, he was also a long way from home. Now, he finds himself in a situation not unlike your own. And I can assure you his troubles total up to a lot more than thirty-seven thousand nicker.' When he sat down again he stubbed out the cigar and caressed his tumbler as he leant back against the leather. Slowly Solomon was coming back to life.

'Unlike you, though, this fish is in a position to find help in other quarters. I got a taste of this one, Tom. And already I know what satisfaction it's gonna give me. Because this fish has come up with a most wonderful arrangement. A risky one. All financial packages have their elements of risk—every businessman knows that—but I hope, with your help, this one can produce magical results.'

So at last it comes. 'What if I won't do it?'

God's Will

'Oh, you'll do it,' he said, chuckling at my audacity. 'You'll do it all right.' Then his tone changed as if he regretted using it. 'Tom, I have a reputation, but you have taken the piss out of me and by rights I should make you suffer. But I owe you... you saved my life, when everybody else abandoned me... you helped me. I can't forget that. No matter what you've done, I can't forget it.'

The words were coming out now less in a stream, more in a broken trickle, but just as I'd seen the change in Levy, I could see the same in Solomon.

'Do you find that difficult to believe? I know what you think of me, boy, but there is dignity in me. Do you understand me? Dignity. Can you see what I'm saying? I'm giving you a way out, Tom. This is what this is. A way out.'

I understood it all and, believe it or not, I genuinely felt he was telling me the truth.

'This man is a foreigner... his nationality is of no consequence.' He wasn't looking at me anymore. Instead his gaze was fixed on the darkness above him. 'He's lived in England for some time now. He's a widower. His wife died a few years ago giving birth to their only child, a small daughter—Lottie—just coming up to four, I am led to believe. Cared for by a nanny.'

His gaze dropped from the ceiling and rested on me. The grin was so wide, I could almost see into his dirty little mind. A nanny. A woman. Of course, it had to be that. If I was good for anything, it was getting the girls. It was a blessing I'd been aware of since my arrival in London, but I had never believed it would come to curse me. Whatever he was planning involved a female and my charm.

'I see.'

'I thought you would,' he replied, lighting up another cigar. 'The arrangement is this. You befriend the girl. She is, you'll be happy to

God's Will

discover, not unattractive. Then you get access to the home, become a familiar face. When the time is right, the child will be spirited away.'

'A kidnapping? Isn't that a little old hat?'

'Done properly it might be very rewarding.'

'So, let me get this right—this man is arranging to kidnap his own child?'

'In a nutshell, yes.'

'What sort of father kidnaps his own kid?'

'A greedy one with little conscience... you'll get on famously.'

I sensed something wasn't right—apart from the abduction of a four-year-old child, that is. It then occurred to me that the emotion he'd shown was possibly less to do with his conscience but somehow allied to this filthy little arrangement.

'I've agreed for you to talk with this man. You'll be informed when.'

At what point I entered the equation, I don't know. Maybe that night we talked at Radstone after his return from the States—maybe before, possibly the night I had heard him and Fenton talking below my balcony, who knows? Either way, he'd got me hook, line and sinker. And he had got it spot-on. I was a little fish in a big dirty pond.

'Is Larry part of all this?' I asked.

'Of course. We've all been aware of his problems, but now they're behind him. Larry's taken over a lot of my going concerns, and for this he has a lot of enthusiasm. I never doubted his loyalty. You may think you're the same. Believe me, you are nowhere near. He's in a different class. Now he sees it. He knows you for what you are.' He sat up and looked at me with eyes full of shame for the emotion he had shown. 'Because, like it or not, you're more like me than him. You're from the bottom. There's a stench about us. We never get rid of it. No matter what we do. You won't be seeing any more of Larry.'

God's Will

'And for my part in this you wipe away my debt? And–'

I didn't want to say it and he didn't want to hear it, so he cut me off. 'The money that will be raised from this little exercise will make your debt insignificant enough for it to be loose change. You make a good job of it and there might be something in it for you as well. Fuck me, you don't deserve it, but there'll be enough to go round. Then, when it's all over you won't be seeing any more of us. Clear?'

'Crystal.'

So there it was. A job packaged beautifully, all ready for dispatch. I was to work my way into the nanny's affections, wait until the time was right, then whisk Lottie away. The German government would provide the ransom. The father would keep us informed of any ruse on the part of the police or the special services and when the money was paid, Lottie would be found alive and well. Perfect.

Only this was nothing of the sort. This particular deal was darker than even I could have expected of Solomon. No wonder he was overwhelmed with emotion that night. This was almost beyond him. It had evil at its heart so dark it sickened even him, but wealth has the ability to brighten the bleakest of thoughts. Even though I didn't know what the real plan was at that point, I still sensed something was terribly wrong. What shocked me more than anything else, though, was Larry's involvement. How could I have been so wrong about him? I suppose Solomon was right. We were poles apart. I was alone again.

'There is one thing you haven't considered.' I said this very calmly, in a vain attempt to show I had some say in my own future. Ridiculous really, but to his credit he gave me my moment.

'And what's that?'

'This nanny. What if she's... batting for the other side?'

'Queer? That's your problem,' he said with a smile. 'But if she is, there's not much hope for you.'

God's Will

'Look, if I'm going to put myself at risk like this, I need some sort of security... ' Through the smoke his eyes sensed my helplessness and I hated the strength it gave him. 'And why don't you just snatch the kid —why do you need me?' I was pleading for my life. I knew that, but even then, ridiculously, I still tried to appear I was Jack the lad. I hadn't learned a bloody thing. 'Look, I could get years for this, you have to–'

Suddenly, like a viper's head, his face appeared through the smoke inches from mine. 'There are two things you don't seem to understand, boy. One, you put yourself in this situation, and two... I don't have to do a damn thing.'

I was so scared, I couldn't move. A blind hatred like that is normally reserved for despots and tyrants, but then maybe that's what he was. Under different circumstances, no doubt, Solomon would have excelled in a uniform loaded with medals.

36

Next morning Maria hung her apron on a peg next to the kitchen door and walked boldly through the shadowy living room to be at Levy's side. Reid studied her behaviour from the relative cool of the open door, looking out onto the back garden. Levy was still in his semi-comatose state and had stirred only a couple of times in the past twenty-four hours: he was still to wake fully.

Reid was touched by Maria's unquestioning loyalty, although it made little sense to him. What did women see in violent men? If she only knew what savagery Levy had brought to the world. He watched as she gently wiped saliva from his beard and tucked the woollen shawl under his chin, even though the room was hot enough to incubate an

God's Will

egg. Reid responded by loosening his own collar and rotating his head with his fingertips. His neck ached. Maria had made up a bed in a spare room adjacent to the kitchen. It was so tiny he had slept with the back of his head against the wall, his head angled to the door.

He had slept fitfully. In a bizarre dream he had found he was a prince aspiring to win the hand of a beautiful young princess. But it was clear that her father, the king, did not see him as an appropriate suitor and had set him an impossible task. Taken to the periphery of the kingdom—a dramatic coastline with monstrous black cliffs and mountainous seas—his mission was explained. He had to guide a flock of lambs across a ramshackle bridge connecting two of the highest cliffs; success, and the hand of the princess, was only to be won by reaching the far side of the bridge with at least one lamb. Watched by the king and assembled dignitaries he had set off, lambs gathered up in his arms, others on his shoulders, the rest crowding around his hesitant feet. The waves crashed against the rocks below and the bridge swayed violently. One by one the lambs begin to fall. Each time he slipped or stumbled, more fell from his shoulders. As his feet crashed through the rotten structure, more plummeted towards the foaming waves. Before long there was only one left. He held it close to his chest as he inched forward, his legs aching and the wind pushing against him… and then he reached the conclusion that his task was not to marry the princess at all but to save the lamb, the solitary lamb, and take it far away and keep it safe.

Reid had woken in a sweat and had sat on the bed for hours. When dawn broke he had wandered into the living room, to find Levy mumbling fitfully in his sleep. He understood then, for the first time with any real depth, how their own actions had coloured their lives. There was nowhere to hide for either of them.

God's Will

Maria stirred him from his thoughts by explaining that he was to help himself to food and drink and that she would be home in time to give Levy his second batch of medicine. Finally she explained that it was important that he waited, that he and Levy had to talk. Reid could hear the caution in her voice. He knew why it was there. She was leaving her husband with a man who, given his history, could ruin their lives.

'Don't worry, Maria,' he assured her gently. 'He is safe. I will take care of him.'

She thanked him and went out. As the car disappeared in a cloud of dust raised from the parched road he walked back to Levy's side, sat down, reached out and violently shook him awake.

Next morning Greene was woken early by the police, who informed him that Denby's beaten body had been washed up at Wapping. Angie had reported Greene's violent visit to Muswell Hill. For nearly three hours at the local station he tried his best to explain that although he had indeed found Denby and even invited him back for a drink, there had been a last-minute change of plan. He was careful with his words. It seemed pointless to tell them that somebody else had changed his mind, that it was probably one of Henderson's men stopping Denby from spilling the beans. In the end it didn't really matter what the police concluded. A young couple who had witnessed the incident on Portland Place with the Ghouls had also witnessed a very tall man dragging Denby towards Oxford Street shortly afterwards. The police had to concede that at five foot eight, Greene was not their man.

That was all he could do for Denby. In a way he had done nothing to hurt him, but because the old drunk had got himself involved with vicious men he was now dead. Despite his own plans, Greene wasn't going to risk his life helping the police find his killer. The shame of that moment on the landing wouldn't allow him to rest, however. He could still hear Denby's pleas as he was dragged away. Coupled with the nightmare he was already struggling with, it pushed him to the edge of insanity. It was as if the nightmare had taken over the whole world. Nothing made sense—Denby's murder, the money, even Henderson.

Throughout the morning Greene sat at his window, watching for Henderson and his men. He saw them around every corner, lurking on rooftops, peering from behind chimney pots. He tried hard to keep awake but kept falling asleep and being consumed by the nightmare once more. If he wasn't in the chair he was pacing up and down, talking to himself. Around ten he heard a hesitant knock and Verecker's soft appeals for him to open the door, but he told him to go. He knew in his heart it would do neither of them any good to talk now.

For the rest of the day Greene studied the figures on the street below. Over time he began to recognise some of them. He even talked to them and waved, but never once did they raise their heads to the madman above. In the evening and into the early hours he occasionally saw the Ghouls hurrying by with their pram. It struck him then that he had never seen them during the daytime. This, he supposed, was the reason they were called the Ghouls—they only came out at night. They occupied his mind because of the incident with Denby the night he died and, for reasons he could not easily explain, they terrified him. Was it possible that they were in some way connected to Denby's murder and the madness that was closing in on him by the hour?

Levy was evidently awake but seemed unable to communicate in any way. He stared out of the window, his grey complexion greyer still since Reid had stirred him from his trance.

'Levy, you probably won't remember me. My name is Reid. Alan Reid. I was the investigating officer for the Steiner murders. Neither of

God's Will

us are in any state to fuck about so I'll get to the point. I know you were with Sickert and Solomon on the night of the kidnapping and if I can prove you were responsible for her death in any way, I will have you carted back to old Blighty yesterday.'

Levy's eyes blinked several times and Reid wondered if this was some kind of communication, some type of code. One blink for yes, two for no? He lowered his face to Levy's and growled at him like a dog. 'Tell me, you bastard. Tell me what happened!'

To his disgust and shock a smile appeared on Levy's bearded face. He sat back, unable to decide how to react.

'Reid. Alan Reid of the Yard.' The tone of Levy's voice was not what Reid had anticipated. It was unexpectedly deep, though it lacked any authority. 'I know you,' he muttered. 'I have read about you over the years. *The obsessed inspector. The man who can't let go.* That's you, Reid, isn't it?' A small chuckle escaped his wet lips and he coughed. He nodded to the tissues by the chair and Reid stuffed a couple into his hand.

Now they had made some sort of connection, Reid sank back into the chair, his emotions suddenly uncoiled.

'You want to know about the kidnapping? You want to know? It lives in me, Reid. It is there every day. I've hurt a lot of people in my life. That's what I do. I have killed men. Two. In fights. They were unplanned. I have no regrets. They would just as easily have killed me. These were not good people. So why should I feel any guilt for that? But that night was like no other. It made no sense. It still doesn't.'

'What happened?'

'I don't know all the details... I only know my part in it.'

'That's all I ask. I need to know.'

God's Will

Levy smiled again, but this time it was empty. 'Okay, mister policeman. I'll tell you. But not until you have fixed us two tall drinks of Maria's delightful sangria.'

37

There is a rattle of coughs from Bepa's throat and Philip is at her side in a second. She is deteriorating at such a rate Sickert can sense death closing in on her. She's fading fast. Philip asks him to make the finale concise.

* * *

I should have been making plans to save myself, but the truth of the matter was I didn't see the danger. I genuinely believed Solomon when he said the kidnapping was a way out for me. He was right. I was more Uncle Vinnie than his father. And I'm still not sure if that's good or bad. There was more to it than that, of course. The ripples of what I'd done still touched me daily, but I tried the best I could to lessen the pain. I had experienced wealth and all that went with it and, although I was guilty of many things, it simply didn't make sense to give it all up and be a no one again. I was nothing more than a common criminal. I no longer thought in an honest way. The truth was I rather liked the criminal life. I had discovered a talent for improvisation whilst acting, but there was no doubt I could put it to much better service as a villain. Over the next few weeks I continued my life as a courier. By then I only had one customer, Fenton.

God's Will

'Good morning, my friend,' he would whisper as he passed me 'the mail'. He had a huge belly and long strands of black hair greased down across his bald scalp. Every time I met him, I had an overriding sensation of wanting to punch him. I really did hate him. I could still remember clearly the conversation below the balcony that night at Radstone, how he calmed Solomon with his advice and sickly charm. Well, a child would now be put in huge danger because of his 'advice'. As Solomon's corrupt adviser I knew he would be heavily involved. Even Levy didn't like him. Levy never said much, but as we pulled away from Fenton's offices one day I heard him mutter something about Fenton giving villainy a bad name. I had to laugh.

The summer of nineteen seventy-six is remembered for its hot summer, but for me it was a grim time. Going on without questioning what my life was leading to was a mistake. I should have sensed what was happening, but half of me wasn't alive anymore. For weeks I waited for the call, hoping that something miraculous would occur to wash away my debt, maybe a heart attack for Solomon or perhaps a sudden visit from the Flying Squad. Anything to stop the plan going ahead—but my luck had all been and gone.

I was sitting at the bar in the Rotella when the moment came. I remember looking up to see Levy at the top of the stairs. He descended like Bogart—I have a theory that all criminals have a movie villain they aspire to. Even though his eyes were on the tables, I knew he was coming for me. As he reached the bar he threw open the lid of his lighter. In the sudden burst of flame he muttered the words I had dreaded and in the glow of light he could have been Bogart himself.

'It's time.'

I hadn't planned to say a thing. I knew the moment would come, and when it did I felt the best policy was to toe the line, but hearing

God's Will

Levy actually speak the words made me want to say something to him, make a connection to him. God knows why, but I did it all the same.

'Why do you do it, Levy?'

Putting away the lighter, he smiled and took the cigarette from his lips. 'I find the hours to my liking.'

Then he winked. It was an odd thing for him to do and it prompted me look at him a second longer. Most of Solomon's people indulged in winks, nods and cheeky smiles, even combinations of all three—but never Levy. He never had to. He was born a fighter and discovered very early on that his size was enough to make such trivialities of communication just that. It was as I considered all this that I realised I was beginning to like the man. Outwardly nothing had changed. This was the same man who had beaten Skelton within an inch of his life and the same man who had humiliated me. But he was also the man who'd been with me when I committed murder. Like it or not, I had to face the fact that there was an affinity between us. We were indeed the strangest of bedfellows.

'Now, let's not keep the gentlemen waiting, Tom.'

At the top of the stairs he opened the door and gave me a faint smile. I should have felt some warmth from it, but it only strengthened my fears. In silence, we worked our way up the building until we arrived at the narrow staircase that led to Solomon's door. For a moment I very nearly found the courage that I'd lacked for so long—to run. Unfortunately the thought of it was the best I could manage. I tapped on the door and was surprised when it opened to reveal Solomon, smiling like a debutante. He invited me in. There was another man on the sofa where I had sat myself only weeks before. At first I couldn't see his face. Then, as the door closed, he turned to me slowly, nonchalantly, a large drink in his right hand. Steiner. He had been part of my life for a while by then, from that night at Milton's with his

God's Will

pregnant wife, on numerous occasions at the Rotella, and of course that first party at Radstone when I had listened to him, Fenton and Solomon from the balcony. Little did I realise then that he and his child would shape the rest of my life.

He was a big man, much bigger physically than Solomon. He had a wide-bridged nose that almost disappeared into a thick moustache of the type so popular at that time. His collar-length brown hair receded to reveal a tanned freckled scalp. I saw all of this, but what I couldn't see was any trace of remorse or anxiety for the coming act. Getting to his feet, he bowed gracefully and offered his hand.

'Herr Sickert. It is a pleasure to make your acquaintance.'

I waited for Solomon to laugh, but even he had been caught up in the moment and looked on with an air of solemnity.

'This is Herr Steiner, Tom, the man I was telling you about. Would you like a drink?'

Christ! There was I was preparing for hot irons and threatening behaviour, and what did I get? Geniality and a cosy chat.

'Please, Tom,' said Steiner, offering me a seat beside him. 'Mr Solomon has told me much about you. You are from the north, I believe. Myself also, but the north of Germany. Hamburg. Maybe you have heard of it.'

'Yes, I know it,' I said, sitting down. 'My dad did his national service there.'

'Did he enjoy his time?'

'Well, if he did, he didn't hang around to tell me.'

There was a moment of tension. Parents and children, of course, being a rather sensitive subject, considering what we were about to discuss.

'I sense a resentment in your voice.'

God's Will

Before I could reply, Solomon pushed a drink into my hand and at the same time made sure I noticed the discouraging look in his eye.

'It was a long time ago,' I said, changing my tone. 'He did what he did. My life's been no less fulfilled because of it.'

Steiner smiled. 'You are a philosopher, Tom. A rare gift in these troubled times.'

His response seemed to ease the tension in Solomon, allowing him to nod in agreement as he sat down himself. This atmosphere of civility confused me. I couldn't understand why they were behaving like this. It sickened me. There we were, preparing to kidnap the man's kid, yet behaving like a group of pensioners on a day out. I should have sensed something was wrong then, but all I wanted was for it to be over.

'Okay, Tom,' said Solomon, handing me a slip of paper. 'This is an itinerary of the nanny's movements. She only has one day off, normally in the week. She drinks with a couple of other German girls at the weekends.'

'Ah, yes, I have a photograph here,' Steiner said, pulling out a small photo from his jacket pocket. 'As you see, she is a rather pretty girl.'

She was that and, if the photograph was any indication, perfectly formed.

'No boyfriends?'

'Just one,' said Steiner calmly, with a broad, sickly smile. I understood then how he'd become a diplomat. 'But he did not last very long. She is quite a studious girl and stays in most times. He got a little bored of her, I think.'

'So you've got your work cut out,' added Solomon. 'But if anyone knows the workings of women…'

He didn't need to finish the sentence: I had caught the contempt in his voice.

'I'll do my best,' I said.

God's Will

'This is all we expect,' Steiner said, his index finger tracing the rim of his glass. 'I feel it is important to say that this is solely a financial dealing. At no point will my daughter be at any risk. It is important you realise this.'

'I understand.'

He handed me another photo. 'And this is Lottie.'

I studied the small black-and-white photograph of a pretty little girl in a light summer dress and my heart sank.

'Anything you want to talk over?' asked Solomon.

'Plenty,' I said quietly, putting the photo down on the table, 'but what would be the point?'

Angry I wasn't behaving as I should, Solomon scowled. 'Now, you listen—'

'No, no, no,' said Steiner, his hands coolly cutting the air. 'Let Thomas speak.'

'Okay. Why is it so important for me to befriend the girl? Why can't you just snatch the kid on the street or something?'

'Because,' Steiner said softly, the way he must have at all those parties and balls, 'that way, my daughter could be harmed. Doing it this way she is assured of her safety. But, more importantly, it shows an element of professionalism behind the kidnapping. Done properly, it will seem you are just one of many players in an elaborate enterprise. If it seems political our governments are much more likely to listen and react accordingly.'

'And what about the girl?'

'What about her?' said Solomon.

'Well, when I've charmed my way into her affections, she'll know everything about me. I'll be the prime suspect. She'll have a perfect description of me.'

God's Will

'And that, Thomas, is all that she'll have,' said Solomon. 'Before the ransom note is even delivered you'll be out of the country. You'll give her a false name and a fictional past. The Old Bill will be looking for members of a terrorist cell, not a northern barman. You'll be well out of it by then.'

Patting me gently on the arm, Steiner reassured me one final time. 'Take my word, young Thomas. This will work most beautifully.'

I must admit, despite my fears, it all made perfect sense. After meeting Steiner I was actually put at ease and, for the first time in weeks, I felt as if a great weight had been lifted from my shoulders.

From that day on Levy and I spent more and more time together. Because of my prodigious rise and fall, he felt pity for me now. I could sense it. He could also see what I'd become. But what he must have realised, but never revealed it to me, was that I was to be the *mark*, the *fall guy*. There was money in this venture, but not for me. Often I've wondered why he didn't say anything or try to help me. The truth of it was that in the criminal world it's dog eat dog. Levy knew that better than most.

I still thought about escaping, but each time I got close I thought of Lottie. And it was from her, or rather the image of her that had had fixed itself in my subconscious, that my idea grew. It was time for me to a make a plan of my own, one fired by Solomon's performance that first night he called me to his office, a performance full to the brim with lies and greed. What he showed that night wasn't empathy. There may have been a thin covering of something like it, but underneath he was hiding pure hatred for me, and I knew that stemmed from the relationship I had with his wife and son.

I also knew that saving his life outside the Rotella had given me time, which I was thankful for, because without it I'm sure I would have been dead months before. But that was Solomon's first mistake. I

God's Will

was still alive and in a position to fight back. During my time with him my instincts had become sharper. From him I had learnt to think in a dishonest way. And it was from that way of thinking that I got an idea that would trap them all.

38

Levy was sitting up now, drink in hand. For half an hour he had told Reid all about Thomas Sickert and his gradual rise through the Solomon empire from general barman at Milton's to his work at the Rotella, thanks to his friendship with Larry. He talked of the night Sickert had saved Solomon and how he had found himself running the organisation after that. Throughout this soliloquy Reid tried to picture it all. It wasn't until Levy described the shooting of Nicki Jainnados in Soho in seventy-six that Levy stopped to down the sangria in one.

'I remember that,' said Reid, in a state of mild shock. 'Sickert did that? We had no idea. No one talked. But you lot never do, do you? Honour among thieves and all that bollocks. But I'm not here for that. You can all kill each other for all I care. You know what I'm here for.'

'Solomon and the diplomat Steiner had some sort of deal. It made no sense. Solomon hated the Kraut. He'd been in a lot of debt to Solomon. Gambling debt. A big one. Originally the kidnapping was simply to pay off the debt, but then they both got greedy. The deal was to get Sickert into the household and organise the kidnapping from within. Come the night of the kidnapping I was to take Sickert and the kid to a safe house near Brighton. The nanny was sent away and Sickert would bring her out.'

'And did he?'

God's Will

Levy's face was greyer now than at any other point. He stared at the floor, his mouth half open, his whole appearance a reflection of his haunted spirit.

'No mister policeman. No, he did not.'

'Why not?'

'Because Larry Solomon appeared before him.'

'And?'

'He shouldn't haven there. He should have been waiting in Brighton.'

'So what happened?'

'I went in. I shouldn't have, but something was wrong and I knew Solomon would want to know. So I went in.'

'And what did you find?'

After a very long pause, Levy stared up at him. 'Carnage.'

Greene slept until early evening when he woke to heavy rain splattering on the long skylight above his bed. He was still drunk, but less so than he had been for a while now. He walked out into the living room and was hit by the stench from the chair by the window. He walked over and looked at the specks of dried vomit and other stains he was too ashamed to recall. He began to sob. There was nothing for him now, he told himself. Nothing at all. If this was life he wanted no more. There had been a couple of brief windows—when he left prison and on the day he had met Fenton's son—when he had believed he could move on with his life, but now he had to face up to the fact that there was nowhere left for him to go.

He walked through to the bathroom. In the cabinet, second shelf down, was the brown bottle of sleeping tablets the prison doctor had prescribed him. He returned to the living room and took off the top. With shaking fingers he placed them in a long line on the windowsill.

God's Will

He poured a large whisky, then held the glass in one hand as with the other he picked up the first tablet and put it in his mouth.

Flight 177 from Malaga touched down at Heathrow at six o'clock British time. Reid's head was in such a state he didn't even know what day it was. His face was bright red from sunburn and he had a throbbing headache. He picked up a copy of *The Times* as he came out of the airport: Sunday 13 February. Had it only been a weekend? Two days, yet he had learnt so much. He bought a sandwich and a bottle of water from a nearby stand and jumped into a taxi. He had a lot to do and very little time to do it in. The chest pains were becoming more and more regular and he was running out of tablets. Maybe he should nip back and see his Ugandan doctor friend? No, first things first. Central London to find Sickert. He knew now with frightening clarity that much of his own investigation had been flawed, and that there was a possibility that Thomas Sickert, the man he had grown to hate, was not after all guilty of the crimes he had long suspected.

39

There is someone in the room other than Bepa and Philip. It is just a feeling. Similar in a way to that day in his room when he sensed a presence at the door. Sickert has slept in the chair by Bepa's bed and is stirred by an odd type of whirring noise off to his left. Something electrical? A motor of some kind. It's the sort of sound he does not readily associate with the ageing building anyhow. It is clear that Bepa is aware of his distraction.

'What is it, Thomas?' she croaks. 'What do you hear?'

God's Will

'Where's Philip?'

'Pip? He's out for a while.'

Her voice sounds very dry. How much longer does she have? And—Pip? That's a new one.

'Shall I continue?' he asks.

Admissions of rape, murder and greed have been met with no comment or judgement. Is that because she doesn't care, or because she is allowing him to cleanse himself of all this self-loathing? Or is there something else at work here?

'Yes,' is the simple response. 'Yes, tell me about the night of the kidnapping.'

* * *

For a week or so after my meet with Steiner and Solomon nothing happened. It was the lull before the storm. Like most men made aware of their mortality, I tried to imagine how the future would unfold. Now it was down to me. I was in a position to end Solomon's reign and help a child I had never met. There was only one problem. Larry. If he had given up the fight and was completely under his father's control it would be almost impossible to help him. But I had to try. Because if I were going to do what I planned there'd be no half-measures; I'd bring the whole fetid structure down on them all. Julia would be okay, I knew that, but Larry would have to be saved.

For a couple of weeks I didn't see him at all. There was always a will-o'-the-wisp quality about him before, but since his return he'd become a veritable spirit. Then, in the first week of July, he turned up at the Rote la. It was early in the morning and most of the boys were sat around the casino, playing cards and waiting for their daily instructions. I wasn't part of the crowd anymore; my status was not too dissimilar to

God's Will

Rimmer's. I was just the errand-boy, and I understood well the importance of my keeping my distance in case one of them got bored and saw entertainment in me. I'd been in that position once before, remember?

Larry entered the room as he always did, confidently and casually, and even before the door closed he was the focus of everyone's respectful attention. As he joked with the other men I was aware how much more confident he was, even compared to the time before his illness. I noticed how I wasn't included. Now his friends were the very people he purported to hate. He had become a very different man to the one I had learned so much from. I wanted to make a connection with him, relive the magic we had before, but in my heart I knew it was over. He would always be in fear of his father, and I think part of his problem was coming to terms with that. He had fought a noble battle but lost the day and, very nearly, his mind. But I loved him still, as I did Julia. I just couldn't let them go.

Later that morning I watched him descend the stairs with Levy after a meeting with Solomon. As Levy read out the daily schedule to the 'fat and muscle' I followed Larry out onto the street. Luckily he was on foot, which gave me ample time to build up the courage I needed. I'd been following him for maybe three or four minutes along Oxford Street when he suddenly turned into a narrow road. Taking this as an opportunity I hurried after him, only to find I'd lost him. Then I noticed a pedestrian walkway below the offices on the far side. Running over, I descended the steps, only to find it deserted. It was as if he'd disappeared into thin air. Then there was a laugh. A mocking laugh I knew well.

'I always said you lacked subtlety.' Behind me, at the entrance, maybe four or five feet above the bottom step, there was a long shelf and a large recess that at some point had been a delivery hatch to the

God's Will

buildings above. Larry was leaning against a drainpipe that ran along one side, arms folded, shaking his head disapprovingly. 'You were following me, weren't you? I mean, this isn't you exercising?'

'I wanted to talk to you.'

Like a cat he dropped effortlessly from the shelf. 'We have nothing to say.'

'It's important. Please.'

'We have nothing to say,' he repeated, heading off along the passageway. It was decorated with beige and red Victorian tiles and as he walked the echo from his shoes surrounded me. I ran after him.

'Larry, please listen to me!'

Slowly he turned. There was a light directly behind his head and it took a moment or two for my eyes to adjust, but in that moment, that moment of fleeting blindness, he seemed like Christ. Through the halo of long blond hair, shimmering with white light, I understood what it was to become a true believer—not in the beliefs, but in the man.

'Do you remember I once said that you and I were the same?' he said softly.

I couldn't speak. I couldn't even think clearly. His voice was all around me.

'Well, I meant every word. You and I are very much the same. Only you have misunderstood one very important contradiction—that your future is not your own. No matter what you do or what you plan it will never work out the way you intend. And fate. We talked of that once. It does exist. Run, Thomas. Run. There is nothing you can do here to make your situation any better.'

As he turned away from me again I wanted, more than anything in the world, to run after him and reason with him. But I knew he was right. Whatever I had to say to him, no matter how relevant or how

God's Will

salient, he would always have the view that fate had already taken care of it.

A week later I made my way to Hyde Park. It was a clear day, when colours throbbed in the heat and sounds danced in the hot air. It felt like a play where I was the leading man awaiting the arrival of my fellow performers. But, like an actor's nightmare, it was a play where I had forgotten the words—if I had ever known them. The curtain was up; there was nowhere to go. The audience was seated and I would be damned whatever my performance.

When I saw them hand-in-hand like mother and child I wanted to run. As they passed I saw the nanny, Olga, was very pretty and true to her photograph in every way. Lottie on the other hand was much taller than I had imagined of a three year-old. For most of that morning I watched them as they walked and played in the bright sun. The birds sang their summer song and the flowers and trees danced in the breeze. Everything would have been heavenly, had one person in the garden not had subversion in mind. Around lunchtime I followed them around the lake towards a small cafe on the waterline. I found a seat not far away and waited for my moment. When it came, however, it was taken by the girl, not me.

'It's a lovely day,' she said.

'Beautiful,' I replied. I fixed my eyes on hers, hoping to set her heart on fire from the start.

'I'm from Germany. People back home always laugh at the British weather, but I find it just the same.'

'Don't speak too soon,' I said, 'it'll probably snow later.'

She laughed and then I heard Thomas Sickert laugh and I knew he felt very proud of himself. But he was no different from Solomon or Steiner. He planned to use the child for his own selfish ends, and there was no guarantee she was any safer with him than them.

God's Will

As I tried to control the anxiety swelling inside, I noticed Lottie studying me. She was always dressed in pinafores, pleated skirts and perfectly ironed blouses. It was probably that, together with her size, that had made me think she was older than she was. Her hair was very dark and always bound in immaculately formed plaits. Her eyes were darker than her hair and I noted the vacant gaze in them. I always had a sense she was looking beyond me, through me, almost. It was very odd, and I had never seen it in a child before.

'This is Lottie,' said Olga.

Smiling down at the girl, I noticed a doll she was hugging against her chest. It was one of those plastic ones with blonde nylon hair and eyes that close shut when placed horizontal.

'Hello, Lottie.'

There was no response whatsoever, and I feared that her innocence had sensed my reasons for being there.

'She's very quiet,' said Olga, filling the silence. I nodded but all I really wanted to do was pick little Lottie up and run away with her. 'She likes you.' I was so caught up in my thoughts, I didn't answer. 'She doesn't smile much... but I can tell.'

Olga introduced herself and I gave her my chosen *nom de plume*. As we shook hands I knew that was it. The contract was finalised and there was no going back. After half an hour or so they left me and meandered in the sunshine until they became dots against a wall of green in the distance. Then they were gone.

To my surprise I felt quite relaxed afterwards. As I considered the journey ahead I felt for the first time that I was doing something good. Of course, I could have stopped it all with a single phone call to the police, but I wanted Solomon on his knees, and I wanted him to know it was me that had put him there. More than anything in the world I wanted to free little Lottie and Julia.

God's Will

In that short time I acted the perfect gentleman. I drew on all my recent experiences, my tried and tested formulas, to gain access to Olga's world. It wasn't difficult, and she was very, very attractive. At first I tried the jokey northern approach. It raised a laugh, but there was more Julia in Olga than Stella. She was a bright girl and I had to thank Larry for all he had shown me. Our mating ground was Hyde Park. It became our place. Each day I waited in the little cafe. Some days they would appear, and some days they wouldn't. I told Olga I was a writer, and to cover myself I copied huge tracts of prose from relatively unknown novels. All of this seemed to work and as the days turned into weeks we became closer and closer. I was actually enjoying myself, even though I knew that somewhere, from not very far away, we were being watched.

Well, they could look all they bloody well liked for all I cared, because I was taking them to a place that would damn them all.

It went on for nearly two months. I was 'in', as they say. My life revolved around my time at the Rotella and meeting Olga. I was tempted to contact Julia on numerous occasions, to tell her everything was going to be okay, that soon she would be free. But I knew better than to ruin everything with a pointless phone call. I needed to see her but it was just out of the question. I was pleased that I didn't weaken, that I managed to stay focused through that time. I was still suffering but I was dealing with it. The pain was holding me, shaping me, like a huge invisible hand—but it wasn't breaking me.

Then, in the shape of a phone call, the moment came. It is ingrained in my memory. I was at the Rotella at the time, being talked into an early death by Rimmer. He hated my guts, but when he was drunk he would talk to anyone. God knows what subject he was on; all I remember is that I was about to go up to my room when the barman handed me the phone. Rimmer didn't even shut up when I stood up and

God's Will

gave the phone back. But I would have gladly allowed him to talk me into the ground rather than make that journey up to Solomon's office.

Levy was the normal bearer of bad tidings and it was odd that he wasn't around that day. He was, as they say, part of the furniture. All thoughts of him disappeared, though, as I knocked on Solomon's door. Inside I found him alone. He was a general the night before a battle and his businesslike handshake nearly made me vomit. It wasn't from fear —I could deal with that. It was the false concern that made me boil inside.

'It's on for next Friday,' he muttered. 'Are you ready?'

For weeks I'd been giving him a weekly rundown of everything he needed to know: where I'd taken Olga, how we were getting on, that sort of thing. I'd been visiting Steiner's home for over a month by then. It was a huge Edwardian house in Highgate. It was a remarkable building and going inside for the first time had made me feel quite patriotic. Why wasn't a British family enjoying this fine example of English architecture? I mused. But then I pictured Steiner being led out of its elegant doorway to a waiting police Maria. Lottie would do a lot better without a father like that.

'And how are you getting on with the child?' inquired Solomon. 'Which way will you take her out?'

So many question, and not a single one showing an ounce of concern for Lottie. She was central to all of our plans, but I knew deep down no one really cared but me. I answered all his queries with the same mock severity in which they were asked. 'It's all in hand,' I would say, knowing that was the only comment I could give with any real conviction. Solomon then explained he needed to go away for a few of days, but assured me he would be back in plenty of time for the act itself.

God's Will

That weekend I took Olga out for a meal. I liked Olga. I had a lot of affection for her, but it was too tied up with other things for me to want to make anything more of it. And what would be the point anyway?

Over the meal she announced she was going back to Germany for a week or two—the following Friday, in fact. I knew then there was no way out. Solomon and Steiner had it worked out in fine detail. The agreed plan was for Steiner to give his daughter some mild sleeping tablets during the evening and I would take her from her bed in the night. Levy would then ferry us to a pre-arranged safe house near Brighton. From there I would make my escape abroad. Of course, I had other plans. And so did they. But what neither side realised until the end was that there was someone else planning yet another outcome for little Lottie Steiner.

40

That August was incredibly hot. The summer of seventy-six has an almost legendary hold over the nation's collective memory. It was as if we had somehow spun out of kilter in the solar system and found ourselves closer to the sun. Each day of the final week before the planned kidnap I travelled over to Highgate to watch Steiner's house from a nearby park.

On the Friday, the day of the abduction itself, Olga invited me round for a goodbye lunch. Her flight for Germany was later that afternoon. As it turned out I got there late because of a tube strike but, waving away my apologies, Olga told me to go upstairs and bring Lottie down for lunch. By then I knew the house like the back of my hand and went directly to her door. Oddly, she wasn't there. Then I

God's Will

heard a noise from the garden and looked out of the window to see her playing on the lawn. As I watched her in the sunshine, all the emotion I'd held back for so long suddenly came out and I started to cry. I also think it had something to do with a fear that I wouldn't be strong enough to help her, that when it came down to it I would be found wanting.

Going outside, I discovered she had moved from the lawn and was standing at the gate at the bottom of a path lined by swathes of white marguerites. The gate looked out onto the road and as I made my way to her I contemplated taking her there and then. I thought that if I moved quickly we would be amongst the crowds before Olga or her father could do a thing. But that thought disappeared when I reached her and discovered I wasn't the only one who had been crying. She had cut her finger and traces of blood had smeared her clothes and the doll she always carried. The cut was quite deep. I don't know how she'd done it; maybe she'd been trying to open the gate onto the street, who knows? But what I found odd was that she showed no emotion. She rarely did, to be honest—there was always a subdued manner about her. It was obvious to me from the amount of blood on her hand that she must be in pain, yet she didn't show it. The tears were running down her face but she looked almost untroubled. It was the oddest thing.

'It's okay, Lottie,' I whispered, squatting down. 'Everything's going to be okay.'

Wrapping a handkerchief round the wound, I took the doll from her and wiped away the blood from its plastic face. As I did so, the doll's eyes opened and I saw some blood had stained one of the coloured glass balls. I was about to wipe that away, too, when Lottie did a very curious thing. Reaching up, she touched my face. At first I didn't know why, but as she brushed my cheek, I realised she was wiping away the remnants of my own tears. It was then that I noticed the similarity

God's Will

between her eyes and those of the doll. There was simply nothing there. But although I couldn't see any emotion in her face, I felt it deeply in her gesture.

Later that day, at the Rotella, I thought of that moment over and over. A part of me felt it meant something, that in a way that moment in the garden was a reflection of the way my life was to be from then on—that I would find freedom in some way. What a fool I was.

Around ten that evening I walked through the kitchens at the back of the casino and out into the dark alleyway behind. It was lined with large grey metal bins and cardboard boxes. Further along, parked in the shadows, was a Mercedes. As it waited for me in the heat of that summer night, I hated it almost as much as I hated Solomon and Steiner. Not that I connected it to the latter because of its German heritage, you understand, but just because it was part of everything that was planned for that little girl. For months Solomon's people had shadowed me. I didn't do a thing without their say-so. They and the Rotella had been my life, but getting into that car I knew I would never return. Even though I was alone, I knew my every step would be watched from a distance—to Steiner's house and then to the cottage on the outskirts of Brighton that Solomon had prepared. Well, good luck to them, I thought, as I started the car and pulled out of the shadows into the bright shimmer of NW3. Good luck to them all.

I'd never been in a Merc before. Solomon was a patriotic type of gangster and normally invested solely in British cars. But if he'd done his homework right (and he usually did) the car would have been bought with cash, abroad, to make it look as if a terrorist cell was responsible. Then driven back by someone who had the intelligence to wear gloves all the time he was in it. It would be someone who knew Europe and had contacts across the continent—a man like Larry, perhaps? Well, I couldn't blame him. He was his father's son, after all. I

God's Will

was independent because of the lack of one. What it must be to be the son of Solomon, I thought…

Larry and Julia were in my mind most of the way, as were Charlie and Olga. But I also had time for Stella and very nearly made a detour to her flat—but I'd given her enough pain for one lifetime. There was even space for that little boy up north. If only he could have seen this, he wouldn't have dared to move away. Of course, there was someone else there, too. She sat in the shadows of my mind, silently watching me, her captivating stare unnerving me and touching me at the same time. *It's okay, Lottie*, I whispered to her, *everything is going to be okay*.

At Highgate Hill I passed the small shabby stone statue of Dick Whittington's cat and remembered Larry telling me about the Bow Bells urging the young man to turn back to London. Putting it down to coincidence, I carried on. By the time I reached the house the moon was high and full and I was in its pull. I knew it would take everything I had to change what was expected of me. Parking the car in the shadows along the street, I walked to the gate Lottie had stood at that afternoon. My plan was to contact the authorities from the house and hope they had enough confidence in what I had to say to go along with the plan until the ransom was handed over. Then I would shop the lot of them. For added assurance I had a revolver in my pocket, one not too dissimilar to the one I had used earlier that year. I'd got it, along with others, when I was the man in charge, and hidden it away.

As I opened the gate I immediately sensed something was wrong, though I had no reason to. Nothing was out of the ordinary. The garden was as still and beautiful as it had been earlier that day. Swathes of marguerites lined the path, and in the moonlight they shone like stars. Yet still I sensed something wasn't right. It wasn't until I reached the house that I had any evidence to back up what I felt. The door was

God's Will

slightly ajar and the lights in the hall were off. Fear took me over completely. I looked back across the garden. Was this a trap? Had they somehow read my mind? Wouldn't they even give me the courtesy of a last stand? As I hovered at the doorway, my eyes slowly adjusted to the gloom. Ahead of me I could see a shape lying on the floor of the hallway at the foot of the stairs. My heart raced and I wanted to run, but I had a responsibility. I wasn't there for myself.

Pushing the door open, I saw the moonlight had pierced the darkness of the house. Then I saw Steiner's bloodstained head. His face was a blur; someone had beaten him so badly he was barely recognisable. I only knew him from his hair and his high, suntanned brow, now red and blue in the silver light. As the image seared itself into my brain I tried to understand what it meant, but it was beyond me. Pushing on, I forced myself up the stairs to Lottie's room. I felt sick and dizzy, and in the darkness I moved like a drunk, each step a stumble. I sensed I didn't have long.

I found the nursery but hesitated at the door. I was, superstitiously I suppose, imagining Lottie in bed with her doll—as if thinking that would make it a reality. I didn't care how she looked, just as long as she was untouched by the horror of what I'd already seen. But reality, I knew, had a tendency to reveal the horror plain and unfiltered. Something, or somebody, was blocking the door. It was only half open and I moved carefully not to disturb whatever it was. Then the light from the window showed me it was Olga. She was lying face down. Stepping over her, I retched when I saw the full horror. I felt faint and collapsed to the floor. Olga's head had been battered in and her long blonde hair was mottled with tissue and dark, almost black, clotted blood.

It simply didn't make any sense. All along I had suspected they were preparing a trap for me—but this made no sense whatever. Not

God's Will

Steiner. Not now. And Olga... why was she even there? Only that afternoon, because of the tube strike, she had joked that she would be Germany before I was at the Rotella. Yet there she was, slumped behind the door. I wanted to get out of there, but the image of Lottie rose up in my mind. I would find her, no matter what. It was all I had left. She was my last grip on reason.

I stood shakily and made my way to the door trying not to tread on Olga's hair. In the light of the moon I saw her blood on my shoes. In that moment I should have been thinking of my own survival, of how that evidence could be used against me, but instead all I could think of was how disrespectful I was being. Out of nowhere, I thought of the bible—of Jesus and of Mary drying his feet with her hair... of heaven... of death

Trying to push the images from my mind, I forced my way out of the bedroom, only to feel my legs give way again when I saw a shape in front of me. I would have fallen onto the landing, were it not for the strong hand that grabbed my arm and pulled me upright. I wanted to speak—to say what, I don't know. Maybe to deny my involvement in the murders, to plead for my life, maybe even to apologise for treading on Olga's hair. In the event it wasn't me who spoke first—it was Levy.

'Where's the car?' he growled. I shook my head, which seems ridiculous now I think about it; it was dark after all. Somehow he got the message. 'Think! Where's the fuckin' car!'

Somehow I managed to mumble an answer as he searched my pockets for the keys. As he found them and the gun, I started to cry. I mumbled over and over for him not to hurt me.

'I didn't kill them, you prick!' he hissed in my face. 'Come on!'

He thrust me down the stairs and somehow kept me from falling over Steiner's body. It only took a matter of seconds to get to the car and a fraction of that time for Levy to start it up. I don't remember

God's Will

much else. The moment had reawakened the sensation I had the day I'd killed for the first time. I was numb, and the inside of the car was the only thing that was important to me. We drove for some time, but I didn't know or care where we were going. I knew what was about to happen. They would kill me, but I wasn't afraid. Only the pain concerned me—the actual physics of how it would be. It was too late for Lottie. I knew in that moment that she would never be found and with that conclusion I had accepted the inevitable.

Oddly, despite my familiarity with that part of the world, it took me quite some time to realise we were on the road to Radstone. I could barely see Levy in the darkness. Other than his solid outline, painted in the orange glow of the dashboard, there was nothing but the smell of sweat and cigarette smoke.

Eventually the car slowed and turned off the main road. This wasn't a road I knew. This one was potholed and muddy. We followed it for maybe five minutes or so and, apart from rabbits scurrying from the headlights, it remained deserted. Finally we turned off the narrow lane and into a wood until we reached an opening with the shell of a dead oak tree at its centre. It was then that I finally realised where I was. We were beneath Baker's Hill. This was the wood Julia and I had used after Solomon's shooting. Here we had hidden ourselves from the world beneath the canopy of the trees. More than that—we had hidden ourselves in the purity of nature. Only the trees and animals had been aware of our secret, or so I had thought. Turned out the world and his wife were aware of what was going on.

Now the serenity of that place would witness a truly secret moment. In a way I was happy it was Levy. We had shared a lot in a relatively short time together, and I felt a unique bond had grown between us. There was no love. There was barely friendship. But there was something indelible that bound us close. As we stopped, a storm of insects and moths hurtled into the beams from the headlamps. I waited for Levy to kill the engine, allowing the darkness and the silence to shroud my final moments. But nothing happened. Levy was so still I could have been persuaded that he had died, except every now and then he would blink. My fear grew. Even at a conservative estimate I would say we sat there for over twenty minutes. Were we waiting for someone? In the end I came to the conclusion that Levy was weighing up my life and death in his mind.

A lot went through my head in those twenty minutes—escape being one of them. Then a shocking thought struck me. It concerned Julia. Did Levy know this spot because she had shown it to him, too? Was I so naïve that I didn't realise what she really was? Was Stella right in what she had said about her? There were so many questions in my mind it got to the point where I couldn't think anymore. Finally Levy spoke, driving everything else from my head.

'Get out.' I didn't reply. I didn't have the guts. I just did as I was told. 'Stand in the light,' he then added, opening his window and revving the engine. As I closed the door the insects and moths whirled about me, like atoms spinning and warped by gravity. But I wouldn't join them until I knew. I stared down at Levy through the open window.

'What happened to the kid, Levy?'

He didn't reply straightaway. Then he slowly turned to face me. 'Your lover boy finally lost it.'

'What?' I was completely staggered by his reply. 'Larry? Larry killed Steiner?'

'And the girl.'

'No...'

'Yes. I couldn't stop him. I was waiting for you across the street when he appeared. He shouldn't have been there. He should have been

God's Will

at the cottage, waiting for you and the kid. It's all for nothing now. All for nothing.'

'But what happened to the child?' I wanted to know before the end, but he wasn't listening to me. He was trying to make sense of what had happened and how it affected him.

'At first I thought Solomon had sent him, but something was wrong. I went in... but I was too late. He was with the child when I got to him...' His voice trailed away into the hum of the engine.

'What happened, Levy?'

'It was dark. He caught me off-balance. I blacked out. When I came round I went back to the car. Then I saw you. I thought you were him coming back. You were lucky.'

From the glow of the light I could see he was nodding and, above the noise of the engine, I heard him muttering a single word, over and over. 'Lucky.'

Then, as if the car had become part of him, it growled angrily and reversed at speed back down the track.

So, despite his views on fate and destiny, Larry had had a plan all along. But what was it? And why did it include Lottie? Was it born from his madness of the previous year? Had he now lost his mind completely? None of it made sense. But out of nothing, I felt there was still a chance of saving the little girl. If he didn't take her to the cottage in Brighton, where did he take her? Radstone? It was possible. I estimated it was a thirty-minute walk from the wood, fifteen if I ran. The moon would light my way, and although it was the last place in the world I should be, that was exactly where I was going.

I ran up to the peak of the hill overlooking Radstone. From there I could see the oatmeal stone of the house in the glare of the moonlight, warning me, it seemed, to stay away. I couldn't.

God's Will

As I reached a row of small cottages huddled against the edge of the road I became aware of a flashing blue light approaching from the north. Gripped with fear, I crouched behind a fence and watched as it sped by. I knew that in London the same would be happening, magnified a dozen times. Soon the truth would be known and my name would be connected to the butchery. I realised then I didn't have long and moved off purposefully into the unknown.

Within minutes I was in the copse by the conservatory outside the house. I was terrified and moved forward very slowly until I suddenly saw a shape moving quickly across the lawn towards the patio steps. At first I thought it was one of the servants, but then I realised it was Larry. He was moving so fast he was in the house before I could do a thing. Almost instantly I heard shouting, but it wasn't until I reached the far side of the lawn that I realised it wasn't Larry's voice, but Solomon's. He was yelling, screaming, though I was too far away for it to hear what he was saying. I climbed onto the patio and kept low until I was outside the door. There I listened, hoping for some sort of explanation for the night's chaos.

From where I was standing I could see Solomon at his desk, but it wasn't until I peered around the opened doors that I saw Larry pointing a gun at his father. He wasn't moving at all. He was so still. All the movement was coming from Solomon as he screamed with rage in his chair. Even from the door I could see the tears in Larry's eyes. I think what really shocked me most was Solomon's reaction to the situation. Most fathers would be surprised to find their only son pointing a gun at them, but this was Solomon, let's not forget. He was screaming at Larry —but not for him to put the gun down, to tell him where the kid was.

'Where's the kid? What's going on? You should be waiting for Sickert. What the fuck's going on? Where's Levy? Where's the kid? Where's the girl?'

God's Will

When he said 'girl' I thought he was talking about Lottie, but then it occurred to me that he was referring to two different people. If Lottie was the kid, the girl had to be Olga. What did he want with her?

'It's over,' I heard Larry mutter.

Solomon stood up abruptly. 'What? What's over? Give me that! Give it here!'

Moving around the desk he slapped Larry across the face. The sound was unbearable. As his father raised his crisply ironed sleeve to do it again, Larry took a step back and aimed the gun at Solomon's head. I waited for the shot. It never came. Instead, the same white linen sleeve pushed the gun out of Larry's hand and Solomon grabbed him by the throat. It seemed ridiculous. Larry was at least five or six inches taller than his father and it wasn't physical strength he lacked. Solomon had a hold over Larry the way his good old dad had had over him. Solomon's father would have been proud of his son. He was a chip off the old block. Not a bit like Uncle Vinnie.

In those few moments I understood the depth of Larry's hell for the first time. 'What have you done? Where's the kid? Is she at the cottage?'

Solomon threw Larry back against the far wall and punched him hard in the stomach, before going back to his desk and picking up the phone. I think he was trying to locate Levy—where, I don't know. Either way, I knew it was a wasted call. Suddenly Larry rushed for the gun, which was lying a matter of feet away from the desk. In an instant Solomon understood the situation and turned to kick his son as he came forward. He caught him full in the face and the force pushed his head back at such an angle I was sure his neck must snap. Larry was on his side with his face away from me when he landed. His helplessness did nothing to stop the onslaught.

God's Will

'You're weak ' Solomon screamed. 'You always have been, you cunt! Weak! Weak!'

Between each word he kicked Larry, hard. I was in the open door now, plain to see. The thing was, Solomon was so caught up in the moment he just didn't look. I was terrified, ready to run and save myself. Yet there was this ball of energy deep inside me growing like a sun, forcing me to face what I had avoided for so long. It grew through me, until I thought I could see its light shining through my fingertips. And I could see those fingertips so very clearly, because they were gripped around the gun. I don't remember picking it up, but there it was, and nobody was more surprised than Solomon when he eventually saw me. The look in his eyes was possibly worth everything I'd gone through up until that moment.

'What the fuck...?' he muttered. The look on his face was almost identical to the one he had shown outside the Rotella, the night I saved his life. Now the circle was complete.

Levy once told me it was always easier killing the second time. He was right. Solomon was dead with the first shot. I only emptied the gun to continue the sensation. For a few moments I didn't move. I was very close to him, looking down at the expensive linen sleeve he had used to cover his face. It was so white. There was no blood there. It seeped away beneath the crispness of the cuff onto the carpet like an expanding crimson halo. The sun that had briefly glowed within me had died. The fear had passed, too. Calmly, I placed the gun down on the table and helped Larry to the door. I took him upstairs and tended to his wounds, then put him to bed. After that I showered and watched as the blood ran off me. I'm not sure whose blood it was, but by then it didn't really matter. Afterwards I dressed and found the whisky Larry had introduced me to on my first visit. We were the only ones now; the servants had been given the weekend off, for obvious reasons. It was

God's Will

clear from the empty wardrobes that Julia had gone, too. Solomon would have sent her away—I knew then I would never see her again.

To my surprise the police didn't initially make any connection to Solomon. That would come later. In fact, his body wasn't found until the following Monday when the servants returned. Within an hour of their arrival, Radstone was swarming with police. They found Larry and me in our little cocoon upstairs. Reid, the investigating officer, was particularly sickened that we could behave so inhumanely. But what he couldn't see was that we were the sane ones. Together we understood the world very well. We were, as Larry once put it, the same.

I didn't understand why Larry's plans had involved Lottie, or how he had disposed of her. But every time I doubted him, I tried to remember what he had gone through at the hands of his father. He was like a fruit that had absorbed the vine; it was impossible to distinguish where the wood ended and the flesh began. The terrible reality was, he was his father's son.

Tending to his injuries over that weekend I understood what it is to care for someone you love deeply. Larry was a good patient, but then it's easy to deal with an empty shell. In a way Larry had died, too. From that night to the start of the trial, I didn't utter a word. It didn't help my case, and it infuriated my defence, but what could I say? I was guilty. I did commit murder; it didn't matter to me who it was. The worst part was knowing that I'd failed to save Lottie. That, for me, was the worst guilt of all. Of course, this allowed the prosecution to paint a rather black picture of two young men organising a scheme so dark it even disgusted me. It's surprising how creative one can be given time to rearrange the facts. I didn't stand a chance. But then it was of no interest to me. They could have reintroduced capital punishment for all I cared. At least in that there would have been an end to the pain. As it was, I was sentenced to twenty-five years for my involvement in the

God's Will

kidnapping and the murders of Steiner, Olga and Solomon. Larry, despite his mental state and the fact that her body was never found, was convicted of Lottie's murder. Traces of her blood were found in his white E Type Jaguar.

* * *

There is a sudden cough and gasp and an awful thud forces Sickert out of the chair. He searches blindly beneath him for the bed or, rather, Bepa's body beside it. He yells for help and after the heavy clatter of feet the door opens. But it is not Philip. The smell and sounds coming from this person are quite different. In a moment Sickert hears the springs of the bed sigh as Bepa's unconscious body is placed back on it. Sickert can see this in detail in his mind and he wants to take off the bandages but he is too afraid to discover who this other person is. Especially now Bepa, this kindly old woman, may be dead.

41

Greene was in hell.

It was as if a heavyweight boxer had been practising jabs on his stomach for a couple of days. He had the mother of all headaches, too; he shook like he had a fever, yet he was freezing cold. His eyes were open but he could not make sense of where he was or why he felt this way. It only got worse when a red-faced devil looking remarkably like Alan Reid popped into view above him.

'Good morning, Mr Sickert.' The look on Reid's face was relaxed, kindly almost.

God's Will

'What happened to me?' he murmured weakly.

'What happened is you tried to kill yourself, you dumb bastard... but I saved you.' He grinned and Greene's heart sank as he remembered the whisky and pills. 'Now that is irony, I think you'll agree. How's about a nice cup of tea?'

If Greene required confirmation that he was now in the afterlife, this was surely it...

In the early afternoon, a full five hours later, Greene finally got up. He was in the living room. Strangely, the chair by the window was gone, though the stench of it still lingered. Reid was leaning against the windowsill, staring at him with his arms folded. He looked relaxed. He had explained how he had got in and why Greene wasn't dead.

'I note from the medication that the sleeping tablets were prescribed by a prison doctor. For obvious reasons, they don't hand out the strong ones. Next time take double and throw in a dozen painkillers. That should do the trick.'

Greene had thanked him for saving his life and for his constructive advice, then he told him to go to hell; but not before leaving enough money to repair the lock he had kicked off the door-frame. It was only then that Reid had told him why he was there and that he had spent the previous couple of days with one Jack Levy. Convinced he was hallucinating from the sleeping tablets overdose, Greene didn't react. Then Reid mentioned Julia and the rest. Greene didn't speak. He asked no questions and offered no cross-examining; there was no doubt Reid had experienced all he described because Greene could see it in his face and hear it in his voice. The two men were in the same place, mentally and in every other way.

It could have been due to these revelations or to his state of mind one day after a failed suicide bid, but for the first time in his life Greene

God's Will

wanted to talk about his involvement in the kidnapping of Lottie Steiner. More than that, he felt an eagerness to explain to Reid that he *was* a killer, that his sentence was justified.

'I don't care,' Reid said at the end. They had been talking for hours. 'Who do you think killed Denby?'

'Henderson, who else?'

Reid frowned and his mouth sagged. 'I don't see it. He's not bright enough. You don't even know if he's in London. I'm a little out of the loop on that front.'

They sat in silence for a while, Greene on a couple of pillows on the floor and Reid on a coffee table.

'Why?' Greene enquired softly. 'Why this obsession?'

Reid didn't speak for what seemed like an age, and in that time Greene watched his face closely. His bloodshot, tired eyes revealed nothing at first; then, quite suddenly, they glassed over and tears began to spill down his red, veiny cheeks. He didn't move—he simply stared up at the window without blinking, and cried. He had somehow opened a door inside that had remained closed for a very long time and all the pain he had kept locked up in that place washed over him. Eventually he got to his feet and walked to the door.

'I once had a child. Becky. I loved her so very much. She died and I would do anything in the world to go back and hold her in my arms one more time.' He wiped the tears from his face with the sleeve of his jacket and then he chuckled. 'I'm dying, Tom.'

Greene was shocked, genuinely so. 'I'm sorry. I had no idea.'

Reid gripped the handle, turned with a grin and tapped his chest. 'Dodgy ticker. We could still find out, you know? Piece it together, you and I?'

Greene laughed gently. 'I don't see it somehow, inspector. But good luck with your search. You know everything now. Nobody knows

God's Will

where Larry took her. She could be anywhere. Anywhere at all. I'm without purpose, and you're dying. Not what you might call a strong combination.'

'Fair enough,' Reid acknowledged, with a nod. 'One final thing. You said Larry spoke on his deathbed. Something about God, you said?'

'It was nonsense.'

'Tell me what he said, exactly.'

Greene shrugged. 'I asked him where he had taken Lottie and he said "God's will".'

'Meaning?'

'Meaning inspector, that at the end he had lost his mind completely. He was an atheist.'

'Strange,' Reid muttered with a shake of the head. 'Better be off. Take care, Tom. And remember, you have a life ahead of you if you choose to live it.'

Then he was gone and Greene felt unusually at ease having spoken the whole truth. Well, nearly all of it. He had lied on one front. There was one thing he still had to do. One more thing before he could rest.

That evening, after showering his emaciated body—he had lost more than two stone over a month—Greene presented himself to the world. The knowledge of Levy and Julia's survival had invigorated him. And so, with a sense of reconciliation with a city he had recently learned to hate, he got a tube and went back in time again, this time not decades but a month or so, back to that first week of freedom. Entering the Duke of Cumberland in Camberwell, there were no flashbacks and there was no sense of dread, no fear that some hidden memory may leap out of the darkness. The ghosts had been laid to rest.

God's Will

He heard Rimmer before he saw him. He wasn't alone. He was surrounded by a group of young men. As he approached, Rimmer broke off from his monologue and took a sip of beer. According to Reid, Rimmer ran weekly tours of gangland London, educating the young of today about how the criminals of yesteryear operated. He had been, as far as Greene could gather, recalling his own time as an East End gangster. His audience was agog, fascinated by the wholly false recollections of this remarkable man. Greene shook his head, appalled by society's fascination with thugs.

'You still walking then?' Rimmer said, wiping the froth from his stubbled lip when he saw Greene.

'Cut the crap, Rimmer, or I'll tell your customers what a gutless little shit you really are.' As he said this one of the kids got up to face him. 'Sit down, son,' he muttered, 'I'm a real gangster.' The young man reluctantly subsided, allowing Greene to get a little closer to Rimmer. He didn't waste the opportunity. Grabbing him by the throat he pushed him back against the wall.

'Where can I find Henderson?'

'He'll find you when he's good and ready!' Rimmer retorted, squirming.

'You see, that's always been the problem with you, Rimmer. You just can't answer a simple question. Now, where will I find him?'

'Here, you're hurting him!' said one of the lads.

Relaxing his hold a little, Greene smiled, happy he'd hurt the old fool. 'That better?'

'He'll have you for this!' Rimmer gasped, giving Greene a pungent blast of bad breath.

'I don't give a fuck. Now where is he?'

'He could be anywhere.'

'Try and be a little more specific.'

325

God's Will

'He's got a restaurant in Soho. It's called the Shangri-La. He's there in the week, occasionally.'

Greene grinned. 'Very good. Thank you for your time.'

As Greene made his way back outside, the kid who had stood up to him followed him out. 'Here, mate, could I–'

'Could you what?' he growled.

'Could I have your autograph?'

Greene was still laughing when he emerged from the underground in Soho fifteen minutes later.

Greene was beginning to suspect the Shangri-La was just that, an impossible-to-find earthly paradise, by the time he located a grubby little restaurant by the same name on Golden Square an hour later. To his surprise it was only a street away from where Milton's once stood. What was even more surprising was that he'd passed it numerous times since his release. It was dark now and he found himself lurking in the shadows in a little park in the middle of the square. He didn't feel any particular urge to kick the door in and face Henderson. It was just that he'd experienced so much over the past weeks, he wanted to get things right in his head before he saw him.

Around ten it started to rain and Greene took it as a cue to do what needed to be done. As he crossed the square a black saloon appeared and slowed to a stop outside the restaurant. He was virtually at the door by then, but hesitated as the occupants got out. They were slightly the worse for wear, drink-wise, and laughing and joking, but one voice in particular was familiar. He tried to focus on it as they approached the door. As they entered the pool of light coming from the windows, Greene saw him as he always had in his mind's eye—maybe a few pounds heavier, maybe a little greyer, but still every bit the gangster.

God's Will

Henderson spotted Greene straightaway but didn't seem to recognise him. Then he stopped and stared at him more closely, and Greene could see from the look in his eye that something had registered in his head and he was now searching to find the name for the face. But he couldn't identify it. It was a very telling moment that, for Greene. More so than he realised.

Greene found himself hating the man even more because he didn't even recognise him. He also hated him because of everything Rimmer had said, and because of Denby. There was hardly enough hate left for himself, for not having the courage to find him the day he met Rimmer at the Duke the first time. For quite a few moments they just stared at each other in the rain.

Greene spoke first. 'Don't remember the face?'

'Should I?' Henderson replied quizzically. Before he could speak again, though, his confident expression changed to one of recognition. 'Little Tommy Sickert! Well, well, well. When did they let you out?'

'Don't give me that. I've just spoken to Rimmer.'

'Rimmer,' he said with a laugh. 'Is he still alive?'

'Save it, Henderson. Now, what do you want from me?'

That earned a bemused glare. Again, that was telling. 'I don't know what you're talking about.'

Greene wanted to appear calm and unruffled, but Henderson's reaction angered him so much he felt the words gushing from him like magma. 'Don't you fucking do that to me, Henderson! Don't you dare!' After dealing with Rimmer so effectively he was feeling a little indestructible and went for Henderson's throat in the same casual manner. Bad mistake. Two men, until that moment standing on either side of Henderson, lifted Greene off his feet and had him up against the restaurant wall before he could even get close.

God's Will

Henderson walked to him. 'What exactly is your problem, Mr Sickert?'

He was only a matter of inches away from him now and, looking into Henderson's eyes, Greene saw something he didn't recognise, something different from all those years ago. Henderson was a changed man.

'Does the name Denby ring any bells?' Greene demanded.

Looking round at his henchmen, Henderson frowned and shook his head. 'Who?'

'Denby. The man you sent sailing down the Thames.'

Up until that moment Henderson had been smoking a cigar, but as Greene said this he threw it away and stepped closer. 'Now listen here, I know you've been through a lot for what you did—and I am not ungrateful for the opportunities that came my way because of it. But hear this. You are nothing to me. Things have changed since we last met. I am now a respectable businessman. You are nothing. You always were. But if you ever embarrass me like this in public again I will come out of retirement and send *you* down the Thames. Is that clear?'

'Shall we do him, boss?' said one of the men.

'No,' said Henderson, his eyes still on Greene. 'I think Mr Sickert has got the message.'

Greene wasn't sure what he had been expecting to achieve but Henderson's reaction puzzled him in the extreme. He had played his hand so well, Greene had no taste for the rest of the game. He didn't look back at Henderson once as he walked away, but he could imagine the look on his face.

Something wasn't right.

Walking through Covent Garden, he tried to clear his head as he watched people hurrying through the rain on their way home. Greene himself was in no hurry. He felt he was somewhere between the end of

God's Will

one chapter and the beginning of the next. He wandered aimlessly until Big Ben rang out the midnight hour. Like waking from a dream, he looked up and realised he was on Shaftesbury Avenue, in roughly the place he had met Stella all those years ago, the day he was nearly knocked down by a bus—the day it had all gone so horribly wrong. Then he recalled how it had all come about because he had taken the wrong turning—and it was that conclusion that led him to another. What if it *was* Henderson? What if he had got it wrong? What if Henderson had realised, too late, that he had nothing stashed away, so he'd sent Denby on a wild goose chase—and the information he'd been given about him, whatever it was, was simply unfounded? Wouldn't Denby then be in the way? Was that why he was killed? Well, if was, it would mean the end of his troubles once and for all.

42

When Greene opened his eyes next morning it was as if he had slept for days. His head was foggy and his limbs heavy but that was merely the aftermath of the overdose. Beyond that he felt at peace. The hell of the last month now seemed like a nightmare. All this stemmed from Reid's visit and knowing his life was no longer at risk. Released from the fear of knowing he was being watched constantly was like waking from a terrible fever. He suddenly saw the world clearly. That night had been the first in months he had not dreamt of the house and the bodies.

Later that day his little Asian friend called with his groceries, to find the madman beardless, dressed and a little less mad. Almost immediately there was a clarity to everything he did. He could almost imagine a future free of pain. He was ready to take Reid's advice.

God's Will

Greene knew now that he would never find out what happened to Lottie, or why Larry had done what he had. These things were beyond him. He would let Reid take that to his grave. Feeling the guilt for himself was enough. He wasn't going to take on Larry's and Reid's as well. The remarkable news that Levy and Julia were still alive had shocked him, but knowing one of them was dying and the other had hooked up with a dodgy copper was some recompense. Nobody, it seemed, had benefited from Lottie's death.

Greene wallowed in a type of conscious serenity he had rarely known. He no longer checked the streets for Henderson's men. There was no reason now not to move on with his life. He had inherited, thanks to his secret benefactor, a rather comfortable life and, if invested wisely, an even brighter future. If the money was from Henderson, well, so be it. He'd been through too much not to want to be happy again. And to think it was all thanks to his one-time tormentor Alan Reid.

A few days later Greene decided to clean the flat and have a clear-out. Most of the afternoon was spent trying to clean the carpet around the chair near the window. It was in such a state it would have made more sense buying another one, but he had no intention of wasting any of his windfall unless he really had to. Around five o'clock it started to get dark and he'd just about finished putting things away when he noticed a small pile of what looked like postcards on the floor, half hidden beneath one of the curtains. On closer inspection he saw they weren't postcards at all, but the photographs he had 'bought' from the Ghouls on the night of Denby's murder. How they'd got on the floor he couldn't say, but there they were in all their blurriness. They'd lain at his feet through the hell of those weeks and he didn't like the association. With the intention of putting them on the improvised rubbish pile Reid had started out on the stairwell, he stepped out into

God's Will

the gloom. Suddenly there was a noise in the darkness. He could see someone further along the landing, but as the bulb had still not been replaced he could not make out the shape through the tenement gloom.

'Who's there?' The silence was filled with apprehension, but he sensed only a little of it was his own.

'Hello, Tom.'

Coming into the pool of light from his room, a familiar face brought a smile to Greene's own. 'Mr Verecker?'

'Sorry, I wasn't intending to spook you. It was just that after those stairs I just needed to catch my breath for a moment.'

With a laugh Greene invited him in and tossed the photos onto a shelf by the door. He led Verecker through to the living room. After the niceties and a brief tour of the now furnished flat they toasted the future, staring out across the city in the fumes of the freshly disinfected carpet.

'Well, I hope you don't mind me calling round. When you didn't answer on the previous occasions I was concerned. Especially after what you told me about this Henderson character and what have you.'

Greene sensed from the way he stressed the latter end of the sentence that he may have heard of Denby's death in the local press. It had nothing to do with Greene, though. Denby got what he deserved. Messing around with gangsters is never a healthy pastime; he knew that better than most. Besides, after his chat with Henderson he had decided his troubles were over and he told Verecker as much. They talked and drank until late, and around midnight he was the only one talking. It was a rare sensation, getting fulfilment from expressing himself. He was coming alive again and he would have talked until sunrise had he not noticed a change in Verecker.

He was standing across from him, leaning against the window, and had been listening to him intently, but as Greene paused briefly to top

God's Will

up their drinks, he noticed tears in Verecker's eyes. Then he started to sob. Greene couldn't believe what I was seeing. What was most upsetting was the sound he made. It was the sort of noise you would expect from a child, not a middle-aged man. He was reminded of Reid's tears the previous day. He simply didn't know what to do.

'I'm sorry, Tom,' Verecker muttered after a while. 'It must be the drink. Brings back the memories.'

'It's okay.' Presuming Verecker was talking about his mother, Greene passed him a handkerchief and leant against the window next to him. 'I'm sorry, I was talking too much. Do *you* want to talk?'

'No, it's not that. I... I like to listen. It's just... it's just that it never happens as you plan it, does it? I mean, I had such plans for my life... do you know, when I was a boy I wanted to be a pilot? The thought of just sitting in a cockpit and flying off somewhere... anywhere, was such a wonderful thing to me. With mother now gone—I mean, I cared for her for years—it's just that...'

'I know... I never planned to go to prison for quarter of a century.'

'No,' Verecker replied stoically.

Greene realised how condescending he had sounded and apologised, but Verecker dismissed it, as Greene knew he would. Mumbling something about an early start, he started to leave but stopped at the opened door and pointed to the photos on the shelf.

'Never took you to be a photographer, Tom.'

'I'm not... and neither is the person who took those.'

Although Verecker was looking at the photos, it was clear his mind was elsewhere. But then it had been all night, Greene acknowledged. At first he simply put it down to Verecker's mother's death and the fact that he would now be alone. Yet from his gaze he sensed something else was lying heavy on his mind. It was difficult to put his finger on it, but there was something eating away at him. He knew the look. The

God's Will

express on admitted anxiety. He'd seen it on his face just before he left that day in Muswell Hill, when he first came to see him. Something was troubling Verecker.

'Well, goodnight, Tom,' Verecker said, finally breaking the silence. 'Keep in touch.'

Watching him walk into the darkness and listening to him tread wearily down the stairs, Greene sensed for the first time that Verecker knew more about his situation than he was letting on. But it was late and he had thought enough for one week. He closed the door and then remembered he still hadn't thrown away the photos. They were like a bad penny. He picked them up but one fell back onto the shelf. As he reached for it, he was struck by something that looked familiar. In lots of ways it was like all the other photographs he and Denby had 'purchased' from the Ghouls, but there was something about this particular one. Like the others, it was out of focus and of nothing in particular, but unlike the rest it was an interior shot. It was possible to make out an antique chair and a table covered in dust in the foreground and, beyond that, high on a bare wall, a painting—well, a small section of a framed canvas, anyway. There was actually more frame than painting, but somewhere at some time Greene had seen that frame before. He tried to think but it was late and he was tired; he just couldn't concentrate. He decided sleep might restore the memory in the morning so went to his bed.

That night he dreamt of himself, Larry and Lottie. But this was no nightmare. They were all children, untouched by the horrors of the world, running through meadows of pure white marguerites, each one, it seemed, grown solely to enhance their happiness. There was no fear there, no dirty red-brick houses, no Steiner and no Solomon. They were children preparing for a life of happiness. As they lay on the slope of a

God's Will

hill staring up at the blue sky he fell into a dream—a dream within a dream.

Next morning Greene woke to find the sun shining brightly through the skylights above his bed. The sky was a deep winter blue, occasionally visited by a puff of white cloud. As he lay in the bed he studied the view for some time. He was only half-awake and remnants of his peaceful, untroubling dreams were still playing in his mind. They contrasted sharply with the image of Verecker's pained expression and the photo of the dusty room with the painting on the wall. And all the time he kept looking at the skylights above him. They reminded him of an artist's studio, light being an essential stimulus to the senses of an artist. Not that he had met many artists in his life. In fact, he would go as far as to say he had only met one.

He would never know if these thoughts in isolation would have led him to the conclusion he reached. It was possible, but if he hadn't seen the photo the previous night, or dreamt of Larry, or even awakened to see the sun shining through the skylights there would have been a very good chance he would never have thought of Larry's self-portrait.

That was what he had recognised in the photograph—a small section of the painting that had hung in Larry's flat. How often had he fallen asleep staring at that portrait? How often had it triggered dreams of Larry being free from his father's hold?

Naked, Greene jumped up and ran through the flat, searching every drawer and box for the photos he and Denby had bought from the Ghouls. There were a lot more than he had realised, but none that shed any more light on the interior of that house or the painting.

All day Greene waited for that strange couple to pass by. Up until then he would have done anything to be rid of them, but out of nowhere they had become central to everything in his life. For three days there was no sign of them. Lately, he realised, he had been seeing them less

God's Will

and less. On the fourth day he became so frustrated he actually went out at night to track them down, not that he knew what he would have done if he had found them. He just needed to see them and follow them to their world, anything to understand the connection between that blurry image and this strangest of couples. Whatever his reasons were, it didn't matter, because they were nowhere to be found.

Could it have been simple coincidence that the photo was given to him of all people? Maybe Denby had slipped it in to force his hand? The more he thought about it the more incredible the possibilities became. Had Larry known them? It was possible. When it came to Larry anything was possible. He did have a fascination for tramps, and wasn't that what the Ghouls were? For days he considered the likelihood of this. It was a long time before he eventually forced himself to dismiss the theory. Due to its size the painting had been probably been bought by some bar owner somewhere in London and used to hide a nasty stain on a wall or something. Maybe the Ghouls had wandered into the building and took the snap whilst it was being refurbished. Greene simply couldn't see how any of this could connect to Larry at all.

Then, very early one morning, as dawn was preparing to break, he saw them. They were like shadows hurrying away from the light, their heads bowed and the black, ageing pram rolling before them. In a moment Greene was flapping into his jacket and rushing out onto the steps. He glimpsed them in the distance just as they turned north onto Portland Place. As he turned the corner himself he saw them again, now maybe three hundred feet ahead of him, this time turning right onto Park Crescent. From there they crossed the busy Marylebone Road to Holy Trinity Church. By the time Greene got there the lights had changed and the traffic was whizzing by. For a short time he could do nothing but watch as the odd pair carried on towards the bustle of

God's Will

Euston Road. When he did eventually get to the other side they were gone, disappeared into the thick flow of morning commuters. He searched for another hour—sidestreets, cafes, but all in vain. As he made his way back to the apartment and the sun rose above the city, he wondered if they really were spirits of the night.

43

Someone was at Angie's door. Ever since Denby's death she had been fearful of Greene's return—she shuddered to think of his real name and his transformation from mild-mannered house guest to violent child-killer. She had contacted the police straightaway, but they didn't seem to care. That had all changed with Denby's murder. *What did Greene say? Where did he go?* Then nothing. She had had to go to the local station herself. They gave her firm assurances that Greene wasn't involved in Denby's death; there was no evidence that Greene was responsible in any way for Denby's demise. They'd had a word with him about his violent housecall, but it was her word against his. *Don't worry, Mrs Roberts. One more act of violence or a threat of any kind and he'll be back inside.* She had scoffed at their naivety—what were mild treats to a man who had butchered an innocent child? The next act of violence might just be the one that killed her.

Yet it was not Greene who was at the door. A quick glance through the living room window revealed the policeman who had called before. Was it Rose, or Reid? The unhealthy-looking one, either way—the tall one with the red eyes and cheeks. He asked her if she had a few minutes. It had only been a week or so but he looked ten years older. Angie led him through and made tea. The cup sat in his palm and he

God's Will

didn't take a sip until he made a small grimace and drank some to wash down a tablet from a vial in his jacket pocket. It wasn't only his eyes and nose that were red now—his whole face was. Sunburn? Red-haired people rarely tanned. It was the old joke. He looked like a lobster.

Angie repeated all she had told the police. She even showed him the new lock and where Greene had held her by the throat beneath the painting on the wall. It was clear from his reaction that he hadn't found what he was looking for. Whatever it was. He had seemed distant, confused.

'Did anyone ever call on Denby?'

'At the beginning, yes. A lot of reprobates, but that stopped suddenly when Greene... Sickert arrived,' she answered bitterly, lighting up her third cigarette since his arrival. She was going through two packs a day thanks to Greene.

'And Greene?'

'Only one. Mr Verecker. A lovely man.'

'Verecker?' Reid frowned, remembering that Verecker hadn't mentioned this. 'Yes, I've met him. Was he Greene's only visitor?'

'Yes.'

'Tell me, did Denby ever meet Verecker?'

'Don't think so. No, he only came once, and Denby was out. He stayed away that night. Meeting friends the other side of London.' Her voice tailed away and the carpet at her feet became her focus. 'Hang on, though. No, Mr Verecker came another time.' She looked back at Reid. 'The day you came. He drove past while you were on the doorstep. I remember now. He slowed down and looked at me, I noticed him over your shoulder but I didn't know who he was at that point. Isn't that funny? I forgot all about that. I wonder why he didn't come in?'

God's Will

'Maybe he lives locally?' Reid muttered. 'Probably just a coincidence.'

Reid thanked her for her time and went out, leaving Angie with the feeling that something she had said had changed his thinking somehow. She could tell from the way his eyes widened when she had talked of Verecker. As long as she lived she would never understand the minds of men.

The more Greene thought about the Ghouls, the more he found himself thinking about the night of Denby's murder. What had he seen in the tramp's eye on Portland Place? Had he seen the man somewhere before? Before his arrest, maybe? Did he work for Henderson or Solomon? Had he seen him inside? Was he an ex-convict? He didn't think so. Did he resemble a brother or father he had met then? Was there a watered-down familiarity of facial grouping or eye shape and colour? No matter how much he tried to convince himself the Ghouls had nothing to do with his past, the more they occupied his thoughts. It *was* Larry's portrait. How and why the Ghouls had come across it he had no idea, but there it was. Other doubts were now growing. In the light of Levy's admission, and knowing Reid was off his case, he felt unburdened a little of his long-felt guilt. In its place his thoughts, like atoms battering against the walls of his mind, fused into clusters, throbbing with intensity until he had to face their glow. One, the brightest of all, was the identity of his secret benefactor. Reid was right; it wasn't Henderson. It was an interesting suggestion by good old Verecker, but Reid knew his stuff. There was really only one person who knew for certain, Fenton. Or… maybe there was another?

The next day was Friday and Greene decided to do a little detective work. Getting a tube to Southwark, he found a pub overlooking Fenton's offices, on the corner of Lant Street. He sat by the window

God's Will

and, with eyes peeled, watched the building across the way. It was dark and sleeting, and in the gloom the ugly mishmash of poorly maintained Edwardian and postwar architecture seemed to close in like giants over the bunches of people waiting at the bus stops. He was there for about an hour and saw quite a few people come and go from the grey Victorian building, but not the one he had come to see. Then, around six, the lights opposite went out and Fenton appeared on the pavement. He was alone, which wasn't good. Deciding to come back on the following Monday Greene finished his beer and went out. As he did so he was nearly bowled over by a group of drunken women going by. It was maybe because of the state they were in they didn't really notice him, which was helpful, because one of them was the reason he was there. It wasn't Fenton he wanted but his dippy secretary, Miss Hawkins.

Following them was easy. He only had to listen and reflect on what a terrible mixture alcohol and youth is. They were singing, swearing, joking, all the time unaware of his scrutiny. He watched them, or rather he watched Miss Hawkins, closely. A few minutes later the girls entered a narrow road and went into a pub called The George Inn. As Greene turned the corner he realised he knew the place. Often when he and Levy dropped off 'mail' at Fenton's offices they would call in there for a pint. The place was ancient. It was originally a coaching house, which seemed to Greene to make it an appropriate stopping place for the drunken mares ahead of him. He ordered a pint of bitter and watched the girls, dressed in extremely tight dresses, from one end of the bar. It was easy to spot Fenton's secretary—she was the one with the huge arse and the lovely face. She was also a little more smashed than the rest.

As they went outside for a smoke, Greene hoped Miss Hawkins wasn't too drunk because he needed to talk to her. His major problem

God's Will

was that he needed to get her alone. Surrounded by her drunken friends, that was easier said than done. For half an hour he watched them. It wasn't a pretty sight. Whatever happened to the fairer sex? he wondered. Then his moment came. Passing her drink to one of the other girls, Hawkins stumbled across the cobbles back into the pub. He had it all worked out, and it went like a dream. Well, the first part, anyway. As she walked past the bar he took a step back and turned to face her. As planned she walked right into him. He grabbed her arms as she fell back and pulled her to him.

'Christ!' she yelled.

'I'm terribly sorry.'

As Miss Hawkins steadied herself it was clear she recognised him. The problem was, in the state she was in, she couldn't remember why.

'I know you!'

'Are you all right?' he said, releasing her from his grip.

'I'm not sure—what you got in mind?' She was giggling, which he took to be a good sign. 'Yes, I've definitely seen you somewhere before.'

'Yes, I have a feeling I've seen you somewhere, too.'

For a moment or two she simply stared at him, her eyes struggling to focus on his face. 'The problem is,' she observed, 'I'm far too pissed to remember my own name at the moment, let alone yours. Now if you'll excuse me... I gotta pee.'

On that she rushed along the length of the bar and disappeared into the toilets. At that point Greene genuinely felt he'd missed his chance. For a few minutes he considered his next move. The girl was obviously too drunk to be of any help, and he didn't want Fenton to know he was prying. Deciding to come back another time, he finished his pint and turned to leave.

'Bloody hell!' said a voice.

God's Will

Quite inadvertently, he had stumbled into Miss Hawkins again. This time on her return. She fell backwards onto the floor with such a bang he was certain she'd broken her spine.

'He's at it again!' she cried.

'I'm so sorry,' he said, picking her up.

'I say you're at it again, Mr... Greene! You're Mr Greene of Muswell Hill! I knew I'd seen you before.'

Buying her a drink, he sat her down. It seemed his timing was perfect in more ways than one. Miss Hawkins was drunk because she was celebrating her new job. She was leaving Fenton's employment.

'But you're not really Mr Greene, are you? You're a Mr Sickert. But don't worry your secret is safe with me.'

'Thank you...'

'Julie.'

'Thank you, Julie. I would appreciate that.'

Her mouth dropped open and she stared at him. 'I just thought. We're going clubbin'. You wanna come?'

'Bit old for that sort of thing. How's your...?'

'Arse? Bloody sore! It's all right, though,' she added with loud laugh, 'I've got plenty 'a paddin'. Anyhow, I would have thought with all that money you got, you'd be clubbin' every night.' Bashfully she covered her mouth with her hand. 'Whoops! Me and me big mouth.'

'It's all right. It's common knowledge now. As I'm sure you must know.'

'Know?' From her tone, which smacked more of curiosity than of suspicion, he sensed she really didn't know at all.

'Didn't Mr Fenton ever tell you?'

'He would never say,' she said, after a loud belch. 'He's very professional, Mr Fenton. He's very cons... cons ..'

'Conscientious?'

God's Will

'That's the fella. I don't like to leave him, but I've got to get on in life. I won't be held back. Between you and me, I was keeping that place going.' Trying his best to stifle a smile, despite his disappointment at realising she probably couldn't help him, Greene nodded profoundly. 'Who did you get the money from, if you don't mind me asking?'

'What? Oh, from... my Aunt Beryl,' Greene lied, his eyes staring off into the distance. 'She always did have a soft spot for me.'

'Oh. Well, if she's got all that money she wants to get her staff some decent clothes. And a bath.'

He was so caught up in his disappointment he didn't really catch what she was saying. 'What did you say?'

'The man who brought the letter. She wants to get him some decent clothes and make sure he has a bath before presenting himself to the world.'

'What man?'

'The man who bought the letter. The smelly one!'

Greene was suddenly alert to her every word. 'Could you describe him?'

'Well, like I said, scruffy and smelly. It's a shame, really, he was quite a good-looking bloke. I like older men, Mr Sickert–' She apologised and lowered her voice to a whisper. 'I mean, Mr Greene. She moved closer to him. 'Sorry, but I'm always a randy cow when I've had a drink.'

'Quite... this man, was he alone?'

'Yes.'

'Was he tall with black hair and a long overcoat?'

'That's him. You know him?'

God's Will

'Er, yes. It's my aunt's... butler, Jenkins,' he lied again, this time a little more imaginatively. 'He's always been a bit like that. Low on hygiene, high on loyalty.'

'Loyalty's a rare thing these days. I could be loyal to a man like you, Mr Greene.' She was now cuddling his arm with her head against his shoulder.

'This man... I mean, Jenkins. Did he say anything?'

'No. Just gave me the envelope, stared at me with these dark haunting eyes, and went out. Never saw him again. I only know all this because next day I had to type a few letters out about finding you. Are you sure you don't wanna go clubbin'?'

Greene walked from Southwark to Marylebone in a trance. His feet were sore and his head was spinning, but for the first time since his release, despite the nightmare, the fearful twists and turns, he wondered if there was a possible answer to be found. For days he had searched for the Ghouls. There was no doubt in his mind that the man Miss Hawkins had described was the man, who, along with his partner, had haunted his life for nearly two months. But what connection had they to Larry and the painting? He still didn't know, but he would go to the ends of the earth to find out. He walked steadily, unmindful of the swathes of commuters and the heavy traffic going by.

He couldn't explain why but he felt he was on his final journey. There was the oddest feeling deep inside him, and that was where all his focus now was, too. Maybe that was the reason he had not noticed the car that had followed him for most of the day. Maybe that was why he had not noticed it park up and had failed to spot its occupant, the tall man who had plans for him long before his release from prison, watching him intently on foot from the other side of the busy road.

God's Will

44

Reid rang Mifty and arranged to meet him in their usual pub, The King's Head on Westmoreland Street in Marylebone. Why they still met there he wasn't sure. He was no longer a copper, and it really didn't matter where they met. Mifty had been one of his most reliable informants and Reid felt it important to protect that source by meeting him away from the covetous eyes of colleagues. Besides, they did a nice pint of London Pride.

Despite a late winter chill, drinkers—mostly doctors and surgeons from the heart hospital across the road—huddled around their cigarettes outside and chatted animatedly. Inside, Reid found that warm familiarity of a lunchtime English bar, with more huddled groups, more private laughter and, sitting alone at the head of the horseshoe bar, his fingertips stabbing away at the tiny buttons of a mobile phone, Mifty.

Despite his reassurances to Greene that he had nothing to worry about, Reid found the whole business oddly troubling. Who had murdered Denby, and why? And as for the money Greene had inherited, that simply made no sense. Taking everything into account, all he could think was that Rimmer was the only way forward.

Reid ordered a pint for himself and a pint of cider for his young snout; his poison of choice. They nodded at each other without speaking, then moved to a quiet corner and got to work. Mifty first.

'Rimmer. Full name George Horatio Rimmer. Lives alone in Camberwell in a small house left to him by his mother. His main source of income is the gangland tour he runs alone. They're not what you might call well-organised, but they seem to bring him a steady income. It seems there's still plenty of interest from punters in all that stuff from

God's Will

back in the day, exclusively blokes though—it's an odd sort of bird who'd get a kick out of gangland thuggery.'

'Not in my experience,' Reid observed, wiping a film of beer foam from his lip. 'Is that it?'

Mifty raised his closed fist to his lips and coughed, melodramatically. Reid knew that there would not be another word exchanged until payment was forthcoming. He produced a bundle of notes from his inside pocket and the atmosphere relaxed, but only for a moment.

'Did you know you were being followed?' Mifty muttered, swiftly checking the notes.

Reid tried not to let his consternation show. 'How do you know?'

'A light blue Fiat, old-looking thing. Pulled over when you did. The driver was watching you as you walked in.'

'I didn't see anyone.'

'You haven't been well. Anyhow, he's gone now,' he said, peering out of the window.

Reid ignored the implied suggestion that he was losing it. 'It was probably coincidence.'

'I would agree, if I hadn't seen the same bloke a week ago.'

Reid sighed inwardly. He *was* losing it. 'How long do you think he's been following me?'

'Maybe for a while, who's to say?' the young man replied, gulping at his pint.

He was full of life, bloated with confidence; what he had observed didn't affect *him* in any way. It angered Reid that the youngster was aware of something he wasn't. How could he not know he was being tailed? He *was* past it. The batteries were running down. What part of him would fail next?

God's Will

'The question is,' Mifty continued, his own thinking clear and untroubled, 'are you willing to pay a reasonable—improved—rate to find out who?'

'How much?'

Mifty, his mouth full of booze, didn't stop to answer immediately. He just raised his eyebrows and widened his eyes as if to say he hadn't even considered an amount. Reid knew he already had and repeated the question.

'What would you say if I said a monkey?' Mifty said after a long pause.

'Five-hundred! I'd say don't be so fucking ridiculous.'

Mifty held his ground. 'I'm sorry, Mr Reid, but that's the price.'

He put down the empty glass and got up. Reid pulled him back down and nodded, wearily. Mifty the victor sat back and waited.

'All right,' Reid conceded, 'you got it.'

'I called round your place for my money in case you were back. But you weren't. As chance would have it your Paki landlord was chatting with someone. The topic was you, and I got a good ear.'

'And it was the same man who followed me today?'

'Definitely.'

'What did this man say?'

'Asked how long you had lived there, that sort of thing. But the odd thing was, the Paki seemed to know him. Said he would see him next month.'

Reid nursed his pint for a minute or so. This made absolutely no sense. He needed more. He was alarmed, but this time didn't let it show. 'And you think that's worth five-hundred quid?' He chuckled, but there was no humour in it. This snippet of information was priceless and somehow Mifty knew it.

'Yes, and so do you.'

God's Will

Reid bristled but slid a pen and battered notepad across the table. A scrawny, vein-mapped wrist shot out of the kagool the young man was wearing but it hesitated above the paper.

'A monkey? You gave your word.'

Reid chuckled again. Now there was humour, comedy almost, at Mifty's dilemma. 'I'll increase it to a grand if you can locate my landlord. He's got properties all over the city and I'm in a hurry.'

Mifty was out of the door without saying another word, leaving Reid alone to reason with contrary emotions. Who the hell was watching him? Any potential answer should have terrified him; he could be in grave danger. This faceless man Mifty had seen seemed to be in complete control, not only of him but of Greene, too. He didn't know why, but a lifetime of experience told him it was so. He felt breathless and a twinge of pain shot across his chest. He popped another tablet, leaving the final one rattling on its own in the vial.

It had been three days since Greene discovered the Instamatic print of Larry's self-portrait, two from the morning he had followed the Ghouls. He was living at the window again, but not in the unhealthy fashion he was before. He was off the drink; he now drank coffee and ate fruit. He had also bought himself some binoculars. This was a changed man. Moreover he was an organised one. He was on a mission to solve a complicated riddle. If there was no sign of the odd couple with the pram by breakfast time he gave up until the following evening. This was only a twelve-hour vigil. He couldn't explain why, but he knew the pair would not appear in the daytime. That didn't mean he thought they were anything supernatural; he was beyond all that nonsense about spirits. He thought rationally now. The new Thomas Greene based his thinking on common sense, on patterns of behaviour.

God's Will

But there was one flaw in this approach. It was designed for a single purpose, to locate the odd couple who had somehow stumbled into his life. It did not allow for peripheral concerns. It narrowed his view of the world and it closed his mind off to unknown dangers. If it hadn't Greene would maybe have spotted the pale blue Fiat parked up the street. He would then have possibly sensed that the tall man who had followed him to Southwark and Miss Hawkins had been with him most of the time ever since. Sitting at the wheel of his car for days, spying on at his window, the watcher's personal hell was one of increasing anger and despair. It was rapidly reaching fever pitch and was now on the verge of blowing both of their worlds apart.

The phone call from Mifty came as Reid was arguing with a battle-axe of a female at St Thomas' Hospital. He needed more tablets. God knew how much time he had left. He didn't even know what the tablets did other than keep the pain and tightness at bay, but they kept him going, allowed him to get through the day without collapsing in a heap as he had at the supermarket. Now he had only one left, and that would not do. This he had explained in detail to the slip of a woman with the upturned nose and over-officious nature in the waiting room, which smelt of malady and anxiousness. *No prescription, no medication* was the unadorned response. Reid explained to her that she was a cow and she told him she knew that, as his *kind* told her so on a daily basis.

His frustration was short-lived, however. Mifty had gold for him. He had located Mohammed in Battersea and would keep an eye on him until he arrived. *And could he bring the money, too?* Reid was there within forty minutes, but without payment. He had more pressing concerns. Mohammed was tucking into egg and chips at a greasy spoon on the Northcote Road. Reid waited until Mifty had sulked off before confronting his man.

God's Will

Mohammed seemed surprised to see him but his voice was composed. 'Mr Reid. What are you doing in this neck of the woods?'

Reid explained why and dressed the words with enough menace to put Mohammed on the back foot. Not that Mohammed let it show, but Reid knew. As he talked between mouthfuls, Reid noticed a dark blotch on the top of the other man's scalp. It looked to him as if a bird had crapped on it and he had never cleaned it away so the stain had darkened on his skin. Why had he never noticed this? he wondered. Was he at last seeing the world clearer? Could it be that solving a riddle, profound and unfathomable until now, would give him another life, one of happiness and peace? Could his heart problem be resolved?

Not daring to wonder at the answers, Reid pressed home the attack. 'A reliable source informs me that a man was asking after me at the flat. Who was it?'

Still Mohammed showed no concern. He hid emotions well, thought Reid. He came across as stupid, but it was a ploy, a disarming kind of ploy, and it worked well. Reid had seen it a thousand times. The Asian popped the final mouthful of yolk-coated crust into his mouth. His diction was hampered and the tone muffled but Reid heard his reply distinctly enough. 'Oh, you mean Mr Lamb?'

He searched his memory but could identify no one by that name. 'How do you know him?'

'Roy? He rents one of my apartments. We have an agreement. He has fallen out with his lady friend so he asks me not to give his name out. I know you can be trusted, Mr Reid.'

Roy Lamb? Reid's never heard of him but there was something curious about the name. He took out the pen and pad for a second time that day and slid it across the plastic table top. 'Address.'

Mohammed began to write without questioning why. 'I have always wondered what you do, Mr Reid.'

God's Will

Reid was too busy trying to understand why the name of a man he had never heard of was playing with his brain to answer at first. 'I suppose you could call me a private detective.'

'Gracious me! You are not representing Mr Lamb's lady friend, I hope!'

'I don't do divorces...'

'My father was a great fan of Raymond Chancellor...'

Chandler, thought Reid, but didn't correct him.

'He had many of his novels. What an exciting life. What was his favourite now?'

Reid picked up the pad and read the words on it before placing it in his pocket. Like the name the address meant nothing to him. But there was something in the name... There was something about it. As he got up, Mohammed followed his ascent with his index finger.

'*The Big Sweep*!'

The Big Sleep, you piss-taker. Reid wanted to slap him, but suddenly his thoughts veered in a new direction as, in his mind's eye, he saw the letters of Roy Lamb's name appearing.

He glared at the seated man. 'How does Roy spell his surname?'

Mohammed looked puzzled at such a strange question. 'Lamb? L, A, M, of course!'

Reid's heart rate increased to an incredibly unhealthy level. In his head the letters began to move around until they fell into a name he recognised.

R. O. Y. L. A. M = MALORY.

That was this man who had organised Greene's stay at Muswell Hill. Somebody was playing a game, and as he looked at the address—Flat 7, 183 Broadstairs Crescent, Brixton—Reid realised he was very close to finding out who.

God's Will

It took Reid an hour to find it and, just as Denby had done a month earlier, he now stood before the door with the faded green paint, wondering what was on the other side. Unlike that of the murdered man, Reid's visit was unheralded. The occupant did not know he was on his way. He checked the stairwell a couple of times before knocking gently on the loose wooden panel—just as Denby had. It made the same rattle, but the hand that made the sound belonged to a man no longer haunted by his past. There was firmness in this fist. A type of benign confidence had grown through the bone, muscle and tissue; Reid's resurrection had opened his eyes and he felt he was on the threshold of something. But what? He knocked again, waited for a moment then tried once more. Inspector Reid was making his enquiries.

He considered the situation for all of three minutes before deciding he could wait no longer. The rattling door had made plenty of noise up until that moment so he felt pretty confident that kicking it in wouldn't draw too much added attention. So that's what he did. One single, good old-fashioned police kick, just above the handle. The door flew open, closed briefly and then opened again with a yawning sigh of defeat. He hadn't lost his touch. He waited for some type of response from the other rooms on the floors below but none was forthcoming. Inside was darkness—complete, suffocating blackness. It pulled at him, it drew him in and, like Denby, he had no defence against it.

Along a short hallway he found a barren living room, another room he presumed to be the bedroom, a bathroom and a small kitchen. In the latter he found a cooker, fridge, cupboards and sink that should have all been condemned in the late seventies. It was a typical Mohammed 'luxury' home. Unlike his own place, however, this apartment seemed unlived in. There was no evidence of human life at all. He checked the bin. Empty. The cupboards and drawers. Empty again. In the tiny

God's Will

bathroom there was more of the same. Oddly, the bedroom door was locked. Most landlords wouldn't have locks on bathrooms let alone bedrooms. This was the tenant's doing and, from closer inspection, a recent addition.

It didn't stay locked for long.

Using the same technique as on the front door, Reid kicked the door open. Again he found darkness but from it he sensed a presence of a kind. He found the light switch and after a short delay a solitary striplight spluttered into life. What he saw in the bright fluorescent light took his breath away. It was as if he was back in his own flat a week or so earlier. To his left was an incident wall. There was a mural consisting of photographs of Lottie, Solomon, Greene, himself—a recent one of him getting out of his car—and another of an elderly man with a large moustache he was sure he had seen somewhere before. These images filled the central part of the main wall, directly across from a single bed and faded mattress. Around the images, not unlike his own set-up, were other pieces of information regarding the Steiner case —newspaper cuttings, magazine articles and, below them, like a tiny city skyline, a row of stacked books on the same subject. Whoever Malory was, he had followed the case in the same way but, if the newspaper dates were anything to go by, for not so long. The latest addition was from the *Daily Express* and comprised a report on the German journalist's claims that the Steiner gold had been secretly shipped to the UK in nineteen seventy-six, despite denials by both governments. The only thing that differed from his own investigation was the inclusion of maps of Kent, Essex and East Sussex on a wall adjacent to the bed, some blown up so they could be viewed easily from the pillow. Night-time reading if he ever saw it.

Why hadn't he ever thought of that? Maybe he wasn't as obsessed as he thought? In a daze he slowly moved around the bed to get a closer

God's Will

look. Names of places, as familiar to him as his own offspring, sprang out before his bloodshot eyes. Radstone, Baker's Hill, Lambourne, the A213—Solomon's house, the surrounding landscape, the local parish, the river and the road that ran through the area respectively. While he had linked particular areas to notes on the periphery with red string, Malory had used green. While he had typed out his comments with fervent endeavour, Malory, a man who could not have been as well versed on the intricacies of the case despite recently released police reports, wrote his in a tiny caterpillar-like scrawl with a perception and understanding that impressed Reid greatly. How he wished in that moment to have some knowledge of graphology, that he might garner some hidden insight into this man's character. What secrets were to be found in those wildly crossed t's, stabbing fullstops and tall proud consonants? Whoever this man was, he understood the case and had made relatively accurate summations, based both on the police reports of the time and, presumably, his own theories. Malory had a bright mind. But what was he doing? Why would someone not part of the investigation be so obsessed? Was there a connection to the case? Was he a vengeful relative who had bided his time having reached an influential position within government? Was that how he had organised Greene's aftercare on release? Or was there some other connection to the Solomon family, or even Greene? It was on that final thought that something stirred within him. He turned and walked over to the photographs. There it was—the old man with the moustache. He knew him from the newspaper reports.

It was Denby!

This all came as such a shock Reid couldn't think coherently. He felt breathless and weak and sat heavily on the bed. His chest suddenly tightened and he felt a sharp piercing ache in his left arm. He gripped it and knew what he had to do. Throwing back his head he swallowed the

God's Will

remaining tablet, dry, then dropped the empty vial on the unadorned mattress. As he waited for the pain to recede he took deep breaths, concentrating hard on the maps in front of him until the moment had passed.

Something else drew his attention. Malory had circled a wide area around London, like an archery target, across all of the maps. In each layer was a time zone—thirty minutes, an hour, and so on up to two and a half hours. The final layer ran as far as Bishop Stortford in the north, the coast in the south and Rochester in the east. Reid stood and examined Malory's furthest boundaries. Why this far? Maybe because Malory knew less than he did and that allowed him to look beyond what was possible? This mysterious figure had about as much chance of finding Lottie's body as he had now. Reid was fascinated, nonetheless—excited almost by the realisation that someone else had such interest in the case. Then he noticed something else on one of the smaller maps of the Rochester area. A name, a placename that seemed oddly familiar to him. His eyes had brushed over words that triggered some memory in him, like a puzzle. Like the name of Roy Lam. He tried to locate the words again but as he did so he heard a noise behind him. Wrenching his focus from the north Kent marshes, he turned to see a tall figure silhouetted in the doorway. He froze, unsure what to do or say, but in the end it wasn't he who spoke first.

'What do you think you're doing?' The voice was deep, steady and familiar to Reid. He didn't reply. 'I asked you a question!'

Either it was the after-effect of the tablet or shock, or possibly both, but Reid could not put a name to the voice. Everything was out of context. Then the man stepped forward into the illumination of the striplight.

Reid's mouth opened slowly and he spoke in a whisper. 'Verecker?'

God's Will

His head spun and in a moment he understood. Of course. Verecker was Malory. Now there was no confusion in his mind. Parts of his brain, rusted and cobwebbed, unused for so long, were once again groaning back into life. Cogs were clicking, wheels whirring, out of control.

'It was you?' Reid didn't move. He simply stared at Verecker, whose towering frame filled the doorway. 'It was you who had Denby watch over Sickert.'

'I don't know what you are talking about. I… I… I sublet this flat. I don't know any Denby.'

'What are you looking for, Verecker?'

'What are you talking about? You come into this flat—or should I say trespass—you kick in the door and make these accusations! How dare you!'

'Is it Lottie? Do you have your own interest in the case? Is that why you befriended Sickert? It was you who organised the house in Muswell Hill. There is no Malory. It was you all along. You had access to prison records. You knew when he was coming out. You're Malory. But why? Why use Denby to watch over them? You know Sickert—you could have just asked him.' There was something in Verecker's eye when he mentioned Denby that made him slow down. The wheels and the cogs came to a standstill. The result was a pattern, a pattern Reid understood perfectly.

'You killed him. *You* killed Denby.'

Verecker had changed. His face was neither passive nor raging. He was mumbling to himself, as if he was trying to make sense of this turn of events. Although he didn't understand what it was all for, a lifetime of experience told Reid he was right and that he had revealed an unlikely killer in this mild-mannered man. *But why?* He glanced back at the wall at all the clippings of the kidnapping and the rumours of

God's Will

torture and cannibalism. He had seen them all before; he had most of them on his own wall, in his own private collection, but there was one subject he did not cover that Verecker had in abundance. The Steiner Gold.

He turned his head to face Verecker again. 'It isn't the child at all, is it? It's the gold!'

Expressionless and quite still, Verecker did his best to defend himself. 'No, you're wrong. I took an interest in the case after what those butchers did that to that little girl. Little Lottie–'

'You fool. There isn't any gold, there never was. It never left Germany.' Reid pointed at the wall. 'That report about the flight is nonsense. The reporter probably got wind that Sickert was due to be released and stuck it on the market to make some quick cash. You bloody fool, Verecker!'

'No,' Verecker murmured, over and over. The rant lasted for maybe thirty-seconds or so and in that time Reid's anger merely intensified.

'Do you think this was a game? A puzzle? Anagrams of names— hide and seek?' He pointed at the maps on the wall and his voice raised to a shout. 'Find the fucking thimble!'

Something dark took Verecker over and for the first time Reid feared for his own life. Without moving his head he glanced around the room for something to defend himself with, something to hold him back, to redress the balance, to make the fight less unfair. There was nothing, nothing at all but a wall full of memories and two haunted figures on the edge of a precipice. Reid looked back at Verecker in time to see the look on his face change once more and his body stiffen. In that same moment Verecker leapt forward, his hands reaching for Reid's throat. Despite his size he was unusually agile. Reid's head smacked against the wall, pain taking his breath away. He felt his body

God's Will

give under the assault. Verecker's strength was remarkable. Reid found himself suspended against the wall, choking for air.

'You're after it, too!' Verecker yelled. 'You don't give a damn about the girl It's the gold you want. That's why you're following Sickert. That's why you've waited for so long. Well, it's mine!'

Reid tried to speak but he could barely breathe. Verecker's thumbs were digging into his windpipe. His chest was tightening, too. He knew this was the end. Verecker's final words were echoes to Reid, whooshing around him like bats at great speed until eventually they passed through him and he was unable to focus on a single thing.

With one hand on Reid's jacket and the other on his throat, Verecker began to batter him against the wall with a terrible howl, like that of a wild animal. Along with phlegm and saliva it escaped through his gritted teeth against Reid's blue lips and bulging eyes. Verecker was out of control.

45

Despite his best efforts Greene fell asleep at the window of his flat during the night. It was brief, a momentary drift into dreamland, but in it he found horrors he believed forgotten. It was Lottie again. He was watching her watching him from the street below. Her black hair fell down her chest like plaited liquorice. She had the doll in her arms as Greene only woke from this torture when his chin hit the windowsill, causing him to spring back to life. Getting his bearings, he stared out into the street... and there they were.

Like human-sized wind-up dolls the pair walked side by side, never once looking round, never once talking, their focus ahead of them,

God's Will

beyond their antiquated pram. Greene hurriedly put on his coat and ran out of the door, wondering feverishly, madly, what connection they had to Larry. Like the time before, he ran out onto Westmoreland Street just in time to see them turning left, north, onto Portland Place. And like before he was too obsessed with their destination to see the blue Fiat parked along the road and a man he knew well watching him from the wheel.

It was just after seven in the morning and the sky was white with winter fog that hung in the cold air around traffic and commuters. This time the Ghouls would not elude him. He would stay close and follow them back to their world, even if it *was* an imaginary one. He closed the gap and was certain they would look back at some point and spot him, but they never did. They seemed to exist in a world of their own. By then he was, too, because if he had been a little more conscious that morning he would have been aware of Verecker striding through the mist not far behind.

Following the same path along Portland Place, past the silent protester, and across Marylebone Road, Greene stayed as close as he dared. After a couple of minutes the couple turned off the high street across Euston Square. In less than a minute they were in Euston Station and heading for the tube. Paying contactlessly, Greene passed through the automatic gates and hurried down the escalator. By this time they were maybe thirty feet ahead of him and he realised from their wordless routine, the man holding the front wheels of the pram and the woman holding the handle, that this was the way they moved around. It explained why they suddenly disappeared and reappeared all over the city. It just hadn't occurred to him that they would travel on the tube— not with the pram. But that was where they had gone, and it was why he had lost them the previous time.

God's Will

Greene arrived on the platform a dozen feet behind them just as a warm rush of air from a passing train swept through the tunnel. As he waited, more and more commuters spilled onto the platform. Fearful he may be carried away from the pair in the tide he slowly pushed through the throng towards them. It was easier than he thought; the smell they gave off cleared a large space around them. He'd been there himself, but it didn't matter to him now. He would put up with anything to keep them in his sight. As Greene got closer he realised he was almost close enough to see into the pram, but before he could get any closer the arrival of another train checked his advance. As it came to a stop there was movement all around him, forcing him ahead of his quarry towards the train. Not knowing the pair's intentions, he looked around to see where they were, and as he did so he caught the woman's eye and something stirred within him for the first time. At first he thought it was fear that she would recognise him but, just as it had been with her partner, he realised it was something much more than that. He turned away and let himself be steered onto the train because it was obvious the Ghouls were getting on it, too.

As the doors closed behind them the Ghouls stood over the pram like guards until the train set off. Again their odd nature and unwashed smell kept people at a distance, which allowed Greene to see them clearly from further along the carriage. But he was being watched, too, by a tall figure in the next carriage—a pair of eyes watching him watching them. From Warren Street to Goodge Street to Leicester Square he was vigilant, anticipating any sudden movement when the train stopped. But it wasn't until the doors opened at Charing Cross that the couple came back to life. Keeping close, Greene began to follow them out, only to be halted by a group of schoolchildren rushing into the carriage. As he stumbled back a young schoolteacher yelled at her charges for their over-eagerness and apologised profusely, but the damage had been done. He had lost sight of them.

Rushing up the stairs to the concourse, Greene searched in all directions for them but there was no sign of them anywhere. He wondered if they were still on the platform and turned, but as he did so he caught something familiar out of the corner of his eye. It was only a fleeting glimpse, but he was sure he saw part of the pram, the ancient black perambulator with large wheels and spokes. Even though the station was packed with commuters, Greene was certain he saw its macabre shape briefly through the crowd. He rushed through the travellers like a wild man. Again he thought he'd lost them, but as he looked beyond the gates to the railway platforms, he saw them. They hadn't escaped him at all. They were getting a train out of London.

Greene thought quickly. He could pay, but he simply didn't know which train they were going to get. Hoping he would have enough time to buy a ticket and get on the train, he waited until they boarded. There was a risk he could lose them again, but he had no choice. They were walking between two trains, on platforms three and four. Then, as he watched, with the sound of his heart beating in his ears, they turned sharply to the right and boarded the train on platform three. Searching the huge information board, Greene looked for the train's ultimate destination. The journey's end struck an obscure chord within him.

In less than a minute Greene had a ticket and was searching each carriage from the platform. He found the couple in the final one and boarded the adjoining carriage so he could see them through the compartment door. He remained completely unaware that Verecker had replicated all of this and was watching him from the next carriage down. Within minutes the train was cutting through the morning mist above the Thames, heading south-eastwards towards Kent. By then it was around eight, but despite a defiant effort the sun was struggling to

God's Will

break through the cloud and mist, which mingled like a blanket above the city. In the subdued unnatural glow, Greene watched the blank faces of the Ghouls as they stared out across the urban landscape, little guessing what hell they were leading him to.

Reid didn't know where he was or even that he had been attacked until he raised his head and the throbbing pain knocked him back onto the bare floorboards. He was lying on his back by the bed, beneath the wall of maps. The floor next to his head was smudged with dried blood. He wondered how long he had been there. He tried to push himself up but couldn't. Then he remembered the transformation of the once mild-mannered Brian Verecker.

Was he still in the apartment?

Not daring to make a sound, he got up. There was no sign of Verecker in this room or the next. It was morning now and Reid concluded his attacker was long gone. He was about to leave when something drew him back to the bedroom, specifically to the wall of maps. He sat down on the bed again. Paralysing flashes of the assault blinded his thinking as he stared up, but he *was* looking. He *was* taking in information—not consciously perhaps, but his mind *was* absorbing details, as it had done the night before. In his brain, Verecker was still battering his head against the wall, but some small part of it was analysing, deducing, finding an answer to a riddle at the centre of his unconscious. It was something he had seen. Two words. A name.

Gad's Hill.

He did not recognise it. Cogs clicked, wheels spun. What was it? Why did the words strike him so? Greene's voice, or rather Thomas Sickert's, suddenly echoed in his mind and increased in volume the more he concentrated upon it. It was a conversation they had had in his apartment on Westmoreland Street the day after Sickert had taken the

God's Will

overdose, the one about Larry in the hospice and the night he had been handcuffed to Verecker...

'You said Larry spoke on his deathbed. Something about God?'

'It was nonsense.'

'Tell me what he said, exactly.'

'I asked him where he had taken Lottie, and he said God's will.'

'Meaning?'

'Meaning, inspector, that at the end he had lost his mind completely.'

The wheels stopped and the cogs clicked one final time as Reid clambered to his feet.

No, Thomas Sickert, he did not say God's will. He did not at all. He said Gad's Hill.

Larry Solomon's final words had not been some profound religious observation; they had been the answer to Sickert's question. He had taken Lottie Steiner to a place called Gad's Hill in Kent.

Reid drove north of the Thames to Sickert's flat in Marylebone. He drove so fast he turned a thirty-minute drive into fifteen. Despite his continued knocking there was no reply from the door at the end of the dark corridor. Had Verecker dragged him away as he had Denby? Had the occupant tried his hand at suicide and been successful? He was about to kick the door in and find out, for a second time, when he heard footsteps on the stairwell. He pulled himself into the shadows and listened as feet approached him in the darkness. He hoped it was Sickert.

'Mr Reid?' said a voice—a familiar one, but not Sickert's. 'I know you're there. I saw you come up.'

Mifty. No doubt staying close so as not to lose his money.

'The money will have to wait. Now fuck off.'

God's Will

'You shouldn't be so hasty. I want my money but it's possible you might want to give me some more?'

'What are you talking about?'

'The man in the blue Fiat. He was here.'

'When?'

'About half an hour ago. Did you know he was watching over Greene? I came thinking you might be here.'

Reid's tired eyes had now become accustomed to the darkness and he could see the contours of the little man's face. His tone mellowed and he moved away from the door. 'Do you know where he is now?'

'He got a train. With Greene.'

'Together?'

Mifty chuckled. 'Course not. He was following him. I thought you might be interested so I followed *them*.'

'Where did the train go?'

Mifty hesitated. Reid had no time for this. Taking the bank card out of his wallet he pushed it into his hand. Seven-two-eight-nine. Take what you like.'

It could have been the dim light but he was certain that the shape of Mifty's face changed, as if the molecular structure of it had transformed due to this huge inducement. When he spoke again the little man's voice had a richly contented tone.

'The train's destination was Rochester.'

Away from the city the mist was so dense it had a hold on everything. It slurred the conscious world into a gloomy intensity, which even affected Greene as he stared out at it. Other than the Ghouls that was all he noticed. The mysterious couple had become central to everything he thought important. As the train juddered through the London boroughs of Greenwich and Charlton and Woolwich, his eyes remained fixed on

God's Will

them. Rochester. Was that a coincidence? He remembered clearly the time he went there with Larry and the day he met Julia. But what connection was there to the Ghouls? As he considered the possible outcomes, he became almost dizzy from excitement and fear.

The further away from the city they went the more the fog smeared the world into a dream. Even when the sun finally peeped through the morning cloud the fog held tight, concealing the towns of Dartford and Greenhithe and Gravesend. They were places he had heard of and read about but had never personally known. At each station he waited with childlike anticipation for some movement from the Ghouls to indicate departure from the train, but his wait just went on and on.

At Gravesend the train was held at a red light for a time but when it set off again it plunged into the mist once more. Greene had no clue that the end of his journey was drawing near. After ten minutes the train slowed to a stop at Higham Station. He had little idea where that was. He knew it was north Kent, but he didn't know where exactly. By then the train was nearly empty. For a moment the Ghouls didn't move, but as soon as the doors opened they suddenly came back to life and hurried out. Greene followed. Out on the platform he watched as they dissolved into the mist beyond the small station house. Then it was his turn. Moving off into the unknown, he was completely unnerved by their proximity in the swirling fog. It was so cold and the mist was so dense he could barely see a thing other than their black shapes moving ahead of him.

Once out of the station they walked down some sort of narrow lane for quite some time. All around him Greene made out the vague shapes of trees and hedges looming over him like giants questioning his reasons for entering their strange world. Now, as he had always imagined it would be with the Ghouls, everything was changed. He had gone from one world to another. They *were* ghosts, just as Denby had

God's Will

described them. Their black shapes diffused by the mist seemed both unearthly and timeless. Away from the train, the station and the world he knew, there was nothing now to reassure Greene that this wasn't hell. Normality no longer existed. London's familiar pace was his reassurance each day, and without it he was lost. All he had was the belief that this eccentric couple could somehow lead him to the final answer.

The pair had walked for twenty minutes or so, but never once did they slacken their pace or look back. Occasionally they passed a small isolated house or cottage and Greene would slow for a second or two, but on they would go, and again he would hurry through the mist after them. Other than a solitary dog walker he saw no one else. On at least two occasions he was certain he heard footsteps behind him, but looking back all he could make out were the haunting black shapes of trees and hedgerows. He realised now they was approaching the coast —not because of salt in the air or any view of the Thames estuary, but due to the blast of a foghorn shattering the morning silence every thirty-seconds or so.

Twice the fog became so dense Greene lost sight of the Ghouls. Then he would hear the unsettling squeak from the pram and he would lengthen his step through the gloom. After some time he detected the vague outline of a wooded hillside. As the track turned away from it he was surprised to see the couple suddenly stop and lift the pram over a stile, in the same way he had seen them do so on the escalators at Euston. Dipping down behind a fence, Greene watched as they walked across a small field and into the wood beyond. When they were at a comfortable distance from him he did the same.

Once among the trees the fog seemed thicker, its dank, lifeless vapour closing in on him like a shroud. He must have been only twenty feet behind the Ghouls now, but suddenly he couldn't see them. He

God's Will

knew they must be just ahead of him as he could still hear the pram, but they had been absorbed by the mist and the darkness of the wood. Then the squeaking of the wheels fell suddenly silent. Greene stopped and peered breathlessly into the mist, his warm breath rising in the cold air. In the damp, leaden stillness of the wood, he couldn't hear anything. Nothing at all. Had they stopped? Were they carrying the pram again? He didn't know, but decided to push on anyway, hoping to catch sight of them along one of the many tracks that led off the main path. In minutes, however, he was lost. The mist and the horizonless thickets around him had conspired to disorientate him completely. He tried to find his way back to the main path, but as he did so he saw a tall, looming shape amongst the trees. He knew straightaway it wasn't the Ghouls. Whoever, or whatever it was, was as breathless as he was and seemingly just as lost. The figure had stopped to rest against a tree and was just a matter of feet away from him, but in the mist the man couldn't see him. Greene remembered the footsteps on the lane. He hadn't imagined it. He knew then he was being followed. He thought back to Denby's murder. Was it his turn now? He held his breath and tried to hide his stocky frame behind a narrow tree.

He had never been so afraid in his life.

Then, just as the groaning sound of the foghorn filled the air, the man, quite without any warning, started walking in his direction. Greene couldn't take the chance he would see him and ran down a slope behind him. There the trees were less dense, and as he hurried forward he could see from the light now breaking through the mist that the landscape ahead was flatter and more open. By that point he had completely lost sight of the Ghouls, but now he didn't care. The need to survive had taken him over. At the bottom of the hill there was a small gravel track that led to some sort of bird sanctuary. He saw a sign on which the word 'Marshes' was all he could make out. He didn't think

God's Will

anything of it—he didn't have time. Hurrying past the small observation hut he heard footsteps on the gravel path behind him. He was gasping and his chest was beating so loudly he was sure it could be heard. On he ran, his intention being to make a wide curving dash and then return to the station through the wood. But the more he ran, the more his old body ached, and the further he travelled, the boggier the ground became. Before long he was stumbling from one muddy patch to another. But he didn't stop. He ran and he ran. Blinded by the mist he was a madman again—not because of remorse or self-loathing but out of fear of the unknown. In his panic he had visions of Denby running close behind him, bloated, blanched white, reaching out for him with swollen hands, wanting to know why Greene had abandoned him. Then he thought he saw Lottie pointing the way ahead.

Suddenly the ground beneath Greene's feet disappeared as he stumbled into a culvert. The sides were so steep he couldn't do a thing to stop himself from plunging into the dark water. The freezing, numbing cold of it took his breath away, though it wasn't deep. Trying to ignore the intense discomfort, he clawed his way back up the bank, gasping in the winter air. Then he saw him, his stalker, peering down into the water maybe twenty feet or so further along the bank. Forcing himself up, Greene noticed a clump of trees in the mist over to his right. Thinking he must be near the wood again, he ran as fast as he could away from his pursuer, though now he was coated in mud and his clothes clung to him like ice-cold treacle. He stumbled repeatedly until finally his foot went over and intense pain shot up from his ankle.

The pain was so intense Greene realised he must have broken a bone. He lay in agony, trying to suppress the urge to vomit and looking up at the trees. He was only thirty feet or so from them, but now he saw it wasn't the wood at all, just a trio of elms on a small raised bank. He couldn't reach them anyway. Not on his injured ankle. In total defeat he

God's Will

fell back, conscious of his pursuer closing in on him. All he could do was wait for the inevitable. The deep moan of the foghorn out in the estuary shattered the morning calm. He had an idea where he was now. Along the Thames meant the North Kent marshes—Dickens country. This was where he would die. This *was* the realm of ghosts.

The sound faded and instead all he could hear above his own breathing was the noise of the stranger stumbling towards him. As he got closer Greene made a monumental effort to control the noise of his own breathing, hoping against hope the man would miss him and carry on towards the trees in the distance. But the effort was wasted; in a matter of seconds he stood before him.

'You shouldn't have run, Tom.'

Greene raised his head and stared in shock at Verecker looking down at him, his face ghostly white, gasping for air.

'I only wanted to talk. You shouldn't have run.'

As the foghorn moaned again Greene's head fell back onto the muddy earth and his heart sank.

Before leaving Verecker's apartment Reid had helped himself to a couple of the maps, one of north Kent and another of the area around Rochester specifically. They sat beside him on the passenger seat as he drove. He glanced down at them so often he soon had them fixed in his mind's eye—Rochester, Gad's Hill, Higham, Strood and the North Kent marshes. According to Mifty the train left at eight-eleven from Charing Cross, which meant it would arrive in Higham, the nearest station to Gad's Hill, one hour later. Or Strood and Rochester, the next two stations, shortly after that. He drove fast considering the foggy conditions and hoped members of his former profession wouldn't spot him. There were so many questions in his head, but one that simply didn't make any sense to him was why mild-mannered Verecker was

God's Will

persuaded there was gold to be found. Why would he believe that? Who told him? Risking his life even further he searched his phone log with one hand for Stockwell—the prison officer who had been with Verecker on the night of Larry's death—for a possible answer.

'I don't know that much about Verecker's career, to be honest,' Stockwell told him when Reid finally found the number. 'Other than a year at Broadmoor Hospital I think he spent most of his time at Brixton ..'

'Broadmoor? Verecker told me he never went there.'

'Don't know why he told you that. He asked for the transfer.'

'When was this?'

'A couple of years ago... is everything all right?'

A year before Solomon died. So Verecker had met Larry. He had spent a year around him. What had Larry told him? Was there treasure to be found, after all?

Reid made good time despite the fog and the morning rush hour, but didn't arrive in the area until the train had passed both Higham and Strood. He parked on double yellows and rushed into Rochester station to await the arrival of Greene and Verecker. A handful of commuters stepped out, but none of them bore any resemblance to either of the men he sought. Clearly they had got off at an earlier station. He rushed back to the car and raced to Higham, which was the nearest to Gad's Hill. It was a gamble but it was all he had.

The station was deserted. If they had got off there he had no way of knowing where they had gone to next. They could be anywhere. As he made his way back to the car a middle-aged man appeared with a tired-looking labrador and made his way to a four-by-four parked nearby. As the man produced a bowl of water and the dog slurped noisily, Reid made his way over.

'Excuse me, are you local?'

God's Will

'I am,' the man replied stoutly.

'Where can I find Gad's Hill?'

'Gad's Hill is an area, not a place. Dickens' former home is called Gad's Hill Place. You can see it from here.' The man pointed towards a mist-shrouded hillock a mile or so away, dotted with trees. 'Just follow the track.'

'Have you been in that area yourself—I mean, walking the dog?'

'Why do you ask?'

'I'm meeting up with a couple of friends,' Reid improvised. 'I'm a bit late.'

'I saw a couple of chaps walking towards the marshes. One was quite tall.'

'And the other one?'

'Didn't get a good view. Come to think of it, they were going in the same direction as the twins…'

'The twins?'

The old man giggled. 'I say twins. Not sure if they are. A couple of local oddities. They don't speak to anyone, push a pram everywhere. They live with their mother in an old farmhouse overlooking the marshes.'

Reid didn't hear the last sentence. He was already hurrying from the car park and down the track towards the hill and the marshes beyond.

Ever since his release Greene had considered many candidates as Denby's accomplice and murderer, but never once, not even for a second, had he imagined Brian Verecker. Even though the former prison officer was trying very hard, Greene could see the guilt in the eyes of a respectable man suddenly caught in the act of a terrible crime.

'Tom…' he muttered with a pained expression.

God's Will

For a moment Greene thought Verecker was going to try to talk himself out of it. But in that same moment Verecker's eyes flashed with fear and hatred for himself for being caught out. Greene was physically exhausted and in great pain from his shattered ankle. All he could do was watch Verecker as he fought with his own demons, the swirling mist and wild, facial expressions turning him into one himself. For the first time since he had left the train, Greene appreciated how incredibly cold he was. He glanced down and saw that there was a sheen of ice appearing across his mud-coated chest. The cold penetrated the layers of clothing; it pierced every part of him. He looked up at Verecker again. For a few long seconds nothing happened. All he could hear was their laboured breathing and the foghorn filling the marshes with its doleful cry.

'It wasn't Henderson at all. It–it was you all along…' Greene stammered. He felt so overwhelmed by the facts, he actually laughed. Then he became serious again. 'It was you who killed Denby.'

For a moment Verecker looked away across the estuary, but when he turned back Greene saw something he never thought he would see from any human being he cared for—pure and simple hatred. Slowly moving towards Greene and muttering, of all things, an apology, Verecker reached out and pulled Greene up from the ground by his muddy lapels. He was amazed at the man's strength and remembered how the former prison officer had dragged Denby from his flat. This must have been how he had deposited his body in the Thames.

For a moment Verecker just held him there, his mind on him but his gaze elsewhere. Then, with a desolate cry, he threw him back onto the ground. Greene stared in bewilderment. In prison he had never seen Verecker use any sort of violence. His temperament had been such that most prisoners would never dream of attacking him. He was the only

God's Will

friend most of them had had, which was what made this moment all the more terrifying.

'Where is it?' Verecker growled, his voice a garbled guttural cry.

'What? What in God's name is it that you want?'

'I know there's gold! He said he had placed it somewhere safe, and one day you would know where. "Sickert knows where the treasure is," he said. He was teasing me, laughing at me. Or so he thought! Now tell me!'

'I don't know what you're talking about.'

'Don't do that! Don't you dare! He told me! He told me it all!'

'Told you what? Who told you?'

'You know! Don't play with me! Larry. He told me about the ransom for the Steiner girl. The treasure. Where is it? Tell me!'

Greene could barely believe what he was hearing. Nothing seemed real. It didn't make sense why he was there. Suddenly everything became too much for him—the marsh, the mist, the madness in Verecker's eyes. And through it all he could hear Larry's mocking laugh. Even from the grave he held power over people. He had told Verecker a story about a ransom. *Treasure.* It had been a sick joke that had festered in Verecker's timid mind. Over time it had evolved into an obsession, turning the most placid of men into an animal. It had made that man start to realise there was more to be had from life than existing amongst society's outcasts. He had forgotten what he was because of greed.

'I've watched you all—Solomon, Denby and, most of all, you! You're pathetic, all of you. Every day I have had to listen to your excuses, your complaints, your bad luck. You make me sick! But now it's my turn. I've waited a long time. Now, where is it?'

Quickly Greene's pity for Verecker changed to disgust. He'd always seen the other man in a different light to other prison officers. Now he

God's Will

saw how he had been deceived. How was it possible for a man to hide such bitterness?

'You fool,' Greene hissed. 'There's no gold. There never was.'

'Don't do that!' Verecker screamed, kicking Greene again and again. 'That's what Reid said—but he won't say another word now. I know what's going on. You know! *I've been left some money, Mr Verecker,*' he said, mocking Greene with his own words. 'You think I'm stupid? You've got the gold. You've come back for some more. Where's the treasure? Tell me!' He was distraught, crying with fury and frustration. Greene sensed that whilst this belief had existed only inside Verecker's head he had been able to rationalise it, contain it, but once he had voiced it out loud it had taken him over the edge. Now it was Verecker who was the madman. 'Please! Please, Tom. Please don't make it even worse for yourself. Just tell me.'

'There's no treasure…' Greene said weakly. He was so, so cold. 'How could you think that? The ransom was never paid. Larry killed them all before I could do a thing—'

'You're lying!'

'No! Just look at the trial. There was never any mention of gold or a ransom—'

'Yes, there was! It was all covered up. To save embarrassment for the two governments. It was in the newspaper. He said you knew where it was, and I've been watching you long enough. I've invested a lot. Now, where is it? Where's the treasure?'

Greene repeated that he knew nothing but Verecker wouldn't hear him. How convincing Larry's particular brand of mockery could be, Greene thought, as Verecker's boot lashed out at him. Now it all made sense—Denby's conversation on the phone, Verecker's visits—all because of a few glimpses of the old Larry. Verecker had clearly spent some time with Larry at Broadmoor at some point and there a little

God's Will

light had pierced the fabric of Larry's madness, but instead of remorseful reflection the bitter syrup of ridicule and cruelty had poured through. He had realised then that Verecker was no different to anyone else, and every man has his price.

No matter what Greene said or how he said it, Verecker wouldn't hear him. By then he had stopped talking anyway. All Greene could do was curl up as Verecker screamed into his face and bent down to punch him. Then, without warning, Verecker stopped screaming and his gaze lifted from Greene. It was as if he was tracing the outline of something with his eyes, somewhere beyond the man lying at his feet, and for one crazy, deluded moment Greene thought he had finally got through to him. For a very brief moment he thought he knew what was going on in his mind. Verecker had seen the emptiness and understood that everything he had done had been in vain.

But he was wrong.

'That couple you were following, the ones with the pram...' Verecker spluttered, his eyes still searching in the distance. 'That's why you're here. They've got it! You're getting it from them. You were with them the night Denby came to you...'

'You fool, Verecker,' Greene muttered, barely able to keep his eyes open, 'you bloody fool!'

Defenceless and almost passing out from the pain, Greene considered what Verecker had become. He was the worst kind of coward, worse even than Denby. For a lifetime he had toed the line, all the time dreaming of another life. It was a perverse morality made defensible by a warped view of the world. Within those prison walls, day in, day out, Verecker had become trapped. In a way he was just as much a prisoner as the rest of the inmates. Greene had mistakenly imagined Henderson's hatred for him, but he now saw the reality of it in Verecker. The man's greed had distorted him. He was without reason,

God's Will

and from the beginning of the attack to the final moments of consciousness Greene knew he had witnessed true hatred and self-loathing in all its brilliant intensity.

46

Sickert is back in his own bed but he has hardly slept at all. Is Bepa dead? Was her fall from the bed her final moment in this world?

It is time to think for himself.

Slowly removing the bandages, taking particular care around his eyes, he gently allows his eyelids to open. The light is too much and it takes at least half an hour for him to fully focus on anything. But he can see. His eyelids are sore and puffy but he can open them enough to focus for the first time on where he is. The room is large, not too dissimilar in size to his old room at Radstone but, unlike that one, this is run-down and dirty, covered with cobwebs and dust. To his left a fire glows in the faint light, the coals crackling in defiance of the howling wind that pushes at the large window beyond the foot of the bed. There is a solitary door off to his right. In his blind, rat-infested world he had imagined an austere room, but it is far from that. Wherever he looks there are dust-coated ornaments and pictures with dancing silky cobweb tendrils—but nothing to give him any real indication of where he is.

Sickert finds that at the window. Of course, he is in Kent. In the distance he can see the trio of trees where he was attacked. With his vision now restored the full horror of the attack is recalled in appalling detail. It was Verecker who attacked him that day he followed the Ghouls from London to Higham. But how did he survive? A robin hopping from branch to branch in the tree outside watches him closely,

God's Will

he wonders if it is the one that found him out on the estuary. He watches it watching him, its dark eyes reminding him again of something from his past. He remembers the freezing fog and Verecker's madness. A chill runs through him. Inside, Verecker had obviously gone out of his way to protect him. It was possible that right from the beginning he had seen some mileage in the Steiner legend, that in some way he might benefit from it one day. He remembered that Verecker was at another prison for a time. He realised now it was Broadmoor. Had he gone there specifically to be close to Larry? If he had, then Larry would have sensed that. He would have seen Verecker's greed as clearly as he had seen his own all those years ago, and from then on he would have toyed with him, day in and day out.

But where is Verecker now?

Something else then occurs to him—the footsteps he heard as Bepa collapsed. And the presence at the door of his own room…

Sickert stumbles out onto the landing. Away from the fire, the cold is intense and he needs to rub his arms and torso to keep himself warm. Across the walls of the house is a black sheen of damp, mingled within the gaudy red swirls of the wallpaper. Here and there mice and rats scurry to their holes. Then the smell of decay becomes less intense. Moving through the hall he becomes aware of the scale of the house. Once it had presumably been a large family home; now it was soulless and in the throes of death. Stopping to catch his breath Sickert notices a balcony ahead of him leading to a wide staircase. He moves tentatively forward and peers down to see a large reception room scattered with furniture, some of it broken, the rest covered in dust sheets. In the centre of the room, next to the staircase, is a large pile of branches, which he presumes is fuel for the huge but now redundant fireplace on the opposite wall.

God's Will

As Sickert is about to carry on along the landing, he suddenly notices the Ghouls' pram sitting by one of the huge bay windows adjacent to the main door. Apart from the occasional rat, the room seems empty. He decides in that moment it is time to find out what lies inside. Struggling for breath, he grips the banister and goes down. As if sensing his fear the wind howls at him from the chimney, but he has come too far to be affected by that. Stumbling across the threadbare carpet he stops and looks down at sleeping eyes and dark matted hair. He reaches down to pull back the filthy old blanket and uncovers the small shape it conceals. There is no life there. There never has been, only a terrible significance. When he picks up the doll the eyelids suddenly open and as he stares at the bloodstained glass eyeballs he understands it all.

Answers break over him like a huge, foaming wave. He doesn't fully understand everything in that moment, but somewhere deep inside he knows enough for tears to start falling from his eyes. He strokes the doll's matted hair and recalls the first time he saw it in Lottie's arms on that hot summer's day in Hyde Park all those years ago.

Suddenly Sickert hears a noise and turns to see the woman he knows as Bepa, her neck heavily bandaged, on the upstairs landing. Alongside her is a man he presumes to be Philip. But he is someone else, too—one half of the Ghouls. That should shock him, as should Bepa's presence—he had thought she was dead—but it is what is hung on the wall below them both that really gets him. There, in all its striking beauty, is Larry's self-portrait. Since finding the photo in his flat it has been in his mind's eye throughout. He can hardly believe he is looking at it once more, especially in this unfamiliar environment. It all seems so unreal.

'Hello Thomas.'

God's Will

Sickert's gaze rises to the woman's face. He knows her as Bepa, yet it isn't her at all. It isn't until he reaches the bottom of the stairs that he realises who she really is. Now he understands what happened to Veronica Wood. He hasn't seen her for over thirty years, and of all the people he might have expected to see in this house, she was the last.

'Come,' she mutters croakily, 'join us.'

By the time Sickert has climbed the stairs again, Philip has led her back to her room. Giving himself a moment to gather his thoughts, he takes a huge breath and follows them. Her room is beautiful but when he looks closer he sees that everything has a coat of dust. Dominating the middle of the room is a large four-poster bed from which lilac silk drapes hang, bunched gracefully at each post with gold-coloured rope. From the door he still can't see her fully, but as he moves towards the bed he finally spots her frail shape amongst the many pink and lilac pillows. As if expecting guests, her hair is neat and her face powdered. From the fireplace, dry air rises towards the high ceiling, stirring the long threads of cobwebs.

On the large Edwardian mantelpiece stand reminders of her beauty in her youth. In the centre of them all is a large picture of Larry. Sickert's eyes widen. He knew Larry adored Veronica, but he never suspected a relationship. They were lovers, and he never knew. He didn't recognise her voice because of the huge growth that had reshaped her throat and larynx. But for a talent for faces he would never have recognised her even now. The cancer has aged her beyond her years, and her body has withered. She is so thin it seems the softest breeze would break her. Yet despite this, and the state of the house, she seems contented, carefree almost.

She continues to smooth the blankets as she speaks. 'They were returning from London and heard someone yelling on the marshes.'

He knows full well what she is talking about. 'How long ago?'

God's Will

'Philip thought someone was stuck in the mud. It happens from time to time. People become disoriented in the mist, you see. But it wasn't that. It was you and another man. He was beating you, mercilessly. A man called Verecker. It was over a week ago.'

He scrutinises her expression. 'How do you know his name?'

Her stare is fixed on the fire, as if she is watching the events she describes. 'He was beating you. He was wild. You were trying to get away. But he was too strong. Besides, your ankle…'

'Philip saved me?'

'No, another. Philip was making his way to you when another man appeared through the mist. He pulled Verecker off you and there was a terrible struggle.'

'Who was this man?'

'They fought in the mist, coated in mud. They fought for their lives.'

'Who was he?' Sickert pleads.

'Reid, Alan Reid.'

'My God. How do you know their names?'

'Because they are both dead. I know in detail what happened because Philip saw it all. Verecker was too strong for Reid, too, but when they fell into the culvert Reid locked his arms around Verecker and threw himself forward forcing them both under the water. They were not seen again until their bodies washed up along the estuary next day.' She finally looks up at him. 'It seems Inspector Reid saved your life. Philip returned with his sister shortly after the fight to bring you here. It was then I realised who you were. Imagine my surprise, Thomas.'

'Imagine mine…' he murmurs, realising how in his shocked state his mind had turned Verecker and Reid and the foghorn into unearthly creatures.

God's Will

'I suppose so,' she says, her voice as frail as her body. 'But it is good that you came when you did. You shouldn't be up, though. You're still not well. Come, sit by me.'

'How did Reid know where I was?'

She sighs softly. 'We will never know.'

Her skin is gossamer-like, the colour of palest pearl. Yet when he looks closer he sees the dirt under her nails and scabs on the back of her hands and arms. Just like the Ghouls. As he sinks into the chair by the bed, he realises he still has the doll. Neither of them speaks. Instead they study one another for some time.

'I still don't understand…' he whispers.

'Do you know where you are, Thomas?'

'The Thames estuary, somewhere near Rochester.'

She nods slowly and points to the window. 'The hill you see beyond the wood is known as Gad's Hill. This place was once known as Gad's Hill Farm…'

Larry's voice suddenly fills Sickert's ears and he places a hand across his mouth as tears well in his eyes. 'Gad's Hill! I misunderstood him!' he cries. 'How could I have been so stupid?'

He understands it all now. Larry saved Lottie and brought her to the tranquillity of this place. The blood they found in his car was from Lottie's cut from the gate at the Steiner home earlier that day. Never once has he considered Veronica to have been part of the scheme. Larry's part of the scheme, anyway. When Solomon bought the Duke, Sickert had thought he would never see her again. But of course he did; it wasn't Julia he had seen Larry with in Rochester all those years ago —it was Veronica.

'You were aware of Solomon's deal with Steiner?' she asks.

'Of course.'

God's Will

'So was Larry, but he knew there was more to the bargain than simple profit. On the advice of Fenton senior, Solomon had Larry break into Steiner's home and find out as much as he could. What Larry found sickened him. Steiner was a serial child abuser—including his own daughter. Larry found photos and films in the safe and decided to save her, using the kidnapping as cover.'

'The original plan was to murder her?'

There is a long, telling pause. Sickert nods as he pieces it together. If they had been planning to dispose of Steiner's damaged goods, they would have done the same to him. And it would all be done to look as if he had planned it himself. A few days after the kidnapping—after the gold had been transferred—a suicide note would no doubt have been found beside his body. Sickert thinks back to the night of the kidnapping, and Levy. Whether he was aware of it or not he was there to take Lottie and Sickert himself to their deaths. Inadvertently Larry had saved many lives that night.

'And Solomon knew that it was more than a kidnapping?' he asks, still struggling to take it in.

'Larry was never sure if all the details were discussed, but knowing his father as he did, he knew she would never be seen again.'

'And what about me?'

'What about you? He tried to talk to you, but by then you had become everything he despised.'

Sickert looks away. Knowing she is right doesn't ease the pain. 'Why didn't he just go to the police?'

'Why didn't you?' she says abruptly. Then her tone mellows. 'I'm sorry. We both know what he became at the end. I don't think anybody could control him. But, Thomas, you must understand there was goodness in him, even at the end.'

'Really? Then what about Olga? The nanny? Why her?'

God's Will

'She knew about the plan, too, Thomas. That was why she was at the house that night. She was to watch over Lottie until the last minute. To make sure everything went as intended.'

Sickert is astonished at yet another revelation and for a moment wonders if the woman in front of him is as mad as Larry became. But in the silence she allows him, he realises it is possible. It was Olga who spoke first in Hyde Park the day he met Lottie, for instance.

'I knew they were building a trap for me, but I never saw her as part of it.'

'It is amazing what lengths people will go to for money. But I don't think she was fully aware of the true extent of the scheme.'

Slowly she is revealing the answers he has sought for so long, throwing open tiny boxes in his mind. He is gripped by what really happened. Now it all seems so obvious. A little like a magician's trick, mystifying until the explanation is revealed. Unaware of his plan to save Lottie, Larry had gone to Steiner's house that night knowing the trap was set for his old friend. Sickert wants to believe that Larry hadn't intended to kill them, that something forced his hand and he had no choice. All he knows for certain is that he found them as Larry had left them.

'But why?' he mutters, still not fully comprehending why he had been left to suffer.

'I'm so sorry, Thomas. I couldn't help you until recently. I had to protect them. We thought we were unable to have children. We had been trying for some time. Ever since we bought this house, in fact. We bought it as an investment shortly after you both met. Thomas, you must understand that we had a wonderful life together. I loved him so very much. Our intention was to sell the house and go abroad with our family. Away from his father and all the villainy.'

God's Will

'And Lottie would be your family?' The smile says it all. Standing up, Sickert tries to find the words that have eluded him so far. 'The woman...'

'Yes, Thomas. It's her.'

She gestures for him to help her to her feet and slowly they walk to the window. Looking out across the marsh it is possible to see two shapes moving towards the house, their arms full of firewood.

'Philip is your son?' he asks, placing the doll on the windowsill.

'Our little miracle... Larry always said he wanted a little boy named Pip. He was born six months after you were both charged. I only saw Larry once after that. I tried to explain, but...'

She doesn't have to say it. He understands. In the state Larry was in at the end, she couldn't have relied on him not to give their secrets away. Luckily for them all, Verecker didn't understand that when Larry talked of treasure he was describing Lottie.

'Why do they go to London? And why the photographs?'

'They live for me. I haven't been outside this house for years. So each week they go into London and take pictures of the houses and the parks and the people, and my beloved Soho. They live for me. They do as they please and they keep me alive with little snippets of the city I love. I think you of all people should understand that,' she adds with a smile. 'Philip allows her to sell some in the pubs. It pleases her. She was abused terribly, Thomas. Terribly. She rarely speaks but she seems content with her life now.'

Suddenly she begins to cough violently. He holds her close and it is almost as if he can actually feel the life emptying from her.

'You came just in time... just in time,' she whispers as he gets her to the bed

'You need to see a doctor.'

God's Will

'As I have said before, a waste of time now.' There is no fear in her voice. No sense that she is afraid of the end.

'What will happen to them?'

'They will look after one another. They do not need me. There is money, as you have already discovered. I'm sorry I couldn't give you more. Fenton will make sure they have what they need.'

'Fenton knows?'

'Larry and Peter Fenton studied at university together. They were close friends before you both met.'

She begins coughing again and he puts her to bed. They talk for some time, until he thinks she has fallen asleep. But as he stands up to go back to his room, she mutters his name.

'Yes, Bepa?'

'You must try to remember him as he was before his illness. He was a good man. A kind man.' Looking down, he smiles and nods. 'I want you to do something for me, Thomas. Will you do it?'

'If I'm able,' he replies, returning to her side. As he places a hand on the bed, she touches it with hers.

'Would you tell Philip all about his father, man to man? He is reserved and distant at times, not unlike his father... but he is quite capable.'

'Of course.'

'Thank you, Thomas. Thank you.'

Tears are falling from his eyes. She brushes them away with her long thin fingers, then smiles and tells him to get some rest.

Next morning she is dead. He had, as she said, come at just the right time.

Gad's Hill was where Dickens lived and died. The Kent marshes was where he imagined Pip and Magwich amongst the mud and the mist. It

God's Will

was also where Larry spent happy times with Veronica. Sickert finally understands in the end.

As the last of the winter snows falls across the bleak landscape later that day, Lottie and Philip bury their mother in the overgrown garden, in the shadow of the house. Sickert recites the poem by Dickens so loved by Larry, the one he performed at the Duke on the day he realised how much he loved him, unaware his love was already given. The final lines affect him deeply.

In my breast alone
Dark shadows remain;
The peace it has known
It can never regain.

Poor Larry.

That evening by the fire, with Lottie silently at his side, Sickert tells Philip all about his father—his generosity, his understanding of the world and his love of the beauty most choose to ignore. And as they talk long into the night Sickert realises it was a little bit of Larry he saw in Philip's eyes that night on Portland Place. There is an oddness about Pip, but from his soft voice and profound enquires about his father, Sickert realises he has found the better part of Larry living on within him.

As Lottie listens, Sickert tries to work out if she remembers him or not. The more he thinks about it, the more he hopes she doesn't. Her abuse has scarred her, stunted her emotionally. She is as uncommunicative now as she was as a child. He can't possibly know what's going on in her head and if the horrors of the past haunt her as his own past has haunted him. He prays to God they don't. Why they

God's Will

are both so unkempt and the house in such a state despite the money they have he doesn't know. It is clearly the way they live. Is it because their parents lived such troubled lives—Veronica herself had killed too, after all—and that instability has been passed down? Yet they have clearly been loved and that is surely more precious than anything.

Next day he returns to London to discover the coroner's verdict on Verecker and Reid is accidental death. It is not clear to the authorities why the two men met there and fought, but drowning was the reason they died. According to the locals, it is common for strangers to lose their way in the mists of winter. A few days after that Sickert makes his way to Highgate cemetery and lays flowers on the grave of Alan Reid. On his stone it reads *Finally at Rest*. Someone, a colleague, most likely Sergeant Calvert, knew him well.

A week later, concerned about Lottie and Pip, Sickert returns to the house only to find it abandoned. Without Veronica they have clearly decided there is no reason to stay. From the entrance Larry's musty portrait stares down at him, and as he looks back at it he finally understands the contrasts in the face. He was haunted. Back then he couldn't see it. But he knows the look. He has seen it in his own face many times. Finally he visits Veronica's room. Without the fire, winter has breached the house's timeless façade, and without her the world he once knew is gone. Apart from Lottie and Philip, the only other things that seem to be missing are the doll and the pram. In the end, Lottie has outlived them all.

Sickert buys the flat in the end—there was no nephew; Verecker had rented it in his own name in order to keep an eye on him. He knows that London will always be his home. To celebrate this he invites Fenton junior out for a drink in Soho. The awkwardness of their previous meeting is gone and they talk long into the night about a secret

God's Will

known only to them. Fenton will never tell where Philip and Lottie have gone. But that doesn't matter to the man from the north, because at last Thomas Sickert, now known to the world as Greene, is at peace with the world.

On the way back later that night it starts to rain and he takes a short cut to the flat along Rathbone Street, through Newman Passage. That area of London that has always held such significance for him. It could have been the wind, or even the drink, but he was certain—certain—he heard the squeaking of Lottie's pram coming from somewhere just out of sight.

The End

Proof

Made in the USA
Columbia, SC
14 March 2018